THE HOUSE OF STARLING

THE HOUSE OF STARLING

BOOK I

CIARA HARTFORD

Copyright © 2024 by Ciara Hartford
Zephi Press, LLC
www.ciarahartford.com

All rights reserved. No part of this publication may be reproduced, distributed, or transmitted in any form or by any means, including photocopying, recording, or other electronic or mechanical methods, without the prior written permission of the publisher, except in the case of brief quotations embodied in critical reviews and certain other noncommercial uses permitted by copyright law.

This book is a work of fiction. Names, characters, places, and incidents either are products of the author's imagination or are used fictitiously. Any resemblance to actual events or locales or persons, living or dead, is entirely coincidental.

First paperback edition: 2024

Paperback ISBN: 978-1-963524-00-0
Ebook ISBN: 978-1-963524-01-7

Edited by Katrina Robinson
Profread by Sara Michelle Rebekah and Lisa Keatley
Cover art and design by Ciara Hartford
Interior art by Ciara Hartford
Map design by Ciara Hartford

For more information, please visit www.ciarahartford.com
Zephi Press, LLC is a publishing imprint created and owned by Ciara Hartford

For Keith.
My first fan, my biggest fan.

I've finally become an author, Dad.

To my readers!

Thank you for taking a chance on this book. As an Indie Author, every reader is appreciated and cherished. But this book is not for everyone. It is intended for adults and may not be suitable for those under the age of eighteen. I like to think that if it were a movie, it'd be rated somewhere between PG-13 and R. Everyone is different in what they enjoy and what they find triggering. Above all else, please protect yourself.

Mature content includes:

» Abduction
» Anxiety
» Post-traumatic stress disorder
» Profanity
» Reference to rape (no actual depictions of)
» Graphic violence including:
  › Torture
  › Blood and gore
  › Dismemberment
  › Evisceration
  › Decapitation

Welcome to Rhend.

N
W
E
S
FORTHAN
RAGGATHAN
DAKARAI HOLD
THE MIDDLELEND
THE WASTELANDS
KEKK HOLD
GLAZMIN
SEBBETT HOLD
SORMIRE

VAIL
THE WILDS
KORTHAN
PARTH
THANDOR
THE MOORS
THE EASTERN PASS
THE OLD ROAD
FOREST
DORMSHIRE
THE HIGHLANDS
RHEND
TREMIRE
JOOSHAWN
LAKE SORMIRE
HARMEND

Sacrifice

She held her tiny elfling in her arms. It was late—or early—she couldn't entirely tell. Everyone else was fast asleep, but she'd been roused to feed this wonderful creature. He was small and fragile, yet deceivingly powerful. She'd fought and sacrificed and waited for him, and now he was here. Perfect. Cherished.

The light of the waning moon slipped through her bedchamber window, pouring shards of white across her son's face as she paced. It reminded her of what she must do—the task she alone could finish. There was one last rift bleeding dangerous magic into this world; it needed to be snuffed out. She'd fulfill that which the guild had set out to accomplish, even if it was the last thing she ever did.

Her brother had been at her side once. Now she went alone. He, like all the other guild members, had given his life to the same mission, and the rifts had taken their price. The cost was non-negotiable.

She placed her elfling, her tiny masterpiece, in his cradle, her gaze lingering on his precious face—his eyes closed once again in slumber. She reached for her father's soul stone resting against her chest, protecting her from the thirst of the rifts. To leave the pendant behind meant death, but she couldn't leave her son unprotected, and she couldn't take him with her. Not for this task.

One day, he would be a formidable Anam Wielder, more powerful than she could ever be. He would hold the strength of generations before him, passed down through succession and careful breeding. Only the soul stone could temper that. It would keep the soulfire within his tiny body at bay, locked within his consciousness until he could learn to control it.

So much damage had already been done while she'd been delayed, struggling with pregnancy. A single battle had changed the course of history, destroying thousands of years of peace between the elves. Not since the humans had scarred Rhend had her people known such hatred.

She squeezed her eyes closed and tried to see anything but the white fire that always burned in her mind. If the guild was wrong about the prophecy's meaning, closing the rifts would be the world's undoing. It was possible she'd be the catalyst for their end, not the savior.

The doubt was as heavy as death.

She said a prayer to the Elder Gods. Maybe someday the power of the rifts could be better understood and protected from those who'd use it for nefarious purposes, but for now, she needed to close the last of them.

Her sweet son shifted in his cradle. With the lightest touch, she traced a pattern across his forehead and down his nose, over and over until he stilled. She stood a moment longer, memorizing the lines of his face, the tuft of dark hair, his diminutive hands that would someday wield amazing power.

It was time to go.

She knew the way, passing unnoticed across the moors toward the forest line, which loomed like a dark blade of shadows separating the earth from the night sky. She wove between trees and rocks on an ancient path, allowing the sounds of the slumbering forest to ease the anxiety that bubbled around the edges of her confidence.

As she approached the last rift, light bled across the broken earth and stained the tree trunks white. Her death was in that colorless flame. She pressed the toes of her boots to the rim of the burning fissure. Trepidation soaked through the soles of her feet and crept up her legs before sitting like a stone in her gut.

She took a deep breath and let it out slowly, methodically, then shook out her hands in anticipation.

It was time.

With her palms down, she drew the fire into herself, feeling her life force struggle against the raw essence that melted into the fibers of her flesh. As with closing the other rifts, tingling began in her fingertips, then poured into her hands and up her arms. The rift's insatiable thirst grated against her consciousness with a sharp dissonance that spoke of sorrow and anguish. It flooded the depths of her being, filling her with doubt, coating her memories in a haze of desperation.

Blood boiled in her veins, pumping like acid through her extremities. A cry ripped free from her lips, but there was no one to hear it. Where once the brilliant white had surrounded her, now there was only a darkness that drew tighter.

This was the cost the soul stone had protected her from: unimaginable pain. Unthinkable pressure as the presence of the rift fought against her mind, desperate to escape its fleshy prison. No elf was ever meant to hold such magic within themself.

She tried to take in a breath, but there was nothing. No air to breathe. No lungs to draw in the air. Her insides had melted. Her vision charred black around the edges until there was nothing left.

Nothing but the memory of her sweet son's amber eyes.

ONE

Prey

S he wasn't a hunter of animals. She was a hunter of Bleck Larin. Today, however, Rae crouched in chest-high grass, many leagues from the fighting. She waited for a very different kind of prey—one without deadly blades and stone-gray flesh. She waited with her mind in two places, arrow nocked, muscles tense.

The setting sun stained the sky pink where it pressed against the earth, bleeding honeyed light over the highlands. Trees dressed in the pale green of early summer cast long shadows, reaching like fingers across the grass. With any luck, deer would make their way out to munch on that grass in the last scraps of daylight, and Rae would be ready.

She didn't need to hunt for food. There were plenty of Shay in Tremire with the responsibility, but Rae's idle hands begged for something to do. She'd been home for three days, and it felt like it had been weeks. Weapons had been cleaned and sharpened, armor polished, arrows fletched. Waiting for her next assignment was torture.

If she had a mission, a battle, a task, she could channel her focus; but without one, she was lost in a sea of details with no reason to collect them. Or, worse, the memories would flood in around the chinks in her confidence—white teeth against stony flesh, amber eyes, ethereal strength honed into merciless killers.

Rae squeezed her eyes closed to clear the shadows of Bleck Larin enemies streaking across the Eastern Pass. Even the scent of soil and spring onions couldn't mask the memory of death and the reality of war. The stain of blood was hard to wash away.

The coo of a mourning dove grounded her in the moment. She opened her eyes, letting the memory of lifeless elves slip away.

The grass moved.

A rabbit bound into her minuscule clearing and sat, content with her presence, nibbling on a fat clover. Rae lost herself in the incessant twitch of its nose and knowing black eyes, which swallowed her whole. She smiled as the creature stood on hind legs and peered up at her, sniffing the air. It knew she was there for bigger prey.

Rae reached, itching to feel its softness. It was something real—here and now—a tiny life as curious about her as she was about it. Her fingers were within inches of it when she shifted her weight, startling the rabbit back into the protection of taller grass. It was a friendship not meant to be. She let her disappointment settle around her like the growing dusk.

Her attention fell back to the landscape, eyes grazing the tips of the grass where the highlands met the Forest of Tremire. The light was fading fast, reluctant stars winking into existence above. The forest seemed to absorb the darkness, plunging Rae into the heavy twilight she'd known since elflinghood. Her home was under that ancient canopy. It offered comfort, peace, and tranquility—oppressively positive things in light of the horrors on the battlefield.

A doe stepped from the protection of the forest's edge, ears angled toward the empty expanse of the highlands, uneven tufts of fur clung to its haunches as it shed its winter coat. It smelled the air and pivoted one ear toward Rae. With practiced silence, Rae drew her bow. She focused on the deer's ribs, her target just back from the shoulder. Taking a deep breath, she held it for a second, then another.

A fawn blocked the kill zone as it sought a clump of tender grass, and Rae eased. A month-old fawn wouldn't survive without its mother. It would starve to death or be snatched up by predators of the wild. Rae was forced to choose the course of the youngling's life, as she'd had to do many times on the battlefield. At least on the battlefield, she was choosing self-defense. When a sword was swinging at your neck, you needn't question if the Bleck Larin were mothers, fathers, daughters, sons. They were enemies. Nothing more, nothing less.

The fawn stepped from the protection of its mother's side and pranced farther out onto the highlands, leaving the doe exposed again. It stamped the dry earth with a cloven hoof, ears twisting as it smelled the breeze. Rae drew the arrow back again. The tension of the string nullified her apprehensions and calmed the ghosts haunting the depths of her conscience.

She was a hunter of prey, in whatever form it took.

It was well past daybreak when Rae finally pulled herself from under her covers. Hadn't she just climbed into them? She dressed in a training jerkin and combed her fingers through her hair, braiding as she moved through her modest dwelling. The fruits of her hunt hung on racks against one wall. The night had been thick by the time she'd finished stripping the carcass of usable meat and fur.

After a quick cup of sun-warmed tea, she grabbed a hunk of truffle bread and stepped out into the tepid morning light. She knew her fellow soldiers would already be an hour or better into training, so she was quick, tearing bites from the bread as she jogged. She avoided the main road, which would be crowded with citizens of Tremire by this time of day. Instead, she chose a less-used trail that wove between the dwellings.

She breathed in the morning scent of dew and blueberry blossoms. No matter where her duties as a soldier in the queen's army took her, this was home. Great ironwood trees stretched hundreds of feet into the sky. Sunlight dripped through meager gaps in the canopy, softening the edges of shadows shifting over the grass. Mushrooms camped around rocks, nestled against well-worn paths that had been carved by millennia of foot traffic.

At the dawn of Rhend, the Shay elves had made their homes from these trees, twisted and shaped by Eishtala magic into modest-sized dwellings. It was craftsmanship sharpened by years of training to manipulate growing things into sensual silhouettes—twisting vines into benches and torch posts and doorways. Rae had been surrounded by such majesty her entire life, yet she couldn't shake the wonder she felt every time she beheld it.

The proving grounds were tucked on the city's southern side, divided from the rest of the forest by a border of ancient stones, mortared in place by moss and honeysuckle. She was greeted with the sounds of wooden practice weapons slamming together, her cheeks flushing with embarrassment for being tardy. She'd never been a morning person, but today she was later than usual.

She swung her legs over the stone wall, then waited stock-still as she scanned the soldiers. Legion Bowrhem stood to one side, his back as straight as the trees, pale-pink, shirtless arms wrapped behind him as he observed the chaos of training. His royal-blue jerkin was crisp and clean, the queen's emblem blazed on his left breast, white hair grazing his shoulders. Legion Bowrhem was the embodiment of Shay strength, with wide, muscular shoulders and a broad chest tapering to tight abs hidden below finely tooled leather. He cut an intimidating profile.

She traced her eyes across the other faces, finding a familiar head of cropped white hair on the far side of the proving grounds. Rae's friend Freck leaned forward, his face inches from another's as he spoke. She smiled at the friendliness between the two. Freck had found a new companion. A smirk blossomed across his lips when he noticed her. She glanced away, her attention falling back to her legion.

Bowrhem had, in essence, a few thousand soldiers to oversee. While Tremire was considered the hub of Shay rule, Bowrhem was rarely more than a league or two from the Eastern Pass, where most conflicts had taken place over the last thirty-two years. A bubble of anxiety rose in her stomach. Why would the legion bless them with his presence?

"You're late." Freck wore the same smirk on his face. "Did you spend the whole night hunting on the highlands?"

She examined her friend, following the dappled, brilliant red shay-marks down his neck to his bare chest.

"Did you spend the night in a new friend's bed?" she teased.

Freck winked. "I don't kiss and tell." He held up a practice sword, raising an eyebrow, and spun another in a clear challenge.

"Oh, Freckles. You're a glutton for punishment."

He swung as soon as her fingers wrapped around the handle. She'd expected as much. He'd been trying to get the drop on her since they'd been elflings. She dodged his strike while he still held the other side of her practice sword.

"Not fair, Dulanii."

He feigned shock, likely at her use of his real name, before twisting away and throwing a snarky wink in her direction.

She let him work his way through the crowd of other training Shay, waiting for the perfect moment to make her move. Turning, he straightened, realizing she wasn't behind him. The smile fell from his face when she winked back.

Like liquid, she flowed into the spaces between combatants, swimming around bodies in motion. This was a dance of elf and blade, one she loved every minute of. She clutched the practice sword with a relaxed hand, knocking the occasional weapon clear. She was in her element as she twisted through the chaos of training Shay—a hunter with prey in her sights.

Freck glanced side to side, searching for an escape, only to find himself surrounded by excited onlookers. Rae gave him no quarter. She slipped under the nearest soldier's practice sword and swung up with her own, catching Freck's downward block with a sickening crack. She didn't hold back, and from the way he flinched, she assumed he'd felt the full force of her strength vibrating through the bones in his arms.

She spun, her hair momentarily obscuring her vision before their wooden blades connected. He backpedaled frantically, leaning clear of her swings. He managed to block her next three rapid strikes to the torso, but the fourth connected with his ribs. Rae winced, knowing full well the pain of taking a hit to the side. Freck, to his credit, did little more than blink, pushing her away as his heels slammed into the stone wall behind him.

Rae gave him a second's reprieve—far more than she'd ever give an enemy—as she calculated her next move. A final strike if the sword in her hand had been made of steel. Freck squeezed his eyes closed, practice sword held out to protect himself. He knew what was coming and that there was little he could do to stop it. He'd lost again.

Years of practiced control, refined by hours of training and muscle memory, stopped Rae's blade just a mere half an inch from his neck. Rae froze in place, letting the power of the blow that hadn't hit its mark ripple through her and into the earth below her feet. Freck's shoulders rose and fell with ragged breaths as he waited, his left eye finally popping open.

"Raemian Starling." Legion Bowrhem's deep timbre cut past the blood rushing through Rae's ears, and she turned to face her legion. The silence as he approached, hands still folded behind his back, was terrifying. "Impressive." He let the words sink in, eyes penetrating her soul. "But perhaps too reliant on flair and individual skill. Not nearly enough on teamwork."

She gazed at Bowrhem's feet, trying to avoid his glare. Rae had never been one for showing off. Never on purpose. Defeating Freck on an almost daily basis, however, was always enjoyable. Those who had watched the duel scrambled back to their usual training, the once-silent practice arena exploding again into shouts of sparring.

"Her Majesty wishes to speak with you after training," Bowrhem said. "I've also been instructed to reassign you to scouting detail as soon as feasible."

"Only myself, sir?" Rae asked as her attention snapped to her legion.

He narrowed his eyes, and she immediately regretted her impulsive question. But Freck had always been assigned with her. They'd been partners from the moment they'd enlisted in the Shay army. They'd been sent on countless missions together—*always* together.

Bowrhem's expression darkened, lips tightening to a thin line. Rae winced. She'd questioned his authority. In front of everyone.

"I was given no other changes in assignment," he said through clenched teeth.

"Of course, sir." She bowed, trying her best to swallow her concerns while holding position as he walked back to where he had stood moments before.

She took a couple of deep breaths to calm her racing heart. Whether from the duel, the assignment change, or the knowledge she'd need to speak with the queen, she couldn't be certain.

"Wait," Freck said, placing a hand on her shoulder and turning her toward him. "What just happened?"

Rae couldn't answer him. At least, not yet.

T W O

Little Starling

ae's legion wouldn't need to tell her twice. Her training helped her weave through Tremire's crowded midday streets. The last thing she wanted was to keep her royal stepmother waiting. Queen Gemma of the Shay wasn't a patient person. She wasn't a lot of things—kind to Rae, for example, though Rae yearned more than anything for her approval.

She didn't want to ruin what little favor she possessed.

The Court of Tremire was bustling. Guards moved constituents in a perfectly choreographed dance of queues outside the massive ironwood tree. Rae was familiar with the process—she'd been summoned by Gemma before—but she usually had some idea of why. Today, it was an unnerving mystery.

"State your business," the guard said. He sounded unenthused to be there, and Rae could only agree. The day was growing hot, and the royal guard armor was heavier and more elaborate than the standard plate mail used in battle.

"The queen requested my presence." She kept her words clipped, noticing the way the guard's eyes narrowed through the slit in his gilded visor as they roamed across her face. He turned with a beckoning motion before cutting a path through the crowd. She followed tightly in his wake, letting the throng of Shay swallow them as they climbed the front steps of the great tree.

Once inside, the noise of chatter intensified to a roar. Most of the royal council's members were positioned against the room's round walls, pressed into cliques. Each group represented a different region of the Shaylands. Important issues were raised by these Shay, but the queen always had the final word. A throne was elevated atop a dais across from the massive double doors. There, with a fake smile plastered across her face, sat Gemma, Queen of the Shay.

She could have been a hundred or eight hundred. Her face was flawless, with high cheekbones, a delicate chin, and a powdery pink complexion. Eyes, like pale-blue diamonds, sparkled with an authority so sharp it could cut steel. Her platinum hair was tamed into an elaborate plait held in place by a diadem crafted from rose-gold vines and leaves that followed the path of the shaymarks dancing across her temples.

Heads turned and voices lowered as Rae was led into the center of the room and then left to prostrate herself.

"Dearest Raemian." Gemma's sarcasm oozed across the polished wood and puddled in front of Rae. "I heard delightful rumors of your latest conquest. A truly stellar performance."

The shifting of feet and murmuring ceased as Rae straightened, remaining at the base of the dais. This was her place—below the queen— always looking up. Gemma crossed her legs, the sheer fabric of her skirt shimmering like the surface of a stream, throwing rainbows across the walls and ceiling.

"Your poor sweet father has been fretting." Gemma made a show of turning her head to the side, a faux pouty lip protruding from her flawless silhouette. "I promised him I'd find you a safer assignment, even though you and I both know where your place is." She looked down a sharp nose, her frozen eyes finding Rae again as she raised one knowing brow. "Killing the scourge of our lands."

No one could deny Rae's superior skills in battle, least of all the woman who had put her there in the first place. Rae's fear had turned into an uncanny talent for self-defense, which had turned into polished proficiency. What frustrated Rae most was that Gemma likely had ulterior motives for throwing her into the army. Rae suspected Gemma needed to get Somin Starling's elfling out from underfoot, and this was a convenient means of doing so.

"I trust Legion Bowrhem has shared your new assignment?"

"He has, Your Majesty," Rae said with a flat voice.

"The change is to happen immediately. First light. Join your new regime in the Middlelend Forest as quickly as your little legs can carry you."

"Of course, Your Majesty." Every eye in the room was affixed on Rae, and it made her skin crawl. She waited on razor's edge, knowing there had to be more.

Gemma shifted her weight, throwing more rainbows across the fragile silence. "You seem...hesitant. Do you have any objections?"

Gods be damned. The Shay were never good at hiding emotions. Rae had hoped she'd kept her face at least neutral enough not to draw attention. The room waited in still silence.

"No, Your Majesty." Rae clenched her teeth so hard after the words left her mouth that she feared Gemma would see the strain in her face.

"Very well." The queen threw her a dismissive flip of her hand. "You may go."

Rae blinked a few times, not believing the meeting had been so easy. She must have missed something. Gemma rarely passed on an opportunity to make an example of her.

"Keep your head down, little Starling, lest you lose it."

She held the queen's glare as long as she dared before bowing low enough to smell the mud on her boots.

On the way home, Rae laid the details of the conversation out in her mind for inspection. Gemma was clearly plotting something. What part Rae would play in this newest game was yet to be revealed.

A familiar mess of snowy-cropped hair peeked from the side of Rae's dwelling as she approached. Freck was stretched out on a blanket of moss, arms folded behind his head, closed eyes pointed to the canopy. She stopped short at the thought of leaving the next day without him.

He must have heard her because he smiled without opening his eyes. "That was faster than usual."

Rae dropped to the earth beside him. "I'm not sure why she needed to speak with me so publicly. I was congratulated for my performance, then told my father worries." She smoothed her hands over the cool moss, running a few tendrils of grass between her fingers. "I leave tomorrow for the Middlelend Forest."

Freck sat up abruptly, stormy eyes alight with an inner fire. "Why are we being separated?" He leaned closer, placing a hand on her shoulder. "Did she give a reason? We've been partners for years, Rae. We go everywhere together."

She shook her head. She should have asked. She'd been given an opportunity to voice her objections, had she not? Rae knew that wasn't true, though. You didn't object to the queen's orders. You followed them and placed a smile on your face and a shield over your heart.

"And your father?"

She held Freck's frosty glare. "I stopped to speak with him first, but he wasn't available."

He was never available when she needed him—not since he'd been bonded to the queen.

Freck let his hand slip from her shoulder, lost eyes gazing off toward the center of Tremire. Rae studied his face, one she'd seen many times—in truth, more than her own. For the past decade, they'd fought side by side against the Bleck Larin. She loved him. She would lay down her life for him.

She followed the path of his bright-red shaymarks as they danced like splashes of freckles down his face, neck, and on to his torso.

"I don't know why you wish to please her." He plucked a clover and pulled it apart before smashing it between his thumb and index finger. "It's not like she actually cares for you."

"She's the closest thing I have to a mother."

He let his head hang a moment before looking up to the canopy. "Just promise me you'll trust your instincts." He glanced at her with a crooked smile. "I won't be there to tell you to stop overthinking."

Rae pursed her lips to keep from smiling. Of course, Freck was right. "I promise."

"And whoever they pair you with, don't get too attached. I plan to be at your side in a week's time."

She pulled a tendril of grass and threw it at him. "Promise."

"Don't let the new regime pick on you." He tousled the hair atop her head, "Short, yes. Weak, never."

She threw a fistful of grass this time. "Promise."

"And give yourself some grace. You don't always have to please the queen."

"You ask too much."

He rolled to his knees and faced her, his expression deathly serious. "Have I? She's taken so much from you." There was a sorrow to his voice that tightened Rae's throat. "Your father, your future, your choice. Why not take me as well, I guess?"

She couldn't hold his glare. He wasn't wrong.

"Enough of this," he said, standing and offering her a hand, a sly smile showing his crowded teeth. "Shall we spend our last evening together moping about? *Or...* sharing a drink with friends?"

Rae took his hand and let him help her to her feet. She dusted her backside before grinning up at Freck, her very best friend, her brother.

"You mean, with *your* friends? You're my only friend, Freck."

They laughed together, linking arms as they followed the path that led into the heart of Tremire.

THREE

The Middlelend Forest

Rae knew she and her new partner were drawing dangerously close to Bleck Larin territory, but the border wasn't a physical line, and their assignment had been clear. They were to scout ahead of the main force and find the source of distant calling.

"Hey." A soft tenor voice sliced the silence open. "For the Elder Gods' sakes, Rae, it's not a race," Gairek gasped, "Can't you slow down?"

His whining was almost more than she could bear. She rolled her eyes but slowed to a more leisurely pace. It hadn't taken Rae long to learn all of Gairek's idiosyncrasies. He was quick-witted but not particularly observant, having already missed telltale signs of the previous scouting missions a league back. He wasn't entirely trusting of her judgment, either.

She glanced in Gairek's direction, finding him quickly. He couldn't hide among the trees with his bright-pink face and brilliant-red hair left long and untamed down his back. At least he wore a shirt, which was more than she could say about Freck. She smiled to herself thinking of her dearest friend. He'd have complained about the pace as well.

"You sure this is the correct direction?" Gairek asked.

Rae stopped sharp, shushing him with a raised index finger. Nothing seemed immediately out of place here—no bootprints or broken branches. No traces of elves. Perhaps patrols or hunting expeditions had passed through this part of the Middlelend Forest before, but not recently. This far north, it wouldn't be Shay in those hunting parties, and they wouldn't be hunting wild game.

The thick canopy, combined with a heavy layer of fallen leaves, kept the shrubs and sun-loving weeds at bay. Saplings thrust themselves toward the sky in their best effort at life, some poking through the cathedral of larger ancient trees if they'd managed to survive the first hundred years. The sentinels of the forest were mystical oaks, maples, and birches, thinner in circumference than the great ironwoods of Rae's home forest, but no less impressive.

She waited, letting the world soak in. This forest smelled different than Tremire, heavy with wet leaves and rotting wood. Ivy and moss clung to everything, hiding entire rocky outcroppings beneath a viridescent blanket. It was wild and enigmatic—the husk of a nut buried deep, waiting to be found by the squirrel that had hidden it.

When there had been peace between the Bleck Larin and Shay elves, this forest had been a shared resource, the innermost depths a mysterious place. Even now, Rae's concern was that the calls heard by her patrol were from a source not entirely of their realm. Stories of magical forces known as rifts were a campfire favorite, but Rae had never had the pleasure of seeing any. Most Shay insisted that the last of them had been snuffed out around the time the warring had begun. That was some thirty-odd years ago, when she'd still been an elfling at her father's knee.

Rae took a tentative step, then they were moving again, Gairek a few paces behind her. She shifted direction to avoid an area where the slender trunks were interrupted by low branches, weaving like intertwined fingers. They reminded her of simpler times—holding her father's hand—the peaceful times before she'd been forced into being another cog in the queen's war machine.

Her mind began to wander, and while she could see Gairek out of the corner of her eye, she was mentally standing at the edge of the Eastern Pass with a bloody sword in her hand. On her last campaign, her morality had burned away, leaving her with only instinctual self-preservation, fed by the echoing cries of fallen comrades. So many times she'd dreamt of battles, terrified by what she was capable of, but never before had she been filled with such regret and self-reproach.

Lost in thought, she nearly missed a soft cry carrying through the stillness. Ripped from her distracted frame of mind, she slipped a little as she skidded to a stop, her right hand clasping the handle of her shortsword.

Gairek had stopped as well, scanning the area before them. He ran his fingers through his hair, his fiery eyebrows crushed together in concentration.

They stood this way for a moment or two, straining to hear what wasn't easily heard. The birds had stopped chirping. Even the crickets had stilled, leaving them in eerie silence, smothered by the scent of decaying earthworms.

"Hello?"

It was a frail voice, female. Based on the volume, she couldn't have been more than a hundred yards away, but sound traveled differently under the trees.

Rae nodded to Gairek and started moving again, calculating every position between herself and her target. She crept on silent feet through the leaves, careful to watch her path for traps as she slid behind a tree and peered around from the shadows.

It was a girl suspended from a juke net. She must have tripped a snare and didn't have a way of cutting herself down.

Rae was frozen. Something was off.

"Hello! I know you're there. I heard you talking!" The girl turned her head, trying to see behind her. "Can you please help me? I've been hanging here for days!"

Rae risked slipping around the tree farther, maintaining the shadows, her eyes never leaving the girl. Struggling for position, the girl reached through the net. A thin ribbon of light illuminated a gray hand.

This was no Shay. This was a Bleck Larin. This girl was an enemy. The color of her skin indicated as much. The creeping instinct to draw her sword wriggled its way up Rae's spine, but she held.

It was possible the girl was Aequus, a neutral elf. They had no sovereign to speak of, just a peaceful collection of all three elven races. But as soon as the word Aequus touched her thoughts, Rae had her doubts. To see one so far into the Middlelend Forest? This place was too hostile for their peaceful ways.

It was more likely the girl was a lost Bleck Larin who had wandered too far from home. Rae's battle instincts began to flow in around her doubts, filling in the cracks of uncertainty. It mattered little who the girl was or how she'd gotten here—Rae was a Shay soldier. She killed Bleck Larin on sight.

She glanced over her shoulder, but there was no sign of Gairek. He could have helped strengthen her convictions like Freck would have. Black and white. Shay and Bleck Larin.

Yet weren't the girl's needs the same as her own? She lived and breathed; required water and sustenance; had a family, a father and mother who loved her. Who had marked the Bleck Larin as enemies in the first place? Were they not elves, as Shay were—as they all were?

Rae shook the thoughts away—more guilt clouding her judgment.

"Please! Some water then?" The girl grasped the side of the net, trying again to turn so she could face the tree where Rae leaned. From the girl's voice and mannerisms, Rae would have thought her little more than an elfling in her teenage years, not yet a woman.

Those nagging questions prevailed. Rae pulled her waterskin from her side and stepped closer, extending only the flask out of the shadow of the tree. The girl squinted, searching for a face to go with the kindness, but Rae kept herself just out of sight.

The girl snatched the waterskin, took several generous gulps, then clutched it to her breast.

"Can you cut me down? Please? I'll starve to death."

Rae remained frozen in place, still struggling against the burden of her choices. Neither was particularly straightforward. It didn't seem like a trap. At the same time, she hadn't heard nor seen Gairek come up from behind. He stayed hidden, perhaps seeing something—or someone—that indicated this wasn't safe. The hair on the back of Rae's neck stood on end. She was missing something. Her distracted thoughts had clouded her usual ability to pick up the smallest of details.

Rae drew her sword and stepped into the light.

The girl, perhaps not prepared for the sight of a Shay, took in a sharp breath, eyes growing wide. Even if this was a trap, the girl was clearly terrified of Rae with a sword in her hand, the Shay Queen's crest prominently displayed over her left breast.

Whatever the girl thought, it didn't matter. Rae had made her decision, for better or worse.

With a single powerful swing, she severed the rope suspending the net, and sheathed her sword in one fluid motion. The girl hit the leaves with a tempered yelp, and Rae gave her a moment to collect herself before she reached down to help her up.

The girl hesitated, studying Rae's outstretched hand with considerable confusion.

Rae couldn't help but smile, a single brow lifting. "If I'd wanted you dead, why would I have cut you down?"

The girl's eyes were so timid and innocent. Like any elfling, she was afraid of doing something wrong, of disappointing someone. Finally, she took Rae's hand, and after the girl was on her feet, Rae noticed how much taller she was than she'd appeared when hanging from the net.

"Thank you." She rubbed her backside, wincing. "Gods, my father will be so worried."

The image of her own father flashed across her mind. A pang of satisfaction gripped Rae. She'd chosen correctly.

"You said you've been hanging for days?"

She could see where the snare was tied to a branch and the crude trigger mechanism. The girl must have been blind not to know what she was walking into. Then again, she was just an elfling, not dressed like a scout or a tracker, but clothed in a maiden's frock and cloak. She probably didn't have the same intuition to ferret out danger.

"I'm going to be in so much trouble. I was..." She hesitated, and Rae glanced over at her downturned eyes, which were veiled with dark lashes. "I was running away." She fidgeted with Rae's waterskin before holding it back out. "He's going to be so angry."

Rae smiled to herself. The longer she spent with the girl, the more satisfied she was with her decision. "I'm sure he'll just be happy you're home." As soon as the words were spoken, Rae's smile slipped from her lips.

She felt them before she saw them, the disruption of the still air brushing across her skin, the faintest scent of sweat. She drew her blade and turned, blocking a broadsword aimed at the soft place where the neck meets the collarbone. She managed to deflect and sidestep clear of striking distance as she faced them. The girl cried out in shock, but Rae's fighter instincts kicked in. Time was already slowing down as her eyes met the fiery brown irises of a Bleck Larin, his mouth masked and a dark hood drawn over his head. He wasn't the only one. She could see the silhouettes of more.

"Get back." Rae moved in front of the girl, who was no longer a Bleck Larin elfling, but Rae's ward, and Rae took that very seriously. She took a few short steps back, enough to allow herself the room to see all four as they melted from the shadows.

These elves weren't wearing the usual deep-red armor of the Bleck Larin King's army. They were clad entirely in black, allowing them to blend into the shadows. Perhaps they were some sect of trackers not associated with the crown?

Gairek should have been among the trees, but there was nothing. Where exactly had he gone?

She didn't get a chance to think further. They were coming in twos.

She ducked under a swinging blade and buried her own deep into the first man's torso, clean through to the other side. He went down hard with a grunt, his partner just behind. Rae used the fallen man's still form as a step to gain needed height, knocking the woman's blade wide and putting an elbow into her eye socket. The woman stumbled, but recovered quickly, blocking Rae's downward cleave. Not prepared for the strength of Rae's swing, the woman's sword was forced to the ground, making an upward counter-swing effortless. Rae's blade lacerated the woman's larynx. She was already looking for the next Bleck Larin as the woman grasped her neck, blood pouring between her fingers.

The third and fourth hesitated, swaying from leg to leg, waiting for an opening. Rae didn't give them one. She slapped the taller man's strike away, using the impact of their swords to slice across his lead arm, cutting deep into the meat of his shoulder. He tried his best to lift his blade to defend with his ruined arm and failed. Rae plunged her sword straight through his throat, then twisted it out the side of his neck.

She leaned back to avoid his partner's sword, the blade passing a hair's breadth from her chin. Bringing her own blade up, she clipped the fourth assailant across the jaw as he tried to evade. He cried out but kept coming. She spun, using the full force of her strength to slice across his abdomen. Entrails and blood sprayed across the leaves at their feet. He could do nothing more than stare blankly at her, amber eyes wide, hands desperately trying to hold himself closed as he sank to his knees and toppled to the side.

She paused, letting the gravity of what she'd done burn into her memory before she turned to the girl. A sharp sting at her neck, like a bug bite, had her searching with frantic fingertips for the offending thing. Instead of an insect, she glanced down at a tiny dart resting in her palm. She'd never been shot with a tranquilizer, but it didn't take previous knowledge to know why the world was suddenly spinning. She stumbled and fell to one knee, her extremities growing heavy. She made what she hoped was firm eye contact with the girl who rushed to her side.

"Run," Rae said.

"Are you okay? What's—" A dart struck the side of the girl's neck, protruding below her hairline. Her eyes rolled as she plummeted face-first to the forest floor.

Rae fought to keep herself upright. Surely Gairek could help? She looked to the trees, searching for his red hair. Instead, she found a dangerously tall, dark figure shift from the gloom, a sword long enough to drag through the leaves hanging from his hand.

"Well, well, well. My lucky day." His accent sent goosebumps down her arms.

Rae met the stranger's golden eyes, dark hair, and cool-gray flesh. He wasn't wearing a mask as the others had, and she was forced to admire his smug smile; the sharp angles of his jaw; his long, slender nose. He'd kill her, and there'd be nothing she could do to stop him. She sank to the ground, managing to roll to her back as she fell.

He reached down, stripping her sword from her limp grip, and threw it aside. Powerless, she could only look at her empty hand as a cold numbness crept over every inch of her body. It took all her strength to keep her eyes open.

A blur of pink and red. The solid thump of a body hitting earth. Rae fought to focus on the face of Gairek, now lying motionless beside her, staring at nothing in particular. His neck was bent awkwardly, drawing her cloudy gaze to the shaft of an arrow protruding from the base of his skull.

A cold blade bit into her chin, forcing her head to face the maskless Bleck Larin towering over her. His smirk should have caused her to squirm with terror, but she was fading fast, her consciousness slipping away like grains of sand between fingers.

"Quite a fighter," he said as he glanced over his shoulder.

Her eyes followed. More Bleck Larin materialized from the forest. All of them in the same black leather, faces covered, amber eyes peeking from hoods.

"What a price you will fetch."

He may have said more, but her world went black.

Bleck Larin Court

The first thing Rae noticed as she came to was that her head was covered with a dark hood. The kind used when one had been taken to a secret location, or execution. The second was that she wasn't moving of her own volition. She was being held upright by her arms, her feet dangling. She shifted slightly in an effort to get a better view, but it was useless. She'd have to rely on her other senses.

The echo of large doors opening and closing told her she was being taken into a massive space, most likely made of stone. This would put her in a handful of places, none of which she wanted to be. Most were Bleck Larin strongholds.

From the footfalls, she could tell that she was accompanied by at least three elves. The footsteps were confident, familiar with the space, sure in their quest.

Whispered voices on either side washed against the walls. Maybe this was some sort of meeting hall or a throne room, which meant she could be in the royal palace. Quite possibly the last place she wanted to be. It was called the castle stronghold for a reason. It was known to be impenetrable and located just inside the Bleck Larin City of Parth.

"Well, Tace, what is so important you needed to interrupt my citizen hearings?"

The voice was youthful, rich. It seemed simultaneously imposing while impossibly gentle. The slightest accent confirmed her fears—it was the same accent as her captor's.

"I'm a citizen. So, I'm attending your hearings." Muffled laughter surrounded them.

At the very least, she could firmly identify that the man known as Tace was the Bleck Larin who had tranquilized her. She could never forget his voice.

"I bring you a Shay, Your Majesty."

Gods, she hoped she'd misheard and that he hadn't addressed the king himself. A ripple of true terror erupted against the inside of her ribcage. She was pushed to the ground, thankful her head was still covered so no one could see her wince as her shoulder slammed into the unforgiving stone.

"A Shay?" The slightest touch of malice whet the edges of the king's voice.

"Not just any Shay. A member of the royal family."

She was in serious trouble. What had given this away? She wasn't the only scout to wear the queen's crest on her uniform.

Her sword. She carried a shortsword inscribed with the House of Starling emblem—five stars encircling a starling in flight. There were only two who held the name, herself and her father, Queen Gemma's bondmate. Few elves carried House names, making it all the easier to identify the ones who did.

She lay limp for a moment before the hood was pulled away, light temporarily blinding her. She squinted past the pain and tried to push herself up, but with her hands bound and the last vestiges of the tranquilizer coursing through her veins, her body didn't respond as it usually would. Instead, she was yanked up to her knees by her hair, an involuntary yelp escaping her lips as the tracker's fingers dug into her scalp. It took a moment more for the fog of the sedative to fade so she could see the king clearly.

She'd heard of him—the mysterious King Mesmal of the Bleck Larin. It was said he hadn't left the castle stronghold since the start of the war. That he was calm, wise, and far older than Rae's stepmother, though one would never know by looking at him—proof that Bleck Larin lived significantly longer than Shay.

Here he stood, the cool-gray complexion of his face framed with raven-black hair tied back tightly in a topknot of considerable bulk, a single shock of white parting the left side. It was bound back with a golden cuff adorned with dragon wings and pinned to the crown of his head. The remainder of his hair hung long in elaborately plaited loops.

Like most Bleck Larin, his ears were much longer than a Shay's and sharply pointed, the tips reaching past the back of his head. The glorious, rich amber-brown of his eyes seemed to glow with an unnatural fire, accentuated by delicate eyebrows that arched in warm curiosity. He had a boyishly thin face, full lips, and a strong yet slender jawline. His expression gave nothing away. Stoic. Beautiful.

His eyes regarded her blood-spattered armor before he dismissed the others milling about the throne room with a curt motion. Before he spoke again, his eyes found Tace.

"Where did you obtain her?" The king's smooth voice was mesmerizing. Even the way his chest and shoulders moved as he breathed was elegant. Formal robes made of supple, creamy-white fabric shimmered as he moved. His ethereal presence was a jarring contrast against Tace's coarse manner.

"In the Middlelend Forest, just within the Bleck Larin territory," Tace said, sounding beyond pleased with himself. Smug and overconfident. "She ambushed my men as we were helping an elfling stuck in a trap."

"He lies." Rae couldn't stop the words from breaking free. They were the desperate words of a prisoner. "*I* was freeing the girl. Tace's men ambushed m—"

Tace yanked her to her feet and motioned toward something just out of sight. Another Bleck Larin stepped forward, presenting her shortsword—still soiled with the gore of elves—to the king, handle first.

Mesmal's eyes lingered on the inscription before he took the sword and leaned it against his throne. His eyes snapped to Rae before he returned his attention to Tace.

"This wasn't wise," he said, thoughts lingering on the careful curve of his eyebrows and the firm set of his jaw. He hid his frustration behind the emotionless mask the Bleck Larin were known for wearing. "Were there others? Shay you may have killed that were with her?"

Tace shifted his weight. "Another Shay dog who met his untimely end."

The reality of Tace's words hit Rae like a wave of frigid water. Gairek was dead. A hazy memory of his empty eyes wafted through her foggy mind. She hadn't known him long, but that didn't matter. It should have been her. With any luck, the patrol division would find him, and the lack of her body would prompt them to search. Maybe, just maybe, her stepmother would attempt to negotiate for Rae's return.

"You may leave, but the woman stays." The king folded his arms.

Judging by the way he hesitated, shifting his weight from one leg to the other, Tace was nervous. She counted his breaths, could tell his heart rate was elevated. Tace stepped to her side, allowing her to steal a glance. A bead of sweat glistened along his brow. He ran a hand over his head to smooth his hair where it was pulled tightly into a small topknot.

"But surely I deserve a prize for my gift, Your Majesty," Tace said, hesitating before continuing. "She killed four of my fighters before she was subdued. Perhaps some compensation for—"

"If you had brought me a gift, perhaps." A flash of anger so brief Rae almost missed it crossed King Mesmal's face. "But you have brought me a problem. Potential conflict that I was not prepared to deal with. You're dismissed."

Mesmal's final command sent a shiver along Rae's tensed shoulders.

Tace drew breath across his teeth. He clearly hadn't expected retribution for his hard work and sacrifice. He grunted through his nose before turning and striding past the other two men, snapping at them to follow.

Rae listened without looking back as their footsteps faded, and a massive door swung shut with a heavy finality that echoed through her very soul. She met the king's stoic stare. They were completely alone—herself and the King of the Bleck Larin. Whatever he intended to do with her, she was bound to find out soon, whether she liked it or not.

"Raemian Starling, daughter of the Shay Queen Gemma. I'd say it's an honor, but now I'm faced with a rather awkward predicament," King Mesmal said. He took a few impossibly graceful steps forward as he spoke. "This might have been more comfortable under different circumstances. As it stands, the daughter of my enemy." He said the final few words through clenched teeth.

"Stepdaughter," she said, dipping her head respectfully, "Your Majesty."

Her courage waned under his heavy gaze, her creeping fears washing over her as his curious eyes searched her face. After a painfully long pause, he stepped forward again. It was startling how tall he was. She was short for a Shay, and he held all the advantage of Bleck Larin height. Something she was only accustomed to while on the battlefield, sword in hand.

"Dare I ask what you were doing on the Bleck Larin side of the Middlelend Forest?"

His eyes lingered on the blood staining her jerkin, still fresh enough she could smell it. The blood of elves. Of Bleck Larin. She knew what he thought of her. The gore of his people was proof enough of what she'd been doing.

"Helping an elfling ensnared in a trap."

She swallowed hard, unsure if he'd believe her and wishing the girl were there to corroborate her story. What exactly had Tace done with her? It was too late to ask. Rae'd have to be satisfied with hoping the girl was alive.

"A Bleck Larin elfling, Your Majesty."

The edges of his temples relaxed, the wrinkle between his brows smoothing, encouraging Rae's confidence.

"She was starving to death," Rae continued. "I gave her water and cut her down. Before I could ask how she got there in the first place, I was attacked by your tracker's men."

He turned his back to her. Not entirely a wise move. Her sword leaned just out of reach against the side of his throne. She could easily edge past him and retrieve it, her mind calculating the exact speed required, the number of steps, the placement of each foot. If she could slip out and leave him alive, how quickly could she run from this place?

"Why release her from the trap? Why not let her starve? Or end her suffering and kill her?" He faced her again, a skeptical tilt to his head. "Has your queen not taught you to hate Bleck Larin? To kill us indiscriminately *on sight?*"

She considered her words carefully. In all honesty, she wasn't sure why. Something had caused her to cut the girl free, some feeling of compassion or pity strong enough that it had overridden her better judgment. It had likely been the guilt that had distracted her in the Middlelend Forest, prompting her to question why the Bleck Larin were her enemies at all.

Yet if she hadn't saved the girl, she could have avoided this entire situation. Gairek would still be alive, and they'd be back with the rest of the Shay patrol.

What did she regret more?

As she held the king's glare with her own, she realized she couldn't explain all of this. She'd have to distill her thoughts as best as possible.

"Because she was only an elfling. I was an elfling once. Weren't we all?" A rightness that she'd not anticipated filled the void left behind by doubt. She tipped her chin up with confidence. "To defend oneself in battle is entirely different from killing an innocent elfling."

The left corner of his lips curled up ever so slightly before his face returned to its same composed expression. It was impossible to know what he was thinking, to gauge what he'd do next, and if there was one thing that terrified her more than a blade to her throat, it was not knowing.

He cocked his head to the side as he approached her again, producing a blade with a deftness that caused Rae to take a cautionary step back.

"I won't hurt you." His hands on her own were warm and gentle. He cut the rope away from her wrists before returning the knife to its hiding place within the folds of his robes. "I'm afraid the years of warring have made our kind most suspicious of one another."

She rubbed her raw wrists, her eyes never leaving his. "Why not kill me and do your people a great service? Surely your generals would—"

He held up a hand to silence her, and she complied, pressing her lips together.

"Why defend your integrity so flawlessly to turn around and suggest such a thing?" He smirked at his rhetorical question, shaking his head slowly. "It wouldn't be a *great service*, as you say. I think peace is possible between our people if we can only put down our blades and use our words."

He watched her with rapt attention as he spoke, relaxing his already stoic expression to one of pure emotionless calm. "I see this potential in you, in fact."

"Potential, Your Majesty?"

"If you weren't capable of peace, why would you have spared the elfling's life?" He smirked. "You're dreadfully young. Do you even know why we fight?"

Did he know her age? What king would trouble himself with such trivial details of his enemy's stepdaughter? Rae didn't have the answer, and he didn't wait for one.

"These last thirty years have been the longest of my reign." His voice was steeped in sorrow that didn't touch his face.

He'd initiated the attack on Dormshire, had seen the death it had caused. The weight of those decisions rested squarely on his slender shoulders. This man had also been present for a long stretch of peace in Rhend and had seen generations of elves come before her.

She shook her head solemnly. She knew too little about the reasons for the first attack on Dormshire. She'd been an elfling then, and now she fought blindly for the queen because she'd been ordered to do so.

"Most don't." He gazed at her with a knowing curve to his lips that made her shiver. "I see so much of your mother in you."

"You knew my mother?" The words escaped before she could temper them, eyes going wide with shock she couldn't hide. She had so little information about her mother. Rae had been too young to remember, and her father had never been forthcoming.

A warm smile bloomed across his lips. "I knew both your parents. Before you were born."

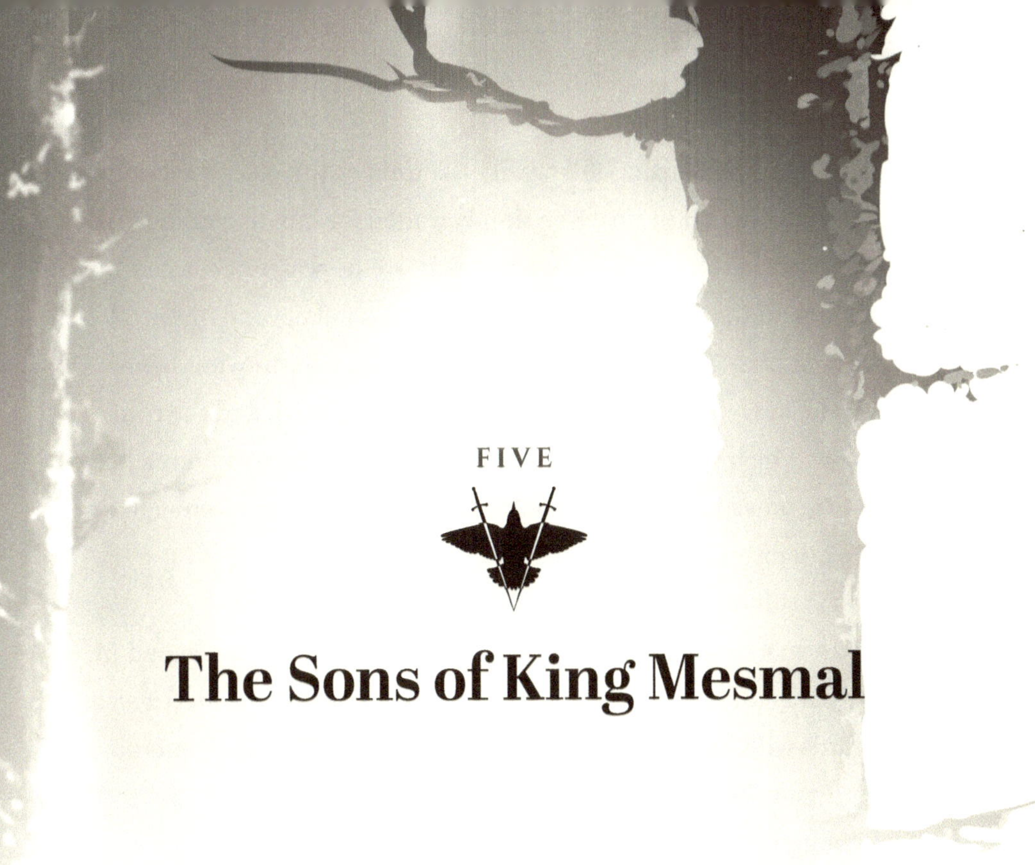

The Sons of King Mesmal

Rae couldn't speak, couldn't move. Her mother had died before she had solid memories.

"I knew your parents quite well, actually...before all this unrest." King Mesmal turned toward his throne.

Rae, unsure if she was meant to follow, stood in place. No matter how much she craved information—begged for it—she was still his prisoner, his enemy.

"I'm surprised Somin would agree to your involvement in the war. Or that he'd be willing to be bonded to the queen, for that matter... after all she's done."

Her mind snagged on his words. What did he mean by *all she's done*? Had it not been Mesmal who made the first fateful declaration of war? The king fell into his own quiet thoughts as he stopped at his throne and turned to face her. Sensing this wasn't the time or the place for asking her many burning questions, Rae simply waited for him to continue.

But when he took a deep breath to do so, he was interrupted by the creaking of the throne room door. From the hall beyond, three tall, strikingly similar Bleck Larin men stepped through, moving toward her and the king. There was no doubt they were related, and the confidence with which they moved spoke of their station. Rae swallowed her nerves. She prayed that she'd schooled her outward emotions enough to hide the mounting anxiety boiling under her skin.

"So the rumors are true," the tallest said as he approached.

If Rae was correct, she knew exactly who this man was. Second in authority only to his father, he was King Mesmal's eldest son. She'd never met swords with him, only seen him from a distance, but his reputation preceded him. He looked less menacing in his formal doublet and soft pants, though choice of garb did little to temper his air of superiority.

He thrust a patronizing hand in Rae's direction, his glare never leaving his father. "You do realize this woman has killed hundreds of your loyal soldiers." He turned his attention to Rae as he stopped only a few feet from her, placing his hands on his hips.

She knew Bleck Larin were tall from an eternity of swinging up at their heads on the battlefield, but being unarmed and surrounded by them was terrifying. These men had strength hidden behind willowy statures. Terribly strict combat training, rigid education, and traditions dictated much of their lives, making every last Bleck Larin a force to be reckoned with.

"She's a grave danger to you," he continued. "Why has she not been thrown in the dungeon? Or, more appropriately, dragged to an execution block?"

He shared much of his father's handsome features—the same clear amber eyes—but his hair was a rich navy, skin slightly bluer in tone. His confidence was both unnerving and perilously attractive.

"Please, Belkin, Raemian isn't here of her own volition," Mesmal said with a flat tone that left little room for concession.

Ah yes, she'd been correct. Prince Belkin. He'd led as high general of the Bleck Larin army for as long as they'd been at war. With an exceptionally strategic mind and fierce determination, he'd kept the Bleck Larin one step ahead of the Shay. Always ahead. It was rumored that he was not only fearless in battle, but ruthlessly deadly. If he possessed one kindness, it was that you wouldn't suffer from your wounds. He would make certain you didn't survive.

"Tace informed us that she was trespassing in the Middlelend Forest. His men found her attacking a Bleck Larin elfling," one of the other sons said, stepping forward. He wasn't as lean as Belkin. His eyebrows were more prominent, and while he had some of his father's features, his skin tone and hair were a softer shade.

Rae guessed he was Roulin. Always in the shadow of his elder brother, but renowned for contemptuous anger. He wore vengeful hatred like a badge on his sleeve, not nearly as good as other Bleck Larin at hiding emotions behind stoic expressions.

"He said he lost four of his own, taking her prisoner."

Rae's hands balled into fists, a sudden need to defend herself washing over her. "I cut the girl down from a trap. The elfling was starving to death from one of *your* tracker's snares." She'd kept her voice as level as possible, but her words still drew resentful glares.

"She's lying," Roulin spat, bitterness leaching from every pore of his cool-gray skin. "What reason would she have to tell the truth?" There was an air of pride in the way he conducted himself—a confidence that came from privilege and affluence rather than feats of strength in battle.

Rae folded her arms. What more could she say? The color of her flesh made her less than elven in their eyes. Instead of arguing, she studied them, taking in every detail: The way they displayed their emotions through words and body language rather than across their faces. The broadswords strapped to their sides, even in the king's throne room. They wore high-neck doublets in shades of deep red and black, with silver and gold embroidery.

"Send her out onto the moors tomorrow and let anyone lucky enough to beat me to her have their chance at revenge," Roulin said, exchanging a smirk with Belkin.

Rae's attention fell to the third son. He hadn't spoken yet. He stood perfectly still, weight evenly distributed on both legs as he watched her carefully. His curious eyes followed the path of her shaymarks, never leaving her. He was shorter than his brothers, but his frame was leaner, built on tight, toned muscles and a warrior's posture.

He matched his father the most in facial features, with the same fiery eyes, stone-gray complexion, and raven-black hair streaked with white along the left side. The same stolid expression on his face and the same impossibly handsome presence.

"You have an opportunity here, Father," Roulin said. "Send a message. Send the queen a finger, a hand, her head. *Something.*"

"Enough!" King Mesmal's raised voice startled Rae, and she took a half step back from him.

With a single word, she understood how this seemingly gentle man could command an entire race of elves.

"I won't punish her for what she's been ordered by her queen to do, just as I would never want my sons to be punished for what I've ordered them to do. She may be Shay, but she's an elf. Her blood runs red, like yours and mine." Mesmal turned toward Rae with a hint of concern in his eyes before it changed to sternness as he directed his attention back to his sons. "Belkin, Roulin, you may leave."

"This is ludicrous, Father." Roulin stepped forward, refusing to back down. "This monster is a murderer!"

"Then so are you. Should *you* be punished?" The king let his words sink in with a pregnant pause. His sons' silence was enough of an answer. "Now," he continued, eyes narrowing, "leave before I think of something else to do with you."

Roulin clenched his jaw, fiery fury simmering under the surface of his flesh as he pierced Rae with burning eyes, holding enough smoldering vehemence to raise the hair on the nape of her neck. He turned and stormed from the throne room. A slam echoed from somewhere down the hall a moment later.

"I fear you'll regret this, Father," Belkin said with clipped words. "Forgive me, but this could be the worst decision you've made since you called your soldiers to arms." He held his father with his eyes as he spoke the last few words, then left, brushing shoulders with the third son as he passed.

The king gazed at the open doors, his expression stolid and his chin raised, allowing the light from the high windows of the room to accentuate his sharp cheekbones, the silence burrowing like maggots into Rae's nerves. Moving only his eyes, he found his third son.

"Gastel, you have nothing to say?" When he finally turned away, the tension building in Rae's shoulders eased. "No accusatory comments? No *remedies* for this situation for me to consider?" Mesmal sat with as much grace as he moved and rested his elbows on the padded arms of his throne, letting his gaze fall again upon his third son.

Gastel didn't respond right away. The mysterious third son of King Mesmal, having never been confirmed by a living Shay, seemed to consider his words more carefully than his brothers. Rae couldn't help but watch him with obvious interest. For more than thirty years, he'd been kept tucked away. What reason would there have been for him to hide?

He took a deep breath through parted lips. "Only that if this is the great Raemian Starling, prized warrior of the Shay army, I've grossly misjudged her." He redirected his words toward Rae as he took a calculated step closer, his eyes penetrating her soul with curiosity so thick it caused her to take in a sharp breath. "I thought you'd be larger based on the stories I've heard. The savageness with which you have dispatched my brother's soldiers." He stepped forward again, emphasizing his height and the same dangerous air of confidence that he shared with his brothers. "You're not what I expected. Forgive my uneducated judgment."

There was an orneriness in Gastel's words that was jarring after the unbridled hatred his brothers had subjected her to. It had an edge of determination, of boldness.

Rae couldn't help but let her stern expression slip. Something about him was so different from what she'd expected—dare she think him affable?

His lips turned up for a split second before settling back into a mask of emotionless reticence Rae was already becoming accustomed to in these Bleck Larin.

"You do understand their frustration, right, Father? I don't agree, but I understand."

The king sighed heavily. "I hate that I do. I fear someday there will be a greater evil neither of our people can handle on our own. We'll need one another's strengths. What good will we be then if we wish only to kill one another?" He didn't wait for a response. "She's to be kept under house arrest in the tower, a sentinel to stand guard."

"Of course, Father. Your will is my deed." Gastel bowed, placing a hand parallel with the ground, thumb against his chest in a sort of salute. "This way, Raemian Starling of the Shay."

Rae took a single step in his direction before the king interrupted: "And Gastel. Thank you, as always, for your steadfastness. What would I do without you?"

"I'm sure you'd get by, but only just." Gastel winked at his father, then turned to leave.

Rae bowed as respectfully as she could before quickly matching Gastel's stride, following a few steps behind. She couldn't help but glance over her shoulder at King Mesmal, who watched her with a knowing twinkle in his eyes as she left.

SIX

The Tower

They wandered through halls with towering ceilings in a strange, boiling silence, questions swimming behind Rae's teeth. As vast as the stone walls appeared to be, the castle stronghold seemed empty—nothing more than a fortress of carefully carved stone to protect a king and his three sons. It was a stark contrast to the small dwellings of the Shay, built in tight clusters, allowing for a closeness and warmth these cold walls couldn't provide.

Her attention was drawn back to the grace with which Gastel moved—his easy gait, the way he turned his head just enough to see her out of the corner of his eye. His hair was pulled back tightly like his brothers' into a small topknot. The cuff securing it was much less ostentatious than his father's. Rae was certain it was an indicator of age, Gastel being the youngest of Mesmal's sons. Until now, no Shay had ever seen him. If the stories were true, she was only a few years older than him.

He silently directed her down an unadorned corridor to sharp-cut stone stairs which disappeared around a tight spiral. Without a word, he nodded, and Rae took the lead, ascending as quickly as she could. After scaling several flights, a small landing with a heavy wooden door broke their climb.

Gastel stepped past and opened the door. "Your suite, Princess." His eyes followed her in.

"I'm not a princess, Your Highness," Rae said with a bow.

She couldn't help but admire the lengths King Mesmal would go to hold her prisoner without throwing her in the dungeon. The room was sparsely furnished—a simple bed across from the door, a wooden chair at a small table, and a vanity with a wash basin. It was a forgotten room in a tall tower, tucked away in an impenetrable stronghold. The most notable detail was a massive window made of intricate stained glass, flanked by narrow sashes that could be opened to let in fresh air.

"Stepdaughter to the queen is still a daughter," Gastel said in a playful tone.

"She never hesitates to remind me I'm not of her blood," Rae countered.

"Meh, royal enough." He smirked, stepping farther into the room. "As my father said, you will be under house arrest. I'm certain only until he can return you safely to your queen." He met Rae's eyes. "Until then, consider yourself a guest."

"A very unwelcome one," Rae muttered.

He straightened, his expression falling. "I, for one, don't find you unwelcome." His eyes never left hers. "But I haven't had the pleasure of crossing swords with you on the battlefield. Perhaps if I had, I'd feel differently."

"Perhaps if you had, you wouldn't be alive to feel anything at all." She found him out of the corner of her eye.

He chuckled, a glint of mischievousness curving his lips as he stepped within striking distance.

Rae's hand fell to her side, the distinct lack of weapon making her shoulders stiffen. He would have had to be blind not to see her posture tighten, ready to strike with her hands should the need arise.

He turned away, inspecting the room, and Rae pried her eyes from the back of his head to gaze over at the stained glass.

The window was magnificent. Glass wasn't a common material used in Shay architecture, so it fascinated Rae all the more. It was a brilliant depiction of life before the war, a landscape along a shimmering river. A massive stone castle loomed on the horizon, framed by ironwood Shay dwellings. There were all manner of elves, Bleck Larin and Shay, even mysterious Trove elves, with their pure-white flesh and hair. Each was thoughtfully animated in such natural and fluid poses. If it weren't for the light streaming through, Rae may have thought it was a painting.

"My father told me that Parth was once home to all elves. He remembers those years fondly. Before the war." Gastel's voice was somber, and Rae risked glancing over at him. "This window used to grace the throne room, but he had it moved here when I was an elfling."

His attention was still cast at the window, and she let her eyes linger longer than she should have on the sharp angle of his jaw, the profile of his slender nose and full lips. Where his father wore a stoic mask, he wore graceful strength. He was beautiful. He met her eyes with a knowing smile, confirming she'd looked a tad too long.

"Perhaps, in our lifetime, Rhend will be like this again." He winked.

Heat rose in her face as she tried to craft a witty retort and failed. She glanced back up at the delicate glass, eyes landing on a pair of elves. The contrast of pink and gray hands joined together was startling.

"I hope you find your accommodations adequate."

His eyes wandered around the room one last time before stopping quite abruptly on her. Where his brothers carried clear hatred toward her, his body language was different—calm, confident, inquisitive. She knew she should hate him, that being alone with him should make her skin crawl. She should be doing everything in her power to kill the secret third son of her arch-enemy. Yet...

A smile crept across his lips. "If I didn't know better, I'd say you were sizing me up." He pursed his lips. "Perhaps you are."

She folded her arms, trying to push away her wretched uncertainty. "Just comparing you to your brothers. You're very different from Belkin and Roulin."

"Thank you." He placed a hand over his heart with mock appreciation. "That might be the nicest thing anyone has ever said to me." Sarcasm stained his words, but she could tell he wasn't being entirely facetious.

It took all her strength not to return the warm smile spreading across his lips.

They were enemies.

"You seem fearless in the face of danger," he said.

"Should I be terrified of *you*, Highness?"

He studied her feet before dragging his gaze the length of her body to meet her glare. A single brow raised as he cocked his head to the side, challenging her to find out.

If her cheeks had burned before, they were on fire now, but he seemed not to notice and finally—blessedly—turned away.

"I'll send someone to assist you with anything you might require." He stepped through the doorway and turned to face her before bowing, his amber eyes twinkling with mischief. "Good evening, *Princess*." And he was gone.

He was definitely not like his brothers.

Gastel's thoughts kept wandering back to the Shay sitting alone in the tower while he dined with his father and brothers. Would she have been sharing dinner with her own family? A friend? Alone in the Middlelend Forest? He had far too many questions considering she'd be but a momentary distraction in their lives. His father had yet to decide whether or how she'd be returned to her people. It was clear, however, that she wouldn't be staying long.

As he sat in the comfortable surroundings of the dining room, he wrestled with the overwhelming need to march back up the tower stairs and ask his burning questions. He had never met a Shay, had never left Parth. Born after the first major campaign of the war, he had never known a time of peace. He relied entirely on tales from his brothers to satisfy his curiosity about the world, but from the moment he'd seen the Shay in the throne room, he'd realized how disparaging Belkin and Roulin had been. Even his father had not been entirely forthcoming.

Having been told his entire life that Shay were frivolous, immovable, muscled meatheads, and lacking any worthwhile intelligence, he was confounded by her. She fit none of these descriptions, and while she'd regarded him with grave caution, she'd also dropped her guard enough to paint a very different picture of a Shay. Dare he admit that he wanted to see more?

"Belkin and I are to head up another small resistance strike at the Eastern Pass in a couple days, Father. Would you like us to return the monster to her people before we annihilate them?" Roulin asked, voice dripping with sarcasm.

Gastel winced, glancing at his brother, his patience wearing as thin as his father's surely was. Roulin was in his typical mood, cranky and critical of how things were being handled, but it was especially grating tonight.

"Roulin." The king slammed his flatware down. "I specifically requested that you not speak this way regarding Raemian Starling."

"A ridiculous request." Roulin pushed himself back and rose out of his seat.

Gastel clutched the edge of the table, knuckles growing white from the effort it took not to jump across and throttle Roulin for his blatant disrespect. Something Gastel was quite capable of doing, even if Roulin was over two hundred years his senior.

"Sit down," Mesmal said, his voice a knife's edge. There was no room for negotiation. "You're worse than Belkin. At least he has the sense to control his temper."

Belkin took a deep breath and folded his hands in front of him as if to further illustrate his loyalty. However, Gastel could see the angry fire in his eldest brother's eyes. Belkin likely agreed with Roulin, but he always managed to control his temper in their father's presence. Perhaps it was a sense of duty, but more likely, it was maturity.

Roulin stepped back from the table, so furious he was shaking. "When that *thing* is gone from this place, I'll return to this table, but until then, Father." He let his words hang thickly in the air, a miasma of hatred settling over them as he left the dining hall.

Belkin stood and bowed, following Roulin from the room, proving he at least had sense enough not to speak so disrespectfully to their father.

"That went well," Gastel said, unable to keep the cynicism from his voice as he relaxed back in his seat.

As Mesmal studied his hands, Gastel wished he could lay his father's thoughts out on the table and see what he truly thought about the situation. But he knew one thing for certain: his father would tell him only what he wanted Gastel to know—nothing more. Though the two of them spent countless hours in conversation, there had been little spoken about the Shay. It was as if his father purposefully kept the Shay from Gastel's world, the reasons for doing so a mystery.

"It seems I've underestimated Roulin's contempt." Mesmal rapped his fingers on the table, his eyes dark with frustration.

Perhaps he'd resigned himself to the idea of his older sons being unhappy with anything less than death for Raemian Starling.

"It wasn't so long ago that we were at peace with the Shay, tenuous as it may have been." His father traced the wood grain of the table's surface with an index finger.

It was perplexing how it could be so easy for Gastel to see but for his father to miss.

"Perhaps it's *this* Shay, Father? Raemian Starling in particular?" There was something in that name, more than the reputation of her proficiency in battle. More than the number of Bleck Larin soldiers she'd slaughtered with her blade. Something that his father was clearly not willing to share.

Mesmal met his questioning glance as he stood to leave. "Perhaps."

We All Bleed Red

An abrupt knock disturbed Rae, but she didn't bother getting up from where she sat cross-legged on the cold stone floor, doing her best to meditate. She'd already been given the evening meal. The sun had set. The servant who had taken away the remains of her dinner had brought her sufficient candles to light the room well into the night if she so desired. There didn't seem to be any reason she'd be interrupted.

Who would climb those stairs at this hour?

Gastel slipped in, closing the door behind him. His blazing eyes meandered across the meager furnishings of the room before finding her.

"What exactly are you doing on the floor?" he asked. His gently upturned lips should have warmed her, but she refused to let her guard down no matter how charming he was.

"I quite like the cold stone on my ass."

His smile intensified. "Is this an affliction all Shay share? Sardonic responses?" He stopped a few feet away, legs spread shoulder-width apart, hands on his hips. "And a lack of interest in proper chairs?"

There was familiar energy in his posture. He stood like a sword-master, poised, ready, and strong. She'd first noticed it in the throne room, comparing him to his battle-tested brothers. He had less of the arrogance of privilege—rather, the confidence that came with years of honing a skill to perfection. Something Rae was well aware the Bleck Larin were known for. Grueling training regimens were perhaps the only thing that could balance against the Gods-given strength of the Shay. His bearing was that of perfection—presence beyond any random elf.

When she didn't respond to his sarcastic questions, he came a few steps closer.

"I believe it safe to say that my brothers officially hate you," he said.

"I honestly expected nothing else." She held his gaze as best she could. The curiosity that emanated from him, the tilt of his head intrigued her more than they should. "Perhaps the fact that you don't is more unusual."

"They can't see past flesh. We're all elves." Seriousness cut through his words, and for a moment, all humor left his face. "We all bleed red."

Goosebumps rose on her arms under his heavy appraisal. She blinked a few times, not expecting this line of conversation. In fact, she wasn't sure what he'd come for. It seemed like a lot of stairs to climb to tell a stranger what they already knew.

The evenness of his breathing and the set of his jaw told her he was completely at ease. He didn't fear her. He was either wretchedly naïve or more than confident in his ability to defend himself.

Gastel looked over at the window, releasing her from the grasp of his attention. "I've always envisioned Shay as cocky, vapid creatures based on what my brothers have told me. Stout muscular beings with bright flesh, bright hair, and brighter attitudes." He crossed his arms. "You're the first I've met, and you don't seem to fit this description in the slightest. Care to explain yourself?"

"Like all Shay, I try to be respectful in the presence of royalty. Otherwise, I'm sure my *vapid* personality would be more evident," Rae said, trying desperately to keep him at arm's length.

"I still find it incredibly hard to believe that you've killed countless Bleck Larin. You seem so...gentle."

Gentle? Had she not tried hard enough to wear the mask of the killer she was? She didn't think *gentle* was one of her hidden characteristics. Not after the Bleck Larin she'd slaughtered. A gentle elf wouldn't have to debate between cutting an elfling from a net and killing her. A gentle elf wouldn't have calculated the steps it took to retrieve her sword and kill the king when he'd trusted her blindly.

She stood from the ground with what she hoped was a warrior's grace. That's what she was. That's what she would always be, and that's what she needed him to see. She needed caution reflecting in his eyes, not curiosity.

"I can't deny my exploits, Highness."

Her attempt at appearing dangerous had the opposite effect.

"Call me Gastel, please, Raemian." He pulled the single chair from the table and sat facing her, crossing a leg and folding his arms across his chest.

Warmth rose to her cheeks at his casualness. She turned away for a moment to recover her composure but immediately regretted it.

"Did I say something to embarrass you?" he asked, smiling wide enough to show his perfect teeth. "It's so hard to tell if you're blushing—your cheeks are already such a lovely shade of pink."

Did he have any idea what torturous heat boiled up inside her? Summoning her strength, she channeled her fighter's instincts before meeting his amber eyes, his single raised eyebrow, his knowing smirk.

"Would your brothers approve of you keeping such company?" She laced her voice with as much menace as she could muster. "Surely I think of nothing but killing your kind." Rae took a calculated step in his direction.

He shook his head in mock disbelief. "You try so hard to be fierce."

"Hand me a sword and see for yourself how fierce I can be."

He let out a short laugh—natural, beautiful—leaning his head back, exposing his throat in such a trusting way.

"You're so different from what I expected. Than I thought any Shay would be," he said.

"You aren't exactly the bloodthirsty demon I'm used to meeting in battle."

She startled herself with the truth in her response. He wasn't what she'd expected at all. Having always been at war, she'd had no way of knowing Bleck Larin were capable of such friendliness.

"Good. I've never been to battle." His smile intensified—if possible.

"Which seems strange with how involved your elder brothers are. Why have you been spared the rigors of war?" The shape of the word war lingered on her lips. A strange word that had carried so much weight in her life—an inky storm cloud hanging low over the latter half.

He hesitated, the smile slipping from his lips. Perhaps she'd found the illusive topic that would drive caution into his heart. They were enemies. He needed to see this, and she wished she didn't need to keep reminding herself.

"By the time I was born, the Bleck Larin had laid siege to Dormshire." He shrugged and looked down at his hands. "It wasn't my father's choice for me to train as a fighter. I begged for him to let me."

"That doesn't explain why you wouldn't join your brothers now."

He stood and took a timid step toward the door. It was clear the conversation had taken a turn he was no longer comfortable with, a sensitive subject that she'd drawn from the depths of family squabbles. She made the mental note, saving this little nugget of information in case she needed it in the future to tame his curiosity.

"At the moment, there doesn't seem to be enough room for three Bleck Larin princes ordering around my father's troops." He bowed and turned to leave. "I should go before I'm missed."

Rae was torn between what should be and what was, worried she wouldn't have another opportunity to speak so candidly with him again.

"Your father seems to trust your opinion. Perhaps he does not allow you to fight because he appreciates your advice?" she asked, causing him to pause midstep. "To be a king, to have the weight of such responsibility upon one's shoulders, I'd think it hard not to have reliable council."

He didn't turn; rather, he found her out of the corner of his eye. "Perhaps." He drew a sharp breath through tight lips. "Or perhaps I don't have it in me to shed the blood of elves."

A stiff posture replaced his confidence as he left, and he didn't look back this time. She hated to admit it, but it bothered her. As if she needed this man to accept her—to *like* her—even though she'd tried more than once to fortify the wall between them.

She'd never preoccupied herself with what others thought of her. It was a quality that drove her stepmother insane. A princess should care. A princess should carry herself in a way that accentuates her best qualities. Rae never bothered. She was, after all, not a princess.

After a few moments, Rae pulled her fiery-red hair from its braid and ran her fingers through it before flopping down on the bed, running her hands over the soft covering. She stared at the rafters high above. How would she spend her time for the rest of the evening, left with only her thoughts and this round room? What was left for her to meditate on?

The burning answer was Gastel. He was beyond perplexing—a smooth sheet of mirror that reflected nothing but her own misgivings. He and his father were a direct conflict with her preconceived notions of who these people were. As much as she hated to admit it, she'd have gladly spent several more hours peppering him with questions, trying to find the missing pieces to the puzzle that was the Bleck Larin. Not that she'd be given an opportunity. She was, after all, a prisoner, and he was the son of her captor.

The angry sorrow that she'd managed to avoid all day washed over her. What was the likelihood she'd see Freck again? Her home? Her father? She pulled herself from the bed, crossed to the window and found the view from one of the opened sashes splendid in the growing twilight.

Parth sprawled out below, a network of crisscrossing streets lit with lanterns that stained the cobbles with a honeyed sheen. Cut stone dwellings lined the walks, windows all shuttered for the night. The streets were empty, a stark contrast to the hustle and bustle of her own home, where the paths between dwellings would be congested with Shay milling about well into the night.

She faced the empty room, focusing on each of the furnishings until her eyes met the door that locked her in, a prisoner of a war that had thus far taken no prisoners. She shivered at the thought of remaining much longer and crept back to the bed, gazing up at the rafters again.

The fear that had consumed her when the hood was pulled from her head in the throne room flooded into every crack of her mental armor. The way the three sons of Mesmal had moved with purpose toward her would be something she would relive for days—more troubling than meeting them on the battlefield. She knew how to face her enemy with a sword, but this?

The indomitable Belkin had seen the destruction she'd wrought against his soldiers firsthand, but Roulin's hatred was deeper. He hadn't been able to hide it from tainting his perfect face. To them, the Shay were an evil blight upon all of Rhend. Shay were nothing more than wicked killers—vile creatures that deserved only death.

A flash of lifeless amber eyes crossed her mind. She couldn't deny what she'd done to their people. Rae stretched her hands toward the ceiling. Was what she'd known her whole life to be right and just, in fact, heinously immoral?

Unable to hold them in any longer, hot tears rolled back across her temples and mixed with her hair as she looked at those hands. They'd taken the lives of elves. Not by choice, but by decree. Would she have done any differently if she'd not been forced into the army by her stepmother?

To excel on the battlefield had been an unintentional side effect of self-preservation. She had not sought the glory of battle, and she certainly had not relished her conquests. Until recently, she had passed them off as necessary, burying her guilt. The Bleck Larin were enemies, to be killed on sight. They didn't have individual names and faces and families.

But King Mesmal had spared her life at her word alone. Gastel was curious and trusting, even if a touch naïve. Belkin, though battle-hardened, seemed to be an honorable warrior. She could only agree with his judgment. She was a monster and didn't deserve any kindness. She deserved the cold, wet misery of a dungeon floor.

She pulled herself from the bed, found a place against the round wall, and curled into herself. A hard sob escaped her lips as she gave in to her self-pity, crying until she slipped into a chao tic sleep filled with nightmares sculpted by guilt and retribution.

EIGHT

Questions Without Answers

Gastel found his father alone in his study, lounging in his favorite chair beside a roaring fire. Instead of a book, his father was reading old correspondence. The aged letters were sprawled out around him on the floor, with several stacked up in his lap and on the side table. Leather storage cases were strewn near a wall, as well as unopened ones, ready to be explored.

"I thought I'd find you here." Gastel sat across from his father in a smaller chair, its arms only slightly less worn from countless talks.

"Something troubles you, my son." His father didn't look up. He could always sense when Gastel was out of sorts. Perhaps a father's instinct, or all the time the two of them spent together in heavy conversation.

Gastel sifted through the thoughts that wrestled for attention in the depths of his mind to find a place to start. "What did you do this for? Why are we even at war?"

It was a question he'd asked before, using other, less accusatory words. If his father was bothered, he didn't show it.

"Here of late, I wonder the same thing myself, but at the time, it made perfect sense." He gave Gastel all his attention. "A great evil had been committed against our people, and retaliation was needed. Perhaps my response was a bit heavy-handed."

Mesmal never seemed fazed by the questioning, never hesitating in his response, but tonight was different. His tone seemed less sure.

Gastel eased back in his chair and stared at the fire, losing track of time as the flames danced around bright coals and stretched into the chimney. He considered his father's words. Some were ones he'd never thought through before. A great evil? So vague. What did he mean by retaliation? His father leafed through the letters in his lap and set another aside. The crinkle of paper brought Gastel back to the present.

"Is there a reason you refuse to send me into battle with my brothers? A real reason? Other than that you trust my judgment and require my advice?"

His father looked up at him with a pointed glare, the usual patience washing away. There was a sternness in the pinch of his lips. "Is there a reason you must know? I need to keep at least one of my sons protected. I can't have you all in harm's way. You are my heirs, after all." He waited for Gastel to speak again, eyes reflecting the golden light.

Gastel couldn't hold his father's stare. He found a pile of papers on the floor far easier to look at. "Why wouldn't you keep your eldest, your heir by birthright? Why endanger Belkin by having him command your army?"

"I have you both where your strengths are best. I trust your advice as much as I trust his strategic battle knowledge. Your empathy balances his warrior mettle."

"What of Roulin?"

His father shook his head, glancing over at the fire. It let Gastel see all of his father's face, to *truly* see him. His age showed. The wrinkles around his eyes and mouth were deeper than they usually appeared. Perhaps it was a trick of the light. Or perhaps Gastel had not wanted to see what had always been there. King Mesmal was growing old. The strain of ruling for centuries was finally taking its toll.

"Roulin would never be able to make coolheaded decisions, much less discuss the direction of a war that he'd see won with unethical techniques. His anger would result in the annihilation of a race he sees no reason to spare."

Gastel's father was right, of course. At least Belkin knew there was rationale not to annihilate an entire race. There were strategic advantages and skills that the Shay possessed that the Bleck Larin did not. A balance that the Elder Gods had intended. The Shay were the only elves capable of manipulating Eishtala magic. While rare, there were those who could use it for healing in miraculous ways. Besides, even the humans had been spared. They'd been restrained by an impenetrable barrier made of magic and barren earth instead.

"Where are these questions coming from this time?" his father asked with a wry smile.

Gastel was certain his father already knew and simply wanted to hear the words.

"Raemian Starling. She's very *perceptive*." Saying her name aloud caused a strange urgency to bloom in his chest, and he glanced away to avoid his father's knowing eyes. "She asked why I haven't gone into battle with my brothers."

His father took a deep breath and let the correspondence in his hand rest against his knees. "She's a strange one. The way she sees people is different. I don't think she always sees Bleck Larin and Shay. She sees a fighter, a nobleman, a king. She's always sizing up her opponent, but I'm not sure she knows who her opponent should be." He smiled more to himself than to Gastel and returned his attention to his correspondence. "What I wish I knew was whether she could ever be *without* an opponent."

"What do you mean?" Gastel followed his father's eyes to the weathered parchment.

"If she could just let herself exist. She's always counting, watching, waiting. I could see it in her eyes the moment Tace removed the hood from her head. She sees everything, hears everything. But can she let that go and just...*be?* Can she stop being a warrior, or is that her genuine and natural state of mind?"

There was a long stretch of silence between them before his father leaned forward, handing him a piece of old parchment. "What do you make of this?"

Gastel took the paper, reading quickly. The details were murky. Nothing seemed to fit quite right. He read it again. "This doesn't feel complete. Like something is missing, perhaps intentionally? Names, maybe? Or titles?"

"I was thinking the same. Much too vague. I fear I missed it initially." Mesmal placed the parchment in another pile. "Now I feel I must go through all these old letters to find where pieces have been left out and see if I can figure out why." Mesmal motioned to the mountains of correspondence around him. "These are all reports from the battle of Dormshire. I couldn't be there in person. Your mother struggled with her pregnancy, and I refused to leave her. Especially after what started all of this."

"What exactly was it that forced you to start a war?"

His father sighed, avoiding his son's eyes. "I'm not ready to explain. Just know that I carry a weight of guilt on my shoulders so heavy I'll never be without its burden."

The silence that followed was deeper than usual. Gastel had over-reached again in his questioning. "I shall leave you to your work, Father. Forgive me for prying."

"You're welcome to pry, my son. I'm just not ready. Not yet." He took a deep breath, letting it out long and slow before glancing at Gastel. "Perhaps Raemian can change things. Then again, perhaps not."

Gastel wasn't sure how or why Raemian could change anything, but his father wouldn't be telling him. At least, not now.

"I'll see you after the citizen hearings, Father."

Gastel left his father's study with more questions than when he'd arrived—and an entire day to dwell on them.

The day passed achingly slow. Rae tried her best to keep occupied, devouring books a servant had kindly provided. Meals were delivered—delicious, plentiful meals—not what a prisoner should be served, which, the longer she spent alone, the more she contemplated. From Mesmal's words, it was clear he intended to return her to the queen. It made her question the king's motivations. After years of war, why the change of heart now?

She stood at the window, spying at the Bleck Larin milling about the streets of Parth. So much space. The market was practically vacant compared to Shay markets. Perhaps it was her bird's-eye view that made it seem that way, but thus far, her impression of Parth was an abundance of vastness while the Shay crammed themselves into tight quarters.

A soft knock drew Rae's attention. The thick pause before Gastel entered did not allow enough time for her to prepare for his presence. She had known him for just over twenty-four hours, and in that time had struggled to force her thoughts onto other topics. He clashed violently with what she knew to be true about her enemy. Worse yet, she found it impossible to dislike him.

"I don't suppose you'd be interested in some company," he said.

She doubted he'd actually leave if she said no. Not with the glimmer of curiosity in his eyes.

"I don't suppose you obtained permission to come this time," she said, hopefully reminding him of his last unsanctioned visit.

"Where's the fun in that?" He took a few smooth steps in and pulled the chair from her table. "Besides." Flipping the chair around, he straddled it. "I'd rather ask forgiveness than permission."

How was it possible that Belkin and Roulin's younger brother was so agreeable? Had they not been raised by the same father? Rae swallowed her intrigue. She needed to build her walls before it would be impossible to do so. She forced her attention back to the city below.

Gastel materialized next to her, silent as death. She took a step back, but he didn't seem to notice as he gazed out the window. She tried not to allow her eyes to linger on his handsome profile, the way his steel-colored skin warmed in the sunlight.

"You really like avoiding me," he said as he turned toward her, leaning against the windowsill.

His crooked smile ignited a fire in her gut. Elder Gods be damned, this was impossible.

Rae's eyes fell to his broadsword. He was close enough—she could elbow him in the face as she retrieved it. The thought repulsed her. Gastel had been nothing but gracious.

"While I appreciate your kindness, Highness, I'm—"

"Gastel."

"Hmm?"

"Like I've said, call me Gastel." He pushed off the wall and walked to the center of the room. "If I had the evening meal waiting outside, would you share it with me?"

She eyed him with suspicious. "I don't think that's a good idea."

"Oh?" His hands found his hips.

"I'm not the best company," she said as she lifted her chin with confidence.

"According to whom?"

"Belkin. Roulin. Take your pick." Gastel's brothers' names slipped out faster than intended.

"Lucky for you, I don't usually agree with my brothers' opinions. But," A wry smile spread across his lips. "I'm beginning to think you'd rather I leave anyway."

"I…" She needed him to leave, but part of her wanted him to stay. "I just don't think—"

"It's fine. Two questions," Gastel said. "Two questions and I'll leave you be."

"You've done nothing but ask questions."

Gastel chuckled. "Two *more* questions, then."

Rae folded her arms. "What kind of questions?"

"Does it matter?" he asked, folding his arms to match hers.

"It does, and that was a waste of a question."

His eyes grew large for a split second before an ornery smile slipped across his lips. "Very well then. I'll make my second one count." He took a heavy step toward her, his eyes holding her glare. "Why didn't you take my sword? If you're so vicious and deadly, why didn't you take it, kill me, and escape?"

Her eyes darted to his sword again.

"Oh, I noticed," he said. "I hadn't realized how stupid I'd been wearing it here until you glanced at it."

She smirked. "Perhaps I should have taken it, if only to teach you not to be so naïve."

"That doesn't answer my question."

She turned away, her cheeks heating with embarrassment. She should have taken his sword, and even if she had left him and everyone else in the castle stronghold alive, she should have taken the opportunity to escape. Rae from a week ago would have. Rae from a week ago would have killed any Bleck Larin in her path.

"Silence is not an answer."

"The kind of question matters," she scoffed.

"Very well." He walked around so he was once again in her line of sight. "If I gave you my sword, what would you do?"

What would she do? She already knew she couldn't kill Gastel, but what about his brothers, the king, the guards, the servants? A nagging voice in the back of her mind kept repeating, *They are all Bleck Larin, the enemy.* Yet, she had been treated with kindness by everyone aside from Belkin and Roulin.

"That's essentially the same question," she finally said.

A smug smile crossed his lips. "I guess it is." He turned to leave. "I'll see myself out. Enjoy your dinner, Raemian."

As he left, a servant brought in the evening meal. Gastel hadn't bluffed about having it outside the door. She turned back to the window to hide her burning cheeks.

NINE

Observations

Rae woke with a start, sitting up from where she'd slept on the floor. Again. The sharp light streaming through the stained glass was a blinding reminder of the time. She rubbed the sleep from her eyes. She'd sat at the table most of the night, digging through one of the books on Bleck Larin history and making mental notes of all that seemed to contradict her own knowledge.

She startled at a sharp knock and pulled herself up, combing her fingers through her hair before calling for the door to be opened.

She'd mistakenly thought it'd be a breakfast delivery. Instead, she found herself face to face with one of the last people she wanted to see in her current state. It was clear Gastel had been awake for hours. She straightened her posture and tried to make it appear less like she had just dragged herself from sleep.

"Did you sleep well?" He left significant space between them and was unarmed, yet still rested his hand where the pommel of his sword would have been.

Smart to leave his broadsword behind this time.

"I slept as well as I could under the circumstances," she said.

She smoothed down the front of her jerkin out of nervous habit, tugging at the bottom. She hadn't bothered removing it to sleep—the tight leather hugging her ribs was a comfort.

"My father wishes for you to join us for the morning meal." He paused as if to think through his next words more carefully. "You're not required; he thought perhaps you'd be lonely."

She was lonely. An unyielding pressure had been placed upon her heart. Here in this room, though it wasn't a dungeon cell as it should have been, she felt oppressively isolated. She hesitated, wondering if there was a reason for the invitation other than kindness. She paused for too long.

"I'll have your breakfast brought to you," he said, turning to leave.

"Wait!"

The word escaped her lips more rushed than she would have liked. She didn't want to sound desperate or vulnerable. *Weakness in the eyes of her enemy? Unacceptable.*

She was unable to miss how he froze and looked down at his feet, pausing a moment before turning. A cool, stoic expression schooled onto his face as he waited for her to continue—his father's face.

"I'll join you. Forgive me. My head is..." She squeezed her eyes closed, trying to clear her mind. "Foggy. I just need a moment." She smiled timidly, but he didn't return it this time. Instead, he nodded and stepped out, letting the door close behind him.

She rushed to the wash basin. The cool water helped wake her as she cleaned the last of the sleep from her eyes. She combed her unruly red hair with her fingers and tied it back at the nape of her neck before gazing at her reflection in the mirror.

What she saw was a Shay girl, shorter than others, thinner, and built with lean muscles. Possessing a slender neck and defined collarbones, which she tried to hide beneath her shirt. The other female Shay were voluptuous and muscular like the men, with full, round faces; wide shoulders; thighs that could run for days; and ample breasts that lured the eye.

She had none of these traits. Other than her complexion and distinct shaymarks that danced along the sides of her face and neck like red lace, she resembled a Shay elfling. She stared with deep blue eyes into the face of a murderer.

That's what she was, wasn't she?

She shook the thoughts away and stepped back. This wasn't the time to question one's existence. Not while a prince waited. Not while a king showed such kindness to allow a prisoner to dine with him. She hurried after Gastel.

Something had changed about his posture. He was stiff, less relaxed, and every step seemed forced. Whatever the reason, it made for a long, awkward trek through the castle stronghold.

When they finally reached the dining hall, Gastel showed her to a chair toward the end of the table before he seated himself across from her, placing both elbows on top, fingers steepled before his lips. He met her gaze with an intensity so strong her eyes watered. Thankfully, she had a new room to regard.

It was a calm room, the walls the color of the summer sky. The farthest wall was bisected by a massive floor-to-ceiling window, frosted with sheer curtains, diffusing the warm pinks and oranges of morning light. The table, capable of seating twenty, was flanked by soft landscape paintings. In her scrutiny, Rae noted the wood finish was worn thin along the stiles and splats of the first few chairs, indicating that perhaps these were the only seats ever used on a regular basis. Four chairs for a king and his three sons.

King Mesmal didn't keep them waiting long. He seemed to float toward them with an unmatched grace. Rather than formal robes, he wore soft black pants; a cotton shirt drawn closed in the front with laces; and a deep-red, high-neck vest embroidered with dragons in glistening silver thread. Sitting next to Gastel, it was hard for her not to compare how much thinner Mesmal was—clearly not a fighter as it seemed all three of his sons were.

"Forgive me for keeping you." He smiled first at Gastel and then at Rae before taking a seat at the table. "And thank you for joining us, Raemian. I trust you slept well?"

"As much as possible, Your Majesty. I'm not used to sleeping within vast walls of stone." She tried to keep her tone light, stripping any accusation from her voice.

Mesmal smiled for a moment before he turned his attention to his son. "And you, Gastel?"

Gastel met his father's kind gaze. "I saw Belkin and Roulin off before the sunrise. They were taking a small contingent force to the Eastern Pass. They hope to be home by evening if all goes well." He took a deep breath, holding it for a moment longer than he should have before releasing it. "It would have been interesting to accompany them."

The moment of tension between father and son was thick enough that Rae held her breath. She had planted this seed by asking Gastel why he didn't join his brothers.

"Your presence is needed here." Mesmal seemed unfaltering in his convictions, confirming what Rae had already suspected: for some unknown reason, King Mesmal was keeping his youngest son hidden away.

"We needn't discuss this again so soon, I should hope." There was a finality in Mesmal's tone that made Gastel sit back in his chair, his posture cowed, eyes averted to his hands carefully folded in front of him.

The silence between father and son stretched mercilessly until servants swept into the room with plates of breakfast delectables, bowls laden with fruit—some familiar, some unfamiliar. Platters of cheese and bread, a tureen of porridge garnished high with nuts and granolas and cinnamon sticks. After all the vessels were delivered, delicate plates were placed before them.

The sight of delicious treats caused Rae's mind to drift to Freck. He was never one to turn down a meal. It was possible he fought against Belkin and Roulin's forces at that very moment. She pushed her worry for him deep down to dwell on later when she was alone in the tower.

"Please, Raemian, help yourself," King Mesmal said, dismissing the tightness in the room with four words. "If there's some other nourishment you require, don't hesitate to ask, and I'll see if my chef can prepare it for you."

There was nothing left of the uncomfortable conversation in his expression—only kindness and his usual comforting calm.

She risked glancing up at Gastel as he reached to take hold of a platter nearly overflowing with berries and nuts. His features were cloudy, strained, eyes downcast, and his knuckles turned white as he gripped the platter. He was trying to hide his frustration, and perhaps he was doing better than Rae thought, but she could clearly tell he was bothered by his father's words.

"I've decided to return you to the queen in two days," Mesmal said. "I'd like to give Belkin time to recover after he returns from his current campaign."

Everything in the room stopped. Gastel froze in place, a fork full of fruit nearly to his mouth. Rae set her own fork down beside her plate and met Mesmal's gaze. Undeterred by his son's reaction, he directed all his attention to Rae.

"I shall send a small retainer of trusted guards with Belkin to take you. Correspondence regarding terms of peace and my personal seal will be delivered to the queen with my highest regards as to your conduct while in my care." He appeared to be waiting for Rae's opinion.

"That's not advisable." Gastel dropped his fork of food on his plate, causing Rae to flinch. "How can you even begin to trust Belkin when he's already voiced his wish for her death?" The words rushed from him.

"I think that's the most forcefully negative feedback I've ever received from you," King Mesmal said with a slight smile that never touched his eyes.

"I can take her. I'm more than capable, with or without the—"

"I need you *here.*"

Gastel's face darkened, brows furrowing, making him appear more like his brothers than his father. He slammed his hands down flat on the table and rose from his seat, sending Rae back in her chair, her hand slipping reflexively to the empty place at her side.

"Let me do this. Let me do one thing for you that doesn't require remaining at your side." Gastel thrust his hand out toward Rae to emphasize. "You'd risk this chance for peace on Belkin and his short temper? One out-of-turn word, one wrong move, and he'll kill her."

Mesmal shook his head, undeterred. "She won't be harmed. I'll return her weapons to her before the journey. If her reputation is accurate, she'll have no problem defending herself against the likes of Belkin, should the need arise, which it won't. You should give your brother more credit."

Gastel straightened, looking over at Rae, his expression softening, and she found herself dreadfully curious about what he thought at that moment. Without another word, he stormed from the dining room.

For a few moments, Mesmal continued eating in silence while Rae tried to sift through the pieces of the conversation. The way each word had been enunciated. The way Mesmal had stayed completely calm. It was obvious from his comment that Gastel wasn't prone to outbursts.

Gastel had a dangerous concern for her well-being. If she should ever meet him on the battlefield, her warrior instincts would always override. Wouldn't they?

"Do you have any objections?" Mesmal waited patiently for her response, no emotion in his voice. "It seems Gastel certainly does. I've never known him to be so forceful in his convictions."

His words confirmed Rae's thoughts, but it didn't cool the strange fear that boiled up inside her. She wasn't ready to be their enemy again.

She hoped the pause to collect herself would be taken as a moment of cool-headed thought. She desperately tried to keep all the tumultuous emotions from her face, but the muscles in her neck tightened with every breath, with every thought that raced through her mind.

She wasn't ready.

"My only concern is whether you wish for Belkin to deliver your declaration directly to the queen," she replied as confidently as she could. "She may not be as interested in returning him safely, as you have been in returning me."

Rae didn't mean anything threatening by her words, only practical information. The queen was far less cool-headed. Even with a declaration of peace in hand, Belkin was the heir to the Bleck Larin throne, the son of the queen's arch enemy—a delicious temptation for a queen who harbored grave hatred for the Bleck Larin.

The king nodded, leaning back in his seat. "A concern I've considered."

He took another bite of his breakfast, chewing slowly and glancing absentmindedly at his plate. It gave her eyes a moment to travel the plains of his face. He wore his age with a grace that couldn't be said for other elders. He could have been another of his sons. Not a single silver thread stained his midnight-black hair, other than the pure white streak he shared with Gastel. He had lines along his eyes and the corners of his mouth, but who wouldn't after what was surely over a millennium of life?

He glanced up at Rae with mischief in his eyes, his lips upturned in a wild, youthful mirth. "I may need your help with something."

TEN

The Power of Fear

Belkin and his regiment rode out at dawn for the Eastern Pass, eager for action. The last time Bleck Larin forces had fought a Shay host this size, they'd taken heavy casualties. Rumors it had been Raemian Starling's contingent made Belkin gnash his teeth. The answer to that troublesome problem sat in the tower at the castle stronghold, but his hands were tied. He wouldn't go against his father's wishes, no matter how foolish they were. What frustrated him more was how Gastel had seemed drawn to the girl. After all the information they'd given the boy, he was still too stupid to see sense.

Today, Belkin led fifty hardened, elite Bleck Larin soldiers. Having two of King Mesmal's sons present was risky, but Belkin was confident this time. After all, the girl was in the tower. While the Shay army had other formidable warriors, none could bring the cold chill of apprehension like her name.

They found the troublemaking Shay loitering along the Eastern Pass. Striking fast and hard, they forced the remaining dozen or so to retreat beyond the Great Oracles that marked the border between Bleck Larin territory and the Shaylands. The city of Dormshire hovered on the mist of the horizon, out of reach without a full-scale army and siege weaponry.

Belkin sat atop his favorite horse, Jore; his first lieutenant, Tildimin, rode beside him. His men stalked the battlefield, rounding up the last few Shay survivors. They'd be interrogated, then slaughtered. It was standard practice. Neither side took prisoners. It was the harsh reality of war or, more importantly, *this* war.

Roulin rode up from behind, a handful of warriors in tow. "There was a smaller force nearly to the moors." He was ill-tempered as usual. It was both his best quality in battle and his worst as a brother. "We managed to keep one alive for you."

One of Roulin's men rode forward, a Shay woman bound and strapped over the back of his saddle like a deer carcass.

"Bring her." Belkin dropped from his horse as the woman was thrown to the ground.

She was badly beaten but still struggled against her bindings with an undiminished will to live. She glared up at Belkin with hatred in her sky-blue eyes, blood still running from her broken nose.

"Just kill me," she spat as he crouched to her level, his face coming dangerously close to hers, willing all his own hatred to burn in his eyes.

He needed her fear to compel her to talk. He needed to know why there were so many Shay brazenly roaming his father's lands. What had changed over the course of a few days to make them so brave?

"Trust me, I'll kill you when I'm done with you." He pushed a lock of red hair from her face, a gesture that may have been considered tender in other circumstances.

There was one line Belkin wouldn't cross, one that he didn't allow his soldiers to entertain. What some of the other forces had been known to do with the women they defeated was immoral. But the *fear* of what he could do to her was something he could use. And would use.

He took his time taking in all her curves. He wanted her to see his eyes travel the length of her body. He wasn't particularly attracted to Shay women, but they weren't ugly, per se. Despite her wounds, this woman may have even been considered attractive. She had a slender jawline for a Shay, long nose, pouty lips. Her full breasts burst from the top of her cuirass; navel exposed from below. Her shaymarks, visible on her toned stomach, wrapped elegantly on to her hips. Strong yet voluptuous.

"Tell me why your forces thought it wise to cross so close to Parth?" Belkin asked.

He left his lips parted, pleased with the terror building in her eyes as he placed a single hand on the inside of her thigh, his fingers meandering.

She swallowed hard, squeezing her eyes closed.

"The queen's stepdaughter." When she opened her eyes again, they filled with tears. Death was one thing; rape, something entirely different. The shame of how her body could be used for his pleasure burned in her hateful glare. "She was kidnapped by you monstrous fucks." She swallowed hard. "The queen will stop at nothing to get her back."

The woman flinched as he leaned closer, his lips mere inches from her neck.

"And if I kill Raemian Starling?" he whispered.

The muscles in her neck flexed as she struggled to pull away from him but couldn't. His hand held her in place at the bottom of her breastplate, his knuckles grazing against the hot flesh of her abdomen.

"She'll invade Parth." The woman struggled hard against him as he brought his knee down between her legs and leaned over her, lips brushing the edge of her earlobe. He could smell her blood, the bitter scent of her sweat—the stench of war and fear.

"With what force? The queen's army is nothing compared to my father's."

She went rigid when she realized who he was. He never wore emblems on his armor, and aside from the cuff on his top knot, he wore nothing that could distinguish him from the other soldiers. The Bleck Larin royal crest was hidden on a silver chain tucked within his shirt. He wished for anonymity. The last thing he needed was a target on his back.

She couldn't stop a sob from escaping. She knew she was already dead.

"The queen will stop at nothin—"

He didn't let her finish. He plunged his dagger to the crossguard up through the softness under her jaw, hot blood pouring from her gaping mouth. He sat back on his heels, letting her slump to the ground. He didn't have time to hear the same words a second time. She was dead before her head hit the earth. His gift, an instant death.

He wiped his dagger in the grass before mounting Jore again, settling back into his saddle as he glanced over to Roulin. They were finished here, but they had more work to do. If there had been Shay on the moors, they'd need to run the length of the Middlelend Forest to be certain no others could endanger Bleck Larin civilians. He shook his head as Roulin reined in his horse.

"They search for the girl. Emboldened by the queen's declaration of a full-scale invasion."

Roulin scowled. He didn't need to tell Belkin how he felt. He'd made it more than clear the day before.

"Looks like we'll be getting home late," Roulin quipped.

They shared knowing nods before breaking away to round up the troops. Midday was slipping away, and they still had much to do.

The Enemy

It was well into the depths of night when Gastel perched himself near the armory gate to wait for his brothers' return. He leaned against the cool stone façade of the stronghold, mulling over everything that had happened. The fact that Belkin would return Raemian to the queen made his blood boil. He was angry and confused, with no idea how to handle any of these emotions properly.

He'd always been content as his father's trusted confidant, never considering there might be reasons he wasn't permitted to leave Parth.

All of that had changed in a single moment.

Everything he thought he knew melted away, revealing a world that had been kept from him like a dirty secret. Shay were supposed to be brainless, beastly elves. Naturally muscular, not having to work nearly as hard for their strength and fighting skill, but lacking in substantial intellect and ability to school their emotions. Yet Raemian was perceptive, calm, clever. Strong, yes. Tight, toned muscles, yes—but beyond everything else, she was refined.

He had not been prepared.

Her power of perception was uncanny. It seemed she could see his fighting prowess simply by watching him move, which made him terribly self-conscious and more confident at the same time. He'd wanted to ask her all the questions his brothers and father had never answered, but she kept him at arm's length, building a wall that she seemed insistent on keeping up between them, making him even more curious.

The sound of soldiers approaching on horseback broke his thoughts. They poured over the bridge from Parth and through the opened portcullis into the stronghold's bailey. A few shy of fifty strong, with a handful of bandaged warriors from battle, streamed in. Belkin broke away and rode toward the armory rather than the stables. Arms crossed, emotions tucked away as best as possible, Gastel stepped from his hiding place, just as his brother reached the gate.

"You didn't have to wait up, little brother," Belkin teased. He was at least good-humored enough to attempt sarcasm.

"How did we fare?"

With a grace that hid the stiffness of hours in the saddle, Belkin swung down from his horse, handing the reins to a groom who rushed out to greet him.

"As well as we could." He strode past Gastel and into the castle, shedding armor as he walked and handing pieces off to a servant who struggled to keep up. "The Shay are out in force. They search for the Starling girl."

Belkin didn't stop, passing through the armory into the main hall without removing his breastplate.

"We managed to interrogate one of them," Belkin said. "Gemma is furious. She needs to be dealt with." It was obvious from his pace he wouldn't be waiting until morning to speak with the king.

A pinch of guilt added urgency to Gastel's step as he walked beside his brother. He knew what his father had planned, and he was the last person that wanted to give this news to the eldest prince.

The reasons Gastel's father wanted to send Belkin instead of him tore at his insides. What possible reason could outweigh the inherent danger Belkin posed to Raemian? Plus, Gastel's worry was selfish. A part of him wanted the task to get out of the castle, which he was rarely allowed to do, and to leave Parth, which he'd never done. He'd be lying to himself if he didn't also acknowledge some part of him wanted every last moment he could steal with the Shay woman.

They wordlessly pressed on through the quiet hall and into Mesmal's private study, where their father was once again pouring over correspondence by firelight. Foregoing the usual formalities, Belkin stood before the king, no bowing, no pleasantries.

"The girl needs to be dealt with. Either you can handle her or I will, but Gemma won't wait much longer before she sends her army. She thinks the girl was deliberately kidnapped." Belkin allowed a poignant pause to emphasize his next words. "We should have sent her head back with your kindest regards, followed by our full might. Now we've lost the element of surprise."

Gastel's attention was drawn to piles of correspondence spread out across the floor and a wide-eyed, cross-legged Raemian. She looked up with brows raised in shock as her eyes met Belkin's.

Belkin took a step back, his face contorting in rage as he drew his sword. The sound of metal scraping across a scabbard's edge was enough to raise the hair on the back of Gastel's neck.

"Calm down, Belkin," Mesmal said, rolling his eyes in a very unkingly way before looking back down at the papers in his lap. Only their father could shrug off Belkin's anger and live. "I needed her eye for detail."

"This is...*insane*, Father. This is..." A strange, exasperated sound escaped Belkin's chest.

Unsure of what to expect, Gastel was frozen in place. Raemian's eyes traveled the length of the saber in Belkin's hand to his face. Not an ounce of fear broke her mask, just a hard expression built on years of battle.

The silence was broken by the sound of Belkin's boot as he slid his lead leg forward, angling his sword. Raemian appeared to be the picture of uncertainty, but Gastel knew she was likely prepared, a snake ready to strike, muscles taut in anticipation. He'd noticed the same posture when he'd stepped a bit too close to her in the tower.

Belkin was the first to move, swinging his saber around his shoulder and down. With unnatural speed, Raemian twisted, reaching for something out of sight beside Mesmal's chair. Belkin's killing blow was halted inches from her face, the sharp sound of metal against metal causing Gastel to grit his teeth. She had retrieved a sword from somewhere. Why his father had the blade in his study was beyond him, but it saved Raemian's life.

Belkin towered over her with her back pressed into the floor, her knees cocked on either side of his legs. Gastel reached for his own weapon but found his hip empty, a decision he never thought he could possibly regret, yet here he was, wishing he had a way of diffusing the situation.

"Leave her," Gastel said, not intending for his words to sound so stern, so foreign to his own ears.

"Stay out of this, Gastel. You know not who she is." Belkin sneered, spitting the last few words through clenched teeth.

With a primal grunt, Raemian thrust to the left side, driving Belkin's blade into the stone floor before she snapped with lithe ease to her feet, hands never touching the ground. Belkin wasted no time, swinging back, the rage of war escaping him. She deflected his blow, using her diminutive height to duck under and strike hard against Belkin's breastplate as she twisted from under his lead arm. Without this last piece of armor, she would have gutted him.

She flowed clear of Belkin's next swing, but his reach was longer than hers, and she couldn't avoid him as he advanced. Their swords came together overhead, faces only inches apart, equally matched in strength as they snarled at each other. Gastel pried his eyes away from them long enough to glance at his father, who was also at a loss for what to do.

Blades skated across each other, steel grinding until they slid apart. Both fighters spun away, only to slam together like equal parts of the same force. Multiple times their swords met, until Belkin was slower to recoil. Raemian caught the edge of his saber's guard with the tip of her shortsword, lacerating his hand and sending his blade spinning across the floor.

With what appeared to be every intention of cleaving Belkin's head free of his shoulders, she swung again, stopping only millimeters from his throat. He could do little more than hold his hands out to his sides, his right dripping blood. Instead of killing him, she glared up at him over the top of her sword. After a few seconds, she pressed the edge against the collar of his shirt, just above his breastplate. She waited, searching for something in Belkin's hardened expression, as all the hatred melted from their faces.

Belkin seemed to accept defeat, taking on the same stoic calm Gastel had seen so often in his father.

"Do it. *Finish me,*" Belkin said, his lips hardly moving, voice barely above a whisper.

Instead, Raemian's shoulders relaxed, and she pulled away, eyes still searching Belkin's as she held her weapon out to her side and dropped it to the ground with a final metallic peal as it hit stone.

With deadly speed, Belkin lunged. Before Raemian could do little more than grab his wrist, he seized the back of her neck and pressed the dagger hard against her throat. Their eyes locked again in a silent exchange of hatred as viscous as blood itself.

She tipped her head back, letting the blade bite into her flesh, lips parting as she calmly observed Belkin's frenzied eyes. "Kill me, Prince. But may you live the rest of your long life wondering why I spared *you* first."

He held her there, all the rage of years at war clouding his eyes, turning them the color of the golden sun. She didn't flinch as he dug the dagger deeper into the soft flesh of her neck.

Time was strange at that moment. It may have been seconds or minutes, Gastel couldn't be certain. Long enough that a line of blood carved a path to her shirt collar before Belkin finally pushed her away and threw the dagger to the ground. He met his father with the accusatory index finger of his bloody hand.

"You play a dangerous game, old man." He looked to Gastel, shaking his head before returning his glare to Raemian. "We aren't finished, Shay." He fled, leaving his saber and dagger where they'd fallen.

Gastel struggled to break free of the paralysis that held him rooted in place. It wasn't so much fear as utter shock. He'd nearly witnessed the death of his eldest brother. If he'd wished for confirmation of Raemian's reputation, he needn't search further. She was a force of strength and battle grit hidden beneath the façade of a timid Shay woman.

As if she could feel the thoughts turning over in Gastel's mind, she glanced at him from the corner of her eye, searching his face for the same answers she'd sought in Belkin's. He would gladly give her the answers if she had asked. Instead, she turned to the king and curtsied.

"Forgive me, Your Majesty. I accept whatever punishment you deem appropriate for my actions."

Mesmal sank back into his chair, rubbing his temples with shaking hands. "You defended yourself, nothing more. Though I must admit, seeing my son's life sliding from the edge of your blade." His face morphed into an expression of tempered anger that lent solidity to his words, sending a chill down Gastel's spine. "You walk a delicate line, Shay."

Rae followed Gastel as she had before, despite knowing the way to the tower. She could feel the apprehension dripping from him and flooding the space between them. It wasn't quite fear; it was something else— something deeper, darker. Firsthand knowledge of what she could do with a blade in her hand, perhaps? She hoped it was enough to tame any curiosity he may have still had.

She touched the place on her neck where Belkin's dagger had pressed and pulled away moist fingers. The smell of her own blood was strange. The blood on her fingertips could have been Belkin's. Almost was, but by the grace of the Elder Gods alone, she had managed to stop herself from killing the heir to the Bleck Larin throne.

The halls were dark at this hour, and the farther they drew away from the heart of the castle stronghold, the fewer torches lit their way. The silence, like the growing shadows, made conversation seem impossible. So, instead, she focused on a speck of light that reflected from something shiny at the back of Gastel's neck.

Distracted by chaotic thoughts, she didn't notice he'd stopped until she nearly ran into him. It was hard to see his face clearly, but what she could see was a concerned curve to his dark brows above the black recesses where his eyes should be.

"I don't understand," Gastel said. "Why didn't you kill him?"

She couldn't answer him. In the heat of battle, she'd wanted his death, prayed for it. It wasn't just self-defense. She'd felt the fury in Belkin's golden eyes and had matched it. She'd gritted her teeth when her sword hit plate armor instead of the softness of flesh, had let the hatred of the last decade of fighting in the Shay army flow through her and poison her vision.

What had stopped her?

A hot wave of disorienting apprehension filled her gut. King Mesmal had been nothing but kind; Gastel, warm and friendly. Bleck Larin weren't what she thought they were. Even Belkin was capable of kindness, in whatever strange form it had taken when he'd dropped the dagger instead of slitting her throat. These people weren't what she'd thought they were—not at all what she'd been led her entire life to believe.

"He doesn't deserve to die." It was all she could think to say—the truth.

"Has he not killed hundreds of your people?"

Gastel's voice held a ribbon of frustration. Or maybe it was confusion. Without light to see all of him, she struggled to read his body language.

"Perhaps in a different time or place. On the battlefield, for certain. But here?" She stepped back, her throat tightening with uncertainty. All her confused thoughts and guilt collected at Gastel's feet.

She closed her eyes, swallowing the anxiety that caused her heart to race, and tried to steady herself with a deep breath, then another. When she opened her eyes again, she saw a man before her. Not a Bleck Larin, not a warrior. A man.

"Today, he isn't my enemy."

TWELVE

The Assignment

Gastel jogged back to the castle after his morning training session. He was sweaty and invigorated, as he always was after stressing his muscles to their limit. But this morning, he felt strange. He had since he'd woken. He wanted to speak with his father before the morning meal, hoping perhaps Mesmal would have some insight.

His father's study was empty, so he headed straight to the dining hall. Perhaps Mesmal had gone early to sit with his tea and thoughts in the quiet before his sons joined him.

As Gastel jogged through the halls of his home, a lingering question from the night before battled his sense of self. Proof of Raemian Starling's reputation had left his brother's words raw and exposed. He couldn't bring himself to believe she was a monster hidden behind short, pointed ears and lacy shaymarks. But he'd witnessed the evidence. And now there was an empty space that had once been filled with certainty.

The double doors stood ajar, and the hushed voices of Belkin and Roulin deep in conversation wafted into the hall. Gastel leaned closer to listen but decided it wasn't worth eavesdropping and pushed into the room, carrying himself with what he hoped was his usual confidence.

Belkin and Roulin turned in unison, two sets of burning eyes. The apprehension that had been growing in Gastel's stomach coated his mouth with a metallic tang.

"Pleasure you could join us, *little brother*." Belkin's voice was stained with menace. Flashes of Belkin and Raemian, blades crossed with searing hatred in their sneers, played through Gastel's mind. Though he didn't fear Belkin, a shiver of caution ran through him. This man would be his king someday. Probably sooner rather than later. Creating an enemy in your future king was never a good idea. Clearly, his eldest brother hadn't cared for his meager attempt to defuse the situation the evening before.

"Good morning, Belkin, Roulin." Gastel kept his voice level as he crossed the room. Perhaps they were discussing something other than the fact that Belkin and Raemian had nearly killed each other?

"Belkin has told me a rather interesting story." Roulin closed his eyes, bringing his hands to his lips as he tried to suppress his anger long enough to continue. "Something about a certain Shay monster being allowed into father's study, and you having the nerve—the *gall*—to have such complacency in the face of your enemy? To tell Belkin to *accept* her presence?"

Gastel's pulse quickened, his hand reflexively dropping to the pommel of his sword—which he'd never leave behind again. He needed to lock his emotions down. Seeing the vehemence flooding across his brothers' faces helped him mask his own.

"Did Belkin mention that he attacked an unarmed elf?" Gastel met Belkin's scowl with a steely conviction that he hadn't been so sure he'd be capable of a moment ago. "She's no threat to Father, and you know it."

Both brothers pinned him with glares of pure disgust, shoulders squared, brows furrowed. They could have been identical twins the way the skin around their eyes darkened to a brilliant shade of teal. Gastel stopped short, knowing he was defeated.

"She shouldn't be toyed with," Belkin said, eyes like daggers. "She's a serious threat in single combat. You saw firsthand last night what she's capable of." An angry index finger jabbed at Gastel's heart. "You and Father don't seem to understand the threat she poses. She isn't an adorable little Shay elfling. She's a raging warrior that wouldn't think twice before slaying you like countless Bleck Larin before you."

"I can handle you. I'm sure I can handle her." Gastel smirked.

His sarcastic response was less than welcome, and he could feel the explosion of fury before either of his brothers moved. Roulin closed the distance first and took hold of Gastel's collar, yanking him hard into his face, their noses nearly touching.

"You could never kill a soul. *You're too soft.* Too naïve." Roulin's eyes were all Gastel could see, with pupils dilated in rage. "She'd destroy you in seconds. She can kill and has killed. More Bleck Larin than you can count. Bleck Larin like you. Like Father." Roulin enunciated each word with precise diction in a low tone that sent another shiver down Gastel's spine.

Roulin held him for another moment to press the point home, then thrust him away.

It wasn't the first time Gastel's lack of battle experience had been thrown onto the floor in front of him. He looked past Roulin and found Belkin's simmering angry face, his arms folded, lips pressed tightly together. He'd let Roulin speak for the both of them.

As if waiting for the perfect moment to enter, their father slipped in from a different side of the dining hall than usual.

"Ah, good morning, Belkin, Roulin, Gastel." He moved with confidence but wore a perplexed expression, avoiding eye contact with any of his sons.

He must have been out in the gardens for a walk. It was the only reason he'd come through the servants' entrance. Was Gastel's father as nervous about tasking Belkin with returning Raemian as he was?

"Shall we sit and dine? We have important things we must discuss."

Gastel sat to his father's left and his brothers across from him, as they always sat. Belkin and Roulin were separated from him in age by over two hundred years, and they had a different mother. It came up so infrequently that it seemed irrelevant, but now that he stared into their angry faces, he wondered if they segregated themselves on purpose. He took a deep breath and stared down at his hands, knowing what was coming.

"Raemian Starling needs to be returned *safely* to Queen Gemma."

Roulin rolled his eyes and leaned back in his chair, making it harder for their father to make direct eye contact.

"I've decided we shall use this opportunity to seek peace with the Shay. To amend the wrongs of our past."

Belkin slammed his fists down on the dining table with bone-shattering force. Thankfully, the servants had not yet set out the breakfast dishes or he would have put his hand through his plate.

"You'll throw away the last thirty years of battle?" He rose, anger boiling in his eyes. "The ground we've gained? All the soldiers we've lost?"

Mesmal waved for Belkin to sit and shook his head. "Belkin, calm down. It hasn't been for nothing. A great evil was—"

"What evil, Father? The woman you took in place of the queen? The elfling you sired outside of bonding? Secrets kept? Promises broken? It is your own mistakes that have brought us to this place!" Belkin's voice was sharp with frenzied accusation.

Gastel snapped to attention. This was new. This was something he'd never heard mentioned before. What was this about the queen? What elfling was Belkin referring to? This was information he'd not been given. Histories he'd not been alive for. A million questions were running through Gastel's mind. There was clearly so much more about the war with the Shay that he was not aware of.

"Well, then, Father, are you going to explain? Your poor, precious elfling is completely lost." Roulin's condescending tone was like rancid syrup.

Gastel, still dissecting what Belkin had just said, hadn't noticed everyone staring at him, his father's expression a stone mask. Roulin wore a smug smile that Gastel had seen before when things had been discussed that he wasn't privy to. It was clear something had been kept secret from him. Something he feared was dreadfully important.

His father looked down at his hands, calmly folded on the table. "I'd prefer explaining everything to Gastel in private. It is between me and him. We have other more important things to discuss for now."

Belkin let out a forced laugh. "What would be more important than—"

"This is, Belkin! *This* is more important." Mesmal's raised voice sent Gastel and his brothers back in their seats. His father smoothed his angry expression back into the carefully cultivated stoicism that was expected of a Bleck Larin king. "You shall deliver Raemian Starling to Queen Gemma. *You* will be my emissary of peace. I shall send my royal seal with you, which you will *personally* hand to the queen."

Belkin appeared as though he were going to interrupt, but their father stood his ground, eyes turning that same devilish shade of angry yellow. It was the first time Gastel had seen him in such a state. He prayed to never experience it again.

"If you so much as *touch* Raemian in a menacing way, you shall spend the next ten years training the new recruits. You will *never* lead my army again, and you will forfeit your birthright and be stripped of your crown." He paused to let the words sink in before leaning toward Belkin, his last few words barely above a whisper. "Do I make myself clear?"

No one moved. No one breathed. Finally, Belkin turned to their father, his expression one of absolute submission. "Yes, Your Majesty."

Gastel couldn't recall ever hearing his brother refer to their father as *Your Majesty*, perhaps always deferring to the fact that Mesmal was his father first and then his king. But today, with this order, he was his king first, the distinction significant. If Belkin didn't do as ordered, Roulin would be king.

Gastel swallowed hard, forcing his frustration down as best as he could. He eyed his oldest brother, who simply stared at his folded hands, accepting his place with grace. There was hope that Raemian would make it home safely. A slim hope, but at least it was something.

THIRTEEN

Soul Stone

Rae had woken earlier than usual, her mind still clouded with details from the duel in the king's study. She hadn't yet bothered dragging herself out of bed. After all, the old down mattress was far more comfortable for lounging than the wooden chair. Seeing as how she could go nowhere and see no one, she relaxed in her soft cotton undershirt and leggings as she read through a bloated manuscript for the third time.

She couldn't help herself, skimming to the pages about the Great Houses. The House of Starling had dwindled to only herself and her father, and in the last several years, she'd been interested in why there were so few that remained. Why had so many elves pulled away from house names? Why did her father cling to theirs with such fervor?

This was her last day before seeing the world outside these stone walls again. While she wasn't excited to travel with Belkin, she was elated at the thought of the sun kissing her skin, a breeze running its fingers through her hair, the smell of moist soil and vegetation.

There had been more than one time over the last few days she hadn't believed she would live to see the sun again. When the hood had been pulled from her head in the throne room. When Belkin had held a dagger to her throat the evening before.

She touched the scratch on her neck. It had scabbed over nicely. For all the Shay's ability to use Eishtala magic for healing, they didn't heal as quickly as Bleck Larin did naturally. Perhaps another gift from the Elder Gods to balance the races.

There was a hard knock, louder than usual. The door flew open before she could respond, and Rae met Belkin's sharp glare as he stepped into the room. A ripple of fear lanced through her. Here in the tower there'd be no shortsword for her to use to defend herself. A steely chill of fight or flight crept over her as her eyes traveled from the weapon strapped to his hip to his amber glare. Remnants of the battle from the night before still swam behind his guarded expression, a seething anger that turned the edges of his irises gold.

He stood perfectly still, wearing a mask of indifference. She knew how he felt about her, how he felt about *all* Shay. Every time he'd been troubled to look in her direction, there had been thinly veiled tolerance in his expression or, more accurately, tempered disgust. The echo of steel against steel in her mind, the resonance of their blades meeting in the king's study only confirmed what she already knew.

"I've been ordered to return you to Queen Gemma in the City of Tremire. We leave tomorrow at first light." He gave a second for his words to sink in. "Your weapons will be returned to you, but I assure you, there shall not be need for them. Your safety is guaranteed. If my father wishes for peace, I will respect his decision with honor becoming of my lineage."

He stopped at the door and looked over at her as she sat on the edge of the bed, her unruly hair whispering over her bare shoulders. Without her jerkin, she felt exposed. He studied her for a long moment, his expression blank. She tried to keep her face as innocuous as possible to match his.

What did he see as his eyes lingered on her face? A warrior? A murderer? Or a vulnerable Shay woman, weak and lonely and...scared? Because she certainly felt like the latter under his heavy gaze. Finally, he raised his eyebrows in an almost humorous way and left without another word.

He had no sharp insults. No threats. Was it an effort to establish some mask of decorum before they traveled to the City of Tremire? Some means of mending a rift between them for the sake of comfort since they'd be forced to endure each other's company through the wilderness of Rhend?

He'd climbed several flights of stairs to give her a message that could have been given to her by anyone. It couldn't be a change of heart, could it? His anger toward her had been sharp, seething, and deeper than any normal prejudice. Whatever the real reason for his change in attitude, she could see through his words.

He said he'd been ordered. It wasn't his choice. His hand was forced. She'd be given her weapons, which was as good a deterrent as any. In all honesty, she didn't fear death at his hands. He was too honorable. If his father ordered it, he'd fall on his own sword. *Honor becoming of his lineage.* The heir to the throne.

She grabbed her shirt and jerkin from the back of the chair, and there was another knock at the door. She bid it be opened but instantly regretted not delaying her response. Immensely self-conscious of how she appeared in her current state of undress, she stood a little straighter, bare arms at her sides.

Gastel was perfectly presentable in a loose, crisp white shirt and black pants. His hair was pulled back flawlessly, but what was concerning was his expression. He seemed perplexed? Unsure? A hint of fear? Definitely not himself. He lingered in the doorway.

"Good morning, Raemian." He was stiff. His words clipped. "I came to make sure you were..." The last word seemed hard for him to say.

"I'm fine."

"I..." He faltered. His eyes followed the shaymarks up her arm and back to her face. "Um..."

She hadn't known him long, but he didn't seem the type to hesitate or lose his train of thought. He seemed abundantly confident. A pang of compassion for his predicament wormed its way into her heart. How often in the last couple of days had she been rendered unable to unearth the perfect words to describe her confused and contradictory thoughts? Too many times to count. Silence had been her friend in all these.

"Forgive me for the way I acted last evening." She broke the silence for him, twisting an unruly lock of hair.

He relaxed back into the Gastel she knew. The one who had surprised her with a kindness she'd never expected to meet in a Bleck Larin.

"I can't fault you for defending yourself, but I can tell you it was terrifying." He took a few steps farther into the room, and a tingle of nervousness flooded through her. His lips curled up as he pinned her in place with his glare. "If I'd doubted your reputation before..."

Heat burned her cheeks. His smile relaxed, replaced with a serenity that caused an explosion of butterflies in the pit of her stomach. *What was this? She had never felt like this. Not for a man. Not for anyone.* It was unfamiliar and tremendously unwelcome. She reached for memories of angry Bleck Larin eyes, mutilated flesh, bloody scenes from the battlefield. Anything to build the wall between them. *Anything!*

She could no longer hold his gaze but had nowhere else to look other than straight ahead into the middle of his chest. Her eyes wandered to an elegant pendant peeking from behind the loose laces of his shirt. She'd never noticed it before. How could she? He always wore high-necked vests, like his brothers and father.

He must have noticed where her eyes had gone because he glanced down. "My mother's soul stone." He reached and carefully retrieved the pendant so he could hold it out for her to see. It caused him to step closer, his warm eyes roaming her face. "It's the only thing I have of hers. She was an Anam Wielder. I was told there are some who wear soul stones to help supplement their powers. My father said it holds a piece of her soul."

"It's beautiful."

Rae marveled at the swirls of purples and reds and blues. Every color twisting and grabbing the light, moving like living stone. She reached up and touched the smooth surface, expecting it to be warm from lying against Gastel's skin. She didn't expect the tiny shock that caused her to pull away sharply.

Gastel chuckled—a deep, warm sound that sent another spark of heat through her.

"Sorry. I guess she doesn't like strangers," he said, letting the pendant slip from his fingers. He didn't step away, and Rae risked glancing up into his eyes.

What she found was mortifying. His smirk kept growing until his teeth showed and left her feeling weak beyond reason. One minute, she was terrified of him; the next, he left her utterly senseless. If he knew half of what he did to her, she'd be devastatingly embarrassed. At some point, he'd stopped being the enemy and had started being Gastel.

"I should go. I wasn't exactly given permission to visit you, but Belkin was in such a state."

He let the words trail off as he glanced up at the stained-glass window. Rae had the overwhelming urge to do the same. This was her last day in this place, and while she wouldn't miss being imprisoned within the cold walls, the emptiness of the castle stronghold, the anger of Belkin and Roulin—she'd miss the beauty of the window. She'd miss King Mesmal's calm kindness, and she'd be lying to herself if she thought she wouldn't miss Gastel's endearing confidence most of all.

"Thank you." She spoke without considering her words. "For your kindness. I..."

She studied the stone at her feet as she pulled the words from her soul. It was something that had continued to surprise her since the moment her eyes had found him. "I didn't know Bleck Larin could be..."

"Nice?" Gastel finished.

She met his friendly gaze, his warm smile. She'd miss him.

"Could be like you."

Time to Go

Darkness had come hours ago, but Rae couldn't sleep. She kept analyzing the day's details, distilling the minutia, trying to see everything. When she closed her eyes, she relived each moment—Belkin's unexpected change in demeanor, Mesmal's hope for peace. Still, her mind always came back to *him*. Gastel's fiery eyes at breakfast, his perfect smile, the way his laugh melted her mental barrier.

If they lived in another time, before all this discord and hatred and war, she might have been allowed to admit how she felt drawn to him. As it was, she'd likely seen him for the last time. It left her with a frigid sense that something beyond precious had slipped through her fingers.

She sat up in the dark room, only a tiny bit of light filtering through the magnificent stained-glass window, compliments of the ambient glow from the city of Parth below. Rain had moved in at midday, as if sensing the mood surrounding the tower. The sound of drizzle on the roof tiles echoed in the rafters like nervously, tapping fingers. Rae would have been immediately lulled to sleep any other night.

She was dressed, refusing to be caught unprepared again by Belkin. A servant had kindly washed her shirt and leggings and had treated the leather of her jerkin, the queen's emblem fresh and crisp over her left breast. Her hair was still neatly braided. She had only to pull on her boots.

She lay back down in frustration. She needed to rest ahead of two long days of travel.

But his smile...

All her life, the Bleck Larin had been angry, distant nightmares, swinging swords at her throat. Her only defense had been instinctual perfection with a blade. And now? She feared that smile almost more than the sword. She'd return home, be sent back to the front, but before defending herself, she'd have to ask questions first. She'd have to ask if the soldier had a family. A bondmate? Elflings? Did he have a smile that warmed a room or eyes that lit the hearts of his friends with joy? Was she kind? Was she forced to fight for her king like Rae was forced to fight for her queen? Was he honorable? Considering would cost Rae precious seconds, which would likely carry a heavy price.

A soft knock brought Rae from her relentless questioning. She crept from the bed and crossed the tower room in the darkness. The door was pushed open, and Gastel stepped inside, a single finger pressed to his lips.

"I can't let Belkin take you." The minuscule light that reflected off Gastel's amber eyes was otherworldly. His cool-gray skin seemed to melt into the shadows of the dark stone walls. "If we leave now, we can be well into the Middlelend Forest before they find you're gone."

He didn't need to tell her twice. She pulled on her boots.

"What of the sentinel?"

He smirked. "He'll wake in a few hours with a headache."

A brilliant fire flared to life, momentarily blinding Rae and throwing the room into warm light. She stumbled back and nearly fell over the chair, catching herself at the last moment. When she looked back at him, he held a gentle orange flame above his open palm.

Gastel had done what she'd only witnessed from a distance. He'd used Anam magic. Where Shay possessed Eishtala, the power to grow and heal, Bleck Larin possessed Anam, the power of fire and heat, wrought from their very souls.

The shadows of his face in the golden light were haunting, the concerned curve of his brows cutting a different image of him. Fear froze her insides. Every muscle in her body tensed with the knowledge that she was alone and unarmed with a Bleck Larin.

"I'm sorry, I didn't mean to frighten you." He shook his hand, extinguishing the fire as quickly as he'd ignited it.

She squeezed her eyes closed, taking a deep breath to clear her mind of dread, focusing on the fact that Gastel had never once threatened her.

"Here, let me show you." A soft breath escaped his lips, and the amber flame erupted above his hand, out of thin air. "It's harmless. Just a soultorch, an Anam magic trick." He let the fingers of his other hand dance through the wafting flames. "Most Bleck Larin have the ability."

She hadn't wholly prepared for the spark of interest that ignited with the flame. "I've only ever seen it from a distance." She reached without thinking. "Is it hot?"

He stepped closer. "Not unless I wish for it to be."

Gastel extended his arm until the brilliant orange flames were below her outstretched fingers. They passed harmlessly through, the tendrils of light licking around her hand in slow motion.

"So strange." Fear gone, Rae placed a hand on either side of his. "I've always wondered."

"I'll heat it for you so you can feel the difference."

He closed his eyes again, took in another breath, and let it out slowly. The flames twisted as they changed, growing brighter, the color shifting from amber to yellow to a brilliant white. Like honey passing through water, her curiosity settled at the bottom of her mind, pushing the last fragments of fear away.

Its warmth wicked into her skin. She smiled up at him, unsure of what to say, as his eyes searched hers. He let the flame burn another moment before twisting his hand, the last of the fire twirling up into the air in a beautiful burst of light, leaving them in the dark once again.

"It's hot enough to melt most metals. I was told mine is particularly powerful, though I've shown no aptitude for Anam magic of any other kind. And trust me, I've tried." He smirked. "As an elfling, I wanted so badly to be an Anam Wielder. Then I would have had something different from my brothers."

"Yet you have something different from them already," Rae whispered. Gastel's brow furrowed, head tipping to the side, unsure of what she referred to. She couldn't help but smile more deeply. "A wish for balance, for peace between our people."

Balance.

The word coated the inside of her mind with a calming rightness.

They stood in the darkness for another moment, the last of her words settling around them like new fallen snow. She realized just how far she had let down her guard. She swallowed hard, knowing it'd be twice as difficult to build the walls again and force herself to see Gastel as anything other than an elf, *a friend.*

He reached for something at his waist, and, for the first time, she didn't flinch.

"Your sword."

He handed her the cherished blade that had saved her life in the king's study and countless times on the battlefield. It would surely save her life again in the future.

A terrible choice presented itself as her fingers curled around the familiar grip. He had just bestowed the very means by which she could destroy the entire royal family of the Bleck Larin. His trust was enough to solidify her decision. He wasn't her enemy. Nor was King Mesmal.

"We need to go," Gastel said.

Slipping her sword into its scabbard, she nodded. She had no more time to waste on such thoughts.

Together, they ducked out and down the winding stairs, stalking through the dimly lit halls of the castle stronghold. They went a different way than she'd ever gone before. As they reached the end of a passage, Gastel opened a narrow door resembling a wall panel and motioned for her to enter before him. As Gastel closed the panel door, the warm glow of his soultorch sprung to life, illuminating a narrow passage that sliced between the walls of the stronghold.

Despite her ability to only see what Gastel's soultorch could reveal, she took one step and then another. She'd never get used to stone structures. Perhaps they afforded the Bleck Larin many more amenities than the trees of Tremire. Could anyone be comfortable knowing their home contained secret passages leading through the walls around them? Despite her own distaste for them, at that moment, she could see their value in spades.

"This way." Gastel passed her, his fingers gliding along her arm to her hand before slipping from her.

They jogged down through the tunnels, descending into the earth below the castle stronghold, coming out somewhere beyond the southern wall of Parth. They were greeted with a cold drizzle and an even colder breeze. Rae regretted not having a cloak to pull around her as they sprinted from the sight line of the city wall and onto the moors. It was going to be a long, chilly night, and they had a lot of ground to cover.

It seemed like hours before Rae noticed vegetation other than tall grasses and scrubby bushes. Copses of stunted trees interrupted the landscape as a hint of light touched the eastern sky. They only had another hour—maybe two—before sunrise, and they'd hoped to be off the moors so they could find shelter and rest for a short time.

They broke the Middlelend Forest just before the sun crested the horizon. Rae insisted they move farther in, instructing Gastel how to move through the trees with as little disruption as possible. Any scout worth her salt would still find them, but the cursed rain became their greatest ally, washing away parts of their trail.

Rae was still concerned about stopping, but if they didn't get at least some rest, she worried that she wouldn't be keen enough to navigate the depths of the Middlelend Forest. She'd traversed deep within these woods before. Once in, it was hard to use the sun or stars to guide the way.

She kept a close eye out for some slight shelter as they picked through the trees. The journey had been slow going for the last hour, the forest dotted with an unusual number of saplings. Finally, Gastel spotted a promising spot. A larger tree had fallen onto another. The two held each other in an endless embrace along the side of a hill. A small area tucked below was mostly dry despite a night of rain.

"I fear we should forgo a fire," Gastel said, letting Rae climb in first.

The space was large enough for two to sleep rather comfortably, albeit close to each other. That couldn't be helped under the circumstances.

"I told you, I'm not a princess; I can sleep anywhere." She winked at him as he settled down next to her.

She stretched out beside him and felt her pulse slow. They'd been jogging as much as possible since leaving the stronghold's tunnels. Her muscles were sore. It had been days since she'd been outside, much less had such physical activity. While it felt good, she wasn't sure she could maintain the same pace after only two or three hours of sleep. They'd have to address that concern after some rest. She glanced over and found Gastel's eyes closed, his arms tucked behind his head. He almost seemed comfortable.

He must have felt her stare because the next moment, he turned his head, eyes open to meet hers. He smiled wryly and then closed them again. "This is the farthest I've ever been from Parth." He took a deep breath, letting it out deliberately. "I had hoped the first time would be under better circumstances."

His breathing stretched into a gentle rhythm as he relaxed. Soft, comforting—the sound of his trust. Rae watched him for a time, not sure how or when she'd allowed herself to be so comfortable with a Bleck Larin, or how he could be so trusting of her after witnessing what she was capable of. She finally let herself drift into a troubled sleep.

She woke with a start. Her sharp movement must have roused Gastel because he met her eyes with concern in his own. He sat up and looked back at her with gentle scrutiny as she rolled to her side and pulled her legs to her chest.

"We should keep moving," Gastel said.

She nodded weakly and pushed herself up beside him, her body more than a little reluctant. The weariness in her legs and back was all too real.

"I'd beg for ten more minutes, but..." She playfully shrugged.

Rae thought she detected a hint of a smile with his raised eyebrows as they pulled themselves out and into the late-morning drizzle.

Old Magic

Gastel couldn't deny he was second-guessing his decision to leave with Raemian. It was a new feeling, this foreboding uncertainty. Confidence, assuredness—these were part of him. A firm grip on reality, on his sword in his hand, on everything he knew. They were part of what made him a son of Mesmal. Now, a nagging doubt seeped in around his lack of answers. The reason his father insisted he never leave Parth, still a mystery. There had to be a reason. The king was horrible at planning, but when he did, there was purpose.

He kept replaying Belkin's heated words the morning before—an affair, an elfling, and the queen's ire? He would force his father to answer for it when he returned. For now, he needed to invest his attention in moving through the Middlelend Forest as quickly as possible. Lost in thought, it was easy to snag an arm on a tree limb or sink to the knee in a muddy bog.

The farther from Parth they went, the more apprehensive he became. Without the declaration of peace and his father's royal seal to ensure its authenticity, he had nothing but his word as proof of King Mesmal's intentions. Words were never enough. He could do little more than trust that Queen Gemma could see reason, but he didn't know—not for certain—and it chilled him to the bone. Or maybe that was just the cursed rain?

Nothing was as it seemed. So much of his life had been in isolation. The longer he spent with Raemian, the more he realized how truly naïve he'd been. And he hated it.

Raemian had the same doubts about his safety, going so far as to ask him to turn back, that she'd go the rest of the way on her own. She reasoned that she'd made this trip before—had been kidnapped from the Middlelend Forest. Part of him couldn't let her. The other part knew there'd be nothing good at the end of this journey, yet he still had to do this. He *needed* to do this...with her.

Raemian stopped short, holding up a fist. She glanced back to check that he was there before scanning the thick forest. This wasn't the first time she'd stopped. What did she see each time? After a long minute, she motioned him closer.

"Can you feel that?" she asked once he drew near.

Gastel tried to see the world through a different lens. There was a heavy scent of muddy soil, jasmine, and rotting leaves. The sun had little chance of filtering through the thick canopy, and the darkness around them was as heavy as dusk. There were fewer saplings, only the great trees that towered over them—the guardians of the forest. The farther they traveled, the stranger it felt, like they were traversing a place not meant for elves.

"A presence?" Raemian's whispered voice broke through Gastel's thoughts.

It *was* a presence. Not a living thing, but *something*. It was faint, but waves of magic wafted through the air around them, hugging Gastel's extremities and sharing the breath he drew into his lungs.

"So strange." She looked up at him, her eyes large with wonder. She held his gaze longer than usual before glancing up to the canopy, her lips parted.

A tickle of apprehension nagged at him again. Something wasn't right. Something older than the trees, than the ground itself. He'd heard tales about the supernatural as an elfling, the magic of the Middlelend Forest, and the reasons it had stood empty for thousands of years. Having never left Parth, he hadn't fully understood the significance—or rather, the insignificance—one felt in the presence of such history. Stone walls, the City of Parth itself, couldn't hold a torch to the resonance of these trees.

"We should keep moving," Raemian whispered. "I can't wield Eishtala, but this feels like magic."

He nodded, and they moved on, side by side, her shoulder nearly touching him for several yards before the trunks of the ancient trees forced them farther apart.

The foreboding presence grew stronger, and Gastel's stomach filled with unease. A vague tingle started at the back of his neck, reaching over his shoulders and into his chest, tugging at the strings of his soul. It wasn't quite Anam. Was it Eishtala? Or some other magic entirely? Something older and more dangerous, perhaps? The foreboding grew around him until Raemian stopped again, this time with her hands spread wide, ready to pull her sword at any moment.

He didn't dare speak or move. Instead, he found her with his eyes alone. She crouched, peering through the trees. He risked turning his head to follow her gaze.

Twenty yards or so ahead, in a thicker part of the forest, where sunlight couldn't penetrate, was a white light that seemed to swirl and twist like fire. If he didn't know better, he'd say it was the shadow of a soulflame. It danced with a life of its own, gyrating and pulsing in slow motion through the branches.

"What…" Her voice was so quiet he wasn't sure her words were intended for him. "What is it?" She stood and started walking toward the light.

Gastel found himself rooted in place, a terrible wave of hot, angry essence spilling over him, drowning him in a pool of energy until he was sinking, helpless.

"Raemian." Gastel gasped between the pulses. "Don't—"

She kept moving, seeming not to have heard him.

"Raemian!" He managed to yell this time, louder than he had intended, but she still didn't acknowledge. Something drew her, while trapping his feet in an invisible binding akin to mud up to his thighs.

"Stop, Raemian!" He could only struggle as she pulled farther ahead, halfway between himself and the white flames.

His desperation to stop her built like an inferno, fed by the branches of the scraggly trees around them. He pulled with all his strength, straining to the point of causing his vision to darken at the corners. As if tearing his soul from his body, he finally ripped his legs free and took several hasty, heavy steps.

He slipped on wet leaves in his mad scramble to catch up. He needed to get to Raemian before she reached the…whatever it was. Deep, heavy magic. That's what it was. It couldn't be Eishtala or Anam—it was something bigger, stronger, something that had no place on this plane of existence. Something that was more dangerous than any weapon, any elf.

"Raemian!"

She stopped this time, eyes wide with shock.

"What is this?" She waited for him to catch up, as he moved impossibly slowly. "It was calling to me."

A crack in the forest floor spilled ribbons of living fire from its depths. The bark of the surrounding trees was charred black, though no actual heat emanated from it. Swells of power oozed around their ankles, leaving strange ripples in the air.

"It isn't Eishtala." Raemian stepped forward, but he put a hand on her shoulder to stop her, gently squeezing.

"All I feel is evil from—" He was cut off.

A blinding screech ripped from the fissure. Gastel doubled over, clutching his ears in agony. He was left with nothing but horrid ringing when it finally stopped. The pause lasted only seconds before the screech began again, bringing him to his knees.

The light pulsed faster, radiating out in violent waves that sprayed the trees with a shower of sparks. It stretched toward him and Raemian with sinister fingers of coursing white energy. Gastel fell forward, barely catching himself before falling face-first into wet leaves.

The wretched sound paused long enough for Gastel to meet Raemian's terrified face. She was saying something, but he couldn't hear her words. He tried to reach toward her, but the screeching exploded again.

Gastel rolled to his back while pressing his hands so hard against his ears that he thought he'd crack his skull. He could feel all the colors of the rainbow while simultaneously experiencing the burn of the brightest white. Instead of soothing blackness behind his eyelids, there were fireworks bursting, colors rolling and shifting like a hundred kaleidoscopes, all dancing and twisting and mashing together.

He screamed until his throat was hoarse, but nothing helped. Nothing kept the brain-decimating noise from destroying all thought and reason. There was no longer a time or place. There was only desperation. He wished for deafness. He cried for reprieve. He begged for death and finally slipped into blessed darkness.

SIXTEEN

Flesh and Soul

A burst of bright light brought Rae's hands up to shield her eyes before she was plunged into darkness. She sank to her knees, feeling with her fingers along the wet forest floor in the direction she'd last seen Gastel. She found nothing but mush and sticks and...the Gods only knew. As her eyes adjusted, she saw his silhouette prone in the muddy leaves.

"Gastel!"

He rolled to his back, thrashing and pressing his hands over his ears.

"Gastel?" She scrambled toward him to help. "What's wrong?"

She hadn't quite made it to him when his body contracted, back arching, mouth agape as he writhed, his eyes rolling to the back of his head before he went limp. Something dark ran from his ears. He was deathly still, his breathing gentle yet shallow. Rae tried to wake him, but even with shaking, it was to no avail.

"Please, Gastel. Hear my voice. Come to my voice!"

He was dead weight.

A forceful voice emanated from all around: "He won't wake until we release him."

"Who's there?" she asked, hovering over Gastel. "Who are you?"

Her eyes searched the murky darkness, but there was no one—only herself, Gastel, the trees, and the rift of dancing light.

"We are all things, yet nothing." The light from the rift pulsed with each word. "We are time itself."

Rae swallowed. The phrases were familiar—some lost, forgotten fairy tale she'd heard as an elfling, or maybe a passage she'd read in a history book.

"He needs to leave this place."

"Why are you hurting him?" Rae tried to keep her voice calm, but her entire body trembled with fear.

"He is not welcome here." There was a menacing harshness to the voice, as if it were many voices speaking as one—some happy, others angry and coarse.

"Why? Because he's Bleck Larin?"

"We care little of his flesh, only his soul."

The flowing ribbons of light coalesced, stitching together into a formless being. It possessed two arms and a head, but where its torso and legs should have been, it was tethered to the fissure.

"He holds the power of devastation." The choir of voices seemed to ebb and flow like waves across a beach. It was a flowing melody one moment, jarring dissonance the next.

"I don't understand."

The being stretched closer, still tethered to the rift.

"His mind and will are strong, but his true soul is sealed."

Rae leaned back, throwing an arm up to protect against the brilliant light that seemed to saturate deep into the fibers of the world. The being held its arms out to its sides as wispy flames danced above outstretched hands.

"He shall wake, but he must leave. He is not welcome here. Not his kind. Never his kind."

"But what kind is that if not Bleck Larin?"

"These words mean nothing. The Sundering grows nigh. The balance has been forsaken. All must be as one."

Blades of light lashed forward from the rift, ripping pieces away from the being one by one, dragging them back into the depths of the fissure.

"He carries many souls. Until he has shed that which is borrowed, his own shall be locked away." The light from the rift built into a blinding crescendo. "He is not welcome here."

Rae shielded her eyes until the light burst out like a gale-force wind, blowing loose strands of hair back from her face. When she dared to look again, all that was left was a gaping, empty crack in the earth—the last wisps of fiery white light wafted up to the canopy.

She held her breath as the blackness eased and the ruddy light of the sun sifted through the thick canopy, illuminating the forest yet again. She sat up straight, glancing back at Gastel's motionless form, and swore under her breath. His breathing was deeper, praise the Gods, but he was still unconscious.

As if dragged from a muddy pit, Gastel came to. He waited and listened for the screeching; the wretched sound had already left a permanent imprint on his mind, thick and heavy like damp clothing over chapped skin. All he heard was the occasional chirp of a passing bird and his own heartbeat. Thank the Gods, the wish for deafness hadn't been granted.

He opened his eyes, throwing an arm over his face to block the piercing light. The world spun around him as he tried and failed to sit up, his extremities three times their normal weight.

"Gastel?" Raemian's voice carried a current of concern. He tried looking in her direction, but again the world spun. "Don't move." A warm hand pressed to his forehead. "Here, let me help you."

A cold memory remained where her hand had just been. She did most of the work, supporting under his neck and back, yet it was still tedious, his entire body screaming.

"Gods." He leaned his head forward as she rubbed the nape of his neck.

"You've been unconscious for a couple hours."

"What was that screeching?" His throat was worn raw. He rubbed the sides of his face, where his skin tightened, pulling away grimy fingers with the telltale rusty brown of dried blood.

"Screeching?"

He met her confused gaze as she worked through his question.

"Didn't you hear the—"

"The rift," Raemian said, gazing over at the dark fissure where the flames had once twisted with unnatural life. "There was a being. It told me you weren't welcome here."

She gazed off into the distance as if trying to remember the conversation, but he knew she could likely recall it with pristine clarity.

"We should go." She looked at Gastel, concern mapped across her face. There was much she wasn't telling him, and at the moment, he didn't have the strength to question. "Can you walk? We need to leave this place. If we can make it to the highlands before dark, I..." She glanced at the dark rift again. "I just think we should do as we've been told."

She helped Gastel to his feet, and though every muscle in his body revolted, he resolved to put one foot in front of the other until he couldn't physically move any farther. May the Elder Gods grant him at least a little strength.

Their pace was painfully slow, yet Raemian seemed beyond patient. She forced them to stop often to rest, even if it was only to lean against a tree for a few moments. She scanned the trees along their route, occasionally scouting ahead.

Gastel, on the other hand, found himself wishing for a warm place to clean up and a soft bed to sleep in. He knew they'd find neither. But the trees were thinning. Hopefully, it meant they were closing in on the highlands and the end of this forsaken forest—a place he wouldn't want to return to anytime soon.

"Do you hear that?" Raemian asked as she paused and glanced toward him.

Gastel's shoulders sank. "Gods, I won't live through another rift." Part of him knew he wasn't being facetious, but he hoped his words had sounded at least somewhat lighthearted.

"No, I think it's water."

She sprang to life, leaving Gastel behind. All he could do was watch with amazement at how she still had the energy to sprint like a lithe deer. He had nothing left. Should death itself stalk him, he resigned himself to accept it with grace.

She disappeared into the trees, and he took the opportunity to stop and rest on a rock almost completely disguised by creeping vines. Leaning his head back, he looked up at the leaves as they twisted and played in the breeze that hadn't penetrated the lower depths of the forest.

Curse this place. Curse this empty husk of a body. Why was he so exhausted? What had attacked him? He had too many questions and no energy left to think things through.

"Gastel!"

He found her easy to spot as she bounded through the trees, using the saplings to twist between the larger trunks and fallen logs. She was a whisper of a long-forgotten memory—grace and light and energy in every step.

"There's a stream!" A brilliant smile was painted across her face. It was contagious, and Gastel felt his own lips turning up.

He stood from his makeshift resting spot and started to trudge in her direction, hoping it wasn't much farther. She'd have to carry him otherwise.

SEVENTEEN

To the Highlands

Water! Thank the Gods! Rae would have preferred a hot bath, but she'd take what she could get. The forest was thin here, leaving the banks bare of trees and littered with smooth stones. The sun slipped low in the sky, casting the stream in shadow and turning the water black as ink.

Before Gastel reached the clearing, Rae pulled her boots and clothes off, lying them flat in the driest spot she could find. She waded out in her undershirt and shorts, wrapping her arms around her chest.

The water was warm for early summer. As she moved deeper, she felt for larger rocks with her toes. She caught the silhouette of her reflection as it churned in the current before sinking to her chin, allowing the stream to flow across her skin.

She hoped the dark water could wash away her fear and apprehensions about drawing nearer to Tremire—nearer to where Gastel would no longer be safe. They were close enough to the highlands that it made her skin crawl. A Shay patrol could find them at any moment. Her eyes scanned the trees before she turned to find Gastel standing on the shore, looking out toward her, a smile tugging at his lips as he pulled his jerkin off. She was quick to turn away, allowing him privacy as he stripped off his damp clothes.

When she turned back her breath caught. She was met with a view of his bare chest, adorned with only his mother's soul stone, water up to the waist of his undershorts. Her eyes grew wide, cheeks warming. Freck rarely wore a shirt, but this wasn't Freck—her closest friend, her brother by choice. This was a Bleck Larin prince with skin the color of mountain granite. A perfect weapon, taller than any Shay. Taller, leaner, and deadlier.

He sank under the water, coming up a few yards from her with his hands pulling through his hair. She stared, unable to help herself, her cheeks growing hotter with every second. It was the way he moved— toned muscles shifting beneath his flesh—the way the water gave his skin a silver sheen. The streak of white in his raven hair appeared to glow as it floated on the surface of the stream around his shoulders.

"Why do you leave your hair so long?" Rae blurted out the first question that came to mind.

He smiled and floated closer. The heat in her cheeks plunged into her stomach. He was only a few feet away, close enough that she could see threads of gold in his amber eyes as they held hers, never wavering.

"Tradition," he said after a long pause. "Yours is long as well."

"I guess it is."

He reached and took a lock of her hair as it flowed with the current of the stream, passing it through his fingers while his eyes followed the length of it back to her face.

"Bleck Larin never cut their hair. It's an indicator of wisdom and standing. A physical representation of our age." He stood out of the water and pulled his hair over one shoulder and down his chest, where it reached his naval. "It grows fast when just an elfling and much slower when as old as my father."

But she was no longer able to focus on the conversation. The water running over his chest and abdomen caused molten butterflies to dance through her.

As a warrior, she was surrounded by perfectly honed, exemplary Shay men. She spent countless hours around them during training. Bare chests and cocky smiles didn't usually elicit such a reaction. What was it about *him* that caused her insides to twist in such a way?

Perhaps it was the almost ethereal quality to his strength—something not quite natural. It wasn't just his physical appearance though. It was his aura of kindness and curiosity; the unsolicited friendship he'd offered; his trust. But the curve of his lips; his thick, black lashes graced with tiny drops of water.

His eyes followed the trails of her shaymarks down her neck and shoulders to the surface of the stream. She plunged her head the rest of the way underwater and held her breath as long as possible before breaking the surface to find he hadn't moved. She was frozen in place as a wry smile broke across his lips.

If he knew what his closeness did to her, he said nothing. Instead, he eased back down into the stream and washed the last of the dried blood from his hair, the weariness returning to his eyes as he ran his fingers over his face and the length of his ears.

"I'll get a fire started," he said as he turned, wading back to shore. "We should rest after we warm up."

Rae hoped her silence was taken as agreement. She was still struggling with words.

Darkness set in quickly after Rae dragged herself from the stream and pulled her leggings and shirt on. She sat across from Gastel at a small fire, eyes touching his loose, midnight strands lying against his chest more than once. Her fingers itched to run the length of them. She twisted her own hair instead.

The haunting cries of frogs mingled with the chirp of insects as the embers died. They would sleep without a fire. They didn't need the light drawing every animal—or elf—to them.

Rae figured they were likely within a league or two of the highlands, but Gastel needed a full night's sleep. He was exhausted from whatever magical being they'd encountered at the rift. She watched with open amusement as his eyelids grew heavy. He drifted to sleep sitting up with his elbows propped on his knees, head sinking between his legs. There was a helplessness about him when her hand touched his shoulder, like he couldn't bring himself to wake enough. She helped him lie back and felt his head for fever.

Before she could pull her hand away, he placed his own over it, his golden eyes opening only enough to see her.

"I'm sorry."

"For what?"

His hand slid off and plopped on the ground beside him. After a breath, she reluctantly pulled hers away as well.

"For being so weak." He let out a long breath that sent goosebumps across her arm where it brushed her skin.

"You aren't weak, Gastel. You were attacked by whatever that *thing* was."

She sat back from him as he closed his eyes again. How much had he pushed himself in order to keep their pace? A pang of guilt raced through her. She should have considered his well-being better.

"I'm the one who should be sorry," she said.

"What for?" His drowsy voice was soft and soothing. It made her want to curl up beside him and wrap herself in his arms.

"For not letting you rest sooner."

He didn't respond, and soon his soft snores were proof he'd succumbed to exhaustion. Her eyes slipped to his gently parted lips. What would it feel like to kiss them? She wanted to slap herself for even considering it. She'd never let physical attraction affect her thinking like this before. She tucked the thoughts away, where they couldn't cloud her judgment, and lay down on the other side of the dying fire.

The cloudless sky, beset with millions of tiny diamonds, spread itself out, a map to the mysteries of the world. Her eyes were drawn to it. Maybe there were answers there. She counted stars until she slipped into a dreamless sleep.

Rae woke to the sound of a crackling fire and the smell of something deliciously meaty. Gastel turned what appeared to be a rabbit on a stick over the hot coals.

"Good morning." His voice held that same gentle quality it had the night before.

Rae stretched and sat up. "Good morning." She began the tedious task of combing through her tangles with her fingers. "That smells amazing."

He flashed his perfectly straight, white teeth. "Good, because it was all I could find."

She scooched herself closer to the fire to ward off the slight chill of the morning air. "How long have you been awake?"

He seemed to concentrate on their breakfast more than necessary. "Long enough to make a fire, hunt, and clean a rabbit." He pulled the meat away from the fire to test it.

He was already dressed, his hair tied back once again. Rae suspected he'd been up far longer than he'd admitted.

"You seem to know a fair amount about hunting and cooking for a prince who's never left his home." Rae propped an arm on her knee, cradling her chin in her palm.

Gastel smiled, his eyes never leaving the roasted rabbit. "Bleck Larin battle training is many things. Weapons fighting, strength training, hand-to-hand combat, battle strategy, and general survival skills." He tested the meat, and this time he didn't return it to the fire. "Just because I don't use the skills doesn't mean I don't have them," he said.

She smiled in spite of herself. "You surprise me, Prince."

"Better than boring you." He ripped a piece of rabbit away and extended it to Rae, his eyes holding hers.

She took a hardy bite, chewing slowly, trying not to think about how he stared at her, the Bleck Larin stoicism falling over his features.

"You'll return to your regiment in the Middlelend Forest after this." It wasn't a question. Gastel's eyes were like amber knives cutting into what Rae had already been fretting over. "Or are you usually assigned to the Eastern Pass?" Gastel asked, his tone darkening.

"I'm not sure where Gemma will send me." Rae met and matched his glare. "I don't usually have a choice in the matter."

He glanced away, and she let her eyes slip along the line of his jaw. She pressed her lips together, desperately trying not to think about how she'd be meeting swords with his brother's soldiers in a matter of days should she be immediately sent back to the fight.

Gastel stood without warning, and she leaned back from him.

"We should get moving. I've heard nothing good about the highlands," he said as his eyes found her.

"I still think this is where you should leave me." She matched his stance, legs shoulder-width apart, hands on hips. The Middlelend Forest was one thing. On the highlands, there'd be no hiding places should they be approached.

He shook his head, stepping forward to stomp out the last of the coals. Several yards behind her, a twig snapped, and Rae turned to listen. The trees were thinner here, but there were still plenty of places for an elf to hide.

A familiar thunk startled Rae, her head snapping in Gastel's direction to see a crossbow bolt sticking out of a tree trunk behind him at head level. Her instincts kicked in, and she lunged, pushing him to the ground and rolling clear. She managed to press her back against a tree before finding him out of the corner of her eye. His hand had fallen to the hilt of his blade.

"Show yourself, Bleck Larin. We know you're there."

Rae peeked around the tree in the direction of the unfamiliar voice but saw no one. She turned to Gastel, who shook his head, indicating he wasn't willing to give himself up.

Another bolt pierced the tree, uncomfortably close to Gastel's chest.

Rae was done. She didn't need to deal with this; she was the queen's stepdaughter. She pulled herself from behind the tree and drew her sword.

"Stand down. We're not a threat."

There was a moment of silence before four Shay elves in full battle armor stepped from behind their respective trees.

"According to the sword in your hand, I'd question that," the patrol's leader snapped, aiming his crossbow at her chest. "Who are you, and why are you traveling with a Bleck Larin?"

"Raemian Starling, and that's none of your concern. He's not a threat."

"Raemian Starling?" The Shay who had spoken looked over at his comrades, a sneer creeping across his face as eight more Shay emerged from the trees. "The queen has been searching for you."

She swallowed back the bitter taste of regret for not forcing Gastel to turn back earlier. His life was now firmly in her stepmother's hands.

EIGHTEEN

Queen Gemma

The walk through the trees of Tremire had never seemed so daunting. Rae could feel Gastel's worried glances every few moments as they were paraded along the worn, earthen trails. He was a Bleck Larin in a sea of Shay. She was certain that being in the minority wasn't something he'd ever experienced, and it was an unusual fear, one Rae knew well. She could only thank Mesmal in her heart for his kindness. Now it was her turn to extend the courtesy and spread peace between their people, but she wasn't so sure she'd have the opportunity—or perhaps, more accurately, the authority.

Tremire was nothing like Parth or the castle stronghold. It was less a city and more a collection of gigantic ancient trees several hundred feet tall, carved and sculpted by Eishtala Masters over thousands of years. Rae wished more than anything that she was leading Gastel through her beautiful home, showing him the delicate craftsmanship these trees represented. Instead, a contingent of soldiers led them directly to the queen. They'd been stripped of their weapons and against Rae's wishes, Gastel's hands had been bound behind his back. It wasn't a good way to introduce him to the Shay. Then again, she'd ended up in the castle stronghold in much the same way.

They were escorted through the groves, past scared and angry faces. Gastel towered over the tallest of Shay. To those who had never seen a Bleck Larin, he was exotic and terrifying. They feared him and hated him, like Rae would have done only a week ago.

The doors to the court were swung open by royal guards in full battle regalia as the procession mounted the steps. How many times had she tried to please her stepmother and ended up here instead? Though Rae had done nothing wrong, the sight of the doors instilled shame in her heart. The friendship she was building with Gastel was forbidden. And while no one could read her thoughts, she feared they were plain in her eyes and every time she glanced in his direction.

They were led into the Court of Tremire, where many elves had been judged. Rae tried to keep her steps confident and sure, but her misgivings were likely written in the crease of her brow and the tightness of her drawn lips.

"Sweet Raemian. My favorite little soldier. I've been so worried."

There was no actual warmth of familiarity to her words, only condescension. Gemma shifted on her throne, drawing attention to the low-cut gown she wore. It was the color of the forest, decorated with embroidered branches and individual sheer fabric leaves that flowed with the light breeze like living silk. Her hair was intertwined with her favorite diadem of rose-gold vines—the picture of royalty.

Gemma quirked a single white eyebrow. "And you've brought me a trophy."

One of the soldiers took Rae's arm and jerked her forward. She'd have gladly volunteered to approach her stepmother willingly if she'd been given the opportunity. In fact, the heavy-handedness of the entire affair grated on Rae's last nerve. Out of the corner of her eye, she saw Gastel struggle against the guards restraining him. She wished she could tell him it'd be okay, even if she wasn't sure that it would.

Gemma glared at her for what seemed like an excessive amount of time before she stood from her throne and stepped forward.

The queen struck her across the face hard enough to throw Rae's head to the side. Her eyes watered, but Rae didn't dare cry out. Instead, she waited until her stepmother's hand dropped before standing up straight.

Gemma struck her again, harder this time, and Rae stumbled to the side.

"You stupid, *stupid* girl." She raised her hand to strike a third time.

"Leave her." Gastel's voice cut past Gemma's, turning every head in the room.

When Rae focused again on her stepmother, the queen was looking past her, eyes wide with shock.

"I almost would have called you Mesmal." Gemma motioned for the guards to bring Gastel closer. "I'm assuming you're one of his precious sons?"

Standing before Gastel, she admired him with a strange mixture of menacing appreciation. She reached to touch his face, her hand dripping with rose gold and gemstones. He pulled away but couldn't go far, wrestling against the guards that held him in place.

"Come now." She took his jaw firmly and forced him to look at her steely, gray-blue eyes, which twinkled with simmering hatred. "Are you afraid I'll maim your beautiful face?" She pursed her lips, tipping her chin up so she still looked down her nose at him. "You aren't Belkin. Roulin then?"

"I'm Gastel."

As Gemma ran her fingers along his jaw, rage festered in the pit of Rae's stomach, threatening to boil over. He didn't deserve to be treated this way, but what could she do?

"You look *so* much like your father." She leaned back, letting her index finger trail painfully slow down his neck to his chest. "Your father, the king who decided I wasn't good enough. Throwing me away like trash." She paused, searching his face, her eyebrows drawing together in thought. "How old are you?"

Gastel hesitated and broke eye contact long enough to find Rae. Something about his age was important. "Thirty-two," he said, the muscles in his neck tightening.

To Rae's horror, Gemma's face grew an impressive shade of pink—a pure and dangerous anger. She'd seen her stepmother like this in the past. Rae tried to take a step forward only to be restrained.

"So it was you!" Gemma's eyes grew round. "The bastard elfling he sired with that whore while promised to me?"

What was Gemma talking about? King Mesmal and her stepmother *promised*? In *bonding*?

All her life, Rae had never known such a union to be sanctioned.

"I heard Mesmal had a third son, but no Shay had seen him to confirm. Yet here you are." A wicked grin replaced the anger on the queen's face. "*A trophy indeed.*" She swept her hand out to a servant behind her. "My blade."

Rae ripped at her captors' grasp, rage exploding in her chest, pulling an arm free for a moment until she was again restrained. She knew what Gemma did with her blade—the *only* thing she did with it. A beautifully sharp kukri was placed in Gemma's open palm, and she raised it to

Gastel's throat, the cool metal resting against stony flesh. His face was washed clean of emotion as he stood like a granite statue.

"Please, Your Majesty." Rae's anguished words sounded as though someone else had spoken them. "Please don't do this."

"I won't *physically* hurt him, dear Raemian."

Gemma slid the razor edge along his neck and pulled it away, leaving a pale scratch. She reached a hand up and laced her fingers into his topknot, then yanked his head forward hard and fast, cutting away his raven hair. When she brought her fist away, it was full. Gastel could only glare, lips parted, eyebrows furrowed in anguish, muscles taut. His remaining hair fell around his face, disheveled and perfectly imperfect.

Gemma handed the mass of hair back to a servant. "Keep this. I shall send it to his father."

She handed the blade back as well, a devious smile crossing her lips as she ran her hands through his loose hair, pushing it out of his face.

"I have never understood why you Bleck Larin wear your hair up so tight." Her fingers lingered on his chin before she stepped back and plopped down on her throne. "Take him to the dungeons, and return my stepdaughter to her residence."

He didn't struggle as he was pulled away from the queen, back through the doors of the court and out into the waiting crowd of Shay.

Rae couldn't take her eyes off him until he disappeared. Then, as though all her energy had left with him, she went limp in the guards' arms. They let her fall to her knees, her fingers splayed out on the floor in front of her. She'd failed. Despite the kindness—no, the *safety* Gastel had offered her—she'd fallen short of providing him with the same.

She squeezed her eyes closed, retreating into herself. This could have been Belkin. This *would* have been Belkin if she and Gastel had not left in the secrecy of night. Would Gemma have done the same to the heir to the Bleck Larin throne?

A sob forced past Rae's lips. *She was a stupid girl.* She'd allowed Gastel to talk her into this without all the details. Of course King Mesmal had a reason for Belkin to escort her. How could she have been so naïve to think he wouldn't?

The guards wrenched her from the floor, dragging her toward the door. Rae fought against them to turn back to the queen.

"They showed me nothing but kindness," she forced through clenched teeth.

She struggled harder and found they weren't nearly as motivated to hold her as they'd been before. She pulled loose and swung herself around to face her stepmother.

"Nothing but kindness, yet you treat him like a common criminal for something he had *no hand in.*" The last few words were raised louder than Rae had ever dared speak to her stepmother.

The dam holding back the last of her emotions burst, her rage flooding from her with angry tears, fortified by every time she'd tried and failed to please her queen.

"Come now, Raemian. It's only hair."

The dismissive tone of Gemma's voice only enraged Rae further. It was only hair—it'd grow back, and thank the Elder Gods he still had his life—but Gemma knew what she'd done. She had disrespected the ardent traditions of the Bleck Larin. A blatant slap in the proverbial face of tolerance and understanding. She had cut away thirty-two years of Gastel's life and had handed it to a servant like trash. It was a desecration of the son that might have been her own had King Mesmal honored his promise.

Rae shivered as a chill washed over her. There'd be no peace, not while Gemma sat upon her hateful throne. Gods help them all, the Shay had been on the losing side of the war. Mesmal desired peace, but after this? Rae's heart hurt with the fear of how Mesmal would retaliate—with what he'd think of her for letting this happen to Gastel.

The queen waved a dismissive hand, and the guards clamped down hard on her arms, dragging Rae from the courtroom.

Pacing in the darkness, Gastel could do nothing but relive what had happened over and over again. The cruel way Gemma had treated her stepdaughter. The utter, broken rage in Raemian's eyes as she had desperately tried to rectify the situation. The way the queen's fingers on his face had made his skin crawl.

Every muscle in his body was taut with anger. He had just enough room to take seven steps and turn, and he'd already done so countless times. Clenching and unclenching his fists, he ran a hand through his cursedly short hair.

He tried to calm himself and focused for a moment on something positive. Raemian's inquisitive eyes when they'd bathed in the stream. Her shyness had been innocent and endearing, filling him with a strange warmth. Now the source of her curiosity was gone—a grave dishonor. Only criminals had their hair cut, and usually only before they were put to death.

He should have listened to Raemian and let her travel the rest of the way alone once he'd escorted her from Bleck Larin territory. How could he have been so stupid? He'd ripped this one painfully slim chance for peace from his father's hands, and for what? His selfish need to spend every moment he possibly could with Raemian. Maybe part of it was to prove he could do something other than spend his entire life in the castle stronghold. His needs and wants didn't seem so important anymore—not when he'd likely never see his father or brothers again.

He slammed his fists into the wall and let rage bellow from him with an angry roar.

"Come now, Gastel, things could be so much worse." The cringey grit of Queen Gemma's voice rose the hair on the back of his neck. "You could be dead."

He'd been too busy wallowing in self-pity to notice her approach. She was flanked by guards, each holding a torch to light her way. Unlike earlier, her platinum hair hung loose around her shoulders, a provocative rhythm tainting every sway of her step. If his previous encounter had been more pleasant, he'd have said she was beautiful with her pale brows and lashes against a powdery-pink complexion. Her shaymarks were like butterfly wings on either temple, stretching from hairline to jaw, eyes a steely blue so light they were almost gray. Her gown hissed as the beaded hem slid across the rough wooden floor like the scraping of a million fingernails across stone.

"I've sent word to your father that you're alive. The terms of your release are in *his* hands now."

"He wants peace," Gastel said without hesitation.

A coy grin snaked across her lips as she wrapped slender fingers around one of the prison bars. Her nails were long, filed to points, and adorned with tiny rose-gold baubles. Each finger was laden with a ring of lavish stones and twisting vines, some that wrapped down the length of her finger and up over her knuckles to the back of her hand.

"Peace?" She leaned closer, and it took all of Gastel's restraint not to pull away. He had to focus to keep his eyes firmly on hers. The plunging neckline of her gown nearly spilled her ample breasts—the likes no Bleck Larin woman would ever be blessed with. "He had an opportunity for peace, and he threw it away, gambling it all on your mother *and you.*"

Her hand slipped from the bar before she turned away from him.

"What will you do with Raemian?" he asked.

She paused, and her posture changed, shoulders angling back before she turned toward him with vicious fierceness in her eyes, all her sauntering seduction gone.

"She'll be sent back to the front where she belongs." Her thin lips turned down, eyebrows furrowed, the ugliness he'd seen in the Court of Tremire visible in every curve of her face. "Killing your kind like the obedient soldier she is."

"She wishes for peace, too."

Her face darkened with anger, eyes narrowing to slits laced with white lashes. "The bars of this cell are enchanted by Eishtala magic. If I'm not mistaken, no Bleck Larin has ever possessed the ability to manipulate it, and no Eishtala Master will dare open this door without my permission. Enjoy your stay for as long as I desire, sweet prince."

She spun away, throwing her hair wide, and rushed from the dungeon without another word. As the guards holding the lanterns followed her out, Gastel was plunged into darkness again.

Turning his palm to the ceiling, he ignited his soultorch. He marveled at the carefully plaited vines of ironwood used to construct the door, the work of profoundly remarkable Eishtala magic. The amber light danced across the surface of the wooden walls, and he smirked, shifting the flame in his palm to bright white.

———

Rae rummaged around in a cupboard for something to eat and distract herself from dwelling on Gastel, likely cold and alone in the darkness of the dungeon. She sat at her table with a piece of hard cheese and a strip of deer jerky. It was better than nothing, but not nearly as delicious as the rabbit Gastel had cooked.

He would probably be starving after being dragged across the highlands by the queen's soldiers. They were given no food or water for the entire day's journey, ripped along at a teeth-gnashing pace. She considered demanding the guards outside deliver at least water and a blanket to Gastel until a sharp knock interrupted her thoughts. Before she had time to respond, the door was thrown wide.

Rae didn't think she'd ever been so happy to see Freck in all her life. She couldn't race across the room fast enough. He wrapped her in his thick, muscled arms and squeezed.

"You're crushing me!" she squeaked out before he released her.

"Gods." He stepped back and took her cheeks in his hands to hold her face still. "When I heard, I thought I'd never see you again." He pulled her in for another hug, this time with less rib-crushing force.

"There was a time I thought the same."

"Gods, Rae." He tucked her head under his chin. "I let you out of my sight one time, just *one* time."

"Okay, okay." She pulled herself out of his arms. "How's my father? Does he know I'm home?"

Freck frowned. "I didn't know you were home until I saw the guards. What are you in trouble for this time? She's never posted guards before."

She shook her head in disappointment. "I really need to speak with him."

"I wasn't even sure they would let me in. Maybe request an audience with Somin tomorrow?" He plopped down on her tiny sofa and patted the cushion beside him. "Come, tell me of your adventures."

Rae pressed her lips together, trying to decide where to start. She told him everything while pacing in front of him. She kept the details as abbreviated as possible—King Mesmal, his sons, the peace the king sought with Gemma. She told him about Gastel and how he'd risked everything to help her return home, but that it had been the worst idea she'd ever gone along with.

"Wait. Let me get this straight. You had an opportunity to take out the *entire* royal family, and you chose to befriend them?" Freck shook his head playfully. "You know we've been at war for the last thirty years, right?"

Rae smacked his shoulder with the back of her hand, a sly smile on her lips. "They were kind to me. I'm not a monster. Not like Gemma." She let her words hang.

"I don't think Gemma would..." Freck paused and looked across the room at nothing in particular. "She wouldn't...would she?"

"She almost did today. She had the kukri to his throat." Rae wrung her hands. "This is my fault. I have to figure out how to make this right."

Freck was on his feet in an instant, taking her shoulders so he could peer into her eyes. "It's not your fault. You've done nothing wrong, Rae." He pulled her in for another hug. "And from what you've told me, neither has he." He held her there for another moment. "Nothing but befriend the enemy, anyway."

She pulled away sharply, finding him flashing his charming, crooked teeth. "Freckles."

He burst into laughter, throwing his head back and slapping her on the back hard enough to send her forward. She joined him, letting the mirth wash away the last bits of anger.

"In all seriousness, request an audience with Somin tomorrow. See if anything can be done." He pinned her with a severe glare. "And don't do that again."

"Do what exactly?" She knew what he meant, but she wanted to hear him say it.

"Don't rush in like you have a battalion at your back. You're so reckless. And for a Bleck Larin? Seriously, Rae?"

She could only smirk.

"I know that look." He turned his head to squint at her from the corner of his eye. "You don't regret a thing, do you?"

She pressed her lips together to keep from smiling.

"Raemian Starling."

"What?" she teased.

"You're hopeless." He shook his head as he reached for a small sack, producing a loaf of honey cake and two large apples from its depths. "Hungry?"

NINETEEN

The Importance of Planning

I trust you've thought this through, Father."

Belkin sat in the saddle with ease, his father on the horse next to him—it was obvious the king hadn't ridden in several years. His father didn't need to travel. Dignitary functions not held at the castle stronghold were few and far between. Plus, the king had Belkin and Roulin to lead his army.

"When have I ever been known to think something through?" his father said, smiling to himself, but Belkin wasn't amused.

"You and Gastel shall be the death of me."

His father had never been the best at planning and strategy. Gastel was the same. This impulsivity was the precise reason Belkin now found himself waiting inside the Shaylands, deep in the Middlelend Forest. For a stupid girl. Not just a girl, a Shay—and not just any Shay—the Shay who had killed hundreds of Bleck Larin soldiers in battle. *His* soldiers.

When Belkin had gone to retrieve her, he'd found the guard unconscious on the landing, the tower empty. He'd immediately gone to Gastel. Discovering his youngest brother was also missing, the truth of the circumstance became clear. Gastel hadn't trusted Belkin to return the Shay safely. Quite honestly, Belkin couldn't blame him. He wasn't sure he trusted himself. One snide remark from her, and he would have done what he'd been waiting to do since the moment he'd seen her standing in the king's throne room—what he'd tried and failed to do in his father's study.

Now this was a rescue mission instead of a peacekeeping one. Rather than waiting for a response from Gemma as to whether she'd accept their request for peace, they waited to hear if she'd negotiate for the safe return of the youngest prince. Belkin and his father knew in their hearts the response wouldn't be favorable.

In classic Mesmal not-thinking-things-through fashion, his father had insisted they leave at once to negotiate in person. Whatever his father's plan was, Belkin had his own contingency plan—a collection of his best warriors, and Roulin at the ready.

They'd taken the Old Road, which, after thirty years of little to no use, was overgrown as the wilderness had reclaimed it. Once near the Shay border, the road had been abandoned in favor of a more inconspicuous route, but doing so had taken them much longer than anticipated.

Belkin knew it would have been faster to cross this section of the forest on foot, but the horses would be needed on the other side. He couldn't expect his soft, out-of-shape father to jog across the entire highlands. He regretted that decision. Jore was a good horse, but something had his dander up, and Belkin's patience was already paper-thin.

Belkin leaned down and patted Jore's shoulder. "Something is strange in this part of the forest. Jore is never this nervous."

"Perhaps he's tired of your negative aura."

Belkin glanced over at his father and found the man smirking. *Smirking!* The crazy, old elf was calling him negative? While they traveled to retrieve their youngest family member from an enraged queen? Enraged because she'd been snubbed by none other than the crazy, old elf beside him.

"Perhaps you should think things through," Belkin sniped.

His father rolled his eyes and looked off into the forest.

Belkin took a deep breath, huffing it out. The scouts should have returned by now. Either they'd been detained by Shay or had gotten lost. Neither scenario was favorable. Nor was the fading light. It meant they'd be making camp in the middle of the forest. For all the talk of thinking things through, nothing was going as planned.

Swinging down from Jore, Belkin pulled his riding gloves off and threw them in one of his saddlebags. He'd do what he always did and fix the problem.

"What do you plan on doing?" his father asked.

It was Belkin's turn to roll his eyes. "I plan on making camp. Get a fire started. Find the scouts. Not necessarily in that order." He drew his saber from the saddle-mounted scabbard. "At least I've planned."

He turned toward his lieutenant, Tildimin, and the handful of soldiers that had stayed behind while the scouts had gone on ahead.

"Stay with the king; guard him with your life. I shall only be an hour at most. If I don't return in that time, take His Majesty back to Parth and direct Roulin to start the full-scale assault on the City of Tremire."

Tildimin acknowledged with a brisk salute to his chest.

Belkin turned to leave but spun back, pointing at one of the other soldiers. "And gather some firewood."

Satisfied that his father was in moderately good hands, Belkin slipped off to find the scouts. It only took him twenty minutes. Both were face down in puddles of bloody leaves.

"Fuck."

Could nothing go as it should?

No arrows indicated a lack of ranged weaponry. Belkin leaned against the nearest tree to cover his backside and scanned in all directions. Nothing. He approached, taking care not to disturb the footprints.

From the look of things, there were two. At least one of them was fairly proficient with a blade. He followed the footprints farther, eyes scanning the tree trunks for the pink of Shay flesh.

"You're on the wrong side of the border, Bleck Larin."

Belkin had never cared for their accent or their prominent muscles. This one had white hair, left loose around his shoulders, and tattoos on his face to accentuate his shaymarks. The sharp sound of steel leaving a scabbard only proved what Belkin already knew. This Shay was stupid, like all the others.

Belkin deflected the first strike with his plate bracer, pulling his saber and meeting steel with steel. The Shay backpedaled and tripped on something buried below the leaves. Before Belkin could exact a perfectly executed killing blow, the second Shay blocked him. She was much shorter but just as muscular as her male counterpart. She, however, seemed able to maintain her footing.

It didn't matter. They were no match for Belkin's superior training and Bleck Larin height. He took turns between the two of them, easily controlling the upper hand, smiling as a pattern in their fighting emerged. He found an easy opening in the woman's defenses, his saber slicing through leather with ease. She went down hard, dropping her sword and clutching her ribs.

The man seemed more determined, but after a few more seconds spent exchanging melee, Belkin infiltrated his defenses and sliced open the man's abdomen—a slow death.

"Monsters." The Shay clutched at his stomach as he sank to his knees. "You're all fucking monsters."

Belkin wasn't interested in conversation. He kicked the Shay to the ground and put his saber through the man's chest. The Shay's mouth dropped open in a silent cry of pain as a ribbon of blood ran from the side of his mouth.

"No more monstrous than your kind, I assure you," Belkin said before turning for the woman.

She whimpered as she scrambled to get away, slamming her back against a tree. Her hand was pressed over her wound, trying to stem the bleeding—and failing. Blood had soaked through and ran down her abdomen. Belkin must have struck harder than he thought. He fisted her red hair and lifted her head, pressing it back against the tree so she was forced to meet his eyes.

"Where does your queen have the youngest Bleck Larin prince?"

Tears left dirty streaks down her cheeks. She swallowed but didn't answer. Belkin shook her head and drove it hard against the tree. It'd have caused even the strongest elf to see stars. Her eyes rolled, then refocused.

"Where does the queen have Gastel?"

She spat in his face.

Wrong move. He brought his sword to her throat.

"I look for my brother. Where does the queen have him?"

"If the queen has him, he's likely dead." She squeezed her eyes closed in anticipation. "Or he's in the dungeons of Tremire. Only an Eishtala Master can open the cell doors. He's there until she releases him."

Belkin sneered and drew his blade across her throat, slicing deep. Her eyes went wide, mouth gaping as blood pulsed from her neck in spurts. He held her head against the rough bark until her labored gurgling ceased and her eyes grew empty before letting her fall to the side.

Belkin wiped the spit from his face and glanced down at the lifeless Shay woman, dead eyes reflecting the sky. For a second, he saw Raemian, and a pang of regret washed over him.

Regret? For killing a Shay? For killing Raemian Starling?

He shook the feeling away. This wasn't Raemian, and even if it was, he had no reason to have regret. Not for killing the Shay responsible for the death of so many Bleck Larin.

He wiped his blade on the woman's sleeve before heading back toward his father. Sliding his saber into its scabbard made the most satisfying sound.

"Rough going?" Mesmal asked.

His father had found a comfortable place beside a warm fire. Belkin ignored his question. It was obvious he'd heard the struggle.

"They likely have him in the dungeons of Tremire."

He looked out through the trees and then back to Jore, who stomped his hind leg. Belkin had hoped it was the Shay making Jore nervous. Glancing back, he noticed his father's expression had taken a much more serious note—not something he often saw from the gentle king.

"We'll give Gemma until tomorrow," his father said.

Belkin nodded. Maybe his father did have a plan.

TWENTY

Simple Requests

R ae's father agreed to receive her shortly after breakfast at his personal residence. She dressed in a simple, form-fitting frock made of blue silk and trimmed in delicate brocade, taking extra care to look her best. Though Somin had never been crowned king, he was held in high regard. Rae always tried her best to show respect for his station, and today, that meant making herself a little more presentable. Once satisfied that she wouldn't embarrass him, she allowed the guards to lead her through Tremire.

She was received by a soft-spoken woman and directed to a lavishly decorated salon. Somin occupied one of the largest and oldest trees in Tremire, and every time Rae visited, it was jarring to see how massive an Eishtala dwelling could be. Downy futons dressed in silk and velvet circled a low, round table in the center, which had been set with two cups of steaming spiced berry wine and a platter of cheese and flatbread.

"My daughter. I've missed you." He flowed across the room and embraced her with gentle arms.

She'd missed him as well, but the display of affection seemed odd. They were no longer close. Not since he'd been bonded to Gemma and she'd been sent to serve in the queen's army. Rae saw her father a handful of times a year, mostly for royal functions, which the queen insisted she attend.

"Gemma says you weren't hurt?"

"Of course I wasn't."

He eased a little and directed her to sit with him. "And King Mesmal? Was he—"

"He was more than kind. He and his sons—well, Gastel—were beyond gracious," she said as she joined Somin on the futons. "They weren't at all as I'd expected Bleck Larin to be."

"When I heard you'd been taken and your partner killed, I—" He choked on his words. "I think we all assumed you'd been kidnapped on purpose."

On purpose? How would a Bleck Larin have known who she was without inspecting her sword?

"How in Rhend were you taken, precisely?"

She gazed down at her hands, embarrassed.

"It doesn't matter." He waved the question away. "I heard Gemma made quite a spectacle of the young prince."

Rae sank further into herself, unable to put the emotions swirling in her mind into words. When exactly had she lost the comfort to speak openly with her father?

Somin tucked an index finger under her chin and tipped her head to face him. "Rae, it's not your fault."

Of course her father would know the guilt she harbored. He had an uncanny way of knowing, even after they hadn't seen each other for months.

Tears threatened, but she did her best to hold them back. "I have to fix this, but I don't know how."

"I will speak with Gemma. Her actions yesterday were heavy-handed." He placed a hand over Rae's. "I fear she didn't think things through." He sighed. "Correction: I *know* she didn't. He's a prince. Even queens must follow protocols when royalty is involved."

"I know Her Majesty won't permit me to see him, but what about you?" Somin shook his head, but she continued: "Just to make sure he has food, water, a blanket, light?"

She tried to keep the concern from her voice, but she doubted she fooled him.

"Sweet Rae, I will do what I can."

She knew full well that while he would try, he'd never go over his queen's orders. To disrupt the careful peace between himself and his royal bondmate would be disastrous. Not just for him, but for Rae as well.

Gastel had spent hours quietly carving away at the ironwood of the cell door with his soulflame and had hardly managed to slice more than an inch deep. He was exhausted from the effort. Even the pathetically meek Anam magic he possessed was taxing. The bars were enchanted by Eishtala, Anam's opposite in every way. Anam used an elf's soul as its source of power; Eishtala used the life force of the world around it. He sat against the wooden wall with his head pressed where his topknot should have been. He needed a break before he could start again.

At the sound of footsteps, his head snapped up. A lone figure flanked by guards with torches approached. It would seem he had a visitor, since he was fairly certain he was the dungeon's only resident. Gastel picked himself up off the floor, the exhaustion of his Anam efforts weighing down his extremities like wet clothes.

"Prince Gastel?" His visitor had a gentle voice, melodic and calm. "I'm Somin Starling, Rae's father."

Of course her father would have such a soothing timbre. As Somin drew closer, the light from the torches revealed just how much she resembled him. The same soft pink complexion and flaming red hair, lacy shaymarks dancing on the sides of his face and neck. Those deep-blue eyes that seemed to see everything.

"Rae asked that I make sure you are well. Have you been provided food and water?"

"I have."

Somin left a few feet between himself and the cell door before retrieving a torch from one of the guards and dismissing them.

"I shall be a few moments," Somin reassured the guards as they glanced at each other. He waited until the light from the torch they shared disappeared completely. "Now that we have some privacy. I'm sure you've already been working on cutting through these bars?"

Gastel took a sharp breath.

"Your mother was a wielder, was she not?"

"So I've been told," Gastel said, certain surprise was written across his face.

"Then I trust you've been trained." His words weren't accusatory—more matter-of-fact.

"I've never possessed the same power," Gastel said.

Somin's brow furrowed in the same way Raemian's would have.

"I have a soulflame, but nothing more."

Somin turned, placing the torch in the wall bracket outside Gastel's cell. Deep shadows highlighted the creases along his forehead. "Have you used it on the cell door yet?"

Gastel hesitated. While Somin was Raemian's father, he was also the queen's bondmate, and Gastel had no real reason to trust him.

"I understand," Somin said.

Gastel's nerves were already worn thin from spending a night in a cell after having been shown no kindness by the queen and her people. Navigating the world of Shay was difficult. He'd only ever known Parth, the castle stronghold, his brothers, and father. Bleck Larin. This was a rough way to learn how little he knew about the world outside his father's fortress. All the history books and correspondence he'd read had not prepared him for how cruel elves could be toward one another.

Somin was quiet for only a moment, but it was long enough for Gastel to second-guess his visitor several times, turning over in his mind what advantage Somin would gain from helping—and whether he was helping at all.

"There's much to say."

"Before you trouble yourself, what assurance do I have that you aren't here on some reconnaissance mission for the queen?"

Somin seemed unfazed by what should have been a rude remark.

"Because Rae cares for you, and while I've done a great many things that haven't always been in her best interest, *this*." He motioned around, indicating the entire situation. "This needs to change." He took a deep breath, exhaling a lifetime of frustration, then met Gastel's eyes. "Where should I begin?"

The air was oppressively still as Gastel waited, unsure of exactly what information Somin could possibly share with him that would sharpen his trust.

"Ah...your mother."

Somin's Secrets

Gastel wished he had Raemian's ability to piece information together, but he didn't. The best he could do was grab and hold the answers to questions his father had never given him.

"Your mother was perhaps the most powerful wielder our world has ever seen." Somin's eyes lit with admiration. "Niminea's responsibilities to the Anam Guild took her all over Rhend. She and Gale, Rae's mother, were close companions. They traveled a lot together until Gale and I were bonded and Rae was born." Somin sat cross-legged outside Gastel's cell with no regard for the fact that he was the queen's bondmate, a king by all accounts. "Surely your father has told you all about her?"

Gastel shook his head. "The pain of her passing was too great." He swallowed, his throat growing dry. "I didn't even know her name." He leaned his back against the wall, eyes finding the shadowy ceiling. There was something about sitting with Somin that reminded him of his father's company, just without comfortable chairs or a roaring fire to help him focus his thoughts.

"I know that pain." Somin seemed to lose himself in thought, then waved the feeling away. "Niminea died closing a rift in the Middlelend Forest just after you were born. She shouldn't have been traveling alone, considering the conditions of Rhend and her ties to Mesmal."

Gastel's attention snapped to Somin's words. The fact that he'd been attacked by a rift and his mother had been killed closing one couldn't be a coincidence. He cursed at himself for not asking Raemian to repeat everything the being had said while he'd been unconscious.

"I'm sorry, I don't mean to be so cavalier with your mother's passing." Somin's words were soft—a father's words.

"No, it's not that, it's..." But again, that creeping feeling that Somin couldn't be entirely trusted wormed its way into his gut. "It's nothing. Please continue."

"There were so many things that seemed to happen within the course of a year. Your father's affair with Niminea was brought to light when she could no longer hide her pregnancy. The rejection Gemma endured in the face of his infidelity was...well, enough to drive her to unfathomable depths." Somin sighed. "Niminea was bedridden for the latter half of her pregnancy—after she learned that Gale was killed in the Culling."

"The Culling?"

"Do you not know of the Culling?"

Somin seemed utterly baffled by Gastel's ignorance, leaving another mark on the lengthening list of histories he wasn't aware of.

"It's the single greatest evil ever committed against the Bleck Larin people." Somin spoke more quickly, a layer of urgency coating every word. "Gemma's rage toward your father caused her to draw a line in the sand—a border, so to speak. When the Bleck Larin that remained in the Shaylands were told they needed to leave, many of them resisted abandoning their families." Somin paused, perhaps deciding on the best words to use. "Gemma gave them five days, then sent troops to rid her lands of what she called 'the Bleck Larin Scourge.' When your father learned what Gemma had done, he called for the full-scale invasion of Dormshire."

Gastel's pulse quickened, pure anger building in the pit of his stomach. He could only imagine how his father had felt. The thought of hundreds of Bleck Larin being murdered for refusing to leave those they loved. Inexcusable. *This* was the great evil his father had spoken of!

"Your father had ruled with a peaceful hand and undiminishable patience—until Gemma took things too far." Somin held Gastel's gaze with grave seriousness. "The Culling was the catalyst, and I, for one, don't blame him for his actions." He swallowed a few times, struggling to continue. "I lost my bondmate and was left to raise Rae on my own, like the other families that had been torn apart."

Gastel frantically tried to piece together all the information as his heart continued to race. "The Culling was Gemma's retaliation for my father's unfaithfulness." He squeezed the bridge of his nose. "How does Gale's death fit into this?"

"Gale was killed by Gemma's executioners in the Culling."

Gastel's thoughts felt thick. "But that would mean—"

"That Gale Starling was Bleck Larin. Yes."

Gastel pushed himself to his feet. "How is that even—"

"Possible? Because there were no laws against a Shay and Bleck Larin lifebond. Your father was to be joined in a lifebond with Gemma, after all. It was thought a lifebond could unify our people once and for all. Tensions since Gemma's father had taken the throne were growing steadily stronger."

The immensity of Somin's words filled Gastel's mind with downy cotton, blurring lines that should have been solid. Burning away barriers that his brothers had painstakingly built as Gastel grew up in a world where elves warred against one another.

Somin stood and faced him. There was a serenity in the man's expression that reminded him of Raemian. But it didn't last. A deep sadness flooded over Somin.

"Raemian deserves the truth," Somin said. His eyes grew misty with unshed tears. "For years, I've been too scared to tell her, for fear she'd hate me—or, worse, hate herself." He shook his head. "I never should've let Gemma send her to the front. I should've refused, but I was a coward."

Gastel shivered with realization. Somin was a Shay capable of loving and creating a family with a Bleck Larin. The fact that Somin had allowed his elfling, a product of that love, to go into battle and kill her own kind without knowing?

Somin considered his next words carefully. "My hands were tied in many ways. The House of Starling is important to the lineage of the royal family. And Gemma exploited that to the best of her ability. Her father committed shady dealings which were solidified when all my siblings were executed under the guise of war casualties."

These were secrets that Gastel shouldn't have been given. Conspiracies that involved crowns and heirs to thrones, swept under the rug of war.

"I was spared by our lifebond agreement. It was the only way I could keep Rae safe, as Gemma sought to eliminate any question of her legitimacy to rule. There's more, but we haven't the time."

Gastel could only stare at Somin as the gravity of the information settled around him. Why would Somin tell him these things?

"Now then." Somin seemed to shake the sorrow and seriousness away in an instant. "If you are indeed the son of Mesmal and Niminea, you should make quick work of these bars."

"I've already tried." Gastel put his finger in the inch-deep slice he'd managed over the last night of attempts. "I've little to show for my efforts."

Somin leaned forward to look at the bars where Gastel indicated.

"That won't do. At this rate, your father will have destroyed the whole of Tremire before you cut yourself free."

"Has Gemma received a response from him?"

Somin shook his head. "I'm not sure, but I think we both know, after this history lesson, how your father responds when people he loves are taken from him."

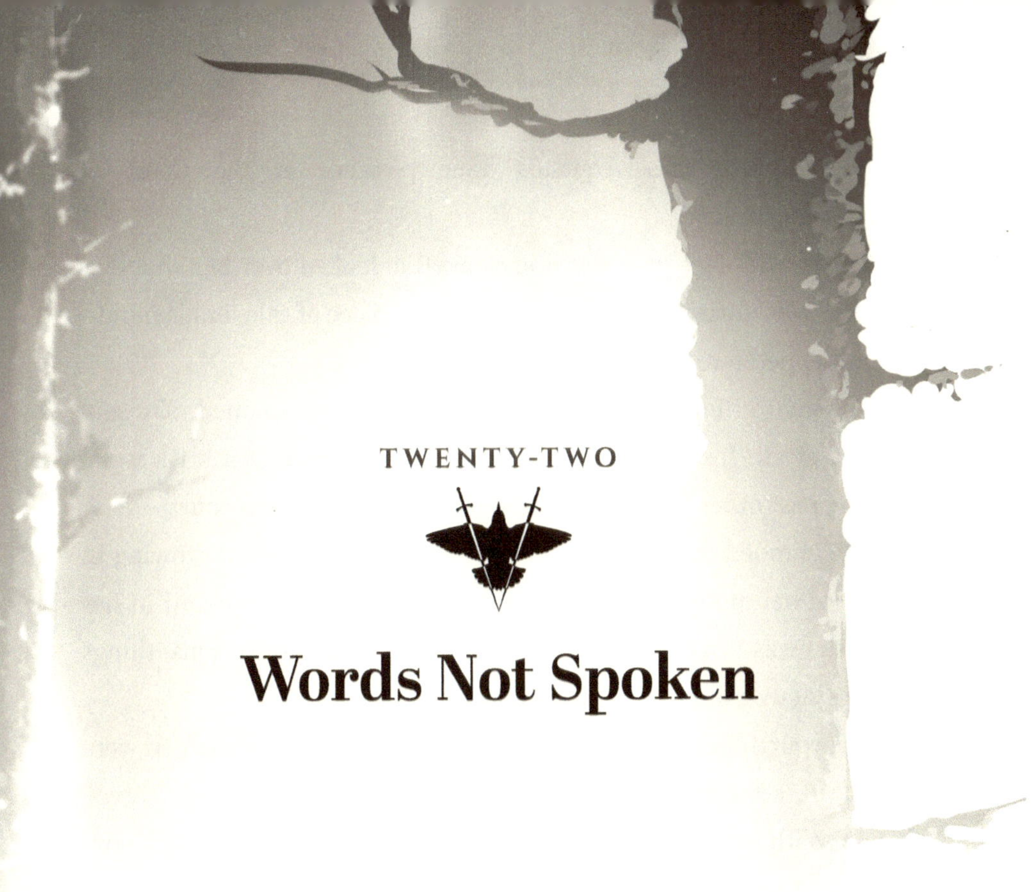

TWENTY-TWO

Words Not Spoken

Rae was beside herself, waiting for any word from her father. It was late afternoon! Surely he'd let her know if there was any news. If there was any...*anything*.

Freck stuffed himself with honey cakes and berries Rae had put out for him. He'd brought news of her next assignment. They would do as they'd always done—protect the Eastern Pass. Dormshire was delicious low-hanging fruit, dangling just out of reach for the Bleck Larin.

"He's probably been detained by Her Majesty." Freck tipped his head back and let a plump berry fall from an arm's length up. "You know how she can be."

A loud rapping at the door sent Rae rushing across the room. She threw the door open, hoping her father was on the other side. Instead, she found one of her stepmother's royal guards.

"Her Majesty has requested your presence at the Court of Tremire immediately."

The guard's face gave nothing away. Rae looked over her shoulder at Freck, who shrugged and popped another piece of cake in his mouth as she stepped out.

The guard didn't tell Rae why she had been summoned. She said nothing at all. Instead, she led Rae through Tremire at a brisk walk, pushing past other Shay milling about the entrance of the court.

Rae climbed the steps to the Court of Tremire, unease growing in the pit of her stomach. As brave as she could be with a sword in her hand, she was lost when it came to the ways of the court. Plus, things hadn't exactly gone well the last time.

The courtroom had been cleared of nobles. All that remained were the queen, a servant, and two guards flanking her elaborately carved throne. With heavy reluctance, Rae crossed the room and knelt, knowing not to rise until she'd been addressed.

"Sweet Raemian, thank you for coming so quickly." As if Rae had a choice. "I thought that since you seem to take such an interest in our Bleck Larin guest, you should be the first to know that I've received word from King Mesmal."

The queen drew the moment out, sipping languidly from a glass of mahogany-red wine, the rings on her fingers chiming against the surface. The queen was trying to force her to speak out of turn. It wouldn't work. Rae had learned long ago that Gemma did what she wanted, when she wanted, to whom she wanted, and no one could change that.

"King Mesmal was exceedingly disappointed to see how callously I handled his son invading my lands." She had a wicked smile plastered across her face, trying hard to bait Rae. Gemma knew Gastel had not invaded her lands. He'd risked his life to bring Rae back safely. "I plan to wait a few more days to respond. Let the young prince rot a little longer in the dungeon. What do you think?"

Rae did her best to tune Gemma out. She focused on the way the fabric of the queen's gown shimmered as she spoke. Light refracted through the wine and left a blood red stain on the table to the side of Gemma's throne. The guard on her left shifted his weight like he needed to relieve himself. There was a fresh chip in the wooden steps leading up to the throne. Afternoon light danced across the floor, cast through the elaborate cutout windows. She focused on anything but the queen.

"I asked you a question."

Rae snapped to attention.

"That's not like you. I know you. You always pay attention. To *ev...ery...thing*. It's infuriating."

Gemma massaged her forehead, causing her white eyebrows to rise and fall with the shifting of her skin.

"Do you know what King Mesmal asked for?" she said, dropping her hand to her lap. "It was unexpected, I should think." The corners of her lips curled up in an ominous grin. "After all he's put me through, this is how he thinks he can solve his little war problem."

As if the war was all Mesmal's problem. It was Rae's understanding that the king had been the antagonist, but she knew he must have had a good reason. The Mesmal Rae had come to know didn't seem like he could order an attack without purpose.

"He wishes for a lifebond treaty." Gemma laughed, a high-pitched, wretchedly fake laugh. "Did you hear me, Raemian?" She pointed at her with a sharply filed fingernail, the rings and baubles adorning it jingling from the speed with which she pointed. "Lifebonding! But not with him. I'm already bonded to your father. *No*. He wishes for a lifebond between you and one of his sons. Any of his sons. He has given me my choice."

Gemma held the end of the word out like the hiss of a sword tip across a floor, then drained her glass of wine.

Goosebumps bloomed across Rae's arms. This couldn't be. *Wouldn't* be. Belkin and Roulin both had such hatred for Shay. After years of war, a lifebond with a Shay? *With Rae?*

"I'm not even sure how to respond to such a preposterous request."

Gemma held her empty wine glass up to a servant, who filled it. She must have finally realized her conversation had been entirely one-sided because she glared down at Rae with serious eyes.

"You've not even asked how my day has been." She held the glass to her lips.

"Forgive me, Your Majesty, I didn't want to interrupt." Rae bowed without looking away. "How has your day been, My Queen?"

"Horrendous. I must decide how to deal with this Bleck Larin problem. I can't leave him in the dungeon forever; they live far too long."

It took all Rae's strength not to lash out at Gemma's attempts to frustrate her. Gastel wasn't a *problem*. He was the furthest thing from.

"Now then, what's your opinion on this whole lifebond agreement?"

She took another sip of wine before setting her glass down and standing. Her dress made it difficult for her to walk, with layers of sheer and ruched pleats tight around her narrow waist, but she took a few steps down toward Rae.

"Perhaps Belkin? Then when he becomes king, you could solidify my rule over all Rhend by killing him."

Not possible. Belkin was a formidable fighter, not to mention the fact that there wouldn't be enough warmth in a lifebond between him and any Shay for him to let his guard down. Even less so with Rae.

"There's no political advantage to a lifebond with Roulin; plus, I've heard he's not nearly as attractive as his brothers."

Gemma stepped closer. Close enough that Rae could smell the queen's sweet wine breath. Rae knew full well what the queen would say next.

"Gastel is deliciously handsome and seems to be the most amenable toward Shay. He is, after all, protective of *you*." Gemma took one of Rae's loose strands of hair in her fingertips and twirled it. "Though I rather like the thought of him at my own disposal."

Rae held the queen's stormy eyes for a moment longer; they twinkled with cunning. Gemma was neither blind nor stupid. Rae had not been able to hide the anger that had simmered and overflowed as the queen had sheared Gastel's raven hair.

Gemma's smile slipped a little, and her eyes traveled the length of Rae, inspecting her for the first time. Rae was thankful she still wore formal attire from visiting her father. Gemma didn't often see her dressed in something so feminine.

"What would your choice be if bonded to one of these Bleck Larin princes?"

"I think we both know the answer to that." Rae immediately regretted the bite in her tone and the quickness of her reply. She tried to recover. "Whomever you should choose for me."

But Gemma had gotten her answer in the words Rae hadn't spoken. The queen spun away, the shimmering folds of her gown slapping Rae's skirt. She plopped down on the throne and reached for her glass of wine, holding Rae's line of sight as she took a sip and pursed her lips.

"Thank you, Raemian Starling, for this little chat. You've been most helpful in my decision on how I should *execute* my response." The corners of her lips curled up in a cruel smile. "You're dismissed." She waved her hand, signaling the guard behind Rae to escort her back to her residence.

Rae turned, but her body had gone numb. Every inch of her shook with anger and terror and hatred by the time she reached the bottom of the steps outside. Had Gemma even heard from King Mesmal? Or had all of this been another one of Gemma's manipulations? Surely she didn't mean to execute Gastel?

She smoothed her hair back out of her face and took a deep breath of the fresh afternoon air. There had to be something she could do, some way to rectify the situation. Even to return Gastel safely would do. Rae had lost all ability to establish even a loose tolerance between the Shay and Bleck Larin, and unless she figured out how to get Gastel out of Tremire, she would lose him, too.

She stumbled to one knee. The guard turned and helped her up with a firm hand on her upper arm.

"I'm sorry, I wasn't paying attention."

The guard gave her a stern look and cleared her throat. Rae knew she'd get no sympathy from her, nor did she expect it. As they approached her residence, however, the guard took her upper arm again and stopped her at the bottom of the steps. She leaned in and spoke with a whisper.

"Her Majesty is cruel to you. She's always been cruel to you. We notice."

The guard gave Rae a sympathetic smile. This was unexpected. Rae would never turn away an ally. She put a hand on the guard's armored gauntlet and returned the smile with a nod. No, this wasn't expected at all, but it gave her hope—something she was in short supply of.

When she opened the door, she was surprised to find Freck and her father sitting at her little dining table. They both looked up, the same pained expression on their faces.

Freck stood and took a few steps in her direction as she crossed to them. He took her in his arms as he had the day before and gave her another of his rib-crushing hugs—something she needed at that moment.

"King Mesmal has responded."

Somin gazed down at the tabletop. "I thought perhaps he had." He took a deep breath. "I checked in on Gastel and found him well."

Rae could breathe a sigh of relief with this news. Her news, on the other hand...

"I think Gemma means to execute him."

She could be wrong. Gods, she *hoped* she was wrong, but after the way Gemma had finished their conversation—the queen seemed determined to inflict as much pain as possible on Mesmal.

"Gemma isn't stupid. If she kills him, she'll see the wrath of King Mesmal like she's never seen before. His gentle nature is the only thing that has saved the Shay from total annihilation all these years." Somin stood. "I need to get back before Gemma notices I'm gone, but there's much I need to tell you, Rae. So many things I should've told you years ago but couldn't."

Freck stopped Somin with a hand on his shoulder and a serious expression, so unlike the warm and bubbly Freck she knew. "Tell her now. You may not have another chance."

The two men exchanged knowing looks that gave Rae a sense of foreboding.

Somin sank into himself.

"I'll give you privacy." Freck took one of Rae's hands and squeezed it. "Have compassion, Rae. He meant only to protect you."

The door closed behind him with a nauseating finality, and Rae could do nothing but stare at it, wishing Freck would come back in.

"Rae, I'm sorry for not telling you sooner."

She hoped she'd washed all emotion from her face as she turned to meet her father's intense eyes. He seemed worried, scared, and defeated all at once.

"About your mother..."

TWENTY-THREE

Anam

With her forehead resting lightly on her intertwined fingers, Rae cataloged everything her father said. Her mother had been Bleck Larin, killed by the queen's executioners in the Culling. The thought of it echoed in her mind. She was half Bleck Larin. Her own stepmother was capable of having hundreds of innocent elves put to death for no greater crime than the color of their skin.

"All of this information just confirms that Gemma will…" Rae swallowed.

Gastel's days were numbered as long as he remained locked within the dungeons of Tremire. He was, after all, the perfect person to use to hurt Mesmal. She met her father's exhausted gaze, trying to keep the urgency boiling in her veins from exploding all over the table between them. He'd just answered every question she'd asked countless times, but there were more forming in their places.

"Why haven't you told me about my mother? Why would you accept a lifebond with the woman responsible for her death?"

"I..." He stammered. "It's complicated."

"What isn't, Father?" Rae did her best to hold the bitterness back from her words. "This entire war is complicated."

He stared at his hands, unable to make eye contact with her.

"How do we get Gastel out?"

Somin stood. Apparently, this answer wasn't as hard to articulate. "He should possess his mother's Anam Wielding abilities. I'm flabbergasted that he doesn't."

"But he does possess her power. He wears her soul stone. He said it contains the last of her soul."

Her father stopped dead, turning slowly toward her. "What?"

Rae squeezed her eyes closed. Before she could say it again, he rushed toward the door.

"He needs to take it off. If there's any of his mother's soul left within the stone, it will lock *his* away." He brought his hand to his forehead, working through the news. "She must have given it to him to protect him."

Rae started to follow, but he turned to stop her, shaking his head.

"You mustn't. I'm going to Gemma. Stay here, please. If anyone can find out what she's planning, it's me. The soul stone changes things. I thought it strange that he had control of his soulflame with no other wielder capabilities."

"How do you know so much about—"

"Call it a strange interest." Her father winked. "Your mother was heavily involved with helping the Anam Guild." His expression turned serious again. "If he can control soulflame while his powers are suppressed..." He took a deep breath, letting it out slowly. "Gods help us, the fire he can rain down. Getting out of a cell will be like drawing open a curtain."

He took her face in his hands. "We can get him out, but we have to do it smartly or he'll have all of Tremire at his heels."

He kissed her forehead like he had when she'd been a little elfling, with all his love filling his eyes, a gentle smile gracing his lips. He wore so much pride in his gaze that her heart warmed a little. This man was her father. Even though he'd made terrible decisions, lied to her for years, allowed her stepmother to send her into war against her mother's people, he loved her.

He turned and rushed out, leaving Rae alone in the quiet of her home with the chaos of information he'd just given her. She had the answers to so many of her questions, but now she wasn't so sure she wanted them. This new reality of her past felt so raw and contradictory to everything she'd always known.

Her mother had been Bleck Larin?

Every breath she took shook with despair. She'd slain countless Bleck Larin in battle. Their lifeless amber eyes—their blood on her hands—flashed through her mind, blurring her vision with grief. She sank to the ground in a heap of tears.

Gods, what had she done?

Cutting through the sorrow was the memory of Gemma's tainted words when Rae had been sent to train with the other elflings. She had not been given a choice. 'S*omin, she will make such a loyal soldier.'* And she had. For years, she had. Now what was she? Truly a monster. Mesmal had every right to hate her—had every right to wish for her death. If ever faced with Belkin's accusations again, she would accept them. Living with this guilt would be so much worse than the darkness of death.

She wiped her tears with the back of her hand as her mind flooded with the memory of Gastel's quirky smile and confident stance. How his eyes had held her in the stream, his concerned gaze as they had walked through the streets of Tremire, his stone-faced acceptance hiding the anger that simmered beneath the surface when Gemma had cut his hair.

If her father was correct, he could be saved, but she wasn't sure how or why. Why would her father help her now? After years of secrets and distance and *betrayal.*

Rae pressed her lips together and squeezed the last tears from her eyes. Whatever her father's plan, whatever the cost, she'd make sure Gastel returned to King Mesmal safely. She had to make this right, now more than ever. She needed to atone for the sins she'd spent half her life committing.

Rae gathered herself and splashed cool water on her face at the kitchen basin, pausing long enough to think through what she could do while she waited. She retrieved a knife hidden behind a loose panel of a cupboard, then collected a set of kunai tucked away under a false bottom in a drawer before pulling her scouting jerkin from its peg.

Gastel pushed himself off the bench and approached the ironwood bars of his cell before he could see who was approaching. It was one torch, one set of footsteps. Usually there were two guards that accompanied visitors. This person had been to see him before.

Somin came into view, a torch in hand and a lump of green fabric slung over his arm.

"You need to leave."

The distress in Somin's eyes was concerning. It was confirmation of what Gastel already assumed would be his fate.

"Just one little problem." Gastel wrapped his fingers around the bars on either side of his face. "Unless you're an Eishtala Master."

"Never mind that. You need to take off your mother's soul stone."

Gastel's eyes went wide. Few people knew about the soul stone. His father, his brothers, *and Raemian.* It meant that she'd told Somin. For the first time since he'd met her, a hard wedge of suspicion split his confidence in two. *What reason would she have to tell Somin?* And why did Somin stare at him with an undercurrent of uncertainty and fear? It wasn't fear for Gastel's well-being. It was fear of Gastel.

Somin hung the torch on the wall and produced a tiny wooden box from the folds of his robes. "Put it in this. Quickly." He held the box up to Gastel with trembling fingers.

Gastel could only glare at the box. He'd never taken his mother's soul stone off. Never. It was the only thing he had of her. He wasn't sure how taking it off now would help him get out of this cell. Instead, he took a step back from Somin, the man's face contorting in urgent frustration.

"Please, Gastel. The soul stone has locked your Anam away. If we don't get you out of this cell and away from Tremire—"

Somin didn't need to finish. He didn't need to look over his shoulder to the entrance of the dungeon, either, but it drove the point home.

A heaviness grew in Gastel's core, coating the inside of his mouth with sandy dread. He stood a little straighter. He knew what Somin was going to say. He'd felt the same when the queen had held her kukri to his neck. A certainty that death stalked him, greedy, ready to drag his soul to the depths of the Great Sheol.

With reluctance, Gastel reached into his shirt and clutched the warm pendant. He hesitated, smoothing his thumb over the polished surface before he finally drew it over his head and extended it out to the box, breath held, heart racing. Surely it was someone else's hand hovering there.

He glanced from the stone to Somin, noting the worry in the Shay's eyes. It was real and solid, a blade at the man's throat. Gastel prayed to the Elder Gods that Raemian had good reason for telling her father about the stone and that Somin knew what he was doing. That this wasn't some elaborate plot to steal Gastel's most precious possession for some nefarious intention.

With a heaviness he didn't fully anticipate, he let the stone slip from his hand and fall into the box with a thunk, the chain dangling from his finger for a second longer. Somin pulled the box away, and as the chain slipped off, the world around Gastel ignited.

TWENTY-FOUR

The Power of Change

Brilliant white flames erupted from Gastel's feet, danced up his legs, and engulfed him. He was brought to one knee, his hands sliding down the bars as he grasped them for assistance. It didn't hurt—there was no pain at all—but the magic, Gods, the power that flowed so casually, so freely around his being, was rich and brilliant and terrible all at once. More than he could comprehend. More than he could ever hope to control. It was ocean waves battering him relentlessly, mercilessly. Tearing down barriers. Ripping away walls. Exposing him with a rawness—a bitter, glorious burning.

"Gastel?"

He looked up at Somin through the inferno around him and saw the man's expression go from concern to terror.

"Gods." Somin backed away from the cell and pressed himself against the wall as if trying to sink into the wood and disappear.

"What's happening to me?" Gastel's voice sounded distant to his own ears. It carried a fullness, a terrifying viscosity that a voice should never have. He closed his eyes and focused for a moment, trying to quiet the roaring of the flames that lapped up around him. He searched for something. An answer? A source?

Something.

Anything.

Shuffling through the doors in his consciousness, he rummaged, desperate. As he moved around his mind, he felt the familiar tug of his soul, the same as when he heated his soulflame, and latched on to it. He had always known it—had always been able to call to it—but now it was a force that took shape and solidified, incessantly shifting. Like a waning campfire that had sparked and grown to engulf the entire Forest of Tremire, it grew until it was an entirely separate being existing within him, patient and helpful, powerful and fierce.

The flames rippled and charred the ironwood black where his hands clutched the bars. His soul nagged on the edges of his mind, waiting, but not so patiently now. Whispering and begging.

It wanted out.

He focused on the ironwood bars, on the walls of the cell, the tree all around him. He took a long, slow breath through his teeth while he let the soul solidify within him, building to a crescendo that pressed at the cliffs of his mind.

When he could hold it no longer, he set it free.

The bars exploded into powdery shards. They sprayed in every direction. White flames rained sparks against the walls, leaving black scorches everywhere they touched. The burning splinters showered down around Somin but left him unharmed, albeit, cowering against the wall, arms wrapped over his head.

Gastel took only four steps out of the cell when the same exhaustion that had consumed him in the Middlelend Forest grabbed hold and sent him to the ground. He held himself on all fours, unable to move, his cropped hair falling into his eyes. His fingers splayed out against the blackened wood, surrounded by white flames. He held himself there for a moment before rocking back onto his knees.

Somin cautiously approached, extending the small wooden box to him at arm's length. "Put it back on." He stooped down a little closer. "You can't control this power."

Gastel could feel the stone's closeness, the soul of his mother rubbing roughly against his own. It created a strange dissonance that grated against his consciousness. He took the box, gazing down at the pendant. It was beautiful. So many times, he'd wondered what his mother looked like, but he could see her now, living in his mind. The semiprecious stone shimmered and danced with its own light. Swirls of purple and red twisted together and moved below the polished surface. Waiting. Needing. The last of his mother's soul remained, always watching over him. He hadn't realized it had also been protecting him, shielding him from his own Anam.

He took the chain in his hand, and the white soulfire died away where it touched his flesh, leaving only his stony-gray complexion. He pulled the chain over his head. The fire extinguished as he tucked the pendant back under his shirt, locking his hungry soul away. He looked to Somin, certain he was unable to hide the weariness that seeped into every corner and crevice of his being.

"Gods, what power." Somin took a timid step toward Gastel and reached out a hand to help him up.

Gastel took it gratefully, grave fatigue leaching into his muscles. With effort, he stood and steadied himself.

"I'm shocked the guards didn't hear that display. We need to leave now."

"How? I can't exactly blend in."

Somin held the green fabric out to Gastel. He was one step ahead. "The Eishtala Masters wear these. You'll have to hunch over to hide your height, but no one should pay you any mind."

Gastel slipped it on, pulling the hood over his head to hide his hair. He followed Somin into the dark passage and shivered as he drew the last of his strength from the depths of his exhaustion. Thank the Gods, this was flight, not fight. He had no weapon. He had only Somin, a cloak, and the will to survive long enough to get out of Tremire.

"How exactly do we plan on getting past the guards?" Gastel whispered. "They allowed one in; they'll only allow one out."

Somin pointed to an alcove up ahead of the door that led out of the dungeon, and Gastel didn't need additional instruction. He pressed himself into the shadows, the green cloak concealing him, and held his breath. The guards' exasperated voices grew louder before they rushed in, their plate armor clanging as they hurried past. Once they sounded far enough down the hall, Gastel ducked out the door and found Somin waiting on the dirt path just outside.

As Somin had promised, they were able to pass without trouble to the smaller, less traveled walks. They followed the trail to a section of the city that seemed woefully trapped in twilight, the canopy of the trees too dense for light to filter through. Strange lanterns threw shards of gilded light across the grassless earth. The carefully manicured paths led to small stoops that nestled below round-top archways.

Somin led him to a door decorated with a bird in flight and pulled Gastel into a lavish sitting area. Gastel ripped his hood back as the door closed behind them and met Somin's eyes with an intensity that he'd not entirely intended.

"I need to see if I can get to Rae. We need to get you out of the city."

The mention of Raemian caused a tightness in Gastel's chest. He hadn't seen her since the queen had cut his hair. Her anguished blue eyes had haunted him. He knew she had likely spent every moment regretting their hasty flight through the Middlelend Forest. He hated knowing he was responsible, that she'd wear the blame for his mistake, his selfishness.

"Stay here," Somin reiterated. "The last place they'll look is here."

Gastel caught Somin's arm as he turned to leave. "Wouldn't they look here first? You were the last person to visit me."

Somin shook his head. "I told them your cell was empty. I doubt they'll suspect me until after they've searched Rae's residence, which I hope they aren't already doing because once she hears about this, she's going to…"

He turned to leave, then glanced back, meeting Gastel's glare with a conviction that Gastel recognized right away—the same conviction he had seen in Raemian's eyes when he'd come to take her from the tower. A desperate certainty.

"Stay here, please. I cannot say this enough. Just stay here. If I don't come for you, wait. I will eventually. If anyone should come to this door, there's a secret hiding place behind the dressing mirror in my bedchamber. The latch to open it is concealed above the golden leaves at the top." He placed a firm hand on Gastel's shoulder. The fear was gone from his eyes, replaced with a gentleness that Gastel had seen so many times in his own father's eyes. "I will come for you. I promise on my life."

The door closed behind Somin, leaving Gastel standing in the middle of the room, unsure of what to do with himself. He looked down at his hands, the hands that had burned with white flames only moments ago. Everything had happened so quickly. He pressed a hand to his mother's soul stone. So many secrets. So many things he hadn't known—about himself, about her, about this terrible war raging between the elven races.

It'd be best if he found the hiding place Somin spoke of. The last thing he wanted was to be found. The remains of how he'd escaped would raise questions he wasn't prepared to answer. He drifted through the dwelling, running fingers over the tops of the sofas arranged in a seating area several times the size of his cell. He let his eyes trace over the curves of the walls, which had been manipulated into swirling patterns meandering like waves, and forced his attention toward a doorway that led into a bedchamber. His attention fell to the mirror, but as he approached it, he froze.

Looking back at him was a stranger.

He reached up and touched the tips of his sheared hair, rough and chaotic around his face. The skin across his cheeks was tight and pale. His eyes were sunken. The amber of his irises, dulled to a muddy brown. He looked as weary as he felt and placed a fist against the glass, squeezing his eyes closed.

So much anger there that he wasn't familiar with or adept at handling. Anger toward Gemma for her hatred and wretched treatment of her own stepdaughter. Anger toward his father for not telling him more about his mother, about his life. Anger toward himself for getting into this situation in the first place. Red-hot rage simmered within him like a thunderstorm, threatening to explode with lightning and hail and winds that tore trees from the earth by their roots. He shouldn't be the angry one. He was Gastel.

Calm. Confident. Steady.

He looked again at the lost eyes staring back at him. He was changed, but he was still Gastel. He took a deep breath, filling his lungs, evening out his tight lips, relaxing his furrowed brow. He let the breath out slow and deliberate with a hiss. It fogged the glass, obstructing his view until it melted away.

Calm. Confident. Steady. But selfish and stupid and…

He took another breath and held it, his mind burrowing deeper into the reflection staring back. He held it until his chest hurt—until he couldn't hold it anymore—then held it a little longer before he finally let it explode past his lips.

Calm. Confident. Steady.

He reached up and felt along the top of the intricate, gilded frame until his fingers found the tiniest latch tucked under a swathe of leaves. He pulled it free, and the mirror swung out to reveal a space large enough for three grown elves to stand. That it had come to this caused him to clench and unclench his jaw. He'd gone from hiding at the castle stronghold his entire life to hiding from a depraved queen in a secret hole in the wall of an ancient tree.

Calm. Confident. Steady.

He promised himself, after this day, he'd never hide again.

TWENTY-FIVE

Escape

R ae stood in her doorway, boring holes into the backs of the guards' heads as they left. They'd ransacked her residence, overturned furniture, pulled open cupboards, and thrown most of her linens and clothing all over the floor of her bedchamber. No space large enough for an elf had been left untouched.

There were no longer guards standing watch at her door, and for the first time since she'd been taken from the Middlelend Forest, she didn't feel claustrophobic. She almost joined the chaotic search for the missing Bleck Larin prince, but she knew who had helped him escape. Hopefully, her father would have information for her soon.

The guards had no sooner stepped foot onto the main street when Somin snuck around the side of her tree, his expression wistful.

"Don't worry; he's safe."

Rae pulled him in and slammed her door, suddenly very aware that if one of the guards spotted him sneaking into her residence, they'd swarm the place.

"What in the Gods' names! They said his cell was completely destroyed!"

Rae must have given her father a severe look because he put a firm hand on her shoulder and shook her a little to bring her back to him.

"He's fine!" Somin collected himself with a few deep breaths, as though he'd been running. Her father never ran. "He's at my residence. They won't find him." He tenderly tucked a lock of Rae's hair behind her ear. "Now, the hard part. We have to get him out of Tremire."

"I'll take him," Rae said almost before he'd managed to finish his sentence.

Somin shook his head. She knew what he was going to say. He was going to tell her the queen would be watching her, waiting for her to do exactly this.

She gave him a stern look. "Yes, I will. I created this mess; I need to fix it."

He cradled her cheek in his hand. "Rae, I can't let you. If Gemma catches you, she'll have you executed. There will be nothing I can do to stop her."

Rae pulled away from his hand with a force that matched her mood. This was no time for sentimentality. A prince's life hung from a golden thread woven around the queen's finger. It was only a matter of time before she twisted just so and the thread snapped.

"Let her put me to death. That's better than continuing to kill my own people."

Somin squeezed his eyes closed, pain washing over his face.

"Father." She took his hand in her own and squeezed. "I know you feel guilty for not always putting me first. For being unable to protect me. But we can't change the past." She closed her eyes to center herself.

"What we can change is the future. I need to do this. I need to make sure Gastel leaves Tremire alive." Any hint of apprehension was gone. She was convicted. "I must make sure King Mesmal knows there's still hope for peace somewhere in this world. Maybe not today, but someday. That there are elves that can see past Bleck Larin and Shay. I must do this! Even if it's the last thing I do."

Her father was quiet for a long time, his eyes searching hers. He pulled back, the turning of his mind's gears clear on his face. He was always good for a plan, always thinking a few steps ahead. It was something she liked to think she'd inherited from him—that keen Starling sense for detail and strategy.

"I'll send Dulanii to get you. He'll know the meeting place. If the queen detains you, I promise, on my life, I'll get Gastel out of Tremire unharmed. If you must do this, then let me help you."

"Father, if you help me and she finds out"

He shook his head with a sweet smile and took her into his arms. She couldn't remember the last time he'd hugged her this way, but she'd missed it. She eased into his loving arms like an elfling, tiny and helpless. He was her father, now and always.

"As you said, we can't change the past. I've gone far too long without protecting you. Far, far too long." His hand warmed the crown of her head as he held her against him. "Now there's a chance to make at least some things right. I can't wash away the hatred and sorrow. But to be the father I should've been for you all this time?" He took her by the shoulders, forcing her to look into his eyes, which were filled with adoration. "I'm going to do this, and if she puts me to death, I go willingly, knowing it was for you and for your mother."

He fled before Rae could thank him for understanding or tell him she forgave him for everything or that she'd never blamed him in the first place. Now she'd have to wait, which seemed so much more difficult.

After a lengthy discussion, Belkin managed to get his father to concede that it didn't make sense for the King of the Bleck Larin to stride into the City of Tremire, unarmed, unguarded, and demand the return of his youngest son. Only a dead man wished to ride directly into the home of his mortal enemy.

Once that was resolved, the bigger problem was...who would? With only four guards, Tildimin, and himself, Belkin wasn't confident that any of them were safe in their current situation. He couldn't leave his father so poorly protected. As confident as he was in himself, if he went, he couldn't expect to make it any farther than his father would before being detained or killed. It made the message they'd received late in the day by hawk all the more troubling. Gemma had declined the offer of peace and had resolved to execute Gastel in five days.

This wasn't acceptable, for innumerable reasons. The largest of which was that Gastel didn't deserve to die. Not for this. Not for anything. He was a harmless boy. He didn't deserve to bear the weight of his father's poor decisions.

Mesmal was beside himself, pacing back and forth within a small stable they'd found on the outskirts of the highlands. They decided against a fire, instead standing in the murky twilight that sifted through the seams between derelict boards. They were just shy of the Forest of Tremire, the line of ancient trees only a few yards away. They'd been careful not to attract any unwanted attention, covering themselves with heavy riding cloaks once they'd ridden out onto the highlands.

Their caution hadn't been needed, however. It seemed the queen had pulled back all her forces. As a defensive strategy, this didn't make sense. If you held the youngest son of your greatest enemy and had threatened to execute him, you'd have scouts, heavy patrol, something. The fact that they'd seen no one was perplexing.

Belkin's patience ran dry as his father crossed in front of him for the hundredth time, incessantly rubbing his hands together, his head bowed.

"Father, please sit down."

But his father continued pacing without acknowledging him. Belkin rubbed his forehead. If they waited for night, at least they'd have the advantage of darkness to help conceal them.

"Perhaps I could negotiate a trade," his father said after an unbearably long bout of silence. "I'm sure she'd rather make an example of me."

Belkin shook his head. He'd only ever known his father to be this way one other time, when Niminea had left before her death. His father had fretted over the woman until he'd mourned. Something Belkin didn't want him to endure again.

"I'll not trade a king for a stupid, spoiled prince."

"Perhaps it isn't your decision—not your trade."

Belkin glared at his father. This was no time for self-sacrifice; this was time for planning.

"I'll get him out. I just wish I didn't have to worry about you sitting here with only five guards. I'd be immensely more comfortable if Roulin were here. I can't take you with me. I can't leave you here." Belkin took his turn pacing.

This wouldn't do. He had to make a choice. Leave his father much less defended than he would care to or risk the time it would take to return him to the Bleck Larin territory. He'd lose two days if he did the latter. Two days was two days the queen could decide to change her mind, move the execution up, decide she'd rather negotiate, send her troops across the highlands. Send her troops directly to Parth.

"I wait for darkness, then I'll go. Reconnaissance only. If I can find the dungeon and I can get him out, I will; if not, we'll at least have more information than we have now," Belkin said, his words rushing from him.

His father nodded. He didn't look entirely pleased, but at least they had a plan.

Belkin liked having a plan.

Farewell

Rae nibbled on some berries and cheese, unable to eat much more. Her stomach was in a million tiny knots, waiting for word from Freck. She'd wiped down the workbench no less than three times, had folded and put away all the linens the guards had strewn about, and had cleaned the floors on her hands and knees. All was quiet outside. The streets of Tremire were empty save for a couple of elves who all seemed to be in a hurry.

A light knock at her door brought her out of her seat. She threw the door open to Freck's stern face and stood aside for him to enter. He gave her a hug, squeezing her extra tight, before holding her out by her shoulders.

"Your father will meet us in an hour on the north side of the road to Dormshire. I know the place." He started to look around. "Do you have your sword?"

She shook her head. "It was never returned to me after Gemma's guards took it. I'm sure it's been placed in the royal armory."

Freck frowned. "If I can find a way, I'll get it to you."

"You speak as though I'm leaving tonight."

"I think Somin intends to beg Gastel to take you with him." A warm hand found her cheek. "He's worried the queen will take her anger out on you when she learns he's escaped Tremire. Even now, she's drawn her guards back." He leaned so he could peek out one of the windows. "They searched every dwelling in Tremire, and now they're loitering outside her residence. Just a hundred or better all standing there, like Gastel is going to attack her or something." He raised an eyebrow. "He didn't seem very intimidating when I met him." His eyes slipped over her face as if making a point to commit it to memory. "I may not have time to give you another hug later, so..."

He took her in his arms and pressed his forehead to hers, eyes slipping closed. Rae allowed herself to exist in the moment, ignoring the nagging urgency. She'd only left Tremire without Freck once before, and that hadn't exactly gone well.

"We should go. We don't want them waiting on us," he said.

They crept around the back of Rae's tree and out into the forest. Freck led her through the darkness without a torch, using only tiny bits of starlight to guide them. It took a solid twenty minutes to find the spot Freck was looking for, and then they waited.

They sat in complete silence, the darkness smothering the normal passage of time. After what seemed like hours, Rae stood, unable to calm her nerves any longer. She folded and unfolded her hands, wishing she had a sword to rest a hand on. She was more nervous than the first time she'd plunged into battle, or the morning of her first day of training. It wasn't like her father to be late.

"I'm sure they're almost here, Rae." Freck's soft whisper burrowed into her skin like maggots. She paced, scanning in the direction of Tremire for signs of movement.

Another few moments passed, and the sensation they were being watched—the creeping tickle of eyes moving across her flesh—replaced her mounting anxiety. She paused her pacing and listened.

"What's wrong?" Freck hadn't moved from where he reclined on a smooth flat rock, his back against a tree. "Hear something?"

She shrugged, not wanting to speak aloud. The feeling grew stronger, raising the hairs on the back of her neck.

Rae felt the cool edge of a blade against her jaw before she saw it. She followed the sword with her peripheral vision. It was a dark-fleshed hand holding the blade. No Shay could blend so perfectly into the shadows.

"You're more trouble than you're worth," a familiar voice hissed. Belkin struck his soultorch and held it so he could see Rae clearly, then looked past her to Freck. "Stand slowly, Shay."

Freck did as he was told, his hands out at his sides to show he wasn't a threat. "She's not your enemy."

"She's more my enemy than you realize." Belkin stepped closer, giving Rae a perfect view of his bitter scowl. So much anger toward her, toward Shay. "Where is my brother?"

"Rae's father is bringing him here, but they're late," Freck said.

Belkin turned toward him with daggers in his glare. "Did I ask you?"

Freck cowered against the tree, unsure of how to handle Belkin's sharp personality. In reality, neither did Rae. She swallowed as he pressed the blade more firmly against her neck. Any harder, and it could break skin—a familiar situation with Belkin.

"My stepmother has been cruel to him. I tried to help, only to be detained as well." Rae closed her eyes, willing Belkin to understand.

This was the last thing she'd wanted. "Gemma's anger with your father runs deep."

He shifted his weight, the blade biting in a little harder, but she could only see him out of the corner of her eye.

"If he dies, his blood is on your hands."

She swallowed hard. The full weight of his words washed over her. She took a deep breath, letting silence fill the space around them for a moment more.

"I accept whatever punishment you deem appropriate for the wrongs I've committed against you and your people, Prince Belkin."

She had promised she wouldn't fight back. After all the evil she'd carried out toward Bleck Larin, all the hatred she'd helped to spread at the queen's behest, she deserved death at the hands of the king's most decorated soldier. Warm fingers snaked around her upper arm as Belkin drew her closer, his blade trembling against her skin as he shook with rage.

Freck took a step forward. "Highness, please. Rae does not deserve to die for this. She was forced to—"

Belkin scoffed, interrupting Freck, "Your friend has too many muscles and not enough brains."

Rae squeezed her eyes closed, her mouth dry. What more was there to say? Other than that she understood there was no difference between Bleck Larin and Shay. Gastel had said it best—they all bled red. Beneath skin of gray or pink or white, they all lived and died and loved and lost. No elf deserved death more than another.

Belkin stepped closer, his breastplate digging into her back, close enough that she could feel his breath on her neck. He leaned so his lips were inches from her ear. "Give me one good reason I should spare your life."

"Because I'll kill you if you don't." Gastel's cool voice cut through the darkness before he stepped into the clearing, striking his own soultorch and instantly heating it to brilliant white. He pulled the hood from his head as Somin stepped into the light behind him. Gastel had dark circles under his eyes, a gauntness to his cheeks. He wore an Eishtala cloak over sagging shoulders.

Belkin glared at his brother and shook his head. "Gods, your hair."

Gastel shrugged, that coy smile Rae found so endearing crossing his face. "It's growing on me." He took a few steps closer, and Belkin pulled Rae in tighter, causing her to take a sharp breath.

Gastel held out his hand. "Belkin, she's not our enemy, but there's an entire city of Shay that would gladly fight you if that's your wish." Gastel let his hand drop to his side. "We need to go."

Belkin held firm. From this angle, Rae couldn't see his face. She could only imagine the wild look in his eyes. One she'd seen before when their swords had crossed.

"Please, Belkin," Somin said.

Belkin shifted so he could see the older elf, his grip loosening. Something passed between her father and the eldest prince. It was an impossibly long moment of wordless communication that flowed between them. Then he pushed her away, hard, pulling his sword from her throat.

Gastel caught her as she lost her footing and held her against him for a moment. She reluctantly pulled away, and their eyes locked. Warm butterflies filled every part of her, but this was no time for silly thoughts. She stood straight, mustering as much confidence as she could, and faced Belkin.

"You need to get your brother out of here." She was proud of her calm words after yet again coming so close to death at Belkin's hands.

Somin stepped toward Belkin, not fearing how the eldest Bleck Larin prince still held his saber at the ready.

"Please, take Rae with you. The queen will execute her for helping your brother escape. And first, she'll torture as much information from her as possible." They all looked to Somin, his eyes brimming with terror and sorrow. "Please, Belkin. For me. *For her mother.*"

The pause that followed was excruciating. Belkin looked off into the shadows, a scowl marring his otherwise flawless features as he considered.

"I'll take her as far as the Middlelend Forest," he said, sliding his saber back into its scabbard. "Then she's on her own." Belkin turned and let his soultorch extinguish, disappearing like a wraith into the night.

Somin didn't move for a few seconds, then pulled Rae to him, holding her eyes with his. "Go to Dormshire. Follow the stream that runs through the city. On the far north side, on the very edge, there's a dwelling made of blue stone. Look for the starling. It was our home before the war when we were a new family."

He hugged her the way Freck usually did, with abandon and rib-crushing strength.

"I love you." He kissed her forehead, then pushed her toward Gastel. "Go, before Belkin changes his mind."

Freck's eyes found Gastel's in the dim light. The two men exchanged a wordless understanding. Gastel nodded before glancing back at Rae, his face washed of emotion. How could he be so calm?

Rae's vision blurred. She'd left home so many times on so many different missions, but this felt different. It was possible she'd never return. She found Freck's anguished face as he mouthed the words *'I love you.'*

She was led away, Gastel's arm wrapped reassuringly around her shoulder. She was only half aware of her steps through the dark forest after Gastel extinguished his soultorch. She heard his voice, but the words didn't register. Her heart broke into a thousand pieces of love and friendship; it might never be whole again. She was leaving her family quite possibly forever.

TWENTY-SEVEN

The Old Road

Gastel's father was already saddled, the accompanying guards waiting with their horses. Belkin stood rigid, a perfect, stone statue, his legs spread shoulder-width apart. He held his horse's reins and the reins of another. Gastel's throat tightened. His family had planned on bringing only one additional elf back to Parth. Of course. Why wouldn't they have?

He took the reins and pulled himself up, then reached a hand down for Raemian. After helping her in front of him, he wrapped an arm around her waist to keep her from falling. Warmth wicked up through him from her closeness, but he smothered it. This wasn't the time nor the place.

Without words or light, they kicked off and let the horses set the pace across the moonlit highlands. It would be a few hours of riding to the Middlelend Forest, and even then, they wouldn't be back in Bleck Larin territory.

It was going to be a long night.

An hour or so onto the expanse of featureless landscape, Gastel noticed Raemian swayed with the motion of the horse as she dozed. He pulled her to his chest, tucking her head against his collarbone. She relaxed against him, smelling like lavender and forest dew. Again, that warmth tried to sneak in around the corners of his vigilance, and again, he pushed it away. He pulled the Eishtala cloak around to cover her, smiling to himself.

Gastel tracked the moon as it crossed the sky and lost himself in wandering thoughts. Raemian would go to Dormshire. There she'd be safe from Queen Gemma for a time, hiding in plain sight among her people. He looked down at the top of her head and the soft flame of red hair. Not a drop of Bleck Larin in her appearance other than perhaps that she wasn't nearly as broad-shouldered as other Shay women or as voluptuous as he'd come to learn. He reevaluated the shock he'd felt when he'd learned who her mother was. He wished he'd had more time with Somin, the only elf willing to answer his burning questions about his own mother.

Her name sounded like a lullaby. Niminea. Thank the Gods his mother still protected him when his father couldn't even tell him her name, couldn't tell him the truth about why the war had started. He was thirty-two and had no knowledge of the Culling, the wrongs Mesmal had committed against Gemma, nor the strength of the Anam within himself.

Just thinking about the power he possessed gave him goosebumps. He had yet to decide if he was going to share this information with his father and brothers. A part of him didn't want them to know he'd been carrying such magic within himself—Anam powerful enough to decimate cell doors enchanted by Eishtala with little more than a whisper of a thought. He shuddered at the memory, and Raemian stirred against him.

He took a sharp breath. He hadn't meant to wake her, but now he was painfully aware of how she snuggled against him, warm and soft. He'd witnessed firsthand the skill with which she could wield a blade, yet she was so timid and gentle and…

No, not those thoughts. They were feelings he couldn't have. Not without the pain that would follow when she left.

A dark silhouette cut across the horizon, looming like doughy storm clouds. The Middlelend Forest swelled in front of them as Belkin turned to the northwest. They were headed toward the Old Road, one of the last remnants of peaceful times, connecting the Shaylands and Bleck Larin territory. It would be easier traveling for the horses than the dense forest, lending hope they'd reach Parth by late morning if all went well.

Part of Gastel was happy to be going home, away from the suspicious eyes of the Shay that watched him with naked hatred. The way they'd stared at him as he was marched through Tremire was seared into his memory.

Yet there was another part of him that dreaded returning. To go back to the castle stronghold meant he might never leave it again. At least not while his father could control his whereabouts. He would have to say goodbye to Raemian, and he wasn't sure he'd be able to watch her leave without following.

As if she sensed he was thinking of her, she looked up at him, eyes sparkling with the last of the moonlight, sleep heavy on her lashes. She leaned up to his ear. Errant threads of longing rippled through him at her closeness. He clenched his teeth. This wasn't the place.

"How long have I slept?"

He looked toward the black treeline, trying to gauge the distance. "A few hours. The Middlelend Forest is just ahead."

She looked out at the looming forest, sharp against the sky, then leaned back against him, filling his stomach with that same yearning. He would have liked to keep her this way forever, but soon enough, he would need to climb down from this horse.

And this wasn't the place.

They broke the forest line and slowed to a trot. The Old Road was in an abhorrent state of disrepair. As an elfling, Gastel had heard tales of how it had once gleamed with perfectly laid stones, quarried and placed thousands of years ago. Now it was strewn with broken pavers and overgrown with vegetation. Certainly easier than traversing through the rough of the woods, but much slower than the open highlands.

They pressed on at a reasonable pace. Raemian took to surveilling the treeline. All Gastel saw was the black of night, foreboding and mysterious, slender trees closing in around them like dark fingers on throats. It made his skin crawl. If she was concerned enough to look, there was a good reason.

Belkin lit his soultorch to provide a modicum of light as the moon set below the trees. It was enough for Gastel's horse to follow without trouble, but not enough for him to see much more than dark silhouettes.

For several leagues, they traveled in silence, trying to listen past the sound of the horses' hooves, backs straight in their saddles, eyes trained on the gloom of the unknown. An eerie feeling, like being watched, smothered any conversation they may have had.

Belkin extinguished his torch and held up a hand, stopping them. They waited, the silence deafening. Not even the sound of insects could be heard. Only the rhythm of Gastel's breath echoed in his ears.

It happened all at once, a rush of white hair, the shine of blades, the whoosh of an arrow passing entirely too close for comfort. Gastel threw himself and Raemian from their horse, gathering her under him and pressing them flat against the overgrown grass.

Stunned stupid, he was unable to wrap his mind around what was happening. Raemian pushed herself up and looked back at him, her face obscured by darkness. He reluctantly let her go as she pulled a dagger from her waist. She plunged into the fray like a wild flame, turning and twisting and finding her path as though it had existed for as long as the Old Road itself.

As she melted into the shadows, it occurred to Gastel that it'd be hard for the Bleck Larin soldiers to tell the difference between her and the enemy. He pulled himself off the ground and frantically checked the saddlebags of his horse for a weapon, but there was nothing. No sword, no knife. Nothing. He was as good as useless. He scanned the horses to see if he could find his father and found him motionless, prone along the west treeline.

His heart plummeted into his stomach. If his father had been killed!

He rushed blindly, recklessly, without thinking of the arrows peppering them from the trees on the east side. Sliding in alongside his father, he found him dazed but unharmed, probably having been knocked from his horse by Belkin. Knowing full well he was no warrior, Mesmal may have chosen to remain where he fell. To play dead was safer.

"Are you hurt?"

His father shook his head and reached under his riding cloak, pulling a long dagger and handing it to Gastel. "You can make better use of this than I can."

Gastel took the blade without hesitation and nodded before throwing himself into the fight, not thinking about what his father's words could have possibly meant, pushing away the thought that he might regret leaving his father unguarded.

There were at least eight enemy Shay with another concealed in the treeline. The archer had managed to incapacitate one of their soldiers badly enough that he was no longer moving. A horse rolled wildly, screams of pure agony bellowing from the beast. This was a type of chaos Gastel had never experienced.

Despite the dim conditions, he didn't dare strike his soultorch. It wasn't worth the risk of being an instant target. Keeping the archer in mind, he used the horses to shield himself as he moved closer to Belkin's position. He hadn't found Raemian, but it would have been hard to see much more than a flash of pale, pink flesh. He turned in time to throw his dagger up and deflect what would have been a killing blow to his neck. In a split second, he was given a choice.

Fight or flight.

He kneed the Shay hard in the gut, sending the man back with a grunt. The Shay approached again with more caution, stepping from side to side. Gastel moved in and out of the man's strikes, ducking and sidestepping out of harm's reach. The Shay's sword was significantly longer than his dagger, making it hard for him to get in close enough to strike. He could better arm himself if he could disarm the Shay.

The man wore an unsettling grin as he kept Gastel occupied. After what seemed like an eternity of defensive maneuvering, Gastel got his opening. He lunged, stabbing through the man's forearm and forcing the Shay to drop his sword into Gastel's waiting hand.

His senses sharpened in an instant as the world slowed. Within the span of a second, he went from defensive to deadly.

He instinctively found the gap in the armor at the Shay's armpit, plunging his newfound blade into the man's chest. Gastel twisted the blade, making a wretched, wet, grinding sound against the metal breast-plate. It crunched through ribs, muscle, and organs, causing blood to gush from the Shay's gaping mouth. Gastel spun to the side, throwing the Shay off the sword, the blade snagging on bone on the way out.

Gods, what had he done?

He'd taken a life.

Whatever had reached in and possessed Gastel was cold and terrible. His breath caught, but he couldn't dwell on it. Not with death all around him. He'd chosen fight, not flight.

He searched the fray and found Raemian pinned against a tree. A guttural roar of pure frustration erupted from the Shay holding her arm against the rough bark. By the grace of the Gods alone, she managed to maintain her grip on her dagger. The man chopped away huge chunks of the tree as she shifted just enough to avoid each blow.

Gastel scrambled toward her in a mad dash to help. Before he made it, she managed to wriggle her wrist loose. Without hesitation, she thrust her dagger up through her assailant's throat, spraying blood down the front of her.

For the first time in his life, Gastel understood what Belkin and Roulin had meant when they described battle lust. Rae's eyes were hollow, full lips pinched into a thin line as she took the man's sword from his hand and pushed him aside. The Shay clawed at his throat, desperate to remove the knife, buried to the cross guard. Her dilated pupils fell to Gastel before looking past him. She darted toward three Shay exchanging swings with the Bleck Larin soldiers that had been behind them.

Gastel looked up in time to see Belkin bury his saber deep in a Shay woman's abdomen, flecks of starlight glinting off her wide eyes. Wrenching his sword free, Belkin sprinted back, leaving Tildimin to finish off another Shay woman and passing Gastel as he headed for the remaining three Shay. Gastel considered trying to find the archer until he remembered Raemian. Belkin was headed in her direction. Just what he needed—a convenient excuse. Gastel followed his brother, finding it easy enough to relieve one of the Bleck Larin soldiers of a feisty, duel-wielding Shay.

Beside him, Belkin swung and split skull, spraying blood and brain, then speared his saber through the chest of another. Gastel swallowed back bile at the sound of the Shay's insides spattering across stone.

He'd never seen this side of Belkin, had only heard of it, had honestly feared it as an elfling. The Vengeful Prince Belkin. Warlord of the Bleck Larin. Future King. Gastel had sparred and beaten him countless times, but the brutal warrior standing beside him now—the conscienceless killer—was terrifying and entirely too real.

Gastel continued trading blows with the duel-wielding Shay woman. He was hesitant after his first kill. He fought defensively, easily drawing away her blows but taking no risks of his own. The tip of a blade pierced through the woman's leather armor at sternum level, startling Gastel enough to step back. She moaned in pain, eyes wide, gurgling as she tried to breathe and failed. Belkin drew his blade from her back and turned as Raemian stood over the last of the Shay, dying at her feet.

She met Belkin's war-crazed glare, and just when Gastel was certain Belkin would charge her—would finish what he'd started in their father's study—he turned to Gastel, eyes glittering with death and starlight.

"This is *war*, Brother. Welcome to the battlefield."

He wore a wicked grin, gore caking the front of his armor and splattered up his neck and face. Wiping his saber with a gloved hand, Belkin slid the blade back into its scabbard. The final scrape of metal across metal sent a shiver of understanding across Gastel's consciousness. This was war, and it was so much more terrible than he'd ever imagined.

The familiar twang of an arrow being loosed caused them to turn to the treeline, but it was too late. The arrow sank deep into flesh.

Homecoming

Gastel would never forget the sound—a wet thunk, a stifled yelp—as Raemian took an arrow for his brother. She swayed, forcing herself to stand against the pain as she stared into Belkin's confused scowl. Some unspoken exchange passed between the warriors before she lost her balance.

"Raemian!" Gastel rushed to steady her.

She seemed strangely calm as she looked up to meet his gaze with distant eyes. "I'll be fine." She swallowed hard, eyes rolling. "Never forget the archer."

She sank to her knees as Belkin stood over them for another moment, scanning the treeline before taking off toward the last Shay. He drew the fire of another arrow and ducked into the forest to avoid any more.

Paralyzed with uncertainty, Gastel hesitated, unable to collect himself long enough to figure out what he should do. His father found them in the darkness and shooed Gastel to the side to help Raemian down to the ground.

"Do you need something to bite?"

"Just get it out of me."

She sucked air across her clenched teeth when Mesmal grasped the shaft protruding from above her shoulder blade.

A soul-splitting cry sliced the night open as Mesmal yanked the arrow from Rae's shoulder, sending a wave of nausea through Gastel. Mesmal tore a strip of fabric from his cloak and pressed it against the wound.

"She'll be fine." Mesmal squeezed his youngest son's shoulder. "She knew what she was doing." He looked toward the treeline where a woman screamed in agony before glancing back. "Let's get her up on your horse. The sooner you get her to Parth, the better."

Every muscle in her slight frame tensed as Gastel gathered her to him. She seemed so small in his arms. A war-hardened soldier a moment ago, now a wisp of an elf as Gastel carried her to his horse. He handed her to his father and swung himself into the saddle before hoisting her in front of him as he'd done before. She moaned in pain, and he fumbled as he tried to grasp the reins. Even with half her faculties, she still knew what to do and leaned hard into him, using his chest to apply pressure to her shoulder.

"I'm sorry," she whispered.

"You shouldn't be apologizing for saving Belkin's life," Mesmal said as he placed his hand on hers where it rested on Gastel's thigh. "Ride ahead and get her to the stronghold. It's only a little farther to the border."

Gastel glanced over at Belkin as he crossed to check on one of the Bleck Larin soldiers who lie motionless along the side of the road. In the light of Belkin's soulflame, Gastel saw something he hadn't expected. Concern? Confusion? The thoughts painted across Belkin's face creased his brow with uncertainty.

"Go. Now."

His father wouldn't need to tell him again.

He rode as fast as his horse could manage on the broken road without using his soultorch. It helped that the sky warmed with the promise of dawn. Every few minutes, he checked to make sure Raemian was conscious, and each time, she'd squeeze his leg where her hand rested. He wanted to check her bleeding, but he didn't dare remove the pressure his chest applied. After a while, his shirt was soaked through, sticky against his skin, the smell of blood burning into his memory.

"Gods, Raemian! Why did you do this?" He hadn't meant to ask the question aloud.

"Because I will live from this, but Belkin could have died." She seemed so matter-of-fact. There was no tremble to her tone, no hesitation. "I saw the archer. I knew I couldn't stop her in time," she said, taking a deep breath and letting it out slow. "I'm sorry."

"Don't apologize." He rested his cheek on the top of her head. "Unless you die. Then I'm going to need an apology."

She chuckled, then tensed, struggling to breathe. After an agonizing moment, she took a deep breath before resting her head back against him.

"And apparently don't laugh."

Ahead, the trees thinned, and Gastel was hopeful they were almost out of the forest and on to the moors. The rising sun threw shards of magentas and oranges across the leaves, making them look more like giant glass sculptures than living things. The oversaturated colors were welcome after a night of riding through the darkness.

As they crossed onto the moors, Gastel urged the horse to a reckless pace. If Raemian noticed, she didn't seem to care. Other than squeezing his leg in response to his welfare checks, she didn't move.

After another hour of hard riding, Parth came into view, the castle stronghold perched above the city like an eerie gargoyle. A whisper of mist gathered at its shoulders and smoothed the cold stone edges, softening the structure, reminding him of the stained-glass window high in the tower. The colors, the way the spires seemed flat against the horizon—Gastel wished he could have spent a few moments admiring from this vantage.

"Just a little farther, Raemian," he whispered more to himself than to her. "Just a little farther."

The halls of the castle stronghold had never seemed so long. As Gastel ran to the infirmary with Raemian's limp form in his arms, he noted how he would have placed it closer to the main entrance. He looked down at her pale face. Her breathing was shallow, eyes rolling with pain. His father had said she'd live, but seeing her now, he wasn't so sure.

If she died...

She had better not die.

He pushed the double doors of the infirmary open with a muddy boot and yelled for assistance. One of the healers came sprinting from a back room.

"She's been shot in the shoulder with an arrow."

He helped the healer pull her jerkin away before laying her prone on a linen-covered table. He dared not look away as the healer cut open her blood-soaked shirt, exposing her slender back. The healer cleaned away the blood with gentle hands, drawing a wince from Raemian.

"She's lucky. This should heal nicely. I'll need to stitch her. She's lost a fair amount of blood, but the arrow missed anything vital." The healer's slender fingers prodded and massaged around the injury, but Raemian remained still. "No punctured lung, only a broken shoulder blade."

The healer gave Gastel a warm nod, then turned and disappeared into the back room.

When he glanced back down at Raemian, she had opened her eyes and was looking up at him with a blank expression, her lips parted. He stepped toward her but stopped, too nervous to come much closer. There was nothing more he could do. He felt so helpless.

He swallowed hard, following the contours of her bloody, exposed flesh with his eyes. Rich, red shaymarks wrapped up from her abdomen and on to her back in a beautiful lacy pattern that disappeared below the waist of her pants. They matched the shaymarks on her face, neck, and arms, the same delicate swirls that danced along her temples. He had a strong urge to trace the shapes.

Her curious gaze moved across his face, falling to his blood-soaked shirt. He was a mess. The fighting plus the ride had left him filthy and frayed.

The vision of the Shay he'd killed flashed before his eyes. The blood, the gore. The empty eyes drained of life. If he could take it back, he would, but he couldn't.

Death was permanent.

The fact that he'd been able to kill instinctually was terrifying. He looked at his hands, clenching his jaw. He'd seen it in Raemian's eyes on the Old Road—kill or be killed. The way Belkin's face had contorted with monstrous rage. To simply defend oneself wasn't enough, and he'd taken that which could not be returned.

Such sorrow filled Raemian's eyes. *Did she know what he was thinking?* She cleared her throat to speak, but the healer stepped back in, hands laden with bandages, poultices, and a needle and thread. She set her supplies beside Raemian and waved for Gastel to join her.

"I need your help, Highness. Can you keep the wound clean of blood as I close it up?"

He nodded but wondered if she actually required his help or if she could tell he needed to do something other than stand and watch helplessly.

It was clear she'd done her fair share of stitching wounds. Once she had Raemian sutured, she applied a poultice to stem further bleeding and protect against infection before pressing a bandage in place. After drinking a warm cup of steeped herbs to help with pain, Raemian slipped to sleep.

"She should rest here for a while, and you should get cleaned up, Highness." The healer's eyes sparkled with knowing. "I won't harm her. It's been a long while since I've tended to a Shay, but I hold no ill will."

Gastel nervously clasped and unclasped his hands, not sure he entirely trusted anyone. The healer laid a gentle hand on his forearm.

"No harm shall come to her, not while she's in my care. I promise. Go clean yourself up and rest, Prince Gastel. She's safe."

He backed away toward the door, glancing between Raemian's sleeping face and the healer's soft, knowing smile.

"I'll hold you to your word." He turned to leave but spun back. "And thank you. I won't forget this."

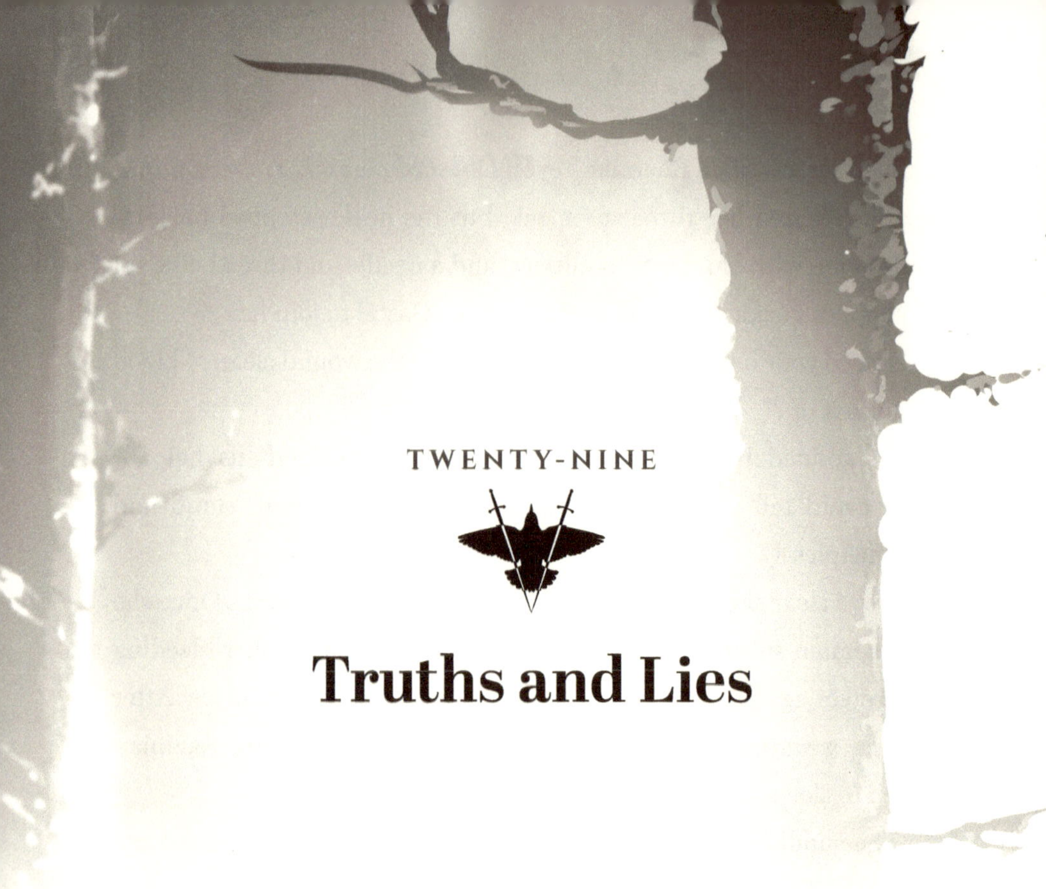

TWENTY-NINE

Truths and Lies

Gastel eased into a steaming tub. Hot water had never felt so good. It had been too long since he'd relaxed in a bath and let the steam curl around him. He thought of nothing in particular, at least until the memory of Raemian's knowing eyes from the infirmary flashed through his mind. It all came flooding back. The hollow stare of death, the musty stink of viscera, his brother's rage-torn expression. Raemian's blood on his shirt. He sank below the water, trying to wash the images away.

Roulin was right. Gastel *was* too soft. While he had the skills to fight, he didn't possess the grit to kill. He couldn't see past the finality of it. He ran his fingers through his hair and tried to soak in the comfort of the water, staring up at the ceiling, letting his extremities float to the surface.

What he'd give to go back in time—not before Raemian, but before leaving in Belkin's place and seeing how angry and vile Queen Gemma truly was. Before seeing the hate in the eyes of the Shay as he was ushered through the City of Tremire. Before knowing what it felt like to take a life.

He poured water over his face and squeezed his eyes closed, but he couldn't rid himself of the memory of empty, lifeless eyes. Then, as if his mind needed more torture, those empty eyes became hers. Her beautiful, pink Shay skin stained dark red. Her full lips parted in a final breath.

He pulled himself from the water. No matter how wonderful it felt, he couldn't enjoy it. He toweled himself dry and threw on clean pants and a crisp shirt before storming from his bedchamber.

He stood in his library—walls built of shelves, littered with books and artifacts he'd been gifted as an elfling. For a moment, they felt more like the trunks of trees along the Old Road. His wet hair dripped down his neck and wicked into his shirt, like Raemian's blood had. In his personal quarters, there was only the smell of paper and leather rather than the stench of battle.

This wasn't the Old Road.

He rubbed his eyes hard with the heels of his hands. She was safe, recovering in the infirmary. He had nothing to worry about. Why did his stomach feel sick? He shook his wet hair out and left it messy and chaotic as he fled his personal quarters. His father and brother should be home, and he knew there'd be much to discuss, no matter how he wished to avoid it. There were questions he'd have to answer. But questions he'd ask as well.

Did his father know he possessed such strong Anam magic hiding under his mother's soul stone? Why had his father kept so much information about his mother from him? Why had he never been given any of the history of this war between Shay and Bleck Larin?

How could his father have lied by omission for years?

For his entire life.

Gastel sprinted through the stronghold, a few startled servants scurrying out of his way. He found his father in his study, weariness marking the lines of his face. It was to be expected after riding through the night and day, trying to bring his heedless, youngest son home. Yet Mesmal smiled warmly and motioned for Gastel to sit.

He didn't sit. Instead, he stood behind the chair he usually occupied, his hands grasping the seat back so tight the leather swallowed his fingertips.

"I hear Raemian is doing well." Mesmal's smile seemed genuine yet restrained.

"She's resting in the infirmary," Gastel said.

Mesmal's eyes wandered over Gastel's hair before looking away, the shame of a disappointed father tightening his lips. He focused on the roaring fire for a moment before returning his attention to Gastel. Propping his elbows on the arms of his chair, he folded his hands together in front of his lips.

"This was stupid. And selfish. But I would have done the same." His father's golden eyes bore into Gastel with scrutiny. "There are things I'm sure you've learned that I had not wanted you to know. Not until I knew how best to explain them." He took a deep breath, his expression melting into his mask of stoicism. "You possess a power you don't know how to control, and enough anger with me for hiding information from you to make it more dangerous than it ever should be."

Of course his father knew. *Of course!* Somin had known; how could his own father not? His mother had been a grea t Anam Wielder, so it made sense he would possess some measure of the same power. Why wait and withhold the knowledge he clearly needed to control his Anam? A simmering rage exploded in Gastel's chest.

"Did you think you could keep me in Parth my entire life?"

That was the only reason Gastel had not managed to learn the truth about his mother or Gemma—or about everything. Clearly his brothers had been sworn to secrecy, his tutors in his youth, everyone in his life. The more he thought about it, the angrier he became. All of this could have been circumvented had he known the truth.

"Did you think I'd never learn?"

"Gastel, I—"

"How can I trust any of you anymore?" Gastel's voice cracked with the anger consuming him.

"I'm sorry, my son. I should have told you." His father's expression remained calm, which only fed Gastel's fury.

"Yes, you should have!"

"Part of me thought I could protect you, that I could think of a way to set things right with Gemma and bring peace to our people before I'd needed to."

"Niminea was my mother. How many times did I ask about her? You always shooed me away."

Gastel squeezed his eyes closed and hung his head before meeting his father's gaze again, his vision fading to a thin line of precariously controlled outrage.

"I'm not an elfling anymore. I didn't even know about the Culling—the real reason we're at war. How is that protecting me?"

He glared at his father, waiting for a response, unsure of what else to say when it'd be better to show him.

He pulled the soul stone from his neck and held it over a side table.

"No." Mesmal stood to stop him. "Your mother said you must never take it off."

"*So you knew!* All this time? You knew what power I possessed? You had me tested by wielders knowing I had only to remove my mother's soul stone, and you let me flounder and fail?"

Searing fury boiled within him, burning through him, breaking him down and reshaping him. In all his life, he'd never been so enraged. This anger wasn't him. It was Roulin and Belkin, not him. Yet it was there. It was horrible and beautiful all at once.

"You've always known," Gastel said with soft words honed by the bitter taste of betrayal. "Does Belkin know? Roulin? Have they known this whole time as well? How can I *ever* trust you again?"

Gastel shook his head in disbelief. They had all lied to him. He dropped the stone. Before the sound of it hitting the table could reach his ears, his flesh ignited in brilliant white flames.

The same surge of unholy energy crawled across his skin, coursing, living within and through him. His soul pressed forward on the edges of his mind, waiting to fulfill his every request.

"How many of you knew?" His voice carried that same faraway quality it had in the dungeon of Tremire. He could see his own reflection in his father's wide eyes. Perhaps he hadn't known how much Anam Gastel truly possessed?

Gastel closed his eyes and tried to extinguish the flames that dripped from his flesh. He pulled it into himself as he did with his soulflame, but he couldn't pull hard enough, and when he opened his eyes again, he was still engulfed in flames—beautiful, terrible, glorious flames.

He closed his hand around the soul stone and felt its coursing, suppressive quality reach up through his arm, its tendrils of strange magic smothering his soulfire. Like before, the fire extinguished as he dropped the soul stone back over his head, leaving nothing but the last wisps of white light drifting lazily to the ceiling. This time, he hadn't blown away an Eishtala cell door, and he felt refreshed rather than exhausted as if the power had restored him.

"Gods, Gastel." It was Roulin's voice from behind him.

Gastel turned his head enough to see both his brothers from the corner of his eye. It was obvious they'd not known either, which gave him at least some comfort. Still not enough to trust them.

"All of you should be ashamed of yourselves." He took a turn glaring at each of them. "Niminea was my mother!" His voice raised with raw accusation. "I didn't even know her name until Somin Starling told me. *A stranger.*" He clenched his fists, anger rippling down his arms. "What a way to find out, while I await death in a dungeon."

He turned to leave, but Mesmal caught his arm.

"If I had known—"

"But you did know, Father." He shook his head and forced a fake smile. "I'm just as stupid and selfish as you, but you knew exactly who and what I am. The least you could have done was give me the same advantage."

He reached up and grasped Niminea's pendant, holding it for a moment before he tucked it into his shirt and left. His father didn't stop him this time, and he didn't look at his brothers as he passed, but he felt their fearful eyes follow him.

Now they knew what he was capable of. What they would choose to do with this new information was up to them.

THIRTY

Rest and Revenge

Days were a blur. Rae slept most of them. She was given herbs to help with pain and sleep, but at the cost of her mental fortitude. This wasn't the first time she'd been bedridden. She'd endured a high fever as an elfling, spending the better part of a week unconscious, the time she'd spent awake imprinted on her memory with razor-sharp clarity.

This wasn't like that at all.

This was a strange waking dream. She would slowly rouse with a swimming head and doughy memories of how she'd gotten there. Strange flashes of blood and Belkin's confused frown. Gastel's concerned expression as he'd watched the healer dress her wound. Mesmal's calm voice cutting through the rough corners of the visions. She didn't like the way she couldn't remember. She *always* remembered.

More than once, she woke with Gastel at her bedside, but when she asked how long he'd been there, he'd smile and avoid answering. He'd take her hand and run his fingers over her knuckles, sending shivers up her arm.

The first time she woke to see him—truly see him—since Gemma had cut his hair, it was hard for her not to notice how different he looked. She'd grown accustomed to the Bleck Larin hairstyle, always pulled back tightly against their heads. It made their longer ears more noticeable, their thin faces more angular. Gastel's hair was unruly and soft and approachable. It was long enough in front that it fell around his temples, framing his face in a way that made his amber eyes brighter, more expressive. She'd always thought him beautiful, like his father, but now? It was dangerous, the attention he could command in her.

Rae's strength was slow to return. At least, it was slower than she would have liked. After what seemed like ages, she was finally able to move around without needing to immediately lie back down. She sat alone in a strange new room, reclined in an overstuffed, leather chair. This wasn't the tower. She'd been made comfortable in one of the guest suites reserved for dignitaries, lavishly appointed with velvet in moody shades of crimson and violet—heavy furniture, leather manuscripts filling bookcases to bursting, a generous seating area framed with a soft wool rug that felt amazing on her bare feet.

She leafed through *A History of Dormshire*, preparing herself for the inevitable journey to her new home. Or was it her old home? Perhaps she'd find some lost part of her mother there, or some long-forgotten piece of herself.

She resolved to lay down her sword unless, by the grace of the Gods, she found work as a bodyguard or mercenary. She was no longer a soldier—not in her heart. Not now that she knew she'd be killing her own kind.

She was elven. Not Shay, not Bleck Larin.

Elven.

A knock at her door broke the silence. Belkin let himself in before she could respond, any emotion hidden under a cold, indifferent mask. He closed the door before crossing to her with unwavering confidence—his usual dangerous posture.

"I came to see how you were healing."

Rae wasn't sure if her shock reached her eyes or not. This hardened war general, who could show nothing but hatred toward her, who had held a sword to her throat with death in his eyes, asked her how she was healing? She swallowed hard, unsure of how to respond.

"This doesn't change anything. You're still a Shay. But I would be remiss if I didn't at least acknowledge your help in the Middlelend Forest."

So he refused to thank her for saving his life. She smirked. That seemed appropriate. Much more in character for him. She'd taken the lives of Shay on the Old Road. Her allegiance in that moment had fallen to the Bleck Larin King, to Gastel and Belkin. A couple of weeks ago, she wouldn't have thought that possible or right. Shay and Bleck Larin. Pink and gray.

She was still learning to find the lines or, more importantly, to see where there were no lines at all. So many things had changed—things that she couldn't unsee and unlearn. Truths that had been kept from her, histories she'd not known.

"A Shay that can kill her own kind." A stony resolve washed over Belkin. "To protect the Bleck Larin King—"

"To protect *my* king." The words had been forming in her mouth the whole time. "Your father is *my king.*"

Belkin tried to smother some shadow of anger that pulled his eyebrows together.

"You knew of my parents, did you not? Before this war?" Rae asked.

Now it was Belkin's turn to be unable to answer. He couldn't hold her eyes and instead glanced over at the window where ribbons of late afternoon light sliced in from between heavy drapes. When he looked back, she saw it—a change in the way his eyes saw her, his anger receding, replaced with confusion and uncertainty. He was conflicted, just as she was, unsettled by the unknown and newly learned. Perhaps he hadn't realized how little she'd known about her mother?

"I did." His glare firmly fixed on her again.

"Then you knew my mother was Bleck Larin."

He glanced down at his feet. Was he nervous? Very unlike him. He was unwavering to a fault.

"*Because I did not.*" She said these last four words slowly, enunciating each with a tight diction she hoped would resonate.

Even though she willed them, *begged* them not to, her eyes filled with tears. Not in front of Belkin. She didn't want to show weakness, not now, and most certainly never to him.

"If I'd known what the queen was ordering me to do." She cursed the ripple of emotion in her voice.

This time, when his gaze found her, it was filled with utter shock. She realized it was possible he hadn't known she'd been unaware of her mother's heritage. So much of his hatred could very well have been from thinking she had chosen to forsake the Bleck Larin half of herself.

"I'll never fault you for hating me, Belkin. Truth be told, I hate myself for what I've done." A single tear burned down her cheek before she managed to bring her emotions in check.

He clenched his jaw. Perhaps he was trying to find words but couldn't. He'd seen so much more than her. He was over two hundred and fifty years her senior. So much history. A lifetime of memories from a world when Bleck Larin, Shay, and Trove elves lived in peace among one another—loved one another. He'd seen Rhend in harmony. He'd also seen the evil one queen was capable of—the damage that hatred and scorn could cause. One powerful person misplacing her own pain had produced so much suffering.

A gentle grin smoothed the edges of Belkin's expression. It was so like Gastel and Mesmal in its authenticity.

"Somehow, Somin managed to raise you well."

Rae pressed her lips together before looking away, unexpected warmth swelling in her stomach.

"Don't hate yourself for something you didn't know. I won't hate you for something you were ordered to do," he said.

From the corner of her eye, she saw his smile widen as he turned and left.

Gastel rubbed his forehead before running his fingers through his hair. Only criminals had their hair cut, and he felt the weight of every furrowed brow, every shocked, round set of eyes looking in his direction.

His father determined the best punishment for squandering what could have been the only possibility for peace with Gemma was for Gastel to attend all formal royal functions, including daily citizen hearings. He sat at his father's right from midmorning until afternoon, listening to people drone on about their problems. Any problem, large or small, could be presented to the king, and Gastel wasn't sure how this had ever been considered wise.

His father expected him to listen, consider, and judge. There were several times when Gastel was asked to make the final decisions for various court formalities, punishments for crimes, or resolutions to disputes. Where once he'd been his father's sounding board, he now felt he played the part of King himself, and he was thankful the weight of that crown would never grace his head.

It took tremendous effort not to tell an old man who had come to spew complaints about his neighbor's attempts to seduce his bondmate that he had no bearing to complain about his current lot in life. All he could think was how Raemian would be so much better than him at pulling out the details of this man's monotonous tale of woes.

Thankfully, Mesmal took his turn and told the old man to try working it out with his neighbor. It didn't seem to sit well, but it was obvious the old man would get no more sympathy today. As a guard ushered the old man out, there was a commotion at the back of the throne room. Two guards flanking a Shay man moved in. They set him on his knees before pulling his head back by his short hair to face the king.

Gastel was out of his seat immediately. This Shay was familiar. He knew those eyes, cropped white hair, the cut of the man's broad shoulders—Raemian's friend who had helped him escape.

"Dulanii?"

Gastel had only spoken with him briefly at Somin's residence before meeting again on the outskirts of the City of Tremire, but he could never forget the man's face and what he'd done to help. He had a wild look in his eyes that superseded the fact that dark purple bruises stained his face, the blood from a broken nose smeared across his cheek. What could he have possibly said to convince the Bleck Larin not to kill him on sight?

"She executed him." Dulanii choked on his words and turned to Gastel's father with tears welling in his stormy eyes. "She executed Somin the day after Gastel escaped."

King Mesmal stood and stepped down from the dais so he could help Dulanii off his knees. It was hard not to notice that Dulanii wore nothing but loose, soft leather pants, boots, and a leather harness that held an empty quiver. His bright shaymarks were prominently displayed down his muscular torso, with darkening shadows left by his being manhandled by the guards.

"You're Raemian's friend?" His father searched Dulanii's face.

He nodded and looked to Gastel. "Is she here? Rae?" He turned back to Mesmal with pain in his eyes. "Forgive me, Your Majesty." He bowed before speaking again. "I mean no disrespect. The queen executed Somin Starling, Rae's father."

Mesmal took a sharp breath and closed his eyes to control his anger. When he opened his eyes again, his face was washed of all emotion. A talent Gastel wasn't sure he could ever master.

"Raemian has not yet left for Dormshire. She's recovering."

"Recovering?" The sadness in Dulanii's eyes shifted to concern.

"She was injured in the Middlelend Forest, but she's fine. Healing well." Mesmal's voice remained calm as he spoke. "For what reason was Somin executed?"

Dulanii shook his head slowly, his eyes falling to the stone tile. "When the soldiers failed to find Gastel, they came for Rae in the night." He met the king's eyes again, but this time they were rimmed with tears. "When they couldn't find her either, the queen called for Somin. I don't know what he told her, but he was executed at dawn the next day. The queen insisted she do it herself."

Gastel's throat tightened as he reached for his neck. He'd felt the cold steel of Gemma's kukri at his own throat.

Dulanii pulled a small box from a pouch at his waist and handed it to Mesmal. "She'll know what this is. It was left for her." Then he pulled his scabbard free and handed the sword to Gastel. "And her sword. I promised her I'd get it to her if I could." He squeezed his eyes closed, holding back tears, and bowed his head again.

"She's the last of the House of Starling."

Gastel couldn't help but glance over his shoulder at Dulanii as he led him to Raemian's rooms. It reminded him so strongly of when he had led Raemian to the tower. But this Shay was nothing like her. He was bubbly and loud and expressive. He wore his emotions openly. Despite being nearly in tears as he'd told of Somin's execution, Dulanii carried a sense of elfling-like wonder as they walked through the castle stronghold.

"This place is huge! How do you find your way?"

Gastel stole another glance. "You get used to it."

Dulanii glanced around and back to Gastel before stopping him with a hand to his chest. Dulanii bit his lower lip and smiled—a strange expression that caused Gastel to quirk his head to the side in silent questioning.

"I understand what Rae sees. You Bleck Larin are handsome once you're out of your armor."

Gastel couldn't help but return Dulanii's smile with a raised eyebrow. Such a strange elf. He wasn't much shorter than Gastel, but he was so much bigger, with wide shoulders and massive, chiseled muscles. Gastel could see how his brothers would be leery of Shay in battle if they were all built like Dulanii. They looked formidable, to say the least.

When they reached Raemian's room, Gastel knocked before holding the door for Dulanii to enter first. He gave the Shay a nod in the direction of the open door, then waited for a moment in the hall as he heard Raemian's excited cry.

"Freck! Gods, what are you doing here? Your face. You've been hurt! Are you okay?"

Gastel came in quietly behind, a silent observer.

"I couldn't let you have all of the adventures without me."

"No hard squeezes," she said as Dulanii gathered her into his arms.

Dulanii took a deep breath and put his chin on top of her head, eyes gazing over at the window of the guest suite.

Gastel held back and leaned against the farthest wall. He'd tried to paste on an amused grin, but part of him was embarrassed to witness their intimate exchange. A flip of jealousy ran through him. He'd come to care for Raemian in a way that was confusing and made his chest tight with longing when she looked in his direction. To see how close these two were, it seemed obvious they had a comfortable relationship.

Dulanii set her down gently before taking her shoulders with his hands, causing her to wince.

"I've hurt you."

She smiled sweetly. "I blocked an arrow. Just a broken shoulder blade is all. Too much adventure."

He joined her smile, running his hand through his snowy-white hair, cut short enough that it stood on end. "You've lived through worse." He glanced over at Gastel, and his eyes went wide. "Gods, Gastel, I'm sorry." He stepped away from Raemian, but Gastel wasn't sure what he apologized for. "Rae is like my big sister."

Raemian looked from Dulanii to him with a timid, knowing smile. When he met her eyes, she faltered, her cheeks reddening.

"Freck, what are you doing here?"

Dulanii brushed away all his concerns and focused on the box, handing it to Raemian, his eyes growing dewy once again.

She glared at him and shook her head. It was clear to Gastel that she knew what it was before she opened it. Her dainty fingers wrapped around a beautiful silver segmented band decorated with scrolling vines and stars adorned with tiny gemstones—an ornate starling with its wings spread in flight in the center segment.

She met Dulanii's eyes again, begging him, wishing him to tell her she was wrong.

"But this is... Is he...?" Her voice quivered.

"She executed him the morning after you left."

A single sob erupted from her, rife with pain. Gastel took several steps forward, but Dulanii was there, wrapping his arm around her good shoulder and tucking her into him. She appeared so tiny against the Shay's massive chest.

"I'm so sorry, Rae. If I'd known she would do this, I'd have...I don't know what I could have done, but I would have done something."

She pulled away from him and met his eyes, her face wet with tears. "You can't go back there. She'll kill you, too. She knows we're close." She placed a hand on Dulanii's bare chest. "You can't, Freck. I can't lose you, too."

Gastel slipped out of the room, his anger simmering. He refused to let Raemian see him in rage. Gemma would pay for all the wrongs she'd committed, but especially for what she'd done to Raemian Starling.

After the waves of anger washed away, he was left with a wretched feeling of jealousy, and he didn't like it. Gastel had no reason to be jealous of Dulanii. He and Raemian had known each other for a few weeks at most. Dulanii, on the other hand, had been her friend for years. Not to mention the obvious: She was Shay. Dulanii was Shay. He was Bleck Larin.

He bit his lip hard and leaned against the wall. He had such a need to protect her, to be near her. He held the memory in his mind of crossing the highlands and her warm back against his chest. The way she had allowed herself to nestle into him, trusting him. The first moment he'd seen her in his father's throne room, she'd looked past his brothers to him, watching *him*, seeing *him* with eyes that missed nothing.

His memories returned to the cell in Tremire. He'd had nothing but time to think while in his cell—all his mistakes, his trivial and selfish needs. That's all this was now, wasn't it? A selfish need?

He had too many thoughts grappling for attention and tearing down his carefully constructed confidence. Pushing off the wall, he jogged down the hall toward the stronghold's entrance, unsure where he was going—somewhere to let out this anger and jealousy.

He took a sharp turn out into the gated gardens, narrowly missing a servant pruning one of the topiaries. He shoved the gate to the main gardens open wide, letting it smack back against the fence in his mad rush through the tall hedges.

And he ran square into Roulin.

THIRTY-ONE

Taking the Bait

Gastel was moving too quickly to stop from being thrown to the ground after plowing into Roulin. With rage building in his chest, Gastel glared up at his brother. He was met with the same viscous anger. Unadulterated hatred simmered behind Roulin's sarcastic sneer.

"Well, if it isn't my idiot, selfish, ass-of-an-elfling brother." Roulin let the last few words hiss past his teeth.

He didn't reach down to help Gastel; instead, he crossed his arms, leaning heavily on one leg. An air of superiority dripped from every pore, only fueling the fire building to an uncomfortable inferno in the pit of Gastel's core.

He embraced the adrenaline coursing through his veins and kicked up from the ground, landing a few feet from Roulin. Their height difference was more noticeable at this distance, but Gastel refused to be intimidated.

"Running away again?" Roulin mocked. "Whatever will Father do without his precious elfling?" He bated Gastel. The real question was whether Gastel would allow himself to be lured. "Or are you waiting for your little Shay whore to heal first?"

Gastel's sword was drawn faster than Roulin could properly prepare. Their blades came together hard—messy and passionate—laced with rage.

"Come now, little brother. You'd defend the honor of a soulless fuck toy?"

Their swords slid apart, and Roulin was immediately pressed into the defensive. Gastel threw his full strength into every strike, driving the sinister smile on his brother's face into a frown of concentration. This wasn't another friendly duel between brothers. Gastel was livid. He let every ounce of his fury guide his sword and stain his vision red.

With proficiency beyond what normal training provided, he flicked the sword from Roulin's hand, sending the blade clattering across the stone path. Roulin stood perfectly still, hands spread wide on either side, the edge of Gastel's blade millimeters from his throat.

"Well, well, well, I didn't realize we had a traitor in the family."

Gastel grabbed the front of his brother's vest and yanked Roulin to his face, the blade kissing flesh. They were nose to nose. Gastel could smell Roulin's hot breath, which stank of yesterday's wine. He cleared his throat to speak, but there were no words. Only searing wrath that burned away his conscience.

"Gastel!"

Belkin's stern voice ripped Gastel from his provoked stupor. He released Roulin and took a step back, but that spiteful smile was still there. With terrifying speed, even to himself, his fist found Roulin's face. Roulin stumbled and landed hard on his backside. Gastel looked down at his brother, the tables solidly turned. Roulin glared up at him, a laceration low on his cheek starting to bleed. Sneering, Roulin spit blood into the grass at Gastel's feet.

"You're just like them. A fucking sack of lowborn shit."

Gastel sheathed his sword, trying to let the madness dissipate. Gods, this wasn't who he was. He didn't take the bait this time.

"I'd rather be like them than you."

He turned, leaving Roulin lying on his back, and sprinted away, jumping over low hedges in his hurry to be rid of the exchange. When he slid into the training arena, he heard the crunch of boots behind him.

"This anger isn't you." Belkin clutched his shoulder to stop him.

Gastel shook his head, glancing at the moors on the horizon. Every part of him trembled with rage. A rush of disgust heated his cheeks. Was he any better than Roulin? This screaming adrenaline felt the same now as it had on the Old Road. This was as terrible and real as the moment he'd taken his first life.

He glared at his shaking hands, fingers spread wide—capable of killing.

"We may not be close, Brother, but whatever this is you're going through."

The look of compassion in Belkin's eyes was real and rare. Perhaps his eldest brother was capable of some level of understanding after all?

Even with this new Belkin standing before him, Gastel was frozen, rendered speechless. The only words he wished to use were the ones on the end of his sword. He squeezed his eyes closed and pressed hard against the bridge of his nose, trying to rid his mind of the image of Roulin's sneering smile.

"Roulin is," Belkin sighed. "Dare I say, a lost cause."

Shocked, Gastel met Belkin's pointed glare.

"Love is rare for royalty." Belkin looked down at his feet and took a deep breath, perhaps struggling to put his own thoughts into words. "I've never felt it. If you care for her, tell her."

Gastel only shook his head. There was no reason to; no good would come of it. Roulin's reaction had been evidence enough.

No, he'd let her go to Dormshire. He'd keep his memories sacred and be satisfied with what he had. The echoes of her smile, her curious blue eyes, the adorable way she blushed when he was near.

"It's not that easy," Gastel said.

"So you do love her." It wasn't a question.

Gastel shook his head again. He didn't know. He wasn't sure he knew what love felt like. It was a word that held little meaning to one who had never experienced it. He couldn't imagine not having her with him, but he knew she couldn't stay. This world they lived in wouldn't allow it. Yet the joy he felt when she was near was immense and pure and wonderful and terrifying and...

"It doesn't matter."

Belkin turned him by the shoulder and glared at him, his simmering frustration returning—the usual Belkin demeanor.

"It matters enough for you to recklessly protect her without thought of your own wellbeing. To do stupid things that only men with lovesick hearts do." He squeezed Gastel's shoulder. "I'm sorry for judging her so harshly."

He met Belkin's eyes, not entirely understanding. He knew Belkin hated her and would kill her if given the chance again. *Wouldn't he?*

"Forgiveness for the things she's done will be hard but not impossible. If Father can see past them." Belkin shrugged, a sheepish arch to his eyebrow.

Gastel glanced back toward the castle stronghold, taking several deep breaths, his eldest brother's hand still on his shoulder.

"You should tell her how you feel. Give her the opportunity to at least know when so much of her life, like yours, has been secrets." Belkin pushed him away and started walking to the castle, turning to walk backward, a teasing smile across his face. "Before she leaves for Dormshire with her muscled, brainless friend."

Rae folded and unfolded her hands, wondering where Gastel had gone. He had left while Freck fought through tears to tell her about her father's execution. After the news had settled and the reality that she was an orphan had solidified around her, she just needed *him*. Even if only his curious gaze from across the room.

Freck had curled up beside her and fallen asleep, exhausted from his journey across the highlands and the Middlelend Forest, his soft snores reminding her of what he'd done to bring her the news. Her best friend had faced death to give her Somin's bracelet—had walked directly into the hands of Bleck Larin to deliver her sword. She was beyond grateful, but now she sat with a jumbled mess of thoughts, the quiet afternoon growing more tedious as it waned.

Careful not to wake Freck, she scooched to the side of the bed, intent on searching for Gastel. As she pushed herself to her feet, struggling a little with her limited arm mobility, he slipped in without knocking. She couldn't help but smile as he silently closed the door.

He loitered against the wall, his gaze touching Freck's sleeping form. Rae searched him for some indication of what thoughts flooded through his mind, but his Bleck Larin stoicism made him impossible to read.

"Can we step out? I don't want to wake Freck," she whispered.

Gastel motioned her ahead of him as he opened the door. They walked side by side in eerie silence as questions bloomed on her tongue, building to a crescendo she could no longer bear. She stopped and turned to face him in the middle of the hall. Her eyes searched his—there was so much she needed to tell him. So many things that had been battling for attention in her mind since they'd left for Tremire. Things she wasn't sure of and things she most certainly was.

Not so long ago, she'd have drawn her sword at the sight of a Bleck Larin and killed him without question. Now? Her entire identity had changed with one misstep in the Middlelend Forest. It made her question everything she'd ever known.

She took one of his hands, an insatiable need to be near him smoldering through her. She wanted to wrap herself into him like she had when they'd ridden across the highlands. The smell of him, like the forest on a spring morning, comforting and familiar. The way his eyes looked at her now, gentle, curious, and longing.

"Gastel, I..."

She couldn't form the words. They were there, but her mouth wouldn't free them. They were sticky like honey, clinging to the sides of her tongue. She could no longer hold his eyes. Instead, she looked down at his chest, where his mother's soul stone rested.

How had things changed so quickly? She'd tried to push him away. Now she felt nothing but fear that she could lose him.

That she could never have him to lose.

Perhaps he knew what she was going to say. No man would put himself through what he had for just anyone, would they? He glanced away before pulling her into a dark room, the light from the hall just touching the floor where they stood. He drew her toward him, hands finding the small of her back. She traced the length of his arm until her fingers found his neck—his skin so much softer than she'd anticipated.

They were close enough to share breath. The need in his eyes as he stared with abandon filled her stomach with a strange mix of apprehension and tantalizing yearning. He cradled the side of her face, tracing along her jaw with his thumb as he leaned closer, eyes falling to her lips.

A throat was cleared from the hall. Rae turned, stepping away from Gastel, hands slipping from him, knowing in her heart this was forbidden.

Rae had forgotten where they were, *who* they were. She pressed her lips together as she met Belkin's glare, and all her apprehension overflowed, her cheeks burning with embarrassment.

"I've been looking for you, Gastel." A single, knowing eyebrow raised. "Father requires you for the citizen hearings. I can walk Raemian back to her suite."

Gastel looked between Belkin and Rae before he left without a word, running his hands through his hair as he walked. Rae couldn't pry her eyes from him, taking in his rigid steps, wishing she knew his thoughts at that moment more than anything. There wasn't time to consider. Belkin waited patiently, a strange smirk spreading across his face.

"I assume he finally told you how he feels." Belkin stepped to the side to let Rae cross into the hall beside him.

Finally? Had it been so obvious? She swallowed hard, not sure how to respond. In the end, she chose silence.

He chuckled, a sound that was even stranger than his cordial demeanor. Rae hadn't been certain that this warlord was capable of humor.

Belkin's stride was as sure as always. She stole a glance at him and noticed the tightness of anger was gone. He looked so much more like Mesmal when his face wasn't tainted with hatred.

"Here we are, Shay Knight of the House of Starling." He bowed at the door to her suite. "Your quarters."

Without another word, he left, the same as always, with war-ready strength in every step.

THIRTY-TWO

Strategist's Mind

Belkin fetched Rae early the day before she and Freck were to leave for Dormshire. He was in a pleasant mood, which Rae was still trying to get used to. Belkin walked with purpose, Rae nearly jogging to keep up with his pace. He was a few inches taller than Gastel, and apparently, all that height was in his legs.

"She's pulled all her forces back. Our scouts haven't encountered a Shay in days."

They passed the throne room and ducked into a more intimate space. Mesmal, with his usual stoic calm, was seated beside a massive table crafted with a topographic map of Rhend. It had three-dimensional cities and forests, mountains to the east, the Wastelands to the west, dividing Rhend from the rest of the world. Even the known entrances to the Trove holds were represented with tiny carved arches made of the same granite as the stronghold.

Rae had never seen a map created with such intricacy. She let her fingers dance over the barren expanse of the highlands. The fields surrounding Dormshire were ripe for harvest. The forests were constructed out of real wood and soft, dyed wool, each distinctly different. Tremire, with tall, wide trees, was mapped out perfectly, down to the earthen paths between dwellings—the Middlelend Forest, with its shorter canopy and thinner trunks, divided by a pristine Old Road. Even the tree city of Soremire was included, nestled far to the south.

Belkin pointed to a handful of locations. "All the usual Shay patrol posts have been abandoned." He pointed to the Great Oracles at the Eastern Pass, another north of Dormshire, a third near the southern entrance to the Old Road near where they'd been attacked. She was well acquainted with the locations, having been posted at more than one.

Rae considered the way the land was organized, the highlands sweeping east, where they opened to a patchwork of fields outside Dormshire. The fertile soils were the largest reason the Shay had fought so hard to reacquire the city after the first siege. Gemma wouldn't risk losing it again, would she?

"She may be planning a full-scale attack," Belkin said, "but we can't see where Legion Bowrhem would try to cross. It'd be foolhardy to bring hundreds of troops through the Middlelend Forest, and it'd take too long to clear it. We have the Eastern Pass under heavy surveillance and plenty of time to mobilize if we saw a large-scale force."

Rae sifted through everything she knew about Gemma's forces. She moved to the west side of the map, searching for something the legion had mentioned about a canyon or a river. Something wide enough for troops to move through, but the trees of the Middlelend Forest nearly butted against the natural plateau that marked the border of Rhend. It was known as the Hill of Tombs for a reason. It'd be devastating to scale with an army; plus, the Wastelands themselves were a fortress of dark sand and monsters that made nightmares blush.

The door slammed behind her. Rae stood a little straighter under Roulin's fiery, contemptuous glare.

"What is *she* doing here?"

Belkin took a deep breath and stepped between them as Roulin approached with his hand on the pommel of his sword.

"We need answers, and she can provide them."

"And you expect her to tell the truth?"

Roulin forced a laugh as he approached the table, glaring past Belkin to Rae, his hatred distilled into the razor edge of a blade cutting through the strategy room. Where Belkin had clearly softened, Roulin's anger seemed only to have matured, expanding into a volcano on the cusp of eruption.

"What glorious insights has she provided?"

Rae ignored his air of condescension, focusing all her attention on the map.

"The secrets of Bowrhem's bedchamber, perhaps?"

"Check your tone," Belkin said, leaving no room for disagreement.

Rae traced the land with her fingers, trying to ignore the brothers' exchange. She'd only been half paying attention the last time she'd been included in the Shay army strategy planning. She vaguely remembered Bowrhem mentioning the west against the Wastelands.

"Forgive me, Highness. The information wasn't directed at me, but I believe Bowrhem mentioned a pass to the west."

She focused on an area that was tucked under the Hill of Tombs and tight against the forest line. There was a narrow canyon where an ancient river had once carved its path through the stone. Based on the scale of the map, there would be enough width for five, maybe as many as ten, grown Shay abreast.

"Do you keep any scouting parties here to the west?" She pointed to a large, flat expanse off the moors with no settlements, farms, or otherwise. A small, unnamed forest hugged the natural ridge, protecting the entrance to one of the Trove holds. It was likely avoided by Bleck Larin and a perfect staging area for an enemy army.

"Not currently." Belkin furrowed his brow as he inspected the area she indicated. "It would take them days to get an army through."

"It's already been days since Gemma drew back her troops. Over a week, actually. She was pulling soldiers back the day Gastel escaped the dungeons of Tremire."

Belkin turned to Roulin. "Send a scouting party and rally the western division. Send word to the eastern to be ready. If she's bringing the full force of her army, we'll need everyone."

Roulin rushed from the room as Belkin leaned on the table beside Rae.

"I've not purposefully intended to make you a spy in this—"

She stopped him with a gentle hand on his forearm, then jerked it away when she realized how casual the action had seemed, how natural, and how he hadn't pulled away from her touch.

"I think we both know how I feel about this war, Highness. Especially now." She covered her father's band and glanced at Mesmal. He'd been quietly observing, his calm presence a comfort. "I only wish there was some way I could stop another battle. I feel Gastel and I squandered our only chance for peaceable negotiations with Gemma."

Belkin turned toward her, his face as expressionless as his father's. "If we can find some way to solve this without bloodshed, we will, but I'll not allow Bleck Larin civilians to be hurt."

Rae looked up into his eyes—those same eyes as Gastel's. Why had she never noticed? She smiled timidly.

His expression changed, softening, smoothing. There was compassion there, and a determination that struck a chord of respect in her heart.

"Thank you, Your Highness," she said.

He placed a gentle hand on her shoulder.

"Call me Belkin."

Gastel had been avoiding everyone, especially Raemian. He tried to avoid his thoughts by filling every waking moment with training in the early mornings, citizen hearings in the afternoons, strategy meetings with his brothers. *Anything.* It helped, but once evening approached, he couldn't turn his mind away.

What did she think of him? He hadn't so much as said hello to her after Belkin had found them together. There were so many things he wanted to tell her, so many things he'd been feeling but had not quite been able to put into words.

Now he had no time left.

The night after he'd nearly kissed her, he'd laid in bed, glaring at the ceiling, feeling the shadow of her breath on his face. The smell of her lingered in his mind. His dreams had been inappropriate at best, taking all his mental fortitude to pull himself from them. Those intelligent blue eyes, the forbidden path of her lacy shaymarks, lips as soft as rose petals.

Gods, how would he drive these images from his mind?

Alone with his thoughts after yet another meal where he'd been subjected to sitting across from her as she dined beside her frustratingly perfect friend, Dulanii. How many times had she caught Gastel staring? Her lips would turn up each time, cheeks brightening. The entire emotional struggle made him feel like an elfling again. It seemed words were no longer sufficient. Not when he could wrap himself around her and keep her for himself.

He pulled his sword from its scabbard. His arms were sore from training for too long and too hard, but it was all he could think to do. If he was moving, he wouldn't be thinking. Because if he was thinking, he would inevitably return to the fact that Raemian would be leaving at dawn.

He paced, sword in hand, trying desperately to focus. Knowing Raemian's mother had been Bleck Larin had destroyed the last of his resolve. He'd managed, for the most part, to bottle up his growing feelings for fear of violating some taboo. Learning she'd been the product of love between a Bleck Larin and a Shay—a love that had been possible once and could be possible again if not for the Godsforsaken war—he couldn't push the thoughts away anymore.

A sharp knock at the door brought him from his ruminations, and he rushed to throw the door wide.

"Forgive me for disturbing you." Raemian's timid eyes met him from the other side, her gaze dropping to the sword in his hand. "I shouldn't have come. I'm sorry." She turned to leave, but he reached for her hand.

"You have nothing to apologize for." He smiled as he sheathed his sword.

What could she possibly think she'd done wrong? She searched his eyes. What was she looking for? Whatever she wanted, she had but to ask, and he would give it to her. Whatever her heart's desire, he would grant it if he could.

"I'm sorry for," Her eyes touched the tips of his hair. "Everything. I can't blame you for hating me."

"I could never hate you, Raemian." He swept a loose lock of her hair behind her ear, eyes never leaving hers.

Without warning, she melted into him, wrapping her arms around his back, her hands finding his shoulder blades and holding him tight.

Her head tucked under his chin. It felt perfect, as though she were made to fit there. He folded his arms around her as securely as he dared. There was more he wanted to say, but words slipped away. Instead, they stood in a silent embrace for several minutes. Minutes that were both blessedly long yet not nearly long enough.

When she stepped back, her face was wet with tears. He feared he'd hurt her in some way, concern flooding back in around his confidence as he searched her face. She only grinned and shook her head.

"I need to find some way to turn back thirty years of blind prejudice and stop Gemma from spreading more hate."

"We...*we* need to find some way."

The fact that she took the weight of Gemma's hatred on her shoulders was concerning. The last thing he wanted her to do was go anywhere near the depraved queen. If Gemma wished to detain her and she was recognized in Dormshire. It was a growing concern. But he couldn't rightly keep her here, where she'd always feel like a prisoner. He had to hope that between her fighting prowess and Dulanii's unfaltering friendship, she'd be safely hidden in plain sight.

"Promise me you won't sacrifice yourself to try and appease her." The words slipped out before he'd thought them through. "She'll execute you, like your father."

"You don't know that."

With paralyzing terror, Gastel realized Raemian had, in fact, been thinking of doing this exact thing.

"That's not a promise."

"I can't promise," she whispered.

He took her firmly by both shoulders and immediately regretted it as pain flashed across her face. It was easy to forget she was still recovering from an arrow wound.

"Raemian. I can't let you go if you plan to give yourself to her to stop whatever she's planning. I can't let you do that."

Sadness moved across her eyes, confirming his fears. "So many people, Gastel. It could be possible to stop so many deaths."

"But you don't know that for sure. You don't know if turning yourself in would satisfy her hatred. You can't take that chance. Please." The desperation was plain in his voice. After she left, there was nothing that would stop her from going directly to Tremire. "*Please*, Rae."

She smiled, and he realized it was the first time he'd used her shortened name. Her smile faded quickly, replaced by a sorrow so deep Gastel wanted to right all the wrongs against her, to heal her, to protect her.

"Gastel, I can't promise you that. If given the chance, I *will* try to end this war." She met his concerned glare with conviction boiling in her deep ocean eyes. "I won't make any rash decisions. This is all I can promise."

THIRTY-THREE

Dormshire

Rae would never forget the way her pink hands looked in Gastel's—a reminder of things that could not be changed easily, perhaps not in their lifetime. He held her gaze with thinly veiled anguish mapped across his usually calm face. He stared for too long with no words. It made Rae's insides twist with the same growing sadness that had plagued her since leaving Tremire.

Freck clasped Gastel's wrist and leaned in to embrace him before Rae and Freck saddled up and turned their horses toward the moors. She hoped the journey ahead would distract her from the sorrow threatening to smother her courage, but she doubted anything could pull her from the raging undertow of melancholy.

The Old Road was deemed the fastest route to the highlands, which after significant discussion was also deemed the safest. At Mesmal's behest, they were escorted on the Bleck Larin side to ensure their safety, but from there, they were two Shay traveling by horseback. If anyone noticed them, no one cared.

They rode tight against the forest line, stopping only once to sleep. The silence between herself and Freck was like a wall of granite. Usually, Rae would have made a point to break the reticence, but Freck seemed guarded and uncharacteristically withdrawn. She resolved to give him his space. He had, after all, lost his home as much as she had.

More concerning than Freck's silence was how often her thoughts turned to Gastel. His eyes had been haunted. If given a choice, he'd never have let her leave. He'd have kept her there with him. Part of that sounded immensely better than traveling away from him, but that wasn't the world they lived in.

Not yet.

They made it to the outskirts of Dormshire by late afternoon on the second day. The haphazard quilt of farmlands morphed into organized fields as they drew closer. Eventually, paths between the plots grew more intentional, some used so much the dirt had been packed into solid clay. The fields were well tended, but Rae was surprised to see there were very few Shay out working in them. In fact, she'd only seen three or four since breaking camp.

The closer they drew to Dormshire proper, the more ominous the lack of Shay became. By early evening, the main road into the city should still have been bustling with people, yet there were only a handful. The gate was sparsely guarded, and Rae didn't see any archers along the city walls.

A creeping concern nestled in her stomach as they passed through the opened portcullis and into an equally empty city. Something wasn't right. A glance at Freck confirmed that he noticed as well.

Once they found the stream Rae's father had spoken of—the only stream that cut through the heart of Dormshire proper—they followed it north as it meandered through the city. The current moseyed along, mocking the urgency Rae felt in every fiber of her being. It had been built over with culverts and careful bridgework as the city had changed over time, but still, it ambled.

They passed through what might have been a particularly seedy neighborhood but found the area derelict. The windows were shuttered tightly, doors boarded up. The last time Rae had been to Dormshire, it had been a bustling metropolis. Every district of the city boasted its own market and craftsman districts. Now it seemed whole swaths were deserted. The carcasses of abandoned buildings gaped like empty eye sockets glaring at those who dared to pass by.

They followed the stream into more affluent neighborhoods with the occasional Shay hurrying here and there. No one made eye contact as their horses plodded through the dirty streets.

The stream carved through the heart of the city's center, near what had once been a Bleck Larin stronghold. Over time, trees had been added and sculpted by Eishtala to bring the Shay aesthetic to the stone structures. Dormshire would always be a strangely eclectic place—a quasi-Shay city built on a foundation of solid Bleck Larin granite.

They continued into the northern district, where the dwellings were comprised almost entirely of stone. Family homes in varying sizes were crammed together in rows sharing walls, some butting against the outer wall of the city. Others stood alone, surrounded by gardens that were still well-tended. Wherever the Shay had gone, they'd left recently.

Freck spotted it first—a pale-blue dwelling wedged between another home and an abandoned garden. With excitement and considerable apprehension, Rae dismounted and approached.

A sense of awe filled her as she stood before the entrance, the starling emblem worn but recognizable, carved into the wooden door. This had been her family's home, her home.

She knocked, but there was no answer. Rae hadn't expected one. Trying the handle, she found it locked. Freck nudged her aside as he drew his dagger and persuaded the latch open, then stepped back for her to enter first.

Rae froze in place. The only home she recalled was the one she and her father had shared before he'd been bonded to the queen. She wasn't sure what to expect. Her mother had been dead for over thirty years. It had likely been devoid of habitation since before Rae had solid memories. She wasn't entirely surprised to find the first room empty, save for a table and chairs covered with sheets of canvas.

She shivered as she realized what this house represented. It had been home to a family torn apart by hatred and fear. A single moment in history was captured in its walls. It echoed the cries of loved ones who had lost their mothers, fathers, and elflings—a time that had shaped the world into the intolerant place it was now.

Rae ran her fingertips along the walls, touching the history, feeling the age, and smelling the sweet, stale air. Dust as thick as boot leather sealed the floors in time—stone hewn from the same granite as the castle stronghold. Rae took a sharp breath. Would she never be rid of the reminders of what she had left in Parth?

"Hello?" Freck called, but Rae knew the dwelling was empty.

Some small part of her was saddened. It was a home. It deserved a family to grace its walls, but it was good they had a place to start, a dwelling to sleep in and consider their own.

"Seems empty at least." Freck stepped around the room, then nodded in the direction of the hall that led farther in. "We should see how the rest has fared."

They moved through and found the rest of the house in the same condition. Dusty, stuffy, sparsely furnished, yet in habitable condition. After the two of them opened some windows, removed the large coverings from the furnishings, and swept up a bit, Rae found herself smiling. This was where Gale had lived before her death, with Somin and a tiny Raemian!

She and Freck stood together in the front room, hands on hips, facing their new home. Finally, the cold sorrow in Rae's heart warmed. Freck glanced over at her, and she met his smiling face.

"Home sweet home," he said.

Unable to resist Freck's infectious optimism, Rae's smile grew until her teeth showed. If there was one thing she was tremendously happy to have, it was his companionship when nothing else was quite right. He lent her a level of comfort that she wouldn't have found otherwise.

"Let's finish getting this place cleaned up, then find the market," Rae said. As much as she wanted to reminisce and think about a time when her family had been whole and happy, they had much they needed to do. "The streets are too empty. The last time I was here, this was a bustling city."

Freck nodded his agreement, and the two of them got back to work. It wasn't long before they were walking their horses up to the nearest stable and searching for the market to acquire supplies and information. They'd need both, but Rae had a foreboding feeling about the latter.

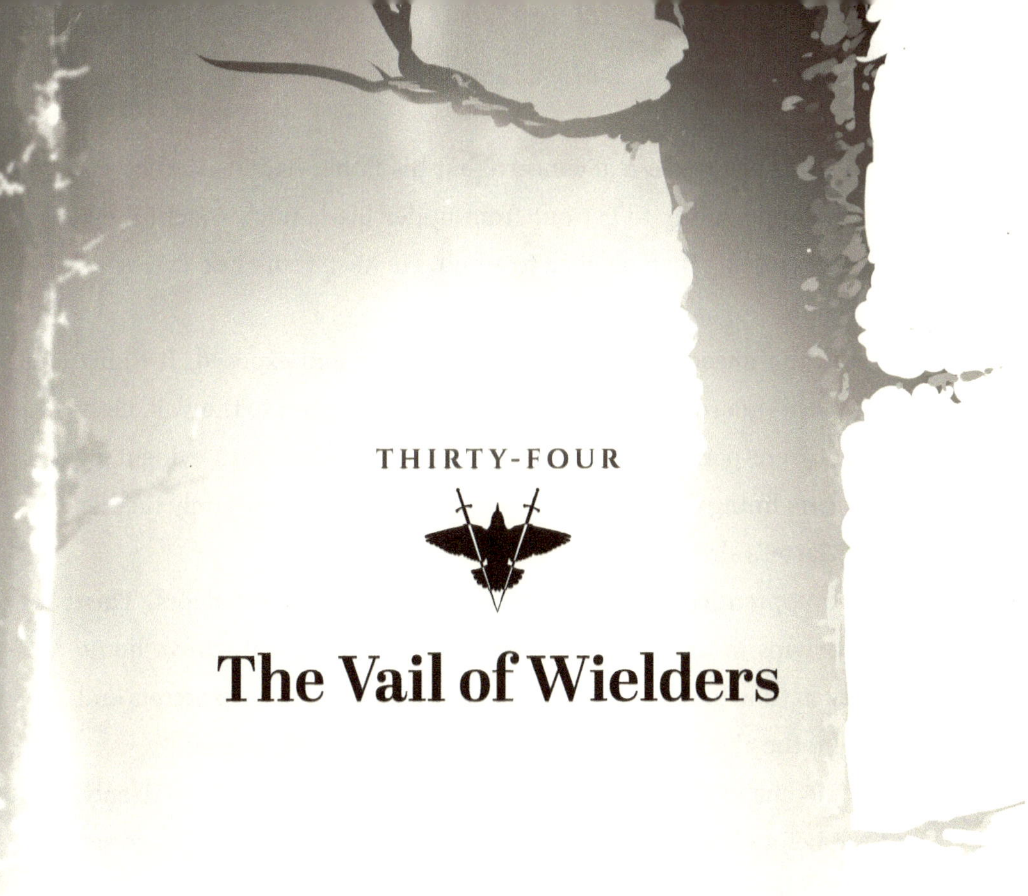

The Vail of Wielders

Gastel left Parth for the second time in his life. If he'd had apprehensions the first time, now the feeling of foreboding was triple. He'd been solid in his conviction to return Raemian, and the knowledge of how that had turned out stained every positive reason he could think for leaving a second time.

The Vail of Wielders was at the very edge of existence, tucked into the northernmost point of Rhend, where the earth met the frigid waters of the Rahven Sea. Clouds smothered the sky with a blanket of downy winter and held the sea mist tight against the earth, leaving a sheen of ice over every surface. While only a couple days' easy ride from Parth, the climate was significantly colder and ideal for training in the use of fiery soul magic.

Gastel pulled the riding cloak tighter around himself to ward off the chill *and apprehension*. Whether he could learn to properly control his

Anam at his age was a real concern, but his father had insisted he go. Plus, the opportunity to get out from under his family's watchful eye was more enticing than he liked to admit. He wasn't sure he'd ever trust them again.

Still, the uncertainty of it all left him raw and exposed. It didn't help that his guards were turned away at the entrance to the Vail. Only wielders were permitted, and this was taken seriously, as evident by the archers lining the parapets. The heavy-handed display only further frayed Gastel's already tattered nerves.

Two apprentices greeted him at the massive double doors. They were perhaps in the middle of their elfling years. It only drove home how much time he'd lost since his father had chosen to keep secrets and deny him the ability to train when he'd been an elfling himself.

"Welcome to the Vail, Highness. I'm Inara." The girl bowed deeply, but not before her eyes found his short hair. "The master wishes to see you immediately."

Inara was a small elfling, not much older than thirteen or fourteen, with keen eyes and a warm smile. The other apprentice, a boy, looked slightly older, but only because he'd already grown into his height.

Gastel nodded. "Of course."

He allowed the boy to take his bag containing additional clothes, a blank journal, and a single novel. He'd been told he would need nothing, but he'd insisted on at least these things and his broadsword. If the last few weeks had taught him nothing else, it was that he should never dive headfirst into the unknown without a means of self-defense.

Inara led him through the wide halls, glancing back every so often. Other than pointing out a few important areas of the Vail like the dining hall and infirmary, she made no small talk. The vaulted ceilings and cold that soaked into one's bones made the place feel emptier than the castle stronghold.

After the abbreviated tour, she directed him to an open door at the end of one of the halls. Within was a study of sorts, lined with floor-to-ceiling bookcases nearly bursting with manuscripts and haphazard scrolls. A desk constructed of the same granite as the walls occupied the center, an ornately carved wooden chair behind. The desktop was littered with more books and scrolls, letters stacked in piles, a curious paper-weight made of purple glass, and multiple goblets of unfinished wine.

"Master, I present Prince Gastel."

Inara prostrated herself on the stone floor before the man known as Master Rayken. Not for the first time, a chill of concern rippled up Gastel's back. With Inara still face down on the floor, Gastel bowed generously. Who'd require more submission than the king?

Master Rayken was old, and it showed. Unlike Gastel's father, the corners of Rayken's eyes were a maze of deep lines. He had bags of dark flesh that drooped down his cheeks, skin stretched until it had lost its elasticity. His once-midnight-blue hair was flecked with silver along his temples. He was skeletally thin with bony fingers that might snap at the slightest pressure. He didn't look like he smiled much; in fact, he appeared to be angry at that very moment.

"You may wait outside, Inara," Rayken said, a chill of superiority staining his raspy voice.

There was no thank you, no kindness. He simply dismissed her. She picked herself up, smiled warmly at Gastel, and stepped out into the hall, pulling the heavy door closed behind her.

"Now then, Highness. You come to hone your Anam Wielding skills." A long sigh of ripe frustration ruffled the scroll in Rayken's hand. "Why your father has chosen to wait until now when you are entirely too old to be properly malleable, is beyond me, but I shall do with you what I can." He set the scroll down, his glare laced with judgments and something more sinister.

"Perhaps we should gauge the level of power your father spoke of in his letter. He mentioned something akin to your mother, which seems highly presumptuous. She was an exception, a rare gem of perfection." He gave Gastel a long once-over, stopping quite abruptly at his hair. "I see the rumors are true. Your hair has been *desecrated.*"

Gastel was growing weary of judgment. It was, after all, just hair. He'd come too close to death to worry about such trivial things anymore.

"In a hundred years, it won't be noticeable," Gastel said.

"Yes, well, hopefully your appearance won't be too distracting to the others." Rayken shuffled through some paperwork, leaving the conversation hanging as though Gastel encroached on the master's precious time. "We shall start with inquiry. I had hoped you'd arrive earlier, but we'll do what we can with what limited time you've left me."

Master Rayken snapped for Gastel to follow as he left the room, leaving Inara in her place against the wall.

They proceeded to the training hall with nothing but the sound of their footsteps. Gastel would have liked to see some kind of equipment. Instead, it was a massive, empty room. No weapons, no shields, just walls devoid of decoration. It made the already-cold Vail feel even more sterile and unwelcoming.

Gastel wasn't sure how his level of Anam ability would be gauged. He'd been tested as an elfling, but always under his father's watchful eye. Looking back now, he was starting to understand the king's protective behavior significantly better.

"Start small. Ignite your soulflame," Rayken said as he faced him.

Since removing his mother's soul stone, his ability to control his Anam while wearing it was becoming easier. It was there when he reached and ready when he called. Gastel did as he was bid.

"Now throw it to me. I assume you can project it at the very least." Rayken's tone was thick with condescension. The man's elitist attitude already grated against the edges of Gastel's shattered nerves.

Gastel had used Anam to light lanterns on a handful of occasions, but it was still an unusual premise for him. Pushing his soul away wasn't comfortable or instinctual. He turned his mind inward and found his soul waiting, as always. When he released the fire, it felt deliberate. Smooth. Easy. He launched his soulflame with more speed than intended, but Master Rayken caught it and rolled it from his palm to the back of his hand and around until the flame dissipated into the chilly air.

Rayken pressed his lips together in thought. "Not terrible for someone with no training."

Without thinking, Gastel had placed his weight evenly on both legs and put his hands behind his back, awaiting his next instruction.

"Two at once."

Gastel furrowed his brow. He hadn't tried this before. He'd always ignited one and shared it between his hands. With this new ease by which he could manipulate his power, he held out both hands palms up and pressed his soul forward. The amber glow heated instantly to pure hot white over his open hands. A shiver of understanding slipped down Gastel's spine. It was *too* easy.

"Pass them, boy."

It was Rayken's tone that Gastel didn't like. Superiority didn't sit well with him. Not because he was a prince. Not because he hadn't had the pleasure of being broken down by masters before. His combat instructor had destroyed him on several occasions. It was because there was no kindness in this man's intentions. Only a love for supremacy.

Gastel did as he was asked and sent his soulflames with terrifying speed toward Rayken. Again, the master caught them.

"Watch your tone," Rayken snapped. "Anam can speak a thousand words, and yours is willful and sharp."

Gastel clenched his teeth. This was going to be a challenge, especially while his mind was on other things. If all had gone well, Raemian and Dulanii would be settling in Dormshire and his brothers would have a defensive strategy against Gemma's army prepared. All while he stood across from an ancient wielder, enduring training he should have had when he was half his current age.

"That's enough for today. We have much work to do with you. This will take longer than I'd hoped."

Rayken seemed more cantankerous than before, walking with purpose back to his study. Inara still stood patiently to the side, her hands folded behind her back.

"Take him to the dorms, then to meet with his overseer, Effrin Kresha."

Inara's expression changed at the sound of this new name. Was it a glint of concern? It was gone as quickly as Gastel had seen it, her gentle smile returning.

Before Inara could pull him away, Rayken clamped down on his upper arm. The old man's grip was stronger than he'd anticipated.

"Kresha shall see to your training. You'll show her the same respect and submission you'd show me. We have rules here. Rules you *must* follow." Spittle caused Gastel to flinch back. "You're an initiate. Not yet an apprentice. I care little of who you are or how old you may be. You're but an elfling in ability."

The master stepped into his study, slamming the door behind him without another word.

If Rayken knew what Gastel could do to him with a single swing of the sword hanging heavy at his hip, the old man probably wouldn't have spoken the way he had. Then again, perhaps Rayken didn't fear traditional steel. Perhaps his powers made him impenetrable to such physical weapons.

"I'd say he gets nicer the longer you know him, but I think we just learn to bend without breaking." Inara's smile was full of gentle understanding.

Her cool blue complexion was fresh and young—such an elfling. It had been a long time since Gastel had been around a young Bleck Larin, not to mention female. Other than the occasional servants or soldiers, the castle stronghold was mostly occupied by men. Courtesans visited on occasion but only stayed long enough to grow bored.

Inara possessed a willowy thinness. She had a long, narrow face, and instead of a topknot, like most grown Bleck Larin, her hair was pulled tight at the nape of her neck with a simple golden clasp, the remaining length plaited.

She led him to the dormitories with the same silent swiftness as when he'd arrived, pointing out the separation between male and female. If one thing was for certain, the entire experience made him feel immensely old. The thought of dormitories and lack of privacy was mortifying. He realized how coddled he'd seem to these elflings.

"Here's your room. Thankfully, Master Rayken saw fit to give you your own space, seeing as how you're a bit older." Inara met his gaze and looked away quickly. Gastel thought he may have detected the slightest color rise in her cheeks.

"Effrin Kresha and the other effrins have their rooms off the main hall. You should learn their names quickly. They'll expect a certain level of respect." She paused, considering her next words. "I can help you with their names tomorrow. For now, just know that Kresha is yours. Each effrin has an initiate and an apprentice. Jad is Kresha's apprentice. You met him when you arrived. You'll get to know him quickly. He'll be helping you quite a bit."

Gastel nodded as he stepped farther in, eyes wandering around the room. This would be his home for the foreseeable future, and he found it exceedingly dull. Stone walls, stone floor. No soft leathers, no tapestries, no warm rugs underfoot. A small bed adorned with what thankfully looked like warm coverings was positioned against one wall. A wardrobe across from the bed was flanked by a single narrow window that looked onto the frigid landscape. A simple dressing table held a plain white washbasin.

"Charming," he said, unable to keep sarcasm from creeping into his voice.

"Master Rayken will want you to remove your sword. It would be best to do that now before I take you to meet Effrin Kresha or she'll be cross." Inara hesitated. "If there's one thing I can say about Kresha, you don't want to upset her." It was the first time Gastel had seen the smile slip from Inara's face, replaced with a concerning sadness. "I wish Master Rayken had paired you with someone else." She rubbed her hands together and gazed down at her feet. "She's possibly stricter than he is."

Apprehension washed over Gastel again, but it was too late. He was here, and he needed to learn how to control his power. He was dangerous, not only to others but to himself. He'd heard of wielders dying because they'd exhausted their souls. He shivered, and it didn't go unnoticed.

"You'll be cold here at first, but it gets better." She opened the wardrobe and stepped back. His single bag rested at the bottom. "Hopefully they'll allow you to use your regular clothing for a little longer. The initiate robes are so thin."

Was nothing pleasant in this place?

By the time Inara led him back to the training hall, it was bustling with wielders. It was clear who the effrins were. They wore heavy sashes of fine blue brocade. Silver embroidery graced the edges of sleeves and collars. The color scheme was easy enough to recognize. Initiates wore orange sashes, apprentices white, effrins blue. There was also a distinct difference in the way the effrins wore their robes, customizing the fit to their own personal preferences.

He immediately sensed who Kresha was. She had twisted Jad's arm behind his head and dropped him to his knees, pinning him in place as she spoke. Her lips nearly touched his ear. When she met Gastel's gaze, she lifted Jad from the ground before thrusting him away, her eyes holding on Gastel, tipping her chin up with authority.

"So hard to get good initiates these days," she said. She sauntered toward Gastel, a suggestive sway to every step. "You must be this prince everyone keeps talking about." Her eyes glanced up to his hair—always his hair—then traveled the length of him, pausing longer than necessary at his lips. "Interesting."

She was nearly Gastel's height and, like Inara, was exceedingly thin, with a long face and high cheekbones. Long pieces of navy hair hung loose around her face. She might have been a beautiful woman if it weren't for the fake smile that reminded him of Roulin. She wore her robes form fitted to her lithe body, a plunging neckline showing the cool-gray flesh between her firm breasts, begging for eyes to see her, seductive and unapologetic.

"I think we'll have *fun* together. Gastel, is it?"

He nodded, trying his best not to cringe. If they wanted him to play this game, he would. He'd do whatever he had to, to get out of this place as quickly as possible.

THIRTY-FIVE

History

The soothing ease of twilight settled around Rae on her third day in Dormshire. Freck was absorbed in sharpening his daggers; the repetitive wet scraping sound was more familiar to Rae than she cared to admit. It reminded her of battles, blood, and empty amber eyes—but also of camaraderie and a place where she'd once belonged: a Shay army she'd called her friends. Could she still? Freck, always, but any of her other brothers- and sisters-in-arms? It felt like eons since she'd stood among their ranks.

She tried her best not to wonder what Gastel was doing that very moment and instead focused on all the information they'd gleaned from the marketplace. Every able-bodied Shay had been conscripted to the queen's army and sent to Jooshawn, south of the Forest of Tremire. Why they'd be sent there, Rae wasn't certain. She couldn't recall anything about a training camp near Jooshawn.

It didn't sit well.

She'd spoken with an old farmer who had said farewell to his only son. Gemma had spread considerable propaganda with the conscription notices, claiming the Bleck Larin were fortifying their forces for a final push into the Shaylands. It didn't fool anyone. People could see how frivolous this latest campaign truly was.

Rae tried to wrap her head around the logistics, the supplies required, the armor that would need to be crafted for the new soldiers. Weapons and materials for housing would have to be considered, not to mention food. How was Gemma able to afford and organize all of this?

It didn't sit well at all.

Reclining on the small futon, Rae pored over a worn manuscript titled The Houses. The manuscript had been a pleasant surprise, collecting dust among the cacophony of trinkets the farmer had been selling alongside his meager supply of summer vegetables. She'd overpaid but considered the additional coin a surcharge for the information he so generously provided.

Skimming the pages, Rae came to the section she was most interested in—The Shay Houses. Hopefully, it'd shed light on the history of the House of Starling and all the houses, for that matter. After reviewing correspondence for King Mesmal, she'd grown more curious. There had been vague references—coded information disguised as ignorance. She'd been shocked to find letters from her own legion among those in the king's collection—references to names and bargaining for prisoners.

The keystone to all of it was something her father had told Gastel in the dungeon of Tremire. Gastel had recounted his conversation while she'd been recovering from her arrow wound, but in her medicated state, she feared she hadn't retained all the information. Regardless, if it were true and the House of Starling had some role within the royal line, she needed to find it.

She flipped back, rereading a few passages, trying to fill in the gaps in her understanding. The House of Moreray, the House of Tremire, the House of Jooshawn—Rae skimmed, searching. Her heart quickened when she ran her fingers over the name. Elegant scrollwork decorated the massive S that sprawled across the page. The curving branches of an ironwood tree wrapped around the sensual shape of the letter, a single starling resting in the branches.

At the time the manuscript had been recorded, Rae's grandfather Somsunder had held the House of Starling. His bonded partner for a time had been another male named Clore. He'd also taken several Shay women as consorts, who had provided him with five elflings. Rae knew of her father's siblings, but they'd all been killed during the first siege of Dormshire. She'd never had the honor of meeting them in person.

She ran her fingers across the page, lingering over the last sentence. *"...the last of the Great Houses."* The pages after were blank, as if left for additional histories to be recorded, but Rae knew there was nothing more to write. Her father had been the youngest. None of the others had had any elflings.

She rolled her father's band around her wrist. Why had the Great Houses faded away? It was a question that wasn't answered in this manuscript. Probably a better question for Mesmal. He was the oldest elf she knew, having lived during times of peace, long before the Culling and perhaps even before the Hundred Years War that had resulted in the banishing of humans from Rhend. It was possible that he'd been the first of the Bleck Larin sovereigns to separate from his house. He would know, and she'd have to be satisfied with asking when given the opportunity to speak with him again. If she were given the opportunity. With a full-scale battle looming, it was unlikely she'd have the opportunity.

Unless...

She closed the manuscript. Gemma's latest scheming seemed to have started when Rae had been taken from the Middlelend Forest—an event that seemed entirely unrelated. Gemma couldn't have had the forethought to put Rae in the perfect place at the perfect time for the perfect abduction.

Or could she?

"I know that look."

Rae jumped. She hadn't expected Freck to pay her any attention. He slipped into one of the chairs at the table and put his feet up on another.

"I'd ask you what you're thinking, but I have a feeling I already know." He smirked. "I miss his handsome face, too."

Rae couldn't help but return the smile. "Among other things."

"The conscription notice is concerning."

She nodded. It wasn't concerning, it was downright terrifying.

"Find anything in the manuscript?" he asked.

"Not much more than I already knew." She slid the book onto the table. Perhaps she'd have better luck with public records?

"You should get some sleep. Maybe Gastel will visit you in your dreams." Freck stood and stretched his arms over his head. "Maybe his brother'll visit me in *my* dreams!"

"Roulin?" The confusion on her face was likely obvious. Freck's taste in attraction was a mystery to her.

He laughed before shaking his head and winking. "Of course not."

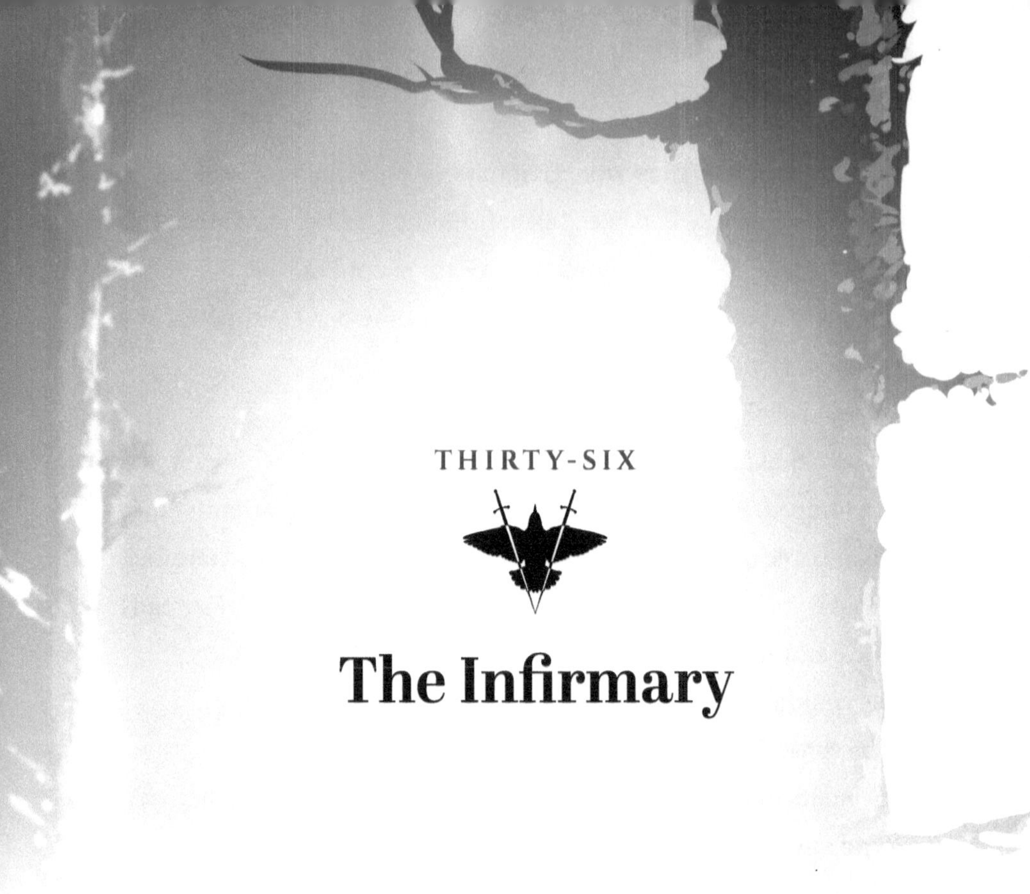

THIRTY-SIX

The Infirmary

Gastel stood alone in the silence of the training hall. The sunrise was still an hour or two away, leaving the Vail in woeful darkness. He had a few hours before the others would file in. It was time to train his body before he had to train his soul.

He was absorbed in forms when someone cleared their throat behind him. He spun, shoulders heaving from physical exertion, to meet Kresha's smirk.

"Did Master Rayken give you permission to use this area outside of training hours?"

He took a few more heavy breaths to calm his heart rate before standing up straight, squaring his shoulders.

"I didn't think I needed to ask permission," he said, hands finding his hips. Her expression changed to one of disgust. "Effrin Kresha," he added, certain he'd pay for his lapse in respect later.

"Perhaps not. I'll review this with him today."

She circled him, inspecting him up and down. Goosebumps bloomed across his arms. Whether from her eyes traveling the length of him or from the frigid air touching his sweaty, hot skin, he couldn't be certain. Kresha made him feel like a horse at auction.

"So this is what a warrior looks like." She licked her lower lip and cocked her head to the side, drawing his eyes for a regrettable second to the exposed flesh of her sternum. "I prefer brains over muscles."

She stepped closer—too close—letting her hand fall to his arm, her fingers tracing along his bicep before slipping down to his forearm.

"But for you, I'd make an exception." Her gaze touched his lips before returning to his eyes.

He swallowed hard and met her glare as her hand slipped from his flesh, leaving a trail of ice. Footsteps interrupted Kresha before she could say more.

"Starting early with him, I see," Master Rayken said. "He needs a lot of molding."

"Actually, Master, he was doing physical training. Is this permitted?" Kresha had a snide way of asking. Maybe she wanted Rayken to deny him this comfort, like all the other comforts they were insistent on denying.

Much the way Kresha had inspected him, Master Rayken looked him up and down, likely noticing his damp shirt and hair.

"As long as he can maintain his initiate training schedule and it doesn't interfere with activities here, I don't see a problem." He glanced at Kresha. She was clearly disappointed. "One indiscretion." The master's bony index finger pointed at Gastel's nose. "And this privilege shall be revoked."

Gastel gave him a generous bow. "Thank you, Master Rayken."

"I paired you with Effrin Kresha because she's my strictest instructor and by far my most skilled. Don't make me regret investing her time and talents on you." Master Rayken's brooding yellow eyes glanced down at Gastel's waist. "And no weapons. Return that thing before training."

"Of course, Master." He'd not even thought of it. It was second nature to belt on his sword each morning.

Master Rayken nodded respectfully to Kresha before stalking away, his thick robes hissing across the stone.

Kresha stared at Gastel, a strange appreciation in her eyes.

"Do you need assistance, Your Highness?" She stepped so close that he could feel the heat from her body. Wandering fingers found the waist of his pants. "There's enough time, I should think," she said, a lusty weight to her words.

His mind pulled away—hard. Thankfully, his body didn't follow. He had a feeling rejection would have only made her even more impossible to deal with. Instead, he placed his hands over hers and moved them away, keeping his expression calm, searching for something to say that wouldn't seem like a direct refusal.

"I've been managing just fine on my own for years, Effrin." With any luck, she'd think he wasn't interested in women.

"Suit yourself, Princeling. The offer stands." She tossed him a sideways glance as she sauntered away.

The distinct lack of wielders in battle had led Gastel to believe that the use of Anam wasn't entirely about death and destruction.

He was revising this opinion.

Kresha showed poor Jad no mercy. He struggled to get up, having been blasted onto his backside by a cheap shot. A trail of charred, brittle flesh down his neck and shoulder smoked.

"Jad, you disappoint. I'd hoped you could help me demonstrate my superior instruction capabilities to our newest classmate," Kresha said. "Perhaps I was a bit too rough?" Her tone was seductively teasing. She paused as Jad's eyes rolled from the pain. "You truly are one of my more pathetic examples."

"Kresha, you know better. Let him see the healer," an especially tall, formal-looking man interrupted.

As promised, Inara kept Gastel apprised of all the Effrins' names, and Effrin Kalbasen was Kresha's mirror opposite; he was calm and patient.

"Mind your business, Kal," Kresha snapped, a feral sneer turning up her lips. "He needs to learn how to defend himself, even when he's injured."

Kalbasen wasn't intimidated. He folded his arms as Kresha drew her soulflame out into a strange planchette-shaped specter that hovered and twisted over her palm, spinning faster as it grew in size and solidity.

She threw it directly at Jad, who leaned forward, protective of his injured shoulder. It never reached its intended target. Instead, Kalbasen caught it, much like Master Rayken had while testing Gastel, and deflected the blast up to the high ceiling.

"Stop showing off." Kalbasen left no room for negotiation.

Gastel learned an important lesson in that moment: Kalbasen was Kresha's senior. This was good to know because Gastel was certain he would never receive any sympathy from Kresha. If he could befriend Kalbasen, there was hope he wouldn't feel constantly under attack.

"I'll walk him to the infirmary," Gastel said as he crouched to Jad's side, helping him to his feet. The boy was unsteady and glassy-eyed with pain.

Kresha shrugged, boredom on her face. She walked away, dismissively waving a hand.

"Thank you, Gastel. I'll mention this to Master Rayken. She's a bit heavy-handed." In a softer tone, he added, "Thankfully, you're older. It won't be so easy for her to push you around."

He gave Gastel a warm nod before returning to training Inara. The techniques they were working through seemed significantly less hazardous, involving what looked like a dome of protective fire and ribbons of soulflame spinning in concentric circles.

Gastel took Jad's good arm over his shoulder and helped him through the halls, trying to remember where the infirmary was. When Inara had given him his initial tour, he hadn't realized how important it'd be to know. Thankfully, Jad was conscious enough to pull him in the correct direction. Gastel had the distinct impression that Jad had been there on more occasions than he'd care to admit.

"I'm sorry. This is probably not how you'd like to be spending your training." Jad's energy waned as they walked.

"No apologies. Apparently, we both got lucky when it comes to effrins," Gastel said, drawing a thin chuckle from the boy.

Gastel froze when they reached the infirmary, eyes meeting a thick slide lock. What reason would there be to lock a healer in the infirmary? Things in this place were most certainly not as they seemed. There wasn't time to dissect the possible reasons. Gastel slid the lock open and helped Jad inside.

The infirmary wasn't like the rest of the Vail. It was green. Extraordinarily green. There were hundreds of leafy plants and vines hanging from hooks mounted to every possible surface of the ceiling rafters. The temperature was several degrees warmer, and the air seemed fresh and clean. Gastel took a deep breath. He was instantly reminded of Raemian—the smell of morning sunshine.

"Jad? Are you back already?" a woman's voice, hidden somewhere beyond one of the curtains of vines, enquired.

The last thing Gastel expected to see was a Shay's bright-pink face emerging from the foliage. Her unruly white hair was pulled back in spontaneous tufts, held in place by twists of vine. She wore the same shimmering green material as the Eishtala cloak he'd donned in Tremire, the fabric flowing like water as she moved. Her calm blue eyes grabbed and held him in place.

"Oh." She placed a hand upon her chest in surprise. "Goodness. I wasn't expecting a prince."

All Gastel could do was nod as she turned her attention to Jad. How had she known who he was?

"She's got to stop this. You're in here almost every day."

Remembering another time he'd spent in a different infirmary, Gastel backed up to let the Shay flit about.

"Highness, can you help him onto the bench? I'm going to need more than ointments for this." She directed her attention to Jad's shoulder as Gastel helped him lie down on the exam table. "Now then. Nothing a little greenery can't mend." She winked.

"Thank you, Master Lorilay," Jad whispered.

The Shay smoothed her hand along Jad's forehead and closed her eyes, taking a calm, deep breath.

Gastel had only seen Eishtala magic performed once, when the bars of his cell in Tremire had been woven closed. He understood the principles of how it was used, but it was a vastly different thing to see.

Lorilay ran her hand down past Jad's chest, hovering just above his navel with fingers spread wide, then paused. Time stood still. Gastel was silent, waiting to see what would happen next. The air moved around him, crackling with energy. Leaves on the closest vines withered and fell to the ground, sounding like crumpled paper as they hit the stone. When her eyes opened, they glowed a brilliant shade of green, illuminated from within by a mysterious light. She focused her hand over the worst part of Jad's burnt shoulder.

The actual act of healing was apparently painful. Gastel stared with morbid curiosity as Jad's eyes rolled to the back of his head. He gripped the sides of the table with bone-white knuckles and arched his back, twisting like a snake strangling its prey. The blackened skin began to change. Gray tendrils wriggled from within, like worms of new skin, gradually filling in the charred crevasses of Jad's flesh. The darker color of his surrounding skin fused and smoothed out to its original gray-blue complexion.

"A little more, Jad. I'm so sorry."

Lorilay focused all her attention on his neck. Her eyes moved under her eyelids, searching for something in her mind. She took another deep breath, and again, the tickle of energy being pulled from the plants moved over Gastel's skin like a summer breeze.

Everything stopped. Jad relaxed, his eyes still closed, lips gently parted. Gastel took a step closer, watching for the rise and fall of his chest before Jad's eyes popped open. He sat up, looking down at himself and his singed robes.

"I'll make mention of this the next time I see Master Rayken," Lorilay said. "There's no reason for you to be in here every day. Plus, I honestly don't think I have enough plants." She took his shoulders and pulled him into a warm embrace, like a mother hugging her son.

"Now then, Highness, something to help with the cold?" She turned her attention to Gastel, sparkling blue eyes seeing everything.

He'd been freezing since coming to the Vail. It was likely a combination of super-thin robes and Wielding not requiring enough physical activity to keep him warm.

"I don't know how I'm expected to survive," Gastel said.

"A warrior doesn't belong in robes. Why have you only now been sent to train?"

She seemed intensely interested, but Gastel wasn't sure he was ready to tell anyone what happened when he removed his mother's soul stone.

"King Mesmal's priorities have changed, and I need to learn to control my powers." He left his explanation vague. "I'm not sure I'm cut out for this type of education."

She nodded, and he sensed that Lorilay didn't miss much.

Jad pushed himself down from the table. The bruising around his neck was almost gone.

"The two of you should get back before you give Effrin Kresha another reason to be cross." Lorilay smiled at them, handing Gastel a glass vial filled with a viscous, purple liquid as she shooed them out the door. "For the cold. Sip a little each morning."

Once out into the hall, Jad slid the lock back in place and met Gastel's critical glare.

"It's the rule. As a Shay, she's to be locked up. I don't agree with it, but I want out of this place, so I follow the rules." He gave Gastel a long, knowing look, pushing past and motioning Gastel to hurry.

But Gastel lingered, eyes firmly secured on the lock.

THIRTY-SEVEN

The Library

Rae left Freck at the market with plans to drum up work for the two of them. They had precious little coin, and if they wished to stay, they'd need to find proper jobs. Rae headed to the old district where she'd heard an extensive library was located, hoping to find more pieces of information.

She crossed into the heart of Dormshire, her gaze wandering over the cracks and crevices worn into the stones of the old stronghold, which now functioned as the council and court. It was smaller than the castle in Parth—approachable and modest, blocky in its construction with no spires, towers, or parapets. Built in a time when elves had no enemies, the front gate was nothing but a gaping mouth, open to the warm breeze. She hesitated, noticing a single armed guard. He wore bastardized royal armor—an enameled breastplate fashioned with the queen's emblem and mismatched helm that no longer had a visor. He must have noticed her hesitation before she hitched her courage because he dropped his spear as she approached.

"State your business." His voice was gravelly, as though he hadn't spoken all morning, and Rae met his narrowed gaze with what she hoped was agreeable confidence.

"Information." Apparently, this wasn't good enough, as the man looked her up and down and frowned but didn't move. "I seek knowledge of the Great Houses. I was told there's a library here?" Before her mind could craft a better story, she settled on a half-truth: "It's for my father."

She hoped the ancillary information would at least advance the narrative that she was in Dormshire to visit family. This wasn't the way she wanted to learn if Gemma had placed a bounty on her head. At least she'd worn a riding cloak, making her scouting jerkin less recognizable.

"The library is at the end of the main hall, to the right." The guard pointed with a gloved hand, his eyes following her in.

She walked as quickly as she could without breaking into a jog, pausing for a moment in front of the oversized door. Nothing but books, dust, and morning light streaming in through the tall windows greeted her. She was otherwise completely alone. The smell of musty old leather and oiled wood enveloped her with eerie comfort.

She stepped past a well-used ironwood desk decorated with elaborate vines, twisted to look like the tabletop was held aloft by minuscule trees on each corner. Stacks of carefully positioned books covered its surface, sorted for return to their places upon shelves.

And the shelves! They were built from ancient trees, something older and more resilient than ironwood—darker with wood grain that begged to be touched. Her fingers trailed across the warm surface, grazing along leather spines as she walked between the towering shelves. She read the titles as she passed, glancing up at the ones she couldn't reach.

"Can I help you find something?"

She jumped at the unexpected voice. Peeking around a shelf, she met the cool-blue eyes of a rather tall man dressed in nobleman's robes. He was thin for a Shay and stood with impeccable posture, an air of authority emanating from him.

"I'm looking for information on the Great Houses," Rae said.

He stepped closer, a knowing twinkle in his eye, as though he'd been waiting for someone to come searching for this exact information.

"There's a collection of manuscripts." He led the way through the stacks as he spoke, indicating the section with a wave. "No one is particularly interested in *that* anymore, what with so few houses, if any, remaining. Not sure you'll find much. The queen's librarian poached many of our manuscripts several years ago." He paused, hovering a moment more. "Is there anything specific about them that you're interested in?"

She tried to keep the shock from her face at learning Gemma had been interested in books. "Just general history, I suppose. It's for my father."

"Ah. I see." He backed away. "I'll leave you to your research. Please let me know if you require any additional assistance. I'll be at the front desk, working on some manuscripts." He flashed her a half-hearted smile before stepping away.

Rae's finger drew a trail in the dust until she found a promising book. She pulled it from the shelf, throwing a cloud of particles into the air, then dropped to the floor with it in her lap. She skimmed the pages. She wouldn't have time to read everything, yet her fingers itched as they moved across the paper, yearning to know its secrets. This manuscript focused on the royal families and how they'd dropped house names in favor of peace between the larger houses. Odd—discord between the houses had never been mentioned. Strangely, there was nothing on the House of Starling, sending a nagging sense of concern into the pit of her stomach.

She leafed through a handful of other manuscripts, starting to feel defeated. She wasn't going to find answers here, at least not in the time she had. She'd promised to find Freck before the evening meal. He was hopefully having more luck finding them work.

Resolved to try one more, Rae pulled a particularly old manuscript from a higher shelf and cracked it open across her lap, fingers tracing across the brittle parchment. Complicated family trees decorated the pages, the House of Tremire's illustrious family members branching out until it abruptly stopped.

There was a name she'd read before—recently, in fact. She brushed over it, a shiver of knowing creeping up her arms. She turned the page only to find the telltale ruffle of a torn page. She flipped through the subsequent pages. Anticipation melted into anxiety as she discovered more removed pages and places where ink had been smeared until it was illegible. A dark mark across another page obscured a reference to something she feared was dreadfully important. It was clear someone had gone to great lengths to hide information, leaving more questions than answers.

She slipped the manuscript back into its place on the shelf, feeling a sudden need to remove herself from the library.

The librarian leaned against the desk, standing straight when he saw her approaching. "Did you find what you were looking for?" he asked.

She shook her head, hoping she was hiding her nervousness.

"I'm sorry. What did you say your name was? I don't think I've seen you in Dormshire."

"I'm not from Dormshire. I'm staying with my family for a while."

He nodded his understanding. "And your name?"

Something was off with the way he pressed her. Apprehension twisted and solidified in the pit of her stomach. She'd had the same feeling when the guard had questioned her outside.

"Lin." She hoped her hesitation hadn't been noticeable.

He didn't reply, just nodded, his expression flattening out into a forced smile. She noticed what she'd hoped she wouldn't. *He knew.* He knew exactly who she was. She wasn't entirely sure how she knew, but his eyes had changed, his posture, the way he held his head. He no longer needed to pretend to be a kind librarian. She bowed respectfully and stepped toward the door.

"Thanks again for your help." She didn't wait for him to reply. Instead, she kept her pace as calm as she could as she walked with forcefully metered steps, feeling his eyes follow her out.

Glancing back at the steps of the stronghold, she saw the librarian speaking with the guard. They looked in her direction, confirming her suspicions. It seemed her time in Dormshire may have just run out. Much too soon.

She hurried through the streets, weaving in unpredictable directions and checking to make sure she wasn't being followed. Running from whatever punishment her stepmother would concoct for her wasn't how she'd wanted to spend her time. After only a handful of days, she and Freck could quite possibly be on the run.

And where could they run to? Rae wasn't sure she could trust going farther into the Shaylands. The risk was too great. After losing her father, she refused to put Freck in unnecessary danger. Going back to Parth wasn't an option either. Perhaps they could find a place to camp in the Middlelend Forest for a time, but Rae feared they wouldn't fare any better than if they tried to join Gemma's forces under assumed names.

A few dwellings down from theirs, she skidded to a stop. From this distance, the door appeared to have been left open. She slipped behind the nearest building and peered out. The cusp of twilight cloaked the nooks and corners in thick shadows, making it hard to see if there was anyone crouched, waiting.

Freck should have returned by now, but there were no lights. Perhaps he'd already gotten back when their unwelcome guests had come to call? If anything had happened to him...but she needn't worry. She, of all people, knew his skill level. A handful of run-of-the-mill guards would be challenging but not impossible for him to handle.

She took a deep breath and crept out from her hiding spot. The home beside theirs had the tiniest slivers of light peeking through shuttered windows. The others were dark and empty.

Facing the street, Rae sidestepped, keeping her back protected against the boarded-up fronts of the empty dwellings. Once in front of the Starling home, she pressed her back against the wall outside the gaping entry and peered in.

The door had been kicked off its hinges, lying in pieces on the floor. Anger boiled in her stomach at the sight of the Starling emblem reduced to pieces. The room beyond had been ransacked. Their meager furnishings had been overturned and broken. The manuscript lay sprawled open beside the upturned table, pages ripped and spread around. There was no sign of Freck, no sign of anyone. A sense of dread for her dearest friend replaced her anger and wrapped itself around her throat as her heart raced.

"Freck?"

She ducked in and crossed to the hall, making her way through the house and peeking in each room. She found nothing but more upturned furniture and debris.

"Dulanii? It's Rae."

The sound of heavy footfalls toward the front of the house froze her in place, feet glued to the stone in Freck's room.

"Raemian Starling, we know you're in there."

The voice sounded vaguely familiar, and then she placed it—the guard who had questioned her at the library.

"In the name of Queen Gemma, present yourself."

THIRTY-EIGHT

Anam Training

Gastel stood across from his effrin with fists at his sides, furious, at the very limits of restraint. He had disobeyed. Again. He had blocked a blow meant for Jad. Apparently, you didn't defend others. It had something to do with the absorption of your opponent's power, but he didn't entirely understand it. He never felt like he was absorbing anything, and Kresha hadn't been particularly forthcoming in explaining how it worked.

For magic that used one's lifeforce, there was certainly a lot of soullessness associated.

"It looks like you won't be doing that silly physical training anymore, Princeling. Maybe now you'll learn to use your brains a little more," Kresha mocked, smiling, clearly trying to make an example of him. "Was it worth it?"

Gastel could only glare at her, all his anger boiling to the surface. Much more baiting and he wasn't sure he'd be able to suppress his growing bitterness.

"I'm not sure mercilessly attacking someone teaches them anything other than hatred," he hissed.

"Hatred has its place." She drew out her fire and held it in her open palm, ready to build yet another attack. "Poor Jad never should have been promoted to apprentice. He doesn't have what it takes. *He's too soft.*"

Gastel took a sharp breath across his teeth. "Perhaps he hasn't had the best teacher," he spat.

Her sinister smile melted into a snarl, ugly and sharp, a blade of uncompromised disappointment burning in her eyes. "And now you get to learn what it feels like to be resurrected."

He tipped his head in confusion. Resurrected? Did she intend to actually kill him?

He was frozen in place with the realization that it was perfectly plausible. She pushed fiery threads into a growing orb of brazen flames, building it into a snake of fire coiled in on itself.

It happened in slow motion. The flames spun and twisted in the air toward him. Gastel knew he couldn't deflect it. He'd try, but he'd fail.

He was never given the opportunity.

A blur of apprentice robes and a shriek of soul-wrenching pain took the direct hit. Inara fell to the ground in front of him, her chest searing with white fire. She arched her back as her body ignited. Another wail of agony broke free of her charred lips as she combusted from the inside out, clawing at her throat until her fingers crumbled into stumps of charcoal. The rest of her skin turned black and sloughed from her petite frame until she was nothing more than a solidified elven-shaped piece of obsidian resting in a mound of ash. Gastel could only watch, mouth agape, heart pounding, eyes wide with blistering terror.

That would have been him if Inara hadn't jumped in front of the blow.

"Gods, Kresha." Kalbasen sent two students running with a wave of his hand.

But who would they be running for? This was beyond Eishtala healing. Inara was dead.

Kresha stood to the side with that same wicked smirk on her face. Not an ounce of remorse, not a moment of sadness.

In his mind, Gastel saw the dead eyes of Kresha before him.

He wanted more.

He pulled the soul stone from his neck and held it out to Jad. "I'll need this back."

His hand ignited in brilliant soulflame the moment the chain slipped from his fingers. Pure Anam rolled up his arms, covering him in beautiful, horrible, glorious white fire.

Kresha's golden eyes grew unnaturally large, her snide smile slipping from her lips. He raised his hands, palms to the ceiling, joy blooming in his stomach as her gaze moved across his flaming form. He wasn't sure what she saw exactly. A man? A monster? A god? The reflection of himself in her eyes was death itself.

Her expression changed, shifting into something raw and exposed. It was the way Belkin and Roulin had looked at him in his father's study. No Bleck Larin should have such Anam.

He didn't want it. Maybe when he'd been younger, but now? He just wanted to be Gastel, the youngest son of the Bleck Larin king. The coolheaded one, the one who had never been to battle, had never taken a life, had never seen the true brutality of Anam.

Had never witnessed an elfling turned into cinders before his very eyes.

He took a single step forward. Whether he wanted this power or not, Kresha needed to be shown the error of her ways. He'd teach her as she'd taught all of her students—with heartless cruelty. He felt a hand on his arm. Kalbasen's fingers turned black where he gripped Gastel.

"No. Not like this. Inara can be revived." Gastel's confusion must have been clear on his face because Kalbasen clarified: "We have a Trove elf, a Svet Priest. He can resurrect her."

Gastel could only stare into Kalbasen's concerned eyes for several seconds as the fire of rage dissipated. He tried as before to draw the soulfire back to himself, coaxing his corporeal soul back into his body where it belonged, but he was unsuccessful. This part of him wished only to be free of its Bleck Larin prison—to burn until there was nothing left to incinerate. It shifted and moved, pulling through him like waves of insatiable wrath, feeding on his fury and hate.

He turned to Jad and reached for his mother's pendant. The boy was all too happy to drop it back into his palm. The fire extinguished as soon as his fingers wrapped around the smooth stone, the same as it always had.

The room was silent until Kresha's gritty voice broke across Gastel's ears. "Well, well, well. Princeling has a soul stone."

And in that instant, he recognized his error. He should have kept his anger in check and waited to see what would happen. Now Kresha knew why he'd been sent to the Vail—everyone did.

"Rayken doesn't know, does he?" Her smirk shifted into genuine curiosity. "How interesting."

He couldn't hold her excited glare. He couldn't look at Inara's smoldering corpse either. Instead, he glanced toward the hall entrance, eyes locking on the pale form of an elf.

The Trove was the size of an eight- or nine-year-old elfling, with extremities that appeared too long for his torso, giving him a gangly, miniature appearance. Against the gray, stone walls his frosty-white complexion appeared to glow, his pure-white hair hanging thin and wispy like spider silk draped over his shoulders. He wore nothing but loose gray pants and a thin strip of cotton over his eyes and walked with confidence to Inara's incinerated corpse, as though he could see her, even with his eyes covered.

The Trove hovered a hand over the smoking remains, breathing slowly, deliberately. Finally, he tipped his head back and took a deep breath as if enjoying the scent of burned flesh and hair.

"She is here waiting, but her body is too badly damaged. Is the healer available?"

His voice carried a deep timbre that didn't match his appearance. It gave him an otherworldly presence that Gastel wasn't sure he cared for.

So this was a Trove elf, a Svet Priest—eerie and mysterious. No wonder they hid from the world.

"I'm here." Master Lorilay rushed into the training hall, one of the other initiates close behind.

"Good. She'll need considerable healing before I can return her soul to her body."

Gastel glanced back at the strange Trove. He wished he hadn't because the Trove turned in his direction, covered eyes facing him. The Trove's expression twisted with shock.

"Niminea."

Gastel was pinned in place, ears filling with a strange roaring, like a waterfall crashing against the cold insides of his paralyzed mind.

"This is Prince Gastel." Kalbasen's reassuring voice cut through the cottony thickness.

"The world has waited." The Trove spoke to Gastel with a frigid, calculated message. "Great Wielder of Anam."

The Trove grinned, sick satisfaction in his upturned lips. No humor. Only a certainty. A knowing so deep and real. He knew the shape of Gastel's existence.

"Great Wielder of Souls."

THIRTY-NINE

At Full Gallop

Rae was frozen in place. It wouldn't be easy to fit through the bedroom window, but it looked like her only way out. That or do as she was told and surrender because drawing her sword wasn't an option. She'd left that life behind. Stepping closer to the doorway, she waited, listening to the shuffling in the street. The guard at the front shifted his weight, his breathing heavy.

"Come on, Raemian; we know you're in there. We have you surrounded."

Weighing her options, none of them seemed favorable. She wasn't particularly interested in standing before Gemma anytime soon.

Goosebumps bloomed down her arms at the sound of clashing steel ringing out in the street. Perhaps they hadn't managed to capture Freck after all? The guard ran from his post at the front entrance, yelling something indiscernible.

She didn't wait for another opening. She dashed down the hall, following the guard out into the street at full speed. As she'd thought, Freck was there, deep in the fray, holding off three guards.

The fourth guard drew his sword as he ran to join his comrades. Rae drew her own, testing its weight in her hand. The world around her slowed, a cold sense of what needed to be done soaking into her flesh. She would protect Freck by whatever means necessary.

Faster than the guard in heavy armor, she sliced across the back of his neck, blade sneaking between the seam of his backplate and helm. He arched his back and crumpled to the ground, face bashing into the dirt road.

Rae exchanged glances with Freck as she deflected a sloppy blow from one of the other guards. Freck's expression changed from anger to genuine relief. He spun, catching one blade and throwing the guard's arm wide before ducking out of the way of another's. If this was any indication of the level of swordsmanship they were up against, she and Freck would make quick work of the rest.

Rae singled out a guard trying to find an opening on Freck's flank. To the woman's credit, she managed to dodge Rae's upward swing, but it only gave Rae a chance to flip her sword and bury it to the hilt in the woman's thigh. She paused long enough for the woman's eyes to widen, then Rae ripped it through the side. Collapsing to the ground, the woman clutched her leg before Rae plunged her sword into the side of the woman's neck, ending her suffering.

Freck traded blows with the last two guards, holding his own perfectly well, but Rae was ready to be finished with the fight. With all her strength, she cleaved the head clean from one guard's neck, his lifeless corpse slumping to the ground at Freck's feet.

The last guard, after having seen what Rae and Freck were capable of, backed up frantically, scrambling to get away. He slammed against the nearest house and held both his arms up.

"Please. Don't kill me. Please."

Freck was angry. Rae hadn't seen such rage in him since the last time they'd fought against a sizable Bleck Larin force. He drove his blade deep through the man's shoulder and into the wall behind.

"Who sent you?" The usually friendly, fun-loving Freck wore a mask of absolute death as he leaned closer. "Who?"

The man squeezed his eyes closed in pain, whimpering as Freck drove the blade farther into the wall behind—steel sliding agonizingly slow through soft flesh.

"Please! The queen! The queen wants her alive. Please don't kill me."

The scent of urine met Rae's nostrils.

Freck yanked his blade out, then jammed his fingers into the wound and pulled the man up on his tiptoes.

"Sorry." Freck plunged his blade into the guard's chest, holding him against the wall as he gurgled and choked on his own blood. "But the bitch can't have her."

Freck let the man slump to the ground before turning to Rae, chest heaving with each breath.

"I'm sorry," Freck said. He leaned against the wall, holding himself up with a blood-slicked hand. "We need to leave, don't we?"

She nodded, then pulled him toward their dwelling.

They worked quickly, cleaning their hands before packing a single bag each and ducking back out into the street under the cover of growing darkness. Rae admired how Freck moved with purpose, his sword drawn as they worked their way through the empty streets of Dormshire to the public stables. If they could get their horses, they'd be in much better shape.

They'd managed to avoid a group of six soldiers running in the general direction of their dwelling, and she was sure there'd be more guards posted at the stables.

Sure enough, as they came into view of the structure, Rae caught a glimpse of two guards, one on either side of the stable door. At least the streets were empty. She nodded in the direction of the guard on the left. Freck didn't need to be told the plan. They'd fought together enough times. She took the guard on the right, covering his mouth and jabbing her dagger under the bottom of his helm into his skull. She lowered him without a sound.

Freck took a slightly more flamboyant approach and tapped the guard on the shoulder. As she turned, he thrust his sword up under her armpit and into her heart. She choked out a scream of pain as he helped her to the ground.

They ducked into the stable, finding their horses but no groom, so they saddled their steeds themselves. Rae wasn't sure she'd ever strapped tack on so quickly in all her life. She prayed she'd remembered to tighten everything as they rode down the main thoroughfare at a dangerous canter. They had only to breach the main gate, which if they were too late would already be locked tightly for the night.

They rode as fast as they dared through the streets, not a word between them, both knowing what they'd have to do if the gate had been barred. While a handful of guards had been easy, the gate force would be something entirely different.

Rae breathed a sigh of relief when she saw the gate was open. There was shuffling and shouting as the guards scrambled to cut them off. Rae nearly ran one man over as he jumped out in front of their horses, but he managed to spring out of their way.

Once through the portcullis, they urged their horses into a hard gallop, driving through the open fields. More shouting and the familiar thrum of arrows being loosed only made Rae spur her horse faster as she and Freck did their best to melt into the night.

FORTY

Voluntary Dismissal

astel didn't leave his room when he woke before sunrise. Instead, he stretched, did calisthenics, and sat in the middle of the cold floor to meditate, trying to rid his thoughts of Inara's charred remains. He needed to temper his anger toward Master Rayken and Effrin Kresha—and all the effrins, were he to be entirely honest with himself. A healer was one thing, but Svet magic? *Resurrection?* This was no way to train. He'd rather hide behind his mother's soul stone for the remainder of his life. He needed to get out of this place before it was him lying in a pile of charred ash on the stone floor.

Gastel jogged to the training hall, getting there just in time.

"Almost late today, Princeling." Kresha tipped her head, a smug smile breaking across her lips. "I'm thinking we test the limits of your power today."

Of course Kresha did. She'd want nothing else than to push until he broke, to learn the full strength of his Anam. Gastel could only shake his head. He was cold, uncomfortable in thin robes, and not interested in her games.

"I think we won't."

He could almost feel the air evaporate around him as the other initiates who had heard the exchange took in sharp breaths at his disrespect.

She frowned. It wasn't her usual malicious frown. It was real disappointment.

"Come now, Gastel. You came to learn to control it. Let me teach you." She took a few steps closer, glittering excitement in her eyes, hands falling to her hips.

"I'm not interested in your method of teaching." Gastel felt the eyes of every elf in the training hall burning into him like a thousand balls of soulfire. "I'm also not interested in dying and being resurrected."

She took two more steps closer, matching his posture. She was inches from him, glaring up at him, daring him.

"I should tell Master Rayken of your insolence. See what he thinks."

Gastel tried to stifle his grin. This was what he wanted. If Rayken turned him away, he wouldn't need to fight his way out. He could leave in peace.

"By all means."

He crossed his arms in contempt and evenly distributed his weight on both legs. He was battle-ready, and judging from the edge of caution in her glare, she knew it.

She stared at him, taking all of him in, but he wouldn't let her manipulate him. Not today, not ever again. When she realized he refused to budge, she stepped back, looking around for the first time at the others, who waited in rapt anticipation for whatever would happen next.

"Oh, go back to training. All of you." She waved them away before pointing at Gastel. "You're dismissed since you *clearly* aren't interested in instruction. I'll be sure to give Master Rayken a full report of your insolence."

A warmth he hadn't felt in days filled his chest. Step one complete.

Being dismissed gave Gastel more than enough time to head back to his room and change into his regular clothes. He stuffed his few belongings into his pack and strapped on his sword for good measure. He planned to attend the midday meal as a prince and then leave the Vail.

But first, he needed to visit someone.

He slipped from his room while everyone was still in training. Rayken was likely hiding away in his study. Gastel moved through the Vail on silent feet until he came to the infirmary and slid the lock open. It took Master Lorilay one look to know why he was there.

"Leaving the Vail already, Highness?"

Her hair was free in glorious waves of snowy white. She was a pretty Shay, her complexion so like Raemian's, her pale-blue eyes holding great wisdom in their depths.

"I can't stay here. I think you knew I wouldn't last long."

He reached for a vine dangling from the ceiling and passed the leaves between his fingers, feeling the silky, smooth warmth of its life.

"I had an inkling." She set the pestle down beside a mortar she'd been working with. "I feel something different about you. A comfort with me that I've done nothing to deserve. As if there's a Shay who holds your heart?"

The smile that had been growing on Gastel's lips was gone in an instant, replaced with narrowed eyes.

"Oh, come now, you needn't hide from me." She quirked an eyebrow at him as she spoke. "This Shay is your balance, Highness. Your steadfastness." She gazed back down at her supplies and started to clean up after herself. "Eishtala and Anam are opposites. Like Shay and Bleck Larin. They balance each other. An ancient equilibrium that has been desecrated over the last thirty years of war."

A comfortable silence settled over them as Lorilay organized a case filled with tiny satchels of dried flowers and herbs.

"I can take you with me," Gastel said.

She shook her head and smiled up at him—so much knowing in the twinkle of those stormy eyes.

"These elflings need me more than I need my freedom." She reached and touched a branch. Gastel felt the surge of life drawing away as its leaves crinkled and fell. When her eyes met his again, they were moist with tears. "I only wish I could help them see that the violence they learn through Rayken only drives them further from balance. Wielding needn't be so destructive."

Her eyes burrowed into Gastel's with some hidden meaning. He desperately tried to grasp it but felt it was just out of reach.

"If not destructive, then what?" He placed his hand on his chest, covering his mother's soul stone.

"Love. Like your mother's." She looked directly at his hand, then back to his eyes. "Protection. Niminea protects you even now."

He took a sharp breath at his mother's name, a name he had not known until recently. A name he had not thought would bring him so much comfort and pain at the same time.

"She protects you from yourself and from others—from Anam itself."

Lorilay stepped toward him, glaring with grave seriousness as she placed a hand on his chest.

It was there all at once. The muscles in his neck tightened as Eishta-la grew and collapsed and grew again, like the waves of the Rahven Sea crashing and pulling away tiny granules of sand. She held him there, as rigid as the stone walls around him. It didn't hurt exactly, just made his face flush and sweat break across his brow. He squeezed his eyes closed against the Eishtala, tearing down walls and rebuilding them. It was heat and magic and *life*.

She stepped away and grabbed the side of a table to steady herself. "Gods. You hold a great power. Your mother was right to protect you. It may never be truly harnessed." She took a few deep breaths, and Gastel reached forward to help steady her as she swayed a little on her feet. "So many souls within you."

"Souls?"

She met his eyes again, the conviction in them terrifying. "You come from a long line of extraordinary wielders, each bestowing their heirs with precious pieces of themselves. At some point, to control the growing power, a soul stone was devised. It can protect the wielder from their own power by locking it away, but it can also protect the wielder from even greater powers, like rifts." Her eyes were daggers. "Niminea died closing the last rift—one to the Eishtala plane of existence—and the rift took its price. I'm certain now that her soul stone was around your neck and not hers. That's the only possible reason she would have died."

He was reminded too clearly of the rift in the Middlelend Forest he and Raemian had stumbled upon. The way it had attacked him, the pain, the dissonance of the screeching that had destroyed his mind and taken all his strength.

"Even dark rifts have latent power. You wouldn't be able to get too close to one." She shook her head slowly. "Not with Niminea's soul stone around your neck." She looked at his chest where the pendant hung under his shirt. "There aren't any rifts open now, though. So much imbalance in the world because of it, too. Niminea and the others in the guild closed them all." She shook her head again. "They threw off the balance, and they all gave their lives for it."

She started putting supplies away again as if the conversation were over, but Gastel had so many more questions. For the second time in his life, he'd found someone who didn't seem afraid to answer them.

"Guild?"

"Oh, there are no more guilds. The old orders are gone, and we've been left floundering." She ducked into a back room and returned, clutching a small leatherbound book. "The old orders were balanced. The Anam Guild, Eishtala Guild, the Svet Guild. They once worked together. Like the Houses of Raggethan, Unnti, and Starling."

The hairs on the back of his neck rose at the mention of the House of Starling. "Why would the guilds close the rifts if it'd cause so much imbalance?"

"The Anam Guild was just doing what they thought was needed to keep Rhend safe." She sighed. "There were better ways, but at the time, it seemed like the only direction. Now we struggle with bigger, older powers.

"Older powers?"

"Ancient magic. Things foretold when the Elder Gods created Rhend."

"I don't follow," Gastel said.

"Good. It's a lot of convoluted nonsense, most of it." She shrugged. "Prophecies make people twitchy. Especially ones that are open to interpretation."

This line of questioning was leading him down a path with an infinite number of doors to open, and he was running short on time.

"You mentioned latent power from a dark rift?"

She frowned, her thoughts seeming to turn inward. "When a rift is closed, the wielder's soul lingers for a time." She tipped her head to the side. "So many questions today, Highness!"

"Since you won't come with me, it's my last chance to ask."

Lorilay glanced down at the book in her hand with sad eyes before she held it out to him. "Take this. It should help you. If nothing else, it will give you guidance."

She smiled timidly as he took it from her hands. Gastel couldn't help but flip it open to the first page. A name was written in beautiful calligraphy.

"Dormel Amfithere?" he read aloud.

Lorilay looked away, her warm smile fading.

"He was my partner, my bondmate until his death. He called it his *Book of All Things Anam*. He was an effrin here and taught beside your mother." When she met Gastel's eyes, he saw so much love. "He was your uncle."

FORTY-ONE

No Rash Decisions

There was something comforting about camping among the trees with Freck. Rae had spent countless missions with him in the Middlelend Forest. Usually without horses and the current of unease that they could be detained by Bleck Larin and Shay alike.

They'd ridden well into the night before Rae felt comfortable stopping to find a place to rest. By the faint light of the moon sifting through the trees, Freck managed to start a meager fire. It was a risk, but he insisted on a hot meal, and Rae was easy to convince. She hadn't eaten since breakfast.

"We didn't fortify your family home." Freck fretted over small things—or perhaps they were just things Rae found small. "Not that we could close the door. Those assholes completely destroyed it!"

Spilling more blood after promising herself that part of her life was passed made it hard for her to focus on something as trivial as boarding up her family dwelling before fleeing for their lives. There was also what Freck had learned regarding Gemma's forces. The entire Shay army was camped outside of Jooshawn awaiting a full-scale attack on Parth. They planned to attack from the west, following the canyon against the Hill of Tombs—exactly as Rae had suspected. What she hadn't realized was that the conscripted soldiers had likely swelled the army to ten thousand strong.

Furthermore, Gemma had relied heavily on the legion's advice and planned to send two contingents as diversions—one through the Middlelend Forest via the Old Road and the other up the Eastern Pass. If Belkin and Roulin had taken Rae's advice to heart, the Shay would be cut off at the Hill of Tombs. Now, Rae worried Belkin might focus all their defenses on the west and leave Parth exposed from the east. Against her better judgment, she and Freck needed to inform him of what they'd discovered.

"We didn't even secure a single shutter," Freck continued, but Rae wasn't listening.

The more she dwelled on it, the more she knew what she had to do.

"Rae, you're stewing. Talk to me."

She met Freck's eyes, which glittered with concern in the firelight.

"She took my entire family, Freck." Rae folded her hands in front of her face, letting her eyes fall to the fire between them. "She needs to be stopped."

"And you aim to stop her single-handed, don't you?" There was an accusatory note in his tone.

"Freck."

"No, Rae. This is ridiculous." Freck glanced into the dark distance. A storm brewed at the corners of his eyes.

"Who else then?"

He only shook his head, looking down at his feet as he pulled his hands to his hips. "I don't know." He faced her, fear and anger written in the crease between his snowy eyebrows. "But it doesn't have to be you."

"This war needs to end, Freck. Gemma needs to be removed from the throne." She searched for the right words to explain. "And I should be the one to do it."

He squeezed his eyes closed, pressing hard on the bridge of his nose. "What madness are you talking about this time? Do what exactly?" He glared, unyielding. "Run headlong into Tremire with your sword in the air? If you're seen anywhere near there, she'll execute you." He swallowed hard, his Adam's apple bobbing. "No, Rae, you can't do this."

But the plan was already coming together. "I can." She met Freck's eyes with conviction. "I must. It has to be me," she continued, even though Freck glared at her with raw anger. "Hear me out. The guard who escorted me before Gemma this last time, I think she was trying to tell me I have support. This, plus the conscripted civilians. I think I could convince them to lay down their arms."

"You've utterly lost your mind."

"If there's no army, there's no war."

"I'm not sure you had a mind in the first place." Freck looked down at his folded arms.

"There's more. The House of Starling is tied to the royal family. Gemma's lifebond to my father was likely a convenient means of tying up whatever loose ends might have been—"

"Are you saying Gemma shouldn't be queen by birthright?" Freck's head snapped back up.

"I'm saying the royal family, when they dropped all allegiance to the Great Houses, was a combination of both the House of Tremire and the House of Starling." Her mind was moving faster than her mouth could. "I think my grandfather was meant to be king, but—"

"But if that were the case, wouldn't Mesmal have known?" Freck interjected. "When the bonding between himself and Gemma was negotiated, wouldn't he have had some kind of knowledge of all this?"

Lifebonds and royalty politics weren't Rae's specialty. For something that seemed so arbitrary to hold such significance seemed archaic to her.

"I don't know. But I must be the one to remove her from the throne."

He shook his head violently. "No, Rae. We need to take what we know to Mesmal, let *him* deal with Gemma. Let him send his army. We both know who'll win. The Bleck Larin are better trained, better equipped, and—as you and I both know—better informed."

Maybe he was right. She placed her hand on her father's bracelet, trying to ignore Freck's poignant stare.

So many secrets floated to the surface, and she was desperate to pluck them up and put them in their rightful place. How much had her father shared with Freck before she'd returned from speaking with Gemma? Regardless, it was time he knew everything.

"My mother was Bleck Larin." Rae waited for him to respond, time dragging out, jagged like the torn edge of a page from a manuscript. "Does that change how you feel about me?"

He turned toward her so quickly Rae flinched.

"Rae. You're my greatest friend. You're a sister to me!" He stepped around the fire, extending a hand toward hers. "As long as you're Raemian Starling, it doesn't matter who your parents were."

He pulled her into his massive arms and squeezed. She submitted, letting his warmth soak in around her apprehensions as he leaned his cheek against the top of her head.

"I love you, Rae."

He didn't release her for a few long and wonderful minutes, filling her heart to overflowing with his unerring friendship. When he loosened his grip, he took her shoulders, forcing her to face him.

"Rae, you can't fault yourself in any of this."

She couldn't look him in the eyes. It wasn't that she felt at fault so much as that she felt a constant undercurrent of guilt for her contribution to the queen's vengeful efforts. She'd taken the lives of countless elves. She'd fought for the queen. Had believed the propaganda, all of which had been completely unfounded. She hadn't thought for herself, a mistake she'd never make again.

The sun had not yet broken the horizon when Rae woke. She lay gazing up at the canopy for what seemed like hours, letting her mind drift through all the possible decisions spread before her. Her heart was a stone in her chest, frozen and immovable. She knew what she needed to do, and as she listened to the soft snores of Freck beside her, she knew when she had to do it.

Freck wouldn't willingly let her go. She'd have to sneak away. Rae would remove Gemma from the throne one way or the other, and while she hoped it wouldn't come to it, she'd assassinate her if need be.

She closed her eyes and saw Gastel's face in her memory—his warm, amber eyes; his soft, unruly hair. She hoped he wouldn't hate her. Not when so many lives could be saved—Shay and Bleck Larin alike. At least she wasn't breaking her promise. This wasn't a rash decision.

This was the *only* decision.

Rae lifted her exhausted body from the forest floor. She removed her father's bracelet and placed it on the pommel of her sword. She strapped Freck's much heavier broadsword to her side before slinging her pack of provisions onto her back. By the light of the dying stars, she led her horse through the trees to the edge of the Middlelend Forest. Though she knew Freck would be sound asleep for another hour or so, she looked back every few minutes to make sure she wasn't being followed.

The sun began to warm the sky as she swung herself into the saddle and turned her horse in Tremire's direction. She prayed to the Elder Gods that Freck would return safely to Parth with their precious intel—and that Gastel would forgive her.

FORTY-TWO

Last Supper

When Gastel stepped into the dining room, he expected an elaborate reaction. He was, after all, not only back in his regular clothes of deep-red brocade and black pants, but fully armed, his pack slung across his body.

He slipped into his usual spot at the table beside the other initiates. Several of them shifted away from him, and he waited as every eye turned in his direction. By the grace of the Elder Gods, he maintained a calm composure even as his heart slammed against the inside of his rib cage.

Gastel glanced up to the head of the table with as much confidence as he could muster and met the master's icy glare, those ancient, yellow eyes always in a state of anger. The two of them stared at each other for a solid thirty seconds before Master Rayken stood and pointed to him, the end of his slender finger glowing with Anam.

"You are no longer welcome in this place."

A wave of relief washed over Gastel. This was exactly what he'd wanted—to be turned away without another ball of fire being lobbed in his direction.

Step two complete.

"You have shamed the Vail," Master Rayken spat.

Kresha rose from her seat, hot fury radiating from every inch of her flesh. Perhaps she'd be punished for not being able to tame him? Perhaps she actually *did* care about his success? She ignited her soulflame as she stepped away from the table. All the sinister games she'd played were gone. She built the soulfire in her hand to a tremendous size in such a shockingly quick amount of time that Gastel almost wanted to stay, if only to learn how.

Almost.

He slid from his seat and faced her, hoping the calm exterior he'd carefully wrapped himself in held as his insides turned to mush.

"Come now, Princeling. Time to leave." Her voice dripped with venom.

Kalbasen drew himself up from the table as well, palpable bitterness crossing his face. "Leave him alone, Kresha. He wishes to go peacefully."

Her high-pitched laugh cut through the room, causing several elflings to scramble out of the way, one of them running from the dining room.

Gastel turned at a soft touch on his arm.

"I'll go with you," Inara said, her timid eyes holding his.

He smiled. He'd hoped she'd leave with him. This poor girl had already been through so much at the hands of these sadistic wielders. The scars from her last unfortunate injury were still shadows on her neck.

He looked back to Kresha as the soulfire left her hand. This time, he wouldn't let Inara defend him, wouldn't let anyone take the blast in his place. He pushed Inara toward Kalbasen, which left him no time to remove his soul stone. He met the Anam with open palms.

The fire bit into his hands, singeing his fingertips, trailing up his wrists, and melting into his arms. But when he looked down, his hands appeared to be completely fine. He took a sharp breath. He had absorbed Kresha's blow and was left with nothing but two hands of coursing soulfire.

He pulled the soul stone from around his neck and tucked it into the pouch on his belt. Impatient to be free, his soul pressed hungrily at the edges of his corporeal body, waiting for his fingers to slip from the silver.

Kresha backpedaled toward Rayken, who stood with his mouth wide and his eyes wider. He clearly hadn't been made aware of Gastel's power, but Kresha knew better. Gastel drew the fire into himself, trying to control it, but like every other time, he was unsuccessful; the flames continued to dance over the surface of his skin.

He turned toward Inara. "Take anyone who wishes to leave, and meet me at the front gate. I must teach my own lesson before we go."

She nodded and did as she was bade, racing from the dining hall.

When Gastel turned back, Kresha had pooled her power again and was building it into a coiled snake writhing in the space above her hands. The fact that she refused to back down was curious. Part of him wondered if she knew something he didn't, but he was certain after having spent most of the day scouring the pages of his uncle's journal that the likes of normal Anam were no match for what he possessed. It had been the same for his mother—something that had caused her much strife when she'd trained within these very walls. Something Dormel Amfithere had documented in detail during his unyielding quest to help his sister control her immense powers.

Master Rayken stepped in front of Kresha and flicked his hand, blowing the fire from her fingers with dangerous ease.

"So you do possess your mother's power." He smiled, one of genuine glee. It may have been the first time he'd smiled in over a hundred years. "Dare I say even more."

Rayken held his hands up, seemingly ripping soulfire from the air and swirling it around himself.

Of course the old master would possess great Anam. Had Gastel been so foolish to think he didn't? The difference was that Rayken knew how to control and manipulate it. Whether that made him dangerous, Gastel was certain he'd find out.

"I shall teach you how to wield this strength, boy," the old wielder said.

Rayken launched spears of soulflame directly at Gastel's heart. At the last second, he managed to roll out of the way and came up with his sword in his hand. The blade was encased with the same fire surrounding his body. Not for the first time, he wondered whether an elder Anam Wielder such as Rayken could defend against steel.

"I don't appreciate the way you teach your lessons here," Gastel said.

He didn't wait for Rayken to mount another attack. He rushed him, sword held ready to block. Rayken managed to throw a meager spear of soulfire in his direction, and Gastel sliced through it, at least satisfying his question as to whether he could defend against Anam with traditional weapons.

He stopped only inches from the old wielder, the edge of his sword a hair's breadth from Rayken's throat.

"I'm leaving. And I'm ready to fight my way out if I must."

The old wielder closed his eyes and drew his fire back into himself, the extinguished flames twisting up into the rafters as he lowered his arms. When he opened his eyes again, all the anger was gone, replaced with a peaceful smile that looked wrong on the old master's lips.

"Leave this place, Gastel, son of Niminea. May the Elder Gods guide your soul."

Rayken turned and left the dining hall, passing Kresha, who simply stood with wide eyes. Gastel slid his sword into its scabbard and pulled the pendant back over his head, extinguishing the flames from his flesh. He looked over at the elflings who were paralyzed against the walls. There was genuine terror written across their faces—real and terrible.

"If you wish to leave, I will take you with me, but we leave now."

He turned to go just as Master Lorilay entered with one of the initiates close behind. They'd probably anticipated carnage but found only a room of startled students and effrins.

Lorilay bowed before she approached, a grin spreading across her face. He returned her smile, warmth growing in his chest. The journal Master Lorilay had given him had contained a wealth of information. He'd already learned so much more about his powers than he had in the hours he'd spent with Kresha.

"Niminea would be proud of you."

He bowed in return and then met her eyes with a seriousness he hoped she noticed. "Thank you. For everything."

She nodded. He wished he could say more, but he didn't have the words ready.

Gastel found Inara and Jad, the only two apprentices who had decided to leave, waiting with a handful of initiates. Inara handed Gastel a cloak, and he couldn't put it on fast enough. Thank the Gods for warmth! He threw it over his shoulders and thanked her with a warm hand on the top of her head.

As the gate opened, a familiar voice wafted down the hall: "I hope there's room for one more."

It was Kalbasen, jogging to catch up, a cloak already wrapped over his shoulders and a bag slung on his back. Gastel grasped Kal's wrist with fervor. He was growing fond of the effrin, quite possibly the only instructor with any compassion for his students. It was a shame he was leaving because Kal was exactly what the Vail needed most.

They turned south, the frigid winds off the Rahven Sea whipping against their backs, urging them forward. The frozen earth gave way to an ocean of ruddy clay scarred with the cracks of drought. If it had been cold within the Vail, it was bitter out, and Gastel pulled the cloak around himself tighter. It'd be a long walk, but worth every league.

FORTY-THREE

Dulanii

The Middlelend Forest cut a line through the otherwise flat expanse of the moors, giving Belkin a chill of caution. He preferred featureless earth. It afforded greater visibility of what was coming. Places like the Eastern Pass, which rolled out from the foothills of the mountains—the dusty plains of the wilds as they melted into the tundra to the north—these places were smooth and endless until they nestled against the horizon. These were the places he liked.

The trees ahead reminded him that they had yet to locate Gemma's army. It felt like failure, and Belkin never failed. With Gastel at the Vail, his father had been floundering. Mesmal was a sentimental old man— far too reliant on his youngest son's albeit enlightened opinions.

Belkin reined in Jore and stopped in view of the Old Road. He'd been riding out each morning to check on the sentinels positioned within the treeline. Thus far, there had been no Shay activity. Today, however, Belkin's chest burst with a momentary rush of joy as one of the sentinels pulled along a tall Shay, shirtless, hands bound. He urged Jore in their direction.

"Hail, Prince Belkin." The soldier saluted with an open hand to the chest, palm down, before yanking the rope to pull the Shay forward.

Belkin found himself looking into a pair of frustratingly familiar blue eyes. Ones he had never wanted to see again. They meant Raemian Starling was in proximity or in trouble; considering that Dulanii was alone, the latter was more likely. He dismounted, cutting the rope from the Shay's wrists, unable to keep the crooked smile from forming on his lips.

"We meet again, Dulanii." He tipped his head back and raised a curious eyebrow at the Shay's bravery. "One of these times, you'll get yourself killed crossing into Bleck Larin territory."

Belkin sensed by the pained expression on Dulanii's face that his explanation for being there wasn't favorable.

The Shay bowed respectfully, eyes falling and holding on Belkin's boots. "Gemma's army is staging in Jooshawn, south of the Forest of Tremire. She plans to send the bulk of her forces along the Hill of Tombs, with diversionary contingents up the Old Road and the Eastern Pass. She has over ten thousand." The Shay looked up, eyes cloudy with concern. "It would have been Rae and me delivering this message, but she's gone to rally the Shay with the promise of peace or to assassinate the queen." Dulanii swallowed hard. "Whichever will end Gemma's reign."

"Fucking Shay woman." Belkin straightened his posture when Dulanii's eyes grew round.

Raemian was a formidable fighter, exceptional at finding meaning in nuance, but clearly didn't understand restraint. She'd surely get herself killed, and if Gastel would be anything like his father when he lost those he cared for, it didn't bode well. Belkin had seen what his youngest brother could do. His Anam was terrifying and uncontrolled.

Belkin turned to the sentinel. "I need your horse." After mounting Jore, he motioned for Dulanii to follow. The sooner they got back to the castle stronghold, the better.

The ride felt longer than it should have been. This wasn't helped by the fact that the Shay riding alongside him garnered a fair number of sideways glances from the smattering of elves they passed. If Dulanii noticed, he said nothing; each time Belkin looked in his direction, he was met with the man's undivided attention.

He was used to riding with Tildimin or Roulin. Dulanii wore an expression like Belkin's father, but with a cloying mirth ready to burst from him at a moment's notice. The Shay should have been nervous about his surroundings. Instead, he seemed curious, his eyes touching everything they passed in Parth.

"Your father's castle looks more foreboding from this angle," Dulanii said as they passed through the opened portcullis.

Belkin had never considered how intimidating his home must appear to those who didn't belong. It had always been a symbol of Bleck Larin strength. As the two of them rode into the bailey and were greeted by a groom, Belkin threw the Shay a sly grin.

"Clearly not foreboding enough to keep you from coming back." Belkin swung down from his horse and turned to Dulanii. "I may need some suggestions on how to keep you pests at bay."

Dulanii handed his reins off and winked at Belkin, a sultry smile turning up his lips. "It'd be my pleasure, Highness."

Belkin shook his head, rolling his eyes as he mounted the steps to the front gate. He moved through the stronghold with purpose, heading to his father's study after finding the throne room empty. Dulanii didn't seem to mind the reckless pace. Instead, the Shay had a spring of confidence to his step that only fueled Belkin to walk faster.

His father was slumped over correspondence yet again. He'd been scouring through old letters for weeks now, and Belkin was beginning to question the man's sanity.

"Dulanii!" Mesmal rose from his seat with a genuine smile, eyes bright with happiness for the first time in days. It was clear he'd grown fond of the Shay in the short time Dulanii had stayed with them before.

Belkin stood stiffly idle as the two men embraced, his father a full head taller but shoulders half the width of Dulanii's.

"Where's Raemian?" his father asked as he looked past the Shay.

"She's gone to confront Gemma and stop this war," Dulanii said.

Mesmal shook his head. "This won't do. Why didn't you stop her?"

Dulanii pulled the sword from his belt. Belkin recognized the pommel, the silver braided wire that wrapped the handle. An engraving of a starling on the ricasso confirmed it. He swore under his breath. Raemian knew exactly what she was walking into and didn't intend to return.

Dulanii knelt and raised the sword to the king's hands, his movements slow, intentional.

"She snuck away while I was asleep. She left her sword and Somin's bracelet."

His father wrapped slender fingers around the band hooked to the pommel and pulled it away, sadness building where the king usually wore a mask of calm.

"Thankfully, Gastel is still at the Vail. If he finds out she's..." Mesmal didn't finish; he didn't need to.

Belkin hoped he'd hardened his expression into his customary unfettered sternness when his father faced him. He wasn't entirely sure how he should feel about Raemian. It had been easy to hate her, but it was growing easier not to.

"This won't do," his father said again.

"Gemma will likely have her executed," Dulanii said, starting to lose his composure. This great beast of a Shay with all his muscles and strength, and he was tearing up? "I've failed her. I shouldn't have slept; I should have—"

Belkin placed a hand on Dulanii's shoulder. "Raemian does not strike me as the type to run blindly to her death. She must feel she can succeed in this, or she wouldn't have gone."

Dulanii's eyes grew large. It was the nicest thing Belkin had said about a Shay in an exceedingly long time. Belkin hadn't been sure he was capable of such compassion toward them, not after years of fighting. He was growing soft.

He faced his father with conviction. "Gemma has amassed an army of ten thousand strong. Dulanii reports that they plan to attack from the west, with sizable diversionary forces from the Eastern Pass and the Old Road," Belkin said, standing a little straighter. "I'll send Roulin with the bulk of the forces to the west and prepare contingency defenses for the diversionary attacks before I join him."

His father's expression went from saddened to serious, lips drawn into a thin line. Belkin had seen him like this once before. *Good.* He needed his father to understand how serious this was. Ten thousand was the largest Shay force they'd ever fought. If they pulled all their trained soldiers to arms, they'd be just shy of three thousand, and Bleck Larin weren't as strong. Taller, yes; better equipped, most certainly; better trained...but there were plenty of traits that Shay elves possessed that could tip the scales in their favor.

His father cleared his throat, the mask of a king falling back over his face. "Send emissaries to all the strongholds and request that any able-bodied and willing Bleck Larin report for battle training immediately," the king said, a dark timbre to his voice. "I shall pull back the armory reserves from Korthan and draw your brother home from the

Vail. You and Roulin will require all the assistance you can get to keep our citizens safe."

It was the first time his father had made such sweeping orders since the first invasion of Dormshire. The Culling had spurred him into action, and it had taken thirty-two years and a real threat to their people to motivate him again. King Mesmal was done with Gemma's games.

Belkin nodded, a plan forming in place. He turned to Dulanii and bowed before leaving the Shay in the company of his father. A few weeks ago, he never would have thought to allow a Shay anywhere near the king, but Raemian had changed that.

Raemian had changed a lot of things.

———

Gastel couldn't help the warm giddiness wrapping around his heart as Parth sprouted up around him. The elflings were weary of walking. Gods, they were all weary of walking, but it was only a little farther.

Elves milling about the busy cobbled streets recognized him, some bowed and moved aside, their eyes lingering longer than necessary on his cropped hair. He returned their courteous gestures, nodding but never stopping.

He was home. Gods, *he was home.* He could jump into action with his brothers. He could worry about the challenges of his Anam Wielding later, when he had more time and, frankly, more interest.

As the castle stronghold came into sight, he quickened his pace. Sweat beaded at Kalbasen's brow, and some of the younger elflings had fallen behind, but it did little to slow Gastel. He was home! As they broke into the main courtyard of the castle stronghold, he turned, walking backward so he could see the others' faces.

"How do you have this much energy after the leagues we've walked?" Kal asked.

"Because I'm home."

Kal shook his head, a sideways smirk crossing his face.

Gastel left Kalbasen and the elflings in the attendance of servants and sprinted toward the throne room. He wanted to speak with his father before he allowed himself the luxury of relaxation. It was empty. Usually he'd be helping his father with the citizen hearings at this time of day. He ducked his head into the strategy room and found it empty as well. The halls of the stronghold seemed particularly sparse of servants as Gastel jogged, a frantic beating of his heart mirroring his urgency.

Something was wrong. Something must have happened.

Gastel knocked timidly on the door of his father's study and heard a calm response from within. He entered to find his father...and Dulanii.

Unraveling

R ae crept into Tremire unnoticed, stalking between the residences near the center of the city. It wasn't until she neared the Court of Tremire that she saw a Shay walking with his head down, moving with purpose. Like Dormshire, the streets were unusually quiet.

The court had been left unguarded, so she slipped in and found it empty. It was truly a beautiful place when you weren't standing before Queen Gemma and her unrelenting glare. The dais Gemma's throne occupied was seamless, appearing to grow from the floor itself. Branches twisted together into a single cohesive structure with vines weaving overhead into the shape of the beloved ancient ironwood tree—the Shay crest pride and joy. An infinity symbol encircled the trunk, added later using lighter sapwood.

Murals fashioned from thousands of tiny pieces of inlaid wood decorated the walls, the panels illustrating the remnants of history with startling clarity. The Elder Gods splitting the races. Bestowing Eishtala magic upon the Shay. The crafting of the City of Tremire. The banishing of humans from Rhend. The crowning of Queen Gemma.

Sheer green fabric, much like the cloaks of the Eishtala Masters, hugged great windows that had been cut through the sides of the ancient tree in intricate patterns that emulated stained glass. Even the floor had been inlaid with scrolling swirls that directed the eye around the court and up to the dais. In the center, delicate lattice patterns bordered a map of the Shaylands with devastating detail. When this room was full of noblemen, attendants, and guards, many of these intricacies were lost beneath robes. Seeing it now, everything in pieces yet as a single beautiful masterpiece of magic and artistry, wound a ribbon of true adoration around Rae's heart.

She marveled for another moment before heading to a small door that led into a strategy room. It had been abandoned in a hurry. A handful of scrolls were scattered about, some strewn on the floor. A book lay open on the long meeting table. Chairs were pulled back and pushed in at different angles.

She stepped around to the head of the table where Gemma usually sat and glanced around the room, trying to see everything from her stepmother's view. The light from a window behind carved a path across a pile of wrinkled scrolls pressed flat. She glanced down at another scroll abandoned on the floor—a map of Rhend. Her attention snagged on a single slip of paper crumpled beside Gemma's chair. It might have been missed if she hadn't thought to walk around the room. Compelled by some strange nagging in the back of her mind, she retrieved it, spreading it out on the table.

"You would still risk everything for pride?
The Sundering approaches.

The Great Wielder lives within another.
It's time to choose your side."

There was no signature, no way of knowing who the note had been from. Rae folded it and slipped it into a pocket before glancing down at the book. She was surprised to see it opened to a page on the House of Starling, the elegant letters standing out in high contrast against the brittle, yellowed paper. She didn't have time to sit and read. It had already been a risk coming to the court in the first place. She slid the manuscript into her pack for later.

As silently as she'd come, she slipped back into the court. The calm, warm fragrance of ironwood stopped her in her tracks. The room changed when empty, amorphous, ready to be molded into whatever she desired. Rae closed her eyes, reminding herself she needed to find and confront her stepmother. Step one in a greater plan for peace.

Ducking out into the afternoon warmth, Rae took an indirect route back to the north of the city. She wasn't certain where to go, but the risk of being found grew greater the longer she lingered. Her feet took her toward the highlands as she analyzed everything she had learned so far. She'd find someplace to collect herself, look through the book, and plan her next move.

She headed west along the rim of the forest, searching for a place to rest for the night. Usually, there were small stables, woodcutter's hovels, or other small structures inside the forest line, but perhaps she was too far from Tremire? Her eyes traced the horizon. She spotted a small shack wedged against a massive boulder.

The unlocked door seemed in good repair, the woodwork freshly painted. She stepped in, glancing around to find it almost empty. A three-legged stool occupied a far corner with a table large enough for a plate of food. Overall, it was clean, with signs of recent use. Hopefully not too recent.

Rae leaned Freck's sword against a wall, dropped her pack to the ground, and plopped onto the stool, a sigh escaping her lips. No sooner had she sat than she heard a voice. She leaned forward, trying to identify where it came from. Looking back toward the door, it sounded as though it came from the wall that faced the rock, but before she could confirm, it stopped.

Minutes stretched as Rae strained to hear the voice again. She eased back against the wall. Maybe it had been her imagination? How could a voice have come from a rock anyway?

Metal grinding against metal brought Rae up out of the chair. She was certain she'd heard it that time. As she reached for Freck's sword, the entire wall swung forward, revealing a pitch-black hole in the rock. A gray-fleshed face materialized from the darkness, meeting Rae with a familiar set of amber eyes.

—+——— ———+—

Gastel looked between his father and Dulanii, a tickle of concern working its way up his spine. "Dulanii? What are you doing here?"

Dulanii stood and gave a friendly yet uncertain wave.

"Gastel!" His father swept forward. "My son, have you followed my summons so quickly?" There was an anxious quality to his question.

"Where's Raemian?"

Dulanii couldn't hold his eyes. Instead, the Shay glanced at the king, his snowy eyebrows pinched with concern.

Gastel's blood ran cold with fear, followed by a flood of terrible, bitter-tasting anger. *He knew it.* She had done what he'd asked, nay, *begged* her not to do. Without another word, he turned and fled down the hall, shedding his riding cloak and his pack as he went. He wouldn't need them where he was going. He needed only himself, his sword, and this burning rage.

Firm hands on his shoulders forced him to stop and spun him around with shocking strength. He forgot how strong Shay could be.

"Gastel, you can't just run into Tremire with your sword held high. Rae had a plan. She had a reason for going."

Gastel squeezed his eyes closed, pressing the bridge of his nose. When he opened them again, he was sure the fury melting his insides was visible on his face.

"She said she wouldn't do anything rash," Gastel said between clenched teeth.

Dulanii seemed undeterred by his rage. If he'd known what Gastel was capable of, he might have exercised more caution.

"She isn't. *She hasn't.* We learned what Gemma's plans are, and Rae truly thinks she can sway the Shay to peace. To remove Gemma from the throne."

Dulanii took a deep breath, letting it out more slowly than Gastel would have liked. He knew the Shay had more to say, and he needed him to hurry up and say it.

"If she can't sway them, she plans to remove the queen by whatever means necessary. For the good of all our kind."

Gastel's entire body felt full of molten metal burning out from a core of solid vengeance. He could see her blue eyes in his mind—her red hair, the color of blood against pale, pink flesh.

"I *begged* her."

"Gastel, you're the last person she'd ever want to hurt," Dulanii said.

His father had caught up to them, and Gastel couldn't risk meeting his glance. Gods, he was angry. Angry that Raemian would put herself in danger, that Dulanii would let her leave his side, even for a second.

Angry at his own lack of knowledge. Angry that any of this, any warring and hatred and death, was something they had to deal with.

"You were supposed to keep her safe." His voice cracked with accusation as he glared at Dulanii.

He hadn't wanted her to leave for this exact reason. Now he felt he couldn't move fast enough. How long since she'd left Dulanii's side? How far was she from Tremire? How much time did he have?

Did he have any time at all?

The picture of what he had to do grew clearer in his mind. He was going to ride through the Middlelend Forest, cross the highlands, and race into Tremire, his fiery soul freed, his flaming sword drawn. May the Elder Gods themselves burn pure within the Anam he'd wield.

"You can't just run headfirst into the Shaylands." Dulanii was stern this time.

"You've already said as much."

Gastel got the distinct impression that Dulanii wasn't used to being the voice of reason but that the Shay was completely prepared to do whatever was in his power to prevent Gastel from making a terrible decision. It was evident in the stony resolve he wore across his face and the firm grip he had on Gastel's shoulder.

The longer Gastel was forced to think about it, the more he realized how right Dulanii was. Damn the Elder Gods, this wasn't how he wanted this to go.

FORTY-FIVE

The Aequus

Rae looked straight into the face of the elfling she'd freed in the Middlelend Forest. The one who had been the catalyst of events over the last several weeks, forcing Rae to reevaluate everything.

"It's *you*!" the girl said, frozen in place. "But they took you."

"I see you managed to make it out of the Middlelend Forest without getting caught in another trap," Rae said, leaning the sword against the wall again. "Was your father terribly cross?"

The girl pressed her lips together as though she'd already said too much.

"My name is Rae, by the way." Rae lifted her hands to show she had no weapons. "I'm happy to see you're alive."

"I'm Geri." The girl stepped out of the darkness and into the shack, pushing the panel all the way open. "And I have no idea how you're alive."

Rae couldn't keep her eyes from looking past the girl into the abyss behind her. It was clear that there were steps that went down, but where did they go?

"It's a long story." Rae threw her a crooked smile and sat back down in the chair. "I'd ask what a Bleck Larin is doing here, but I have a feeling I know." Rae gave the girl her undivided attention. "Which begs the question: why would an Aequus run away?"

"That's also a long story." Geri's candor was disarming.

"I guess we start easy then." Rae crossed her legs. "What's down there?" She indicated with a tip of her chin.

Geri glanced over her shoulder as if to confirm what Rae was asking about. "That?" Her eyes were large when she turned back. "That's um..."

"I was only looking for a place to rest for the night before I leave for Jooshawn."

"What's in Jooshawn?"

"Hopefully, the queen." At the mention of Gemma, Geri seemed to sink into herself, shoulders collapsing. Rae knew she needed to elaborate. "I need to stop this war."

"Oh." The hesitation on Geri's face blossomed into a warm grin. "In that case, you should meet with Freya. She can probably help you."

The last time Rae had gone near this girl, it hadn't ended so well, but Rae didn't have many options. This Freya individual sounded better than nothing.

"I hope she can." She grabbed her pack and sword as Geri motioned for her to follow into the darkness.

Rae was glued in place, gritting her teeth. She wasn't one for underground passages. Plus, this could easily be a trap.

Geri didn't wait for her to consider her options. The girl descended into the shadows as Rae waged battle with herself over whether the risk was worth another potential ally. In the end, she realized she needed everyone she could get and plunged into the unknown.

There was no handrail, so Rae grasped the carved stone walls to guide her. As if Geri had heard Rae's thoughts, the girl struck her soultorch; the eerie, amber light burst across the surface of cut granite converging around them.

The floor of the cave eventually leveled out to smooth, less carved, more naturally derived stone and led into a massive cavern with a vaulted ceiling lined with delicate stalactites. Rae's breath caught as she realized every inch of the ceiling was encrusted with clear crystals growing from the stone itself. They reflected the fire from Geri's soultorch and sprayed shards of broken rainbows across their path.

"So beautiful!"

Geri looked back with a wide grin. "The Trove elves know how to find the best caves!"

Yes. Yes, they did.

A light grew ahead as they left the crystal-studded cavern behind, entering another narrow, winding cave, the mouth of which was flanked by torches. Rae thought she might have heard voices, but it could have been the distorted echoes of their footfalls.

They rounded a corner and met a Bleck Larin and a Shay sitting at a low table and speaking with soft voices. When they saw Geri, they smiled in greeting, not bothering to stand. When their eyes fell to Rae, however, both men were on their feet in an instant, swords rasping as they left scabbards.

"She's a friend!" Geri gestured for the men to put their weapons down. "She's the Shay who saved me in the Middlelend Forest."

The Bleck Larin stepped forward, motioning with his sword tip to the weapon on Rae's hip, which, to her credit, she'd managed to keep her hands away from.

"Drop your sword."

Rae held both hands up in a show of peace before pulling Freck's obnoxiously large blade from its scabbard, setting it at her feet.

"She's a soldier, Geri. You're an idiot," the Shay said. He did not sound nearly as friendly. He pointed to the royal emblem embroidered on Rae's leather scouting jerkin.

Geri's expression fell, marked with desperate devastation.

"I was, but not any longer." Rae ran her hands down the front of her scouting uniform. "A good leather jerkin seemed a waste to destroy for the sake of an emblem that means nothing to me anymore."

Rae was spared further interrogation by the gentle voice of a Shay woman who stepped from the cavern beyond: "I can remove the embroidery if you'd like. These men get a little jumpy when they see Gemma's emblem."

Gods knew how long the woman had been listening. She showed no fear, no hesitation. She approached with a welcoming smile, hands outstretched to take Rae's into her own.

"I'm Freya. Welcome, and thank you for saving Geri's life in the Middlelend Forest." She looked over her shoulder at the men. "She was sure you'd been taken by the Bleck Larin trackers and, most likely, long dead."

These people didn't need to know that she *had* been taken and that she'd been dragged before the king himself. She wasn't ready to trust them with the knowledge that she'd found a friend in King Mesmal, that her loyalty to his people was currently far stronger than her ties to Queen Gemma and the Shay. That the reason she was no longer in the royal army was because her own stepmother had forsaken her, executed her father, and would kill her as well if given the chance. They didn't need to know any of this.

Not yet, anyway.

"I'm Rae, and I'm immensely happy that Geri made it home safely." Rae let the tiniest seed of trust begin to germinate as she bowed to Freya. "And I would love to have the embroidery removed."

Freya nodded as she turned, and Rae followed her deeper into the underground compound. They stepped into a larger chamber where Bleck Larin and Shay sat together at a long table on the far side. They looked up at her out of curiosity, then went back to their conversation.

"They won't bother you, dear. They trust who I trust." Freya had a wide grin and caring eyes that showed hints of age at the corners. Her shaymarks clung tightly to her hairline, wrapping all the way around her forehead and blending into brilliant red hair tied loose at her nape. Her lips seemed to rest in a constant upward curve, joy radiating from her crystal-blue eyes.

She led Rae toward a workstation along one of the walls. Needles, scissors, and other sewing implements were sprawled out on the tabletop. Bolts of fabric were stacked beside it; scraps of leather overflowed from a basket on the shelves carved into the stone behind. There were bins with spools of thread and yarn, others with basic healing supplies and bandages, and jars with herbs and unlabeled powders. Things for fixing clothes and for fixing elves.

"You may want to take it off. It'll make it faster and safer for you," Freya said with a wink.

Rae unclasped the toggles and pulled her jerkin off, handing it to Freya with full confidence. "Shay and Bleck Larin living together seems…" She couldn't find the words.

The group at the table kept glancing in her direction—not maliciously, but with the same curiosity she felt toward them.

The room was sparsely furnished. A crude kitchen with a long utilitarian workbench and open shelves faced Freya's workstation. In the far corner, tables with seats enough for twenty elves sat across from a small, comfortable sitting area. There were a couple of bookcases laden with more than just books. Nothing was extravagant or overstated.

Freya motioned for Rae to sit before pulling a tiny, hooked blade from a drawer. She used it to deftly cut away the embroidery threads one by one.

"We call ourselves Aequus."

Rae's attention snapped back to Freya. To hear the word spoken solidified what Rae had already assumed.

"We're neutral elves. We don't side with Shay or Bleck Larin, though at least Mesmal is a shade more becoming. We don't have a sovereign. And we like it that way."

As Freya's hands removed the queen's emblem, Rae let her mind work through the meaning of the word. Neutral. Impartial and unbiased.

"You fought for Gemma. Why have you chosen to abandon that life?" Freya tucked a stray lock of her hair behind an ear and continued her work.

Freya seemed to expect an answer, watching Rae from the corner of her eye and listening to everything—every word, every intonation. The placement of Rae's hands in her lap, the way she looked around the room. Rae could see the same eye for detail in this woman as she had.

She pulled the words apart, dissecting the question. What answer could she give? To explain to a stranger how she'd not been given a choice when she'd first been sent to fight but how she'd finally found the voice to stop was challenging.

"I can no longer condone what the queen asks of me." Keeping the tremor from her voice was difficult. "To continue fighting in her war and forced to leave everything I know and love behind. I'm not particularly pleased with my options."

The emblem slowly disappeared from the front of her jerkin, one thread at a time. Rae hadn't anticipated the weight she'd carried until it fell away with each piece of gold thread. She gazed down at her hands in her lap, stained so many times with the blood of elves, the edges of her eyes pooling with tears until the lower third of her vision was obscured.

"This is your past now," Freya said.

Her nimble fingers cut away the last of the threads and pulled them free. Freya massaged the leather, closing some of the pinholes so that only the slightest indication remained, and held the jerkin out for Rae to inspect.

"See? Only a whisper. You will know what was there, but others need not. You have changed. Grown. And you will continue to do so." Freya leaned forward and placed a hand over Rae's. "You can choose to forgive or continue to punish yourself, but I think we both know you wouldn't be here if you didn't have a good heart."

Rae pulled on her jerkin, the cool leather stretched tightly around her, hugging her curves—or lack thereof—with protection and comfort. She spread her hands down the front, then met Freya's eyes, a grin spreading across her face.

"Thank you. For this and for your words."

Freya put her tools away and swept the loose threads with her hands into a waste bin, throwing away the last of Rae's former identity.

"Now then, it's time for the evening meal. Would you care to help us prepare?"

FORTY-SIX

The Measure of Friendship

Gastel had forgotten how it felt the first time he'd crossed the Middlelend Forest's depths, the strange way the trees muffled the sounds of life. The smell of earthworms and wet wood and growing things.

Birdsong followed him and Dulanii from high in the canopy. Smaller animals scurried away, their manic rustling the only evidence of their existence. Thankfully, this time there was no rain to soak into Gastel's bones, but there was also no Raemian scouting ahead, twisting through the forest, her red braid streaming behind her.

It took an hour under the trees for Gastel to lose the anger that compelled him to plunge into this latest quest. Now he was left with a hollow place in his stomach. He hadn't been home long enough to properly greet his father, to speak with Belkin about defensive efforts, to say farewell to Kalbasen, Inara, and the initiates.

"You're not what I imagined." Dulanii plucked Gastel from his thoughts after a lengthy silence passed between them.

"How you imagined?"

"Yeah." Dulanii glanced over his shoulder, a sly grin spreading across his lips. "Belkin isn't exactly friendly."

"You probably wouldn't be either if you had to deal with Roulin regularly."

They chuckled together, the last of the tension between them evaporating into the trees.

"My image of royalty is based purely on Gemma, but you and your father are so *nice*." Dulanii slowed, letting Gastel catch up to him. The two men walked side by side. "I've spent the last several years fighting Bleck Larin, and I never once wondered if they could be friendly." His voice dipped. When Gastel glanced over, he saw that Dulanii's face was drawn. "I never stopped to ask if Bleck Larin were just like us, if they had friends and families and—"

Gastel stopped abruptly, grasping the Shay's shoulder. "I knew nothing of the world outside Parth a few weeks ago, Dulanii. We can only know what we've been allowed to learn."

A smile crept across the Shay's face. He shook his head in wonder. "I get it now."

"Get what?"

Dulanii hummed with knowing, resting his hands on his hips before he continued through the trees at a much slower pace. "I get why Rae didn't kill you." Dulanii glanced up at the treetops high above. "Can you imagine the rewards she'd have received? Gemma never seems pleased with her no matter how well she performs in battle." His eyes found Gastel's again. "I might not have been so softhearted with such accolades on the line."

Dulanii's bluntness forced a kernel of caution into Gastel's mind, his fingers itching to reach for his blade. Raemian had always seemed overly courteous. He couldn't ignore that she'd been perfectly capable. The duel with Belkin in his father's study had been proof enough of her prowess. Something else had held her back.

"She saw you. Past your skin. Something more of us should do," Dulanii said. "Plus, you Bleck Larin are attractive when you're not swinging a sword at my neck." He winked.

They walked for a while in silence, Dulanii glancing back every few moments to make sure Gastel was still there. It was a companionable quiet, solidified by the rhythmic sound of their feet crunching through leaves.

"Rae really likes you."

Gastel raised a single eyebrow at the man.

"She tries to hide it, but I know her. She has never..." Dulanii let the words hang, his snowy eyebrows drawing together. "Let's just say, she's careful with her friendship."

Gastel clenched his teeth, the press of time squeezing his chest. They needed to hurry.

Rae sat between Freya and Geri at dinner, smiling often as she took in the banter. It was different from the solitude she'd grown used to as of late. This was like old times, when she and Freck had been in training. There was warmth and fun here that she hadn't realized she'd missed.

Each personality came to life. Geri, by far the youngest, was oblivious to the fact that she was a Bleck Larin living in hostile Shaylands. Freya, as she'd aptly indicated when introducing herself, was the acting leader. Perhaps there was more to it, but Rae suspected the others needed someone to take charge and Freya was more than capable. Geri's father, Tor, was a quiet Bleck Larin. His demeanor reminded Rae much of Roulin without the sharpness of hatred. A cold superiority surrounded him in an unapproachable shield.

Druevgar was the Shay who had guarded the entrance to the compound. He usually went by Druev. In fact, the only person who called him by his full name was Lokryn, the Bleck Larin who had been with him. The two of them seemed to have a similar friendship as she had with Freck, and their constant teasing made Rae smile despite herself. The others sat farther down the table, so Rae could only catch scraps of their conversation.

"So, Rae, where are you from?" Geri asked over the din of chatter.

Rae leaned toward Geri so she wouldn't need to speak so loudly. "I live in Tremire now, but my family had a home in Dormshire when I was an elfling." The table went silent, making the last of Rae's words too loud.

"So your parents live in Dormshire?"

"Oh, no, my mother died when I was an elfling." She looked at Geri, aware that every eye in the room was on her. "My father is deceased as well." She needed to direct the conversation differently. "But I have a close friend I've been traveling with until recently. He's—"

"Please don't say dead."

The table exploded with laughter, and Rae couldn't help but smile at Geri's innocence.

"No, he's delivering a message."

It was hard to explain things without giving information that she wasn't ready to provide.

"Is he still a member of Her Majesty's army?" Druev's question cut through the smiles from the others at the table. A layer of distrust coated his words. He folded his arms across his chest and glared at her.

Druev looked so much like Freck that Rae wondered if they might be related. He had cropped white hair and a fighter's build—trim torso, thick shoulders. Tattoos decorated his neck, disappearing beneath the collar of his shirt, the style of which was common practice among soldiers.

"He was, but like me, we no longer see eye to eye with Gemma on the direction of the war." She held Druev's hard stare until he broke, looking over at Freya instead.

"Come now, Druev," Freya said. "We didn't judge your past service to Gemma when you came to us." She stood and took her bowl with her. "Perhaps you should give Rae some grace."

Druev narrowed his eyes at Rae before Lokryn jabbed him in the side.

"It's true, Druevgar." Lokryn smiled from ear to ear as Druev tightened his crossed arms and sighed. The Bleck Larin sat several inches taller than Druev, his dark-green hair hanging in loops secured at the nape of his neck rather than a topknot.

Rae summoned her courage. It was time she shared more of who she was.

"Actually, my full name is Raemian Starling." She paused to let this sink in. If Druev had fought in the army in recent years, he'd likely know her name. Sure enough, he dropped his arms and sat up a little straighter, all emotion leaving his face.

"I've fought in the queen's army since she forced me into service. When I saved Geri a few weeks ago, it was the first time I hadn't killed a Bleck Larin on sight." Rae's eyes fell to the stew in front of her, letting her focus on something other than the glares from every elf in the room. "Something changed. Something caused me to ask questions I'd never asked before."

Rae looked up, meeting Druev's softening expression with a sternness of her own. "I was taken to King Mesmal by a bounty hunter, but instead of killing me, Mesmal attempted to use my safe return as a means of negotiating peace between the Shay and Bleck Larin." She swallowed to give herself a moment to collect herself because while she'd accepted the next part, it was still hard for her to say aloud. "Gemma has no interest in peace. Instead, she executed my father, her own bondmate, for helping me rescue King Mesmal's youngest son from the dungeons of Tremire."

Silence. Not even a breath was taken.

"I want justice. For my father, for myself, and for every elf who's felt the pain of loss from Gemma's hatred. If I can, I will stop this war by whatever means necessary."

She wanted someone to say something. Anything. Instead, the silence lingered.

"Rae." Geri leaned against her shoulder. "I'm so sorry." The sweet girl wrapped her arms around Rae and squeezed. "You're the bravest person I know."

Rae stole some time alone in the main common room after dinner. She skimmed the pages of the manuscript she'd taken from the court, trying to find the place where it had been left open. Soft footsteps approached so she pulled the slip of paper she'd found from her pocket to use as a marker.

"Seems the others have taken a liking to you." Rae glanced at Freya as she plopped down onto one of the cushions beside her. "Druev just asked me if I thought it wise for you to travel to Jooshawn alone." A sly smile crept across Freya's face. "You didn't have to share so much if you didn't wish to."

Rae set the book aside for later. "I think they needed to know."

"It was brave of you." Freya took a deep breath as if preparing herself for a harder conversation. "I hadn't realized who you were. Your mother was Bleck Larin, wasn't she?"

Rae tried to hide her initial shock, but she was sure nothing much slipped past this woman.

"An elf's dominant appearance always follows the father," Freya said with a matter-of-fact inflection to her voice. "You're Somin Starling's elfling. I knew of him and his bondmate before the queen. I'm sorry you lost him."

Rae nodded but wasn't sure how to respond.

"Interesting reading for one such as yourself." Freya tapped the cover of Rae's book with her finger.

"This was in the meeting room at the back of Gemma's court." Rae reached down for the book and flipped it open to the position she'd marked. "It was opened to a specific page that referenced the House of Starling."

She handed the manuscript to Freya, who was instantly more interested in the slip of paper. Her face drained of color as her eyes tracked across the words.

"Where was this?" Freya's fingers brushed the rough edge of the parchment.

"Crumpled on the floor in the same room. Do you understand the meaning?"

Freya's eyes grew wide. "This..." She looked up at Rae as if seeing her for the first time. "This speaks of the Sundering!" She bolted to her feet, pulling Rae with her. "We need to find Tor!"

Freya dragged Rae down the residence tunnels. The hall was cold, lit with the occasional dim soultorch, casting eerie shadows along the tunnel walls. Rae wasn't sure if the goosebumps blooming across her arms were due to the temperature or the fear that flooded Freya's expression. They burst through a door at the end, nearly falling into a room not much larger than Rae's residence in Tremire. Before a word could be said, Geri's father was on his feet.

"Tor. The Sundering."

Tor reached for the paper Freya extended out to him. He read it aloud, his Bleck Larin accent more prominent than Rae had noticed at dinner.

"You would still risk everything for pride?
The Sundering approaches.
The Great Wielder lives within another.
It's time to choose your side."

He stared at the words a little longer before meeting Freya's glare. "Where did this come from?"

"Rae found it in the Court of Tremire. It must be to the queen, but who'd have sent it?" Freya's eyes were glassy with fear.

Tor rubbed his forehead in frustration. "The Great Wielder lives within another?" He looked at the note again. "How is that even possible?"

"Without knowing for certain who they were to begin with." Freya said.

Memories of the being from the rift she and Gastel had encountered forced themselves to the front of Rae's mind.

"The Sundering grows nigh. The balance has been forsaken."

Tor and Freya turned in Rae's direction simultaneously. She hadn't meant to say the words aloud.

"Where did you hear that?" Tor's voice was so quiet Rae almost missed his question.

"In the Middlelend Forest. There was a rift."

Tor and Freya looked at each other and then back at Rae, Tor sitting with an unceremonious flop.

"That's impossible." He found Freya with his eyes alone. "The Great Wielder died closing the last of them."

Rae knew who the Great Wielder was. While she'd spent days in bed recovering from her arrow-induced injury to the shoulder, Gastel had kept her company. There was nothing to do but talk. It seemed her father knew a great many things about Gastel's mother that he had freely shared while Gastel was still imprisoned in Tremire.

"That Gemma knew of these things—the consequences of her actions for all of elvenkind—and still held her ground against Mesmal?" Freya put a hand to her forehead. "There must be something we can do."

Rae put a comforting hand on Freya's shoulder. "I plan to stop Gemma. You worry about figuring out what else must be done to stop the Sundering you speak of."

"I don't know how one elf can change the tide of an army. How do you plan to do this?" Freya shook her head, eyes filled with concern. She hadn't known Rae for long, but it seemed she'd already adopted her as one of her own.

"I think there are far more than we know who wish for peace." Rae glanced at her hands for a moment before continuing: "My name also has resonance. The greater challenge is Gemma. I must convince her to abdicate or forcefully remove her from the throne."

"The Shay and Bleck Larin alike must be tired of fighting and dying and losing their loved ones." Freya closed her eyes, which glistened with unshed tears. "I lost my sister and my father at Dormshire. My bond-mate and my son in the Culling." Freya motioned to Tor. "Geri's mother left Tor after years of bonding to join Gemma's army."

Tor glared at Rae, a mixture of fear and anger creasing his forehead, his silence speaking for him.

"This is why I must do this," Rae said.

Freya turned and took her arms, a motherly sweetness warming her expression. "I'm not sure I can let you go to Jooshawn."

"I don't think you have a choice. I left my greatest friend behind so I could do this. I've gone against the wishes of someone I care dearly for." Rae pressed her fear away, settling a shield over her heart. "It's this or spend the rest of my life running from my stepmother. I've already accepted my fate. With Rhend in the balance, I've even more reason to restore peace between the Shay and Bleck Larin."

Freya closed her eyes, taking a calming breath. "Then stay tonight. Rest, and leave when you're ready. Perhaps you can help us determine what else must be done to stop the Sundering—if there's even a way."

Rae nodded, glancing at Tor, whose face had settled into the customary impermeable mask of the Bleck Larin. Rest was the last thing on her mind after this conversation.

FORTY-SEVEN

In the Open

Gastel was exhausted. He wasn't entirely sure how Dulanii could continue to stand upright without assistance. After a short night's sleep on the Middlelend Forest's southern edge, they'd tackled most of the highlands in rotating bursts of jogging and sprinting. Now, they rested in the thin shade of a squat tree.

Each time Gastel crossed the highlands, he grew less fond of it. The flat stretch of scraggly grass and clay wasn't quite a desert, but it might as well have been. It didn't help that the sky was relentlessly cloudless.

Dulanii paced as Gastel sat cross-legged in the shade, trying to catch his breath. The Shay's brows were knitted together, eyes cloudy with frustration.

"Please, Dulanii, sit and rest. You must be as hot and exhausted as I am."

"I don't know how she thinks she can stop an army. The whole army, Gastel! How?" Dulanii shook his head and raked his fingers through his white hair, the sweat causing it to stand on end. "She's been researching the Great Houses. She found something, but she didn't share all of it with me. Gods, I wish she'd have just talked to me." He stopped and glared at Gastel. "She never wants to trouble anyone. She's always been like that. Seeing everything, putting pieces together that others miss, but never sharing the burden."

"If she thinks she can, there's likely a good reason. We need to trust her." Gastel wasn't sure he believed his own words, but he willed them true. "We should continue to the forest edge before too long. We're very visible out here." The last thing Gastel wanted was to be dragged back to the dungeons of Tremire.

The forest loomed ahead. Massive ancient trees towered hundreds of feet above the ground. The tree line ran unbroken east and west, as if the Elder Gods had planted it in a perfect row.

Dulanii pointed to a small shack on the edge of the highlands. "We could rest there until tomorrow and start fresh at dawn."

Gastel nodded. The thought of having a roof over his head was pleasing. Dulanii set the pace, and the two began jogging the last leg, eyes scanning the horizon for movement. So far, they'd seen no one, but Gastel knew it was only a matter of time until being a Bleck Larin became problematic.

They were nearly to the shack when Dulanii came to a screeching halt. A single Shay woman stepped from the forest line. Gastel stopped short, but there was nowhere to duck out of sight. She watched the path at her feet and hadn't seemed to notice them as she walked in the direction of the shack. Perhaps she'd only see Dulanii and not the stone-gray-skinned elf with him?

Wishful thinking. She looked up and froze in place, likely petrified with fear at the sight of a murderous Bleck Larin.

Dulanii jogged toward her, waving. "Hey! We're friendly!"

She took a few hesitant steps back, perhaps thinking she could make a break for the treeline. Gastel walked slowly, giving Dulanii an opportunity to ease the tension.

It was obvious from his hand motions that Dulanii was explaining Gastel's presence. Whether the woman reacted favorably or not, he'd find out soon enough.

"We're looking for a friend. She may have passed through here on her way to Tremire." Dulanii glanced back at Gastel as he came within earshot. "She's kind of a small, unassuming Shay."

The woman had yet to speak, her attention lingering on Gastel's short hair a little longer than it should have. They were knowing eyes, missing nothing. Eyes like Raemian's.

"Why come this deep into the Shaylands, Bleck Larin?" Her words held a razor's edge—accusatory and untrusting.

"As Dulanii said, we seek our friend."

She wasn't listening to him anymore. Her attention fell fully on Dulanii. "What's your name?"

"I'm Dulanii. We're looking for Raemian Starling. Do you know her?"

She looked between Gastel and Dulanii with narrowed eyes. "She left this morning for Jooshawn. She stayed with us last night."

"Us?" Gastel asked and saw a moment of hesitation flash across her face.

"Yes." She watched Gastel carefully. "There are a handful of us." She cocked her head to the side as she continued to inspect him. "Rae didn't mention a Bleck Larin friend other than the king."

Of course Raemian hadn't. She'd never give unnecessary details. Apparently, not even to Dulanii, her most trusted friend.

"Unless you're the king?" She glanced up at Gastel's mop of unruly hair. "I'd think having your hair desecrated would be a grave dishonor."

"I'm not the king." It was his turn to hesitate, but they'd come too far for him to stop taking risks now. "I'm his youngest son."

She stood back from him for a moment, searching his face again, a strange mixture of speculation and amusement in her expression. "Seems rather risky for you to come this far into the Shaylands, don't you think, Highness?" She put her hands on her hips, a coy smile turning up her lips.

"You must not have noticed, but there aren't exactly a lot of scouting parties around these days."

"Roulin, is it?" she asked.

Gastel shook his head. "I'm Gastel. Roulin is considerably grumpier than I."

"There was a rumor the king had a third son. Pleasure to meet you." She matched his grin. "Come along. You shouldn't loiter in the open." There was a warmth in the way she motioned for them to follow.

Sure enough, she led them to the shack and ushered them both in before ducking in behind them. Without thinking, Gastel ignited his soultorch.

"Hey, watch that flame in here." Dulanii's terrified face was even more animated by the flicker of the flames.

The woman seemed unfazed, and Gastel suspected she'd been around Bleck Larin on more than one occasion.

"It's harmless, Dulanii." She extended her hand over the flame, and Dulanii watched in horror as her fingers passed through. "My name is Freya. My watchmen will be standoffish. I'll handle things." She looked them over one more time and thankfully approved of whatever it was she did or didn't see. "Your friend Rae had the queen's emblem on her jerkin, but I see you choose to go without."

She admired Dulanii's bare chest with a wink then turned, feeling along the wall until she released a hidden latch with a soft click. A panel opened to reveal a pitch-black tunnel descending into the depths of the earth. Dread wicked up Gastel's spine. How had he gotten here, standing in a tiny shed with a strange Shay woman who seemed to know Raemian?

Dulanii didn't hesitate and disappeared into the darkness. Swallowing his fear, Gastel followed into the abyss.

The Great Wielder

We shouldn't be wasting time. We should be following." Gastel was moving before he'd finished speaking, his frustration tight like a drawn bow.

Freya held a hand up to stop him, a sidelong smile floating across her face. "Patience, Gastel."

His shoulders were rigid. Through all the introductions to the strange collection of elves who called themselves the Aequus, he'd felt his nerves pulling tighter and tighter. They needed to go, or they'd never manage to catch up to Raemian.

"I don't know if you've noticed, but you don't exactly blend in up there." Druevgar had thus far proven himself to be immensely knowledgeable of the Shay army's workings but very distrustful of Gastel. "I'll go with Dulanii. We can blend in, and we know the way the Shay army operates."

Gastel shook his head sternly. "I can't let you do that."

"I'm not entirely sure you have a choice, *Prince.*" Druevgar's sharpness gave Gastel reason to stand a little straighter.

Unfortunately, the Shay was right. Druevgar understood the value of a prince. The lives of royalty could be used for good and most certainly for evil. If Gastel were captured, he could be used to negotiate on a completely different level. His father would cave to any demands—something he'd nearly done already.

"It's settled then. Dulanii and Druev will go to Jooshawn to find Rae." Freya looked between the men until her attention settled on Gastel. "And Tor has questions for you. We'll keep you busy."

More questions? Gastel could already feel his patience disintegrating. He needed to do something other than talk about hypotheticals and opinions. He'd promised himself he'd never hide again, and that's exactly what he felt he was doing.

He glared at Freya. He'd allow Dulanii and Druev to go, but he refused to be happy about it.

Rae smelled the encampment long before she saw it. From the scarred earth and how the land had been stripped bare for leagues, she assumed they'd been there longer than originally anticipated. A semipermanent fence had been erected, more for order than to keep anyone in or out. She slipped between fence posts rather than trying her luck at one of the guarded entrances.

Most of the warriors—men and women alike—sat around campfires, surrounded by tents and crates of food and supplies. They polished armor, sharpened weapons, ate, laughed. A part of her warmed, seeing the trappings of war. She missed the camaraderie.

She crept around the camp's outskirts, trying to get a better view of how it was organized—whether there were winding paths that meandered through or an order to the madness of soldiers and gear. She tried to determine the hierarchy, grabbing snippets of conversation to analyze later.

"She's mad if she thinks this is the final push."

"How long do you think it will take us to cross through the Western Pass?"

"It's not so much a pass as a creek; it'll take forever."

Rae managed to slip from tent to tent. She was passed by a handful of soldiers, but thankfully, with her hood pulled up, she was just another Shay and went unnoticed.

"I miss my bondmate," a weary voice said from a solemn crowd crammed around a smaller fire.

Their tents weren't as large or as well constructed. These were not trained soldiers excited for battle. These were conscripted civilians wishing they'd never left home.

"She always made the best rabbit stew."

"My mother makes the most delicious breads you've ever tasted."

"I hope we're home before the fields need taken off. My father is too old for that sort of work."

These people belonged with their families, not camped in a field waiting for their vengeful queen to send them to their deaths. These were the Shay she needed—the ones forced to be here.

Now she needed to see if she could find the royal guards' camp—or one royal guard in particular.

Gastel sat across from Tor and Freya, his hands folded in front him. He tried to keep his expression as impassive as possible, but the things these two elves told him seemed like fanciful fairy tales. They spoke of Elder Gods and magic turning the tide of history. Things his tutors had told him when he was an elfling—the Great Houses and guilds, alternate planes of existence, prophecies, and balance. The only reason he hadn't yet passed them both off as crazy and left the compound to follow Dulanii was that Master Lorilay had said something to the same effect. She, too, had mentioned balance, his mother's role in the guilds, and the closing of the rifts.

"The Elder Gods foretold of a Great Wielder. One unmatched by any other." Freya splayed her fingers out on the table between them. "A product of many generations of ancestors before her. She'd throw the world off balance. Through her deeds, a great power would blanket our lands, growing and growing until it was out of control. Wars and hatred and prejudices fed and formed over centuries, turned into truths overnight. Everything would build until our world could handle it no longer and would instead tear itself apart. It's known as the Sundering."

She watched Gastel closely, but he did his best to keep his thoughts guarded.

"Your father, the king, was in love with a wielder of significant power, was he not?" Tor asked. He was a bit more direct. "Did he not have an affair with her while promised in lifebond to Gemma, the product of which was this war *and you*?"

Gastel couldn't hold the man's glare; he glanced down at his folded hands instead. "I didn't even know my mother's name until a few weeks ago. My father refused to tell me anything about her."

"This doesn't change what you are. If your mother was a wielder, then you'd hold that power as well," Tor said.

Freya laid a gentle hand across Gastel's. "What Tor is trying to ask is whether you possess a proficiency in Anam magic, beyond what a normal wielder would possess. If your mother was who we think she was and you possess an unusually great power, it is very likely your mother was the Great Wielder."

Freya's hand lingered on Gastel's. She had a matronly way about her, but it didn't cool the anger that built in the pit of his stomach.

"And if she was?" He looked from Freya to Tor as his frustration grew.

"Why can't you simply answer the questions?" Tor asked

"What difference does it make what I am?" Gastel slammed himself back from the table and stood, causing Tor and Freya to lean back, their eyes going wide. "What does it change? What's done is done!"

Gastel was weary of holding his anger in check. Every question Tor asked was like a fingernail scraping across the cave wall. It didn't help that the guilt he harbored for letting others do what he should have done himself was tearing away his conscience.

Freya stood, extending her hands out in his direction. "Forgive Tor. He's not the most patient."

"Clearly."

Tor crossed his arms in frustration.

"I'm Gastel, son of Niminea, a powerful wielder. Whether she was this Great Wielder you speak of, only the Gods know." He glanced to the side, needing something other than Tor's angry face to focus on. "I never knew her. All I have of her is this." He pulled the soul stone from his shirt.

Tor's eyes grew wide as he pushed away from the table, pressing himself against the cavern wall behind him.

"A soul stone," Freya said. "I've heard of them but didn't know any actually existed."

Freya stared at the pendant, no doubt mesmerized by the swirling light under its smooth surface. She blinked a few times as if to clear her mind, then met Gastel's eyes.

"Rae mentioned a rift. She said it spoke to her. Has she ever mentioned this to you?"

Gastel smiled to himself. Of course Raemian wouldn't have told them. She'd protect him until the bitter end.

"I was with her." He paused, his fingers itching to trace the side of his head, remembering the crusted blood he'd washed away. "The rift is dark now. Only a charred fissure in the earth."

"Have you ever taken it off?" Freya asked, her eyes returning to his pendant.

"I have."

He pulled the soul stone from his neck, holding it up so he could see the dancing life within it. He knew what would happen when his fingers no longer touched the pendant—the brilliant-white soulflame that would engulf him. He wished there was some way to explain, but he knew Tor would need to see. The man wasn't the type to trust the words of strangers.

Gastel set the pendant down on the table and stepped away.

Reconnaissance

Rae found the encampment's inner circle easy enough. Most of the large tents flew standards with the queen's crest. Rae lingered along the edge, certain the queen's tent was the massive octagonal structure complete with a foyer the size of some of the lesser soldiers' entire tents. But Gemma's tent wasn't Rae's target. She sought one of the royal guards. More specifically, the woman who had escorted her back after her last encounter with her stepmother—her best hope of a possible ally.

One of the guards loitering around the central fire stood out to her as he spoke, his ornate, inlaid helm tucked under his arm. Rae knew him. He was one of Gemma's favorites, a ruggedly handsome Shay named Neffriss. Unfortunately, Rae was certain the woman he was speaking with was the guard she was looking for. She needed the woman alone. She settled into the middle of a partially obscured stack of crates on the outskirts of the circle. The way these guards were chatting and drinking, it was going to be a long night.

Her ally's name was Solena—at least, Rae hoped she was an ally. The only problem with the current plan was that Solena was almost always paired for guard duty with Neffriss.

In the few hours she'd observed the comings and goings of the guards, she'd learned a great deal—names and titles, the general rotation schedule maintained to provide Gemma with constant security, and the position of Solena's tent directly to the right of Gemma's. These weren't ideal circumstances, but Rae was running out of options.

"Solena."

Rae perked up in time to see Solena's head turn in the direction of the voice.

"Neffriss said you should get some rest; he and I will take next watch." It was another guard Rae had observed in conversation with Neffriss earlier.

Solena lifted herself from the side of the fire and bid the others good night before ducking into her tent.

Rae took a deep breath before slipping from her makeshift hiding spot. She wanted to catch Solena before she had a chance to fall asleep. Rae wasn't concerned about her ability to overtake Solena so much as the ruckus a close-quarters scuffle would make. Canvas walls hid nothing.

From experience of setting up the same style tents at other encampments, Rae knew there was usually a cargo flap at the back. If this one had been constructed properly, it'd be easy enough to sneak through. She steadied her nerves with a few deep breaths. There'd be no turning back once she went in. If she were wrong, Solena would likely take her directly to Gemma. She said a silent prayer to the Gods before she ducked in.

Solena was midway through removing her armor and wore nothing but an undershirt, leggings, plate cuisses, and greaves. She stopped short at the sight of Rae and reached for her sword, freezing before grasping the handle.

"Raemian Starling?" Her voice was barely above a whisper. "What are you doing here?"

"I'm here to try and stop this war. To bring peace—if I can rally these soldiers." Her words sounded grandiose, even to herself.

Solena shook her head solemnly. "I fear we've come too far for that. Where were you two weeks ago?" She met Rae's glare with a weariness in her eyes, then started to remove the rest of her armor. "Too many years of fighting have turned these Shay bloodthirsty. You know the feeling of impending battle." Solena's eyes seemed glued to Rae. "They want Bleck Larin blood, and the queen has promised it to them."

Rae knew the feeling well—the intensifying anticipation, the electricity one felt before the charge, the elation of winning. It was surreal and sensual the way bodies twisted and moved together in a dance, ending in the bitter bliss of death. The way weapons came together in a fiery clash of brute strength was so satisfying. It was known as battle lust for a reason.

Solena pulled her snowy-white hair free of its braid and rubbed her scalp. The woman did a fantastic job of feigning fearlessness, but Rae could see the caution reflecting in her eyes. Solena knew what Rae was capable of. She'd heard enough to have a healthy fear. What Rae needed more was Solena's courage and trust.

"Gemma is determined to have Mesmal's head on her wall. She wants his sons crucified." Solena sat on the side of her cot. "I've only seen her this angry one other time, and I think we both know how that worked out." She could only be referring to the Culling. "She needs to be stopped. I'm not entirely sure how a coup hasn't already taken place."

Rae glanced around at the stale food and half-empty bottle of wine reflecting the light of a single candle. Trunks and chests had yet to be packed for the journey into the Bleck Larin territory. How long had they been there?

"This isn't like anything you've fought in, Raemian. This is insanity. She's swelled the numbers of soldiers to such an extreme—"

"But so many of them are untrained. They're civilians who would rather be with their families. They haven't chosen to fight for her cause; they've been forced to." Rae tried to keep her voice as quiet as possible, but a surge of hot anger boiled up inside her. If nothing else, the Shay army needed to be informed of what they faced.

"When they're thrust on to the battlefield before thousands of hardened, well-trained, and properly equipped Bleck Larin soldiers, do you honestly think they'll stand their ground for a queen who's done nothing but twist the truth for her own gain?" Rae shook her head. "They need to know. Let them choose their path. At the very least, let them know what that path leads to."

Solena stood and folded her arms, pacing in the small space beside her cot. "I'm just a royal guard. I have no authority. We'll need to involve someone who can make orders." Solena pulled her arms apart and folded her hands together, intertwining each finger as she thought.

Rae's breath caught as she remembered King Mesmal's correspondence. There had been letters from Bowrhem. Confusing, almost friendly letters. It was possible she could have another, very powerful ally if she dared to risk it.

"They've been ordered to arrest you on sight. Gemma has a plan for you." Solena met Rae's eyes. "She's always been so cruel to you. I don't know what you could've done to deserve such—"

"It's not what I've done; it's who I am." Rae stood and walked to the back of the tent. Solena needed to get some rest, and Rae needed more information.

"I'll see what I can do. If nothing else, I'll try to find someone with authority who won't drag you directly to the queen," Solena said as she pulled the blankets back and slipped under them, meeting Rae's eyes one more time. "Use caution coming back here. If Neffriss sees you…"

Solena didn't need to finish.

———

Gastel was pacing again. It was becoming progressively harder to remain pent up in a cavern with a bunch of strangers, especially when he knew Raemian was out there in Gods only knew what danger. The situation was far too similar to his time spent in the dungeons of Tremire.

Freya ducked in, but he didn't stop; he merely looked up at her from the corner of his eye as he continued pacing.

"Gastel, we have word from Druev and Dulanii. They haven't found Rae, but they're certain she hasn't been captured."

The tension in Gastel's shoulders eased, but not enough.

"Would you like some dinner?" Freya asked.

"I'm not hungry."

Without the sun peeking through windows, he had no sense of time. He needed something to do. Anything other than dwell on how helpless he felt.

"Gastel, you need to eat. You'll only destroy your strength if you don't."

Freya took a shy step closer to him. She'd been strange toward him since he'd shown her and Tor the level of Anam he possessed. Tor had all but refused to speak to anyone since, hiding in his quarters and having Geri bring food into him. But Freya? Other than treating him with significantly more caution, she'd thankfully not shunned him entirely.

"I know." He stopped and ran his hand through his hair. He hadn't eaten since waking. "I just can't stop thinking it should have been me to go with Dulanii."

She shook her head. "You know that wouldn't have gone well."

It didn't change that it *should* have been him. Just like it didn't change that Raemian should never have gone to single-handedly stop a war.

"Come, Gastel." Freya placed a hand on his upper arm, a knowing glint in her eye. "Have a morsel; then you can come back here and continue your fretting."

The woman was the epitome of kindness and patience. No wonder Raemian had trusted her so easily. He nodded and put his hand over hers. He'd do this for Raemian, not for himself.

He followed Freya out into the common room where a bowl of stew was thrust into his hands before he could slip into a chair beside Geri. It smelled like rabbit and fresh carrots, yanking him back to the morning with Raemian on the edge of the Middlelend Forest.

"Why did you cut your hair?" Geri's question ripped him from his memory. She was adorably blunt. It was clear she had less tact than her father, which was shocking because Tor was downright abrasive.

"Geri, stop it. That's no way—"

"It's fine." Gastel waved it off. It didn't matter. He took another spoonful of stew to give himself a moment to consider his words. "Gemma cut it."

"Wait." Geri's eyes grew round as she looked back at Freya, who was on the other side of the table. "Like, Queen Gemma?"

"Yes."

She searched his face as if to beg him to be joking.

"I was returning Raemian after she'd been captured by a tracker in the Middlelend Forest. Gemma cut my hair instead of my throat." He winked, and Geri's cheeks turned violet.

"We heard rumors about that." Lokryn was a practical Bleck Larin. He'd thus far stayed out of Gastel's way, perhaps sensing the tension building within him. "Heard she used that fancy kukri she executes people with—that she had it to your throat. I bet Rae went insane."

"Lokryn!" Freya scowled at him, but Gastel didn't care.

It was all true. He remembered the moment as clear as if it had just happened. It was a nightmare he relived daily—the razor edge sliding harmlessly across his skin. The way his hair had fallen loose around his face.

"It's fine." He scooped up another mouthful of stew and held it in front of his lips. "If it's true, it's true."

"Brave thing, running headfirst into Tremire," a Shay whose name Gastel had missed chimed in. "Gemma has a hate for your kind like nothing I've seen. Especially you. Your father is one thing, but you're the product of what he did."

"I don't know about brave. Stupid, maybe," Gastel said.

He looked away, feeling their eyes on him. He wasn't the brave one. Raemian was. She knew what lay ahead of her, what Gemma would do to her when she was caught, and she still ran straight into the belly of the beast. He slid the bowl back from the edge of the table and stood.

"Thank you for dinner."

"Your Shay is brave," Lokryn said.

Gastel met his somber eyes. It was the first time Raemian had been called *his*. A burst of pride melted into his tense muscles. He swallowed as his eyes roamed the other faces around the table. It was clear that in the short time they'd known Raemian, she'd become one of them.

FIFTY

Bowrhem

Solena was on duty when Rae crept into her spot among the crates. Just before sunset, she heard Neffriss's voice as he returned from wherever he'd been. He flirted with one of the female guards before donning his helm and stepping away, hopefully to relieve Solena. Rae had the sinking feeling she was running out of time.

Slipping from her hiding spot and sneaking around to the tent, she found Solena in the same state of undress as she had before, but at least this time the woman had a warm smile for her.

"Good," Solena said, slipping her greaves off and a fresh pair of leggings on. "I'm to take you to Legion Bowrhem. Things have already been set in motion." Solena pulled her boots on and directed Rae to follow. "I bet you're pleased to know you aren't the only Shay ready for this petty war to be over."

Rae pulled her hood up once again and fell in beside her. Who'd question her if she was escorted by a royal guard? No one—unless they wanted to be going in the same direction.

It was a quick walk through the encampment to where the legion and some of the lesser generals' tents were collected. No one milled about here. There was no chitchat, just a small, lonely fire likely used only for cooking. A single guard posted outside the entrance to the legion's tent brusquely nodded as Rae was led in.

Bowrhem was bent over a massive map sprawled across a table, weighed down on the corners with random objects. A small stack of crates held what looked like the remains of a meal at the far corner of the tent next to a royal-blue upholstered chair—perhaps the most lavish piece of furniture in the tent. Armor, polished and ready, rested on a stand with three swords leaning against it, their tips nestled in a woolen rug. A network of small oil lamps hung from the ceiling, illuminating the tent with honeyed light. There was no cot, no bedding, no personal belongings. Bowrhem either slept in another tent or stowed these things away when not in use.

He straightened, looking from Solena to Rae and then back down at the map, his expression unchanged. "Solena tells me you have information regarding the Bleck Larin forces."

Rae was hesitant, unsure of what Solena had told him. She cursed her lack of forethought to ask. Solena must have felt the same way.

"There's far more—"

"I asked Raemian." Bowrhem straightened and folded his arms, his eyes piercing into Solena. His gaze shifted to Rae and softened.

She swallowed. There was no turning back now. "King Mesmal desires peace," Rae began. Solena tightened, confirming this wasn't what she should have started with. Nevertheless, she continued,

"He knows about the diversionary attacks and the invasion from the west."

Bowrhem's brow furrowed, eyes frozen on a single spot on the map. His silence was unnerving. Rae had always found him intimidating, but the aura of command around him was terribly imposing.

"How did you come by this information?" He met her gaze, a flicker of anger crossing his brow.

She straightened her posture out of habit. Once a soldier, always a soldier. "I spoke with him at length while held at the castle stronghold. He was more than amicable toward me."

Bowrhem's hands found his hips, chin raised, jaw set. "Might I remind you we're at war with the Bleck Larin? Fraternizing with their king? Your enemy?" His eyebrows rose out of curiosity even though he'd just accused her of treason. "What proof do you have?"

Gods, what proof *did* she have? She had nothing. She'd traveled all this way and had nothing to prove from where she'd come or the days she'd spent in Parth. She had nothing of the Bleck Larin. Nothing but memories, and...

She had memories!

"He shared correspondence with me from the battle of Dormshire. Details about the first advance. Letters from you regarding prisoners." She let her words sink in, his eyes narrowing.

"Anyone could know these details. It's common knowledge that we negotiated for prisoners before General Belkin stopped *taking* prisoners." He folded his arms again.

Rae tipped her chin up, summoning her confidence. "One of those prisoners was your son. I know you personally requested that Mesmal release him, appealing as one father to another." She paused long enough to find the last piece of evidence, perhaps the most significant. "Your warning about the strength of Gemma's forces. You left out names, but there were locations, times, numbers—"

"That's enough." He glanced at Solena before returning his merciless glare to Rae. The information he'd shared thirty years ago could easily be considered treasonous. They'd been the actions of a desperate father. "Why would Mesmal send you to negotiate peace?"

"He didn't. I've come on my own." She swallowed. This was the hard part. She'd given her evidence, and now she needed his support, even if it meant the guarantee that he'd do nothing and order his men to stand down. "To save the conscripted civilians from an early death against a highly trained Bleck Larin army. One that will be waiting on the other side of the Western Pass."

He took a few steps around the table, and Rae's hand fell to the pommel of Freck's sword.

"I'm not going to attack you, Raemian." He let his fingers trail along the edge of the map. "For thirty years, I've watched Mesmal draw back his forces when he could have easily destroyed us." There was a gentle quality to his words; all the harshness of leading as the legion of the Shay army had washed away.

"I wonder how much Mesmal foresaw when he negotiated a life-bond treaty with Gemma. Our world faced such strange changes at that time." His eyes searched Rae's with scrutiny so thick she couldn't blink, couldn't swallow. "A silent war between dying houses. Crowns changing hands. I think you know what I speak of."

Her eyes grew wide. There were so many facets to Bowrhem.

The guard standing outside the tent stepped in and whispered something in Bowrhem's ear. He looked down at the map, clenching his jaw in thought before he met Rae's gaze.

"She has your friend, Dulanii, and plans to execute him and another defector at her earliest convenience."

When Gemma had executed her father, Rae had been unaware until days later. It was different this time. Knowing her stepmother had Freck, she'd frantically pulled a mask of indifference over the seething emotions boiling in her chest. It had the distinct taste of a trap.

She lay awake well into the night, strategizing how she could get to Freck before the queen's kukri was at his throat. She lost herself in the stars peeking through the trees above. Her wandering thoughts fixated on Freck's snowy-white hair pressed against his head after training, the way his arms felt wrapped around her in one of his customary hugs, the hope in his eyes in Dormshire.

Hope.

Hope for something better than this.

After speaking with Bowrhem, Solena had led her away in silence. There had been no words, no plans, or future visits coordinated. It was as if Solena and Bowrhem knew that if Gemma held Freck, Gemma held Rae. In other words, it was hopeless.

A thick darkness crept over her heart. There'd been a glimmer of hope in Bowrhem's words before the news of Freck. It was confirmation that Bowrhem's stern, immovable loyalty wasn't where Rae had thought it to be. It lay with the Shay people and his soldiers, not Gemma. If Rae had Bowrhem's support, she likely had the support of the entire army. She couldn't forsake that.

But if she could get to Freck before the execution?

It was worth the risk, at the very least, to survey the situation and see if there was a chance he could be rescued. She owed Freck that much.

She was up and moving before she could second-guess herself.

It wasn't hard to find where he was being held. Gemma had him shackled to a pole outside her tent with another Shay. Rae knew he'd be under heavy guard. There was no reason to display them so publicly other than to entice her to free them.

She crouched in her usual place amongst the crates. The fire the royal guards loitered around had died down to angry coals, and the guards were gone. Only the usual ones remained. One outside the entrance to Gemma's tent, another likely just inside. Two more around the back.

Her eyes fell upon Freck's fretful movements, struggling to get free of the solid iron securing his hands over his head. His feet were barely flat on the ground. It'd be a long, sleepless night for him.

The memory of Gemma's kukri flashed before Rae's eyes. That deadly blade—how many lives had it taken? She saw her father's loving face when she'd left him on the north side of Tremire. She'd lost her mother and her father to this dreadful queen. Now she'd lose her greatest friend.

Despite knowing she could handle four royal guards, the risks were too great. She had to hold firm—to do what she'd come to do. A conviction grew in the pit of her stomach. Gemma had to be removed from the throne. Her wickedness had grown bottomless.

After several more minutes of thinking and fretting over Freck fumbling with his restraints, Rae couldn't bear to watch him struggle any longer. She pulled herself up from the crates and slipped around the back of the tents.

She didn't get far.

FIFTY-ONE

Martyr

He begged and pleaded, but Freya wouldn't let Gastel leave the Aequus compound. Not yet. He could have managed to get out if he truly wanted to, but part of him knew they were right to keep him.

Sporadic information from Druev had been flowing back from Jooshawn. Nothing of great significance—no word of Raemian, no rumblings of any change in plans. The Shay army would break camp within the next few days. Gastel could only hope his brothers were ready.

"Do you have a moment, Highness?" Freya's calm voice yanked him from his brooding.

"Of course." He set the book aside he attempted to distract himself with and followed Freya into the room she and Tor had previously interrogated him in.

"Tor has been scouring through information." She slid a book in front of him. "When Rae was here, she had more insight." She opened it to a specific page marked with a slip of paper. "In fact, Rae found this book in the queen's court."

The slip of paper caught his eye. He read it twice, turning the words over in his mind.

"You really think I'm the Great Wielder returned?" The Trove elf's words from the Vail whispered through Gastel's thoughts.

She nodded. "We do."

"What difference does it make?" He ran his hands across the page. Another book. That's all he seemed to do in this place: read and answer questions.

"You said you knew of a rift?" she asked.

"I don't know what it could have been if not a rift." His eyes fell to the note again, pouring over the handwriting. He'd seen it before.

"Can you describe it?"

Freya reached a kind hand across the table and placed it over his. "It's okay. Another time."

"No." He squeezed his eyes closed, dragging the details forward. "It was like soulfire pouring up from a crack in the earth." He let the memory wash over him, reliving just enough but not everything. "There was a terrible screeching noise that brought me to my knees. I blacked out." He opened his eyes and saw the blank expression on Freya's face. "Raemian was unharmed."

"And you say it's dark now?"

"Yes, but I was told the remnants of a wielder's soul could have been what Raemian and I experienced." He looked at the note again, but try as he might, he couldn't remember who the handwriting belonged to.

Rae was frozen in place, face-to-face with Gemma's favorite.

"Raemian Starling." In the low light, Neffriss looked more like a demon than a Shay. "You had to know this was a trap." He drew his blade slowly, silently.

Rae wrapped her fingers around the handle of Freck's sword, pulling it halfway from its scabbard, but stopped. She could kill him. She could kill the other four guards as well. She could likely make it out of the camp before anyone managed to catch her, but she didn't come all this way to run. She came to confront Gemma and stop a war. She bit her lip, her mind working overtime. There had to be a way to salvage this, save Freck, and stop an army. She refused to accept that there wasn't. She let her sword slide away.

"Take me to the queen."

The smile slipped from Neffriss's lips. He'd wanted a fight.

Rae let Neffriss lead her past the pole where Freck was chained. To her surprise, she found the other Shay was Druev. How was the Aequus here? She hadn't a clue, nor the time to consider it further before meeting Freck's gaze.

Her heart crumbled.

He'd been beaten badly. His nose was bloody, one eye swollen shut. He had a large gash on his ribs which still oozed into the waist of his pants and purple bruising down his torso. Worst of all was the defeat in his eyes. She knew he'd do it over and over again to save her, as many times as he could.

She didn't deserve his loyalty.

She was thrust to the ground at her stepmother's silk-slippered feet, trying to cobble together a plan between the flashes of panic in her chest.

"Ah, sweet Raemian. Always the martyr." The queen took three steps closer. "I knew you'd come to save your precious friend. So, so predictable."

Rae risked looking up at her stepmother and received a swift kick to the face in answer. Another kick, this one to her chest, sent a bolt of pain across her ribs. Her eyes watered as she squeezed them shut.

"Bring the posts."

Rae didn't try to get up. She preferred the hard ground to another assault. She could have fought back, but part of her still hoped there'd be a way out of this. She just needed to put the pieces together.

But those pieces grew ever more slippery with blood.

She was seized by the shoulders and dragged to her knees. Fingers dug into her scalp as her head was pulled back, forcing her to face Gemma. Rae had been in this same position not so long ago, in a different world filled with a different type of fear.

"Did you know that your father begged for his life? Begged for your life." Gemma plopped onto a plush divan, taking up a lock of her own hair and twirling it around her index finger, a wicked smile spreading across her lips. "What should I do with you first?"

Two guards entered, carrying a stand that was set before Rae. It appeared to be an upside-down table with only two legs perpendicular to the base. It was what the queen called the posts—a cruel restraint used to hold an elf immobile while tortured. Rae had heard of it but had never seen it.

Her jerkin and shirt were cut away, leaving her exposed in nothing but her undershirt and leggings—vulnerable and powerless. Her arms were drawn over the wooden mounts and secured with leather straps across biceps and forearms, locking her upper body in place. Straps were woven between her legs, pulling her thighs against the same posts, biting into the delicate skin on the inside of her legs. The only thing that could move was her head, which she hung in defeat.

Rae couldn't stop the tears from collecting at the edges of her eyes. The panic that had been a mild tickle was now a raging fire in her core as she realized there'd be no getting out of this. Not this time.

"Bring me my rod."

FIFTY-TWO

Mercy

Rae must have lost consciousness because when she woke, the first thing she heard was Legion Bowrhem's stern voice. His tone was level, but from the pitch, Rae could tell he was desperately trying to control his anger.

"If you make an example of her in front of your soldiers, it will demoralize—"

"I don't particularly care what my soldiers think," Gemma hissed. "They aren't here for their brains. They're here to do as I say. That's their purpose."

"It's not advised."

"I didn't ask for your advice."

Rae managed to pry her eyes open. The shadow of Bowrhem in full battle armor was an amorphous blur. Gemma was an outline of soft pink flesh and creamy silk.

"Even your royal guards don't understand why you have always made an example of the girl. What are her crimes?"

"I don't need crimes. She's mine to do with as I please."

"Then release the other two. They've done nothing wrong."

"I've a credible source that says they're spies."

"Spies for whom?"

Bowrhem was pushing his luck. Rae had never heard anyone speak to the queen in such a way without punishment.

"Isn't that obvious, Bow? The enemy."

Rae tried again to focus on the two elves in front of her.

"And who is the enemy, exactly?"

"She is!" Gemma pointed an angry finger in Rae's direction, and while the two elves remained a blur, she could see that jabbing finger perfectly. "She is my enemy!"

"She's your stepdaughter. She's never been your enemy. She has dedicated her life to your service, and you've been nothing but cruel to her in return."

While Gemma's voice had risen several octaves, Bowrhem's remained level. Firm. Almost annoyingly calm.

Gemma turned, causing Rae to flinch, the straps holding her biceps stretching the mutilated skin of her back. She drew a sharp breath across her teeth and tried to relax, but her shoulders and hips ached. How long had she been strapped to the posts?

Long enough to be beaten bloody and for wounds to clot. Too long. She'd lost precious time. Time she could no longer afford to waste.

"She's a traitor, Bow. You need proof? She removed the Shay emblem from her uniform. Probably thinking of killing me with every stitch she pulled away."

Rae shivered as a breeze from someone moving past brushed across her bloodied flesh.

"Majesty, do you wish for the traitors to be brought in?" It was Neffriss's voice. Of course it was Neffriss.

Rae struggled again to see them, but her head swam with terrible exhaustion.

"Yes. Perfect. They need to witness what happens to a betrayer whom I once called family."

Gods, watch what? Rae had already been beaten with the rod until bloody and broken. What else would Gemma do before she executed her?

"And bring my brand."

This time, the cold chill wasn't from air moving across open wounds.

"If your intention is to execute the girl, why torture her first?" Bowrhem asked, his voice still carrying a stern calm.

"I have questions."

"Then ask them. She may be more than forthcoming."

"I'm not sure what's gotten into you, but when I'm through here, we may need to address your fealty. You're dismissed." Her words were laced with venom.

For a thick moment, Bowrhem didn't move, and Rae held her breath. If he pushed back now after having been dismissed.

The air licked the tears that wet Rae's face as Bowrhem left the tent without another word. She thanked the Elder Gods that he hadn't said more on her behalf. Gemma's temper knew no bounds. Rae didn't think the queen was above executing her legion before this final push in her vengeful war.

Spending a night strapped to a pole had extinguished the fire from Freck's and Druev's souls. Instead of struggling, they let the guards push them to their knees. Rae wanted to see Freck one last time before they lost their lives together—not in battle, side by side as warriors, but as traitors. His stormy-blue eyes framed by snowy lashes. Those prominent shaymarks he loved to show off.

Her vision failed her. He and Druev looked like pink Shay-shaped blobs shifting stiffly as they struggled to kneel. She could hardly tell them apart. They were the same height and build. Both shirtless, the same white hair cut short. Red stained down their sides from their shaymarks. The only hint of difference was the slightest shadow of purple from Druev's tattoos. She tried to speak, but her voice was a strange squeak. Her tears threatened to make it even harder for her to see them.

The embroidered fabric of Gemma's gown scraped across the hard-packed dirt as she approached. Rae turned her head to glance behind but was met with blazing pain in her neck.

"You can tear my crest from your clothes, remove it from your armor, push it from your mind, but I will give you one that can never be removed."

Rae tensed as Gemma's hot breath brushed over her ear.

"Not until your soul burns within the depths of the Great Sheol will you be rid of me, my little starling." Her stepmother's voice was laced with a strange, lusty delight.

Rae swallowed, but her mouth felt like it was lined with sand. She'd seen the brand. If Rae remembered correctly, it would fill the space between her shoulders with an ancient tree. Rumor was that Gemma had added the infinity symbol when she'd taken the throne.

Because she would be queen forever.

Because Rae had failed.

There was silence for an agonizing moment. Then she smelled it—the bitter phosphorus of hot metal as it hovered over the ruined flesh of her back. Excited breaths escaped Gemma as she prepared to further desecrate Rae's skin.

"Mercy, please, Majesty." It was Freck's desperate voice. Not worried Freck or even scared Freck. This was defeated Freck, begging for his friend through tears and heartache.

Gemma didn't respond, and Rae braced herself for the pain she knew was coming.

And it was so much worse than she could have imagined.

FIFTY-THREE

For the Wicked

Seething white light lanced behind Rae's eyes; she arched her back as much as the posts would allow. Time had stopped, replaced with a constant searing agony that she couldn't escape. Unconsciousness would have been a blessing bestowed by the Elder Gods themselves. She tried to hold back a scream, but it ripped past her lips, the sound frayed and distant to her own ears.

"Stop, please, stop!" Freck's voice tore through Rae's smoldering affliction. It was a beacon. If he could speak, he could breathe. And if he could breathe, she could endure.

The acrid smell of burning flesh and hot blood filled Rae's nose. It was a smell she knew from war, but this time it was *her* flesh. *Her* blood.

The burning ebbed as the iron cooled. When the metal was peeled away, it took chunks of cauterized flesh with it, ripping open the charred wounds. Rae emptied her stomach, sending another wave of agony through her body.

Gemma handed the brand off to a guard, then stood to admire her work. "It suits you."

Rae was losing consciousness but fought hard, trying to think of some way to save Freck and Druev. Her eyes fluttered, her vision growing dark around the edges.

"Take these two out and strap them back up. I need some rest before I slit their throats."

The relief that flooded Rae was pure, knowing she still had time to think of how to get her friends out from under the queen's wrath. It was a balm smoothing over the battle she waged against her own pain. She let the world slip away.

When Rae woke, her eyelids were crusted shut. She tried to bring a hand up to clear the sleep away, but her wrist was bound. Tugging a little harder only caused the wounds on her back to pull open, sending a kaleidoscope of lights behind her eyes. She eventually managed to pull her other arm out from under herself and rub away the debris.

She was in a small tent, alone, one arm shackled to a central post. She tried to sit up, but searing agony prevented her from doing much more than lift her head. Shay milled about outside, their excited voices driving a wedge of despair into Rae's heart. She'd failed to do what she'd been certain she could do. What she'd *had* to do. The metallic taste of defeat coated the inside of her mouth, devouring the last scraps of her hope.

Rae had not anticipated seeing Freck. He was supposed to go to Parth to deliver information to King Mesmal. He'd have been safe there. Why had he tried to find her? And with Druev? It meant Freck had likely met Freya and the other Aequus. If Gemma learned of the Aequus involvement, she'd surely retaliate against the peaceful elves.

Rae bit her lower lip, tasting blood. Enduring Gemma's wrath would have been so much easier if no one else had suffered it with her.

"I'm so sorry, Freck. I failed." She hadn't meant to say the words aloud.

Heavy boots approached, and a familiar face peeked in.

"You're finally awake!" Neffriss said with a disgusting level of cheer as he stepped in, hands on his hips. "Gemma will be pleased. She's been waiting to execute your friends." His voice dripped with sickly sweet sarcasm.

Frankly, Rae was tired of knowing Nefriss existed. Under different circumstances, she'd have stabbed him in the throat already. Rae choked back a sob as he yanked her from the ground, ripping open scabs across her back like hot blades. She clenched her teeth as she struggled to remain upright, her head swimming with fresh agony.

It wasn't a public execution. It was, however, not entirely devoid of an audience. It appeared Gemma had invited her entire royal guard and several lesser generals. From where Rae knelt on a makeshift dais, she could see the gravity of the situation reflecting in their frosty expressions. Treason was never tolerated, but these weren't the faces of Shay watching traitors being executed. These were the faces of Shay watching their friends and comrades die.

It gave Rae the tiniest sliver of hope.

"For the crimes of espionage, desertion, and high treason against Her Majesty, Queen Gemma, Druevgar of the Shay is sentenced to death by Her Majesty's desire."

Neffriss's voice was like a dull blade sawing through bone as he read the sentence.

"For the crimes of espionage, desertion, and high treason against Her Majesty, Queen Gemma, Dulanii of the Shay is sentenced to death by Her Majesty's desire."

Freck tightened at the sound of his real name. To be called a traitor after all the years he'd flawlessly dedicated himself to Gemma's war? It was sickening.

And it was Rae's fault he was here.

A cold realization settled over her as she took the blame upon herself. She could accept her own death far easier than his.

"For the crimes of espionage; desertion; high treason against Her Majesty, Queen Gemma of the Shaylands; conspiracy to assassinate the sovereign; and disobedience of the highest regard, Raemian Starling of the Shay, spy for the Bleck Larin king, is sentenced to death by Her Majesty's desire."

The faces that turned in her direction were ones of astonished denial. The crimes she'd been accused of were the ultimate disgrace. She'd been a model soldier—decorated for her skills in battle and dedication to her comrades in arms. Perhaps it was hard for those in attendance to believe she'd committed such crimes.

Yet, in all honesty, she had.

She *had* committed high treason. She *had* given Belkin pertinent strategic information. She *had* plotted to assassinate the queen if only to end Gemma's tyranny. And she'd do it all again if it meant getting closer to peace between the Shay and Bleck Larin.

Rae straightened her posture as best as she could, feeling the sticky dampness of blood soaking through her undershirt. She forced the panic burning in her chest down deep, as she had for years on the battlefield. She would accept this with the same grace she'd promised herself she'd maintain if she ever faced the end of Belkin's sword again.

Letting the crowd fade away, she closed her eyes, squeezing the fog of pain to the edge of her consciousness. She needed only a moment of crisp clarity.

There it was!

An idea—small at first, warm in the depths of her abdomen, growing and circulating like the blood that flowed through her veins for at least a little longer.

"Do the accused have any last words before Her Majesty determines her desired execution?"

Compelled by the seed of hope slowly germinating, Rae cleared her throat.

FIFTY-FOUR

Last Words

A sea of eyes fell upon Rae. If she hadn't intended to speak before, she certainly had to now.

"The one whom you call queen is not your rightful sovereign." Rae's words carried a gravelly quality—the voice of someone who had screamed herself hoarse.

Whispers and shifting drew Rae's attention through the crowd to a familiar face. Bowrhem stood at the back, arms crossed, jaw set. A single nod of approval filled her with confidence.

"Another Shay possesses a claim to the throne," Rae said, scanning the faces and seeing that her words had the desired effect. She had commanded the crowd's attention. "Not so long ago, the House of Starling held the crown. Clore Tremire ripped it from—"

"My father picked up a crown Somsunder Starling had thrown away. He was a coward. Like your father. Like all of you Starling sacks of shit."

Gemma stepped forward and stood between Rae and Druev, the kukri held at her side. "The House of Tremire is the rightful royal family! It has ruled with strength and—"

"Tyranny is the word I believe you mean to say, Stepmother. Or would you prefer lies? Deception? Bigotry? Jealousy? How about—"

"You know nothing of what you speak! Nothing of ruling and politics. Your father was the same. Happier to spend his days tangled in my sheets rather than at my side."

Rae blushed at the mention of her father, but she swallowed the memory of him. She needed to focus on the present. The way the soldiers glared with undivided attention. The way the queen's face had turned a brilliant shade of magenta. The determination in Bowrhem's expression.

Druev took a nervous step forward, drawing Rae's attention past Gemma. "You all willfully follow a sadistic butcher who wears a crown and calls herself your sovereign!" He spoke with confidence, ignoring the queen as she turned toward him with icy death in her hand. "You should be ashamed of yourselves! The hatred, the attempt at genocide you have condoned under her order. This should have ended so lo—"

The queen sliced into Druev's throat without waiting for him to finish. It happened so fast, yet Rae felt she'd watched in slow motion. She looked away as blood pulsed down his bare chest. He tried to breathe, the desperate gurgling drowning out everything else until his lifeless body slapped against the dais.

"Any more last words?" Gemma's voice was lusty with challenge.

Rae's time was up. This was her last opportunity, and she screamed internally, using every ounce of her mind to solve the puzzle that lay before her. How to get Gemma to abdicate before Freck was next.

"Prove to your people that you're the true queen." Rae grasped at frayed threads. "Prove to your people that you're not just a murderer whose father stole a crown."

Gemma's eyes narrowed as she nodded to the guard who stood behind Rae. A firm hand lifted her from her knees, tearing open fresh scabs and drawing a helpless yelp of pain.

"I don't have to prove anything to anyone, least of all a traitorous bitch such as yourself." Gemma took a silky step in Rae's direction, thankfully having forgotten Freck.

Rae begged the Elder Gods for another minute, another thirty seconds. She twisted the rope binding her wrists behind her back, testing the tightness. Straightening her shoulders, she ignored the burning as her wounds were stretched.

The queen took another step closer, and Rae's world slowed.

"You have been a thorn in my side for far too long." Gemma's eyes were wild with fury. "I sent you to die on the battlefield, but you always came back, clever little starling."

Gemma didn't notice how the guards in the crowd stirred, the soldiers shifting their stance, hands on hilts, eyes trained forward. Tight lips. Held breaths.

"I should have killed you myself so long ago." Gemma took two more steps. "Removed the last tiny bit of opposition to my rule."

Rae's senses sharpened as her stepmother drew closer, calculating the perfect moment, the number of steps, the exact distance she'd need. One breath. Two breaths.

"Your father was easy to subdue. He had no lust for a crown. But his siblings?"

The rush of blood in Rae's ears made Gemma's words sound as though they were filtered through heavy fabric.

"I had no choice but to send them all to the battlefront. A convenient *accident*."

There was more shifting in the crowd as Gemma continued to implicate herself. Rae couldn't have planned a more perfect public confession. Did Gemma realize what she was saying and to whom she was saying it to?

"And I would have done the same with your father, but he was so desperate to protect you, his sweet little elfling."

Gemma stopped just out of easy striking distance.

"All because your grandfather decided he couldn't give up his wretched house name." Gemma's electric eyes never left Rae. "And the long game was won. My father had endured years at Somsunder's side, bonded to that lunatic who prattled on about balance and houses and guilds. It was rather ingenious the way my father managed to rip a millennium of rule away. So easy. So truly simple."

Rae closed her eyes and let the world recede for a fraction of a second, collecting herself.

"And now you get to watch the person you love so dearly die for your treachery." Gemma turned toward Freck, her platinum hair whipping around her shoulders.

"I said, prove to your *people*. Not me." Surprised by how calm her voice sounded, Rae continued: "Prove to the civilians you've ripped from homes, the mothers and fathers who will never see their elflings again—the elflings who have lost their mothers and fathers. Prove to them that you're worthy to be their queen because from where I stand, I see only a sadistic monster responsible for the greatest unrest Rhend has ever seen—for no better reason than because she didn't get what she wanted."

Gemma's shoulders went rigid with rage before she spun back to Rae, a feral growl erupting from her throat.

Rae lunged, unhindered by fear or affliction, taking two steps before turning her back to the queen, reaching blindly with bound hands for the kukri. The blade bit into her hand, a slight miscalculation, but as suspected, Gemma was completely unprepared. Rae's other hand managed to curl around part of the handle, and as she twisted away, the kukri came with. She snapped the blade between rope and flesh, freeing her hands.

Rae turned in time to see Neffriss spring forward, attempting to put himself between her and Gemma. It was a valiant act, but it didn't melt the frozen certainty of what Rae knew she had to do. She'd never held the queen's blade, and for a cold instant, she swore she could feel the death it had wrought seeping into her palm.

The rasp of swords leaving scabbards filled the air as every royal guard drew their weapon. Rae swung up, the kukri tangling with Neffriss's broadsword. She punched him hard, sending him back into Freck. Both men crumpled onto the platform as Rae sidestepped, slamming her elbow into Gemma's face. Neffriss scrambled to his feet, doubled over in pain, racing to protect his queen.

Rae had a choice to make. Was she willing to kill him to remove Gemma from the throne? Neffriss was, after all, doing what he'd been trained to do—protect his queen. He was another example of Gemma's manipulation.

Before Rae could cut Neffriss down, a bolt buried itself in the side of his neck. Gemma screamed, staring into the hollow eyes of her most loyal guard before he collapsed at her feet.

Rae pointed the tip of the kukri at Gemma, the evil current vibrating up through her arm and into her shoulder, begging for blood. As quickly as time had slowed, it sped back up, slamming Rae into the moment all at once.

"For the crimes against her people, murder and torture of her own citizens, assassination of the true sovereign, and disobedience of the highest order, Gemma, Queen of the Shay, is sentenced to death by the desire of her people." Rae paused long enough to steady her breathing.

"Or to abdicate, be stripped of her title, and remain under house arrest for the remainder of her days."

"Your choice, Gemma." Bowrhem's voice sliced through the crowd, drawing a fair number of heads as he cocked his crossbow. "Perhaps your last choice."

Rae eased back from Gemma as the queen shook with seething madness. Slowly, hypnotically, Gemma turned, glaring back at Bowrhem.

"You. Of all people." She spoke through tight lips, a sob on the edge of her words. "I trusted you."

"And your people trusted you." He aimed the crossbow, and the color drained from her face.

"Wait! Wait!" Panic drove Gemma's anger away. She brought her arms up defensively.

"Choose wisely, Stepmother," Rae said, disgust sharpening her words.

Gemma's head snapped in Rae's direction, pure rage dancing across her face. She pounced. Her pointed fingernails sank into the flesh of Rae's neck. Rae acted on instinct, cradling the kukri along her forearm. She swung over the top of Gemma's arm and through her stepmother's left eye socket. Gemma shrieked as she crumpled at Rae's feet, clutching her ruined eye as blood poured between her fingers and down her cheek.

"Abdicate and live," Rae said with unfaltering confidence, drawing Gemma's good eye. "Or the next throat this kukri cuts is yours."

The air was still, attention firmly adhered to Gemma as she sobbed, crimson tears soaking her satin gown.

"I do. I…I abdicate."

The rush of soldiers jumping up on the dais was chaos—a raging sea of armor and hands. Gemma's arms were restrained as she struggled and wailed in pain. Her pleas for help were ignored as she was dragged from the dais.

Solena materialized at Rae's side, placing a gentle hand on her shoulder before jerking it back, likely noticing the blood soaking through Rae's undershirt.

"We need to get you to a healer," Solena said.

"Where's Freck? Help him...help Dulanii first."

But Freck had already been freed. He was there, seemingly from thin air, leaning forward so Rae could rest her head against his chest. He didn't wrap his arms around her. Instead, he held her head with a gentleness that she needed at that moment.

"Are you okay?" His words were soft, just for her, calmer than they should have been after having come so close to death. She gazed up at him and smiled. He returned it with that wonderful grin she was so fond of before guiding her head back against his chest. "You're okay."

Solena said something else, but Rae's mind could no longer register the sounds as words. They seemed to come too fast and heavy, like wet snow. All the adrenaline of a moment ago had drained away and left her with a husk for a mind and a broken body.

Gemma had abdicated. It was done.

Freck was alive. She was alive.

And it was done.

FIFTY-FIVE

The House of Starling

The closer Rae drew to Tremire, the more anxious she became. By the grace of the Elder Gods, a sadistic tyrant had been removed from her throne. Unfortunately, there was no Eishtala Master powerful enough to heal the wounds that over thirty years of war had inflicted. Only time would soothe the scars hatred had carved between the elven races.

The conscripted civilians were promptly released from service and sent home to their families, but there was still an army of trained Shay soldiers to consider. They'd been promised a battle that would make the past thirty years worth every ounce of blood and tears.

And then it just *didn't happen.*

Rae wasn't sure there were any words that she or Legion Bowrhem could give the soldiers that would cool the lust for battle they carried in their hearts. The Shaylands could very likely plunge into chaos. Plus the worry that the Sundering Freya had mentioned had already been set in motion when the rifts had been closed. They'd stopped the fighting, but the damage had been done. It would chafe like the fresh scars on Rae's back rubbing against the inside of her shirt.

She rode a borrowed horse, Solena close behind and Bowrhem ahead. Her legion, who knew more than he'd let on about the House of Starling's connection to the royal line, kept Rae close at all times. There was part of her that knew what that meant—a responsibility that had fallen to her that she wasn't in the slightest bit prepared for.

"I thought it'd feel different coming home," Freck said from his horse beside her.

Rae glanced over at him, the shadows of abuse at the hands of Gemma's royal guards stained his rosy complexion with large, purple patches.

"It feels heavier this time." He tipped his chin up a little as an angry Shay yelled something not quite loud enough to hear over the din of cheering and horses' hooves.

He was right. It did feel heavier. Shay lined the main path into the city; however, not all looked happy to see them. As she searched the crowd of people, she noticed a gray-skinned face. There was a Bleck Larin here! Their height and dark hair helped them stand out like a midnight blossom in a field of soft pink petals.

Ahead, the great Tree of Tremire came into view, and her heart skipped a beat. At the base of the steps was Freya. Thank the Gods. Rae would need her guidance on how to navigate undoing the potential catastrophe that still hung over their heads.

She took a deep breath in an attempt to calm her nerves. The real danger was only beginning. If events of the Sundering should come to pass, stopping a war was only a small piece of the greater need. Restoring balance to the magic of their realm was another thing entirely. Rae feared much would rest on Gastel's shoulders. She was certain he was the Great Wielder returned. The last thing she wished was to place such a burden on him, especially while he was away learning to control his Anam.

Rae caught Freya's eye and nodded. After she dismounted, Rae practically fell into the woman's arms.

"Thank you for your help. Your guidance was invaluable!" Rae spoke into her ear before releasing her.

Freya wore a wide smile. "You're the one we should be thanking. Your bravery has brought us here. I see Bleck Larin in this crowd. I never thought I'd see them in Tremire again." She nodded toward the doors to the courtroom. "There's much that must be discussed, but I made a promise that I'd give you a moment alone."

Rae wasn't certain what Freya referred to, but instead of wasting time with questions, she climbed the steps and slipped into the Court of Tremire.

The breathtaking beauty of the empty court grabbed her and held her frozen in the silence. She took a deep breath, her eyes following the white stains of light dancing on the ground as a lazy breeze moved through the leaves outside.

"You promised."

Rae knew that voice.

She spun to meet his amber gaze, the last person she expected to see in Tremire. She anticipated anger, frustration, a furrowed brow. Instead, she was met with an ornery grin as Gastel leaned against the wall with his familiar air of confidence, his midnight hair falling around his forehead, threatening his eyes.

How was he here? The words to ask were stuck in her throat as she admired the curve of his jaw and his slender, strong stature. She blinked a few times to confirm he wasn't her imagination.

"I promised I wouldn't do anything rash." She stepped toward him, eyeing how he straightened, evening his weight between his legs.

"And this wasn't rash?" He folded his arms, cocking his head to the side. He didn't move; instead, his sly smile dared her to close the distance.

"There were significantly more rash approaches I could have taken, I assure you." As she drew closer, the muscles in his neck tightened. She paused when she was close enough that she could reach out and touch his flawless face. She'd forgotten how beautiful he was.

The smile slipped from his lips, and he took the last step as if he couldn't wait any longer, pulling her into his arms. The warmth of him—the smell of morning sun and sandalwood washed away any concerns she'd had moments ago. She tucked her head under his chin, sinking into every part of him, wrapping her arms up his back. She hadn't realized how much she'd missed him until his hand cradled the back of her head, fingers trailing the length of her hair.

There had been a moment—had it been weeks now?—when she hadn't been sure she'd ever see him again. And before that, a time when she'd tried to push him away. *Never again.* Deep down, she knew that restoring peace between the Shay and Bleck Larin meant that she would never again have to question or hide her feelings.

He pushed her back to face him, her body screaming to return to the warmth of his arms. He took her chin, gently tipping her face so she was forced to look into his eyes and the glorious fire they promised. He held her there, a stoic mask shielding his emotions, staring until his eyes fell to her lips.

Butterflies erupted in her core, searing through her as the backs of his fingers swept across her cheek before tangling in her hair. He took her face with both hands, unbridled hunger flashing across his face before his lips met hers.

Gods, his lips were perfect—every bit as soft as she'd thought they'd be. She let the moment swallow her whole. A hot yearning threatened to boil over inside her as his fingers traced the line of her spine to the small of her back. He pulled her body tight to him, his unyielding muscles fitting perfectly against her. Solid. Safe.

She wanted more of him. She *needed* more. So, when he pulled away, she yearned to run her hands over his strong shoulders. To taste his breath. To thread her fingers through his hair, to hold him here with her forever. To kiss him again. Her body ached for his touch as she leaned toward him again.

The door to the court swung open, and Rae jerked away. He had a way of making her forget where she was.

"Raemian, the council of Shay have arrived." Solena's eyes darted to Gastel, and she straightened a little. A moment of understanding wafted across the royal guard's expression before she glanced back to Rae. Solena's single raised eyebrow only caused Rae's cheeks to burn hotter. "They wish to speak with you immediately."

This was what Rae dreaded most. Politics. Her life hadn't been spent at court, learning the ins and outs of running a kingdom. She was loath to take the responsibility.

"She'll see them at once," Gastel said without hesitation. "I'd be honored to submit myself as arbiter."

Solena nodded. "Of course, Highness. It'd be fitting to have a member of Bleck Larin royalty present." She gave Rae a warm nod before she turned and left.

"I hope I've not overstepped." He took Rae's hand, entwining their fingers as he gazed down at her. "You seemed hesitant."

In all honesty, Gastel's calm confidence was exactly what Rae needed, and not just because the memory of that kiss still seared her insides.

"I have no experience with," Rae made a circular motion to indicate Gemma's empty throne room. "This."

He matched her pace as they crossed to the meeting room, her hand still coupled with his. It was comfortable, natural. She took a seat to one side, and he looked down at her with a single raised eyebrow, shaking his head slowly.

"And I've already done something wrong?"

Gastel nodded in the direction of the head of the table. "Today, you sit in the place of power."

Rae slipped into her new seat, where Gemma would have sat, and Gastel took the chair to her right. Her heart already raced with misgiving. She met the first councilor's glare, a man she'd seen before, the high chancellor of Glasmin. He was followed close behind by a woman Rae hoped wasn't as angry as she appeared.

This could prove to be harder than stopping a war.

⁂

He knew it was selfish, but Gastel refused to let Raemian out of his sight. The moment she had melted into his arms in the Court of Tremire, everything had clicked into place. When he learned she'd been tortured at the hands of Gemma, that he might have been able to save her from all of it? It tormented him.

As she stood before Legion Bowrhem, a pang of possessiveness gripped him. Gastel had to use every ounce of strength not to step between Raemian and her legion. Some part of him was certain Bowrhem's loyalty was an act—a final cruel plot of Gemma's.

"We can't leave the throne unoccupied, and you know as well as I do who it should fall to." There was an unexpected gentleness to Bowrhem's demeanor that took Gastel by surprise. He'd expected someone more like Belkin in demeanor. "You're the next in succession."

Raemian closed her eyes and took a deep breath. Gastel could tell this wasn't what she wanted, and he completely understood. He'd lived his entire life knowing that his eldest brother, Belkin, would be king, but also that if something should befall both Belkin and Roulin, the burden would fall to him.

And that's what it was. A burden. You were a slave to your crown and your people. You had immense power but no freedom.

"I'm not a queen, Bowrhem. It'd be a great disservice to the Shaylands if I took the throne."

"I don't know if I agree." Bowrhem directed his attention to Gastel. "What do you think is her best course of action, Your Highness?"

The man had a genuine respect for him that seemed out of place. Bowrhem was, after all, the legion of the Shay army—the commander who had sent soldiers into battle for the last thirty-two years against Belkin's forces.

"I can't make this decision for Raemian." Gastel held the legion's gaze, "I know I wouldn't want the distinction any more than she, and I've spent my entire life knowing there was a slim chance the crown could fall to me."

Bowrhem braced both his hands on the table before sighing and pinning Raemian with his glare. "We must put someone on the throne. We invite all manner of unrest otherwise. The Shay can't afford that. No kingdom can."

"A likely solution would be for you to rule." She held Bowrhem's stare with conviction. "The Shay trust you. They know you. You have commanded the Shay as long as Gemma has been our queen. Longer, perhaps."

Bowrhem shook his head again. "This is exactly why I shouldn't. My ties to Gemma could lead some to believe that nothing has changed and bigotry toward Bleck Larin can continue." He squared his shoulders.

"I think it's better that a fresh face, unassociated with Gemma, take the reins."

"I wouldn't be a fresh face. The troublemaking stepdaughter of the queen? I've had a price on my head for how long now?" Raemian paused, her fingers tapping the edge of the table. "No, that'd only cause half the Shaylands to suspect I'd planned the coup to take the crown for myself the entire time."

Bowrhem nodded. "There must be someone who can lead, at least in the interim until a definitive decision can be made." His voice carried a defeated tightness.

Gastel saw the moment the answer lit up Raemian's face. He knew what she'd say before she said it.

"There's one person who'd be well suited." She turned back to her legion. "Freya of the Aequus."

Farewell

Rae stood outside her father's residence, hand resting on the door handle, but she couldn't bring herself to go in—to see everything he had left behind. He'd had the forethought to remove his bracelet and place it where Freck had found it. What other secrets had he left behind for her to discover? She took a deep breath and turned the knob.

Rae half expected to find the residence ransacked. Instead, it was neat and tidy, as if someone had been there that day to clean. She passed through to his bedchamber, where his bed was made, the curtains open—locked in time.

She found the mirror Gastel had told her about and felt along the gilded leaves at the top until her fingers crossed a tiny latch. She took another deep breath, letting this one out slowly. The mirror swung forward, revealing a cubby large enough to hide a couple of elves. There, on the ground, was a plain wooden box with a simple silver latch, engraved with the same starling crest she'd known her entire life. Just as she'd thought, he'd known he would go to his death and he'd known that Rae would find a way to avenge him—to make things right. Or at least as right as they could be made.

She stooped down for the box, holding it against her chest before walking out to the lounge and plopping down on one of the same futons Rae and her father had sat on only a few weeks ago. If she'd known it would be the last time she'd see him, she might have said more, asked more questions, and stayed a little longer. Told him she loved him.

Rae placed the box on the table in front of her and stared at it. Another deep breath. With a heavy heart, she flipped the latch, not knowing what kinds of treasures her father would have thought important enough to place inside. With trembling hands, she lifted a letter from the top and unfolded the parchment. Her eyes crept across Somin's beautiful handwriting; his voice echoed in her head in the calming tenor that had guided her through her elfling years.

My dearest Raemian, my starling in flight,

> *I'm sorry for a great many things. Not the least of which was failing to tell you about your mother. She loved you so very much. You were her shining star, her summer breeze. I would ask for forgiveness, but I'm not deserving of it.*
> *May you find your balance, and may it bring you peace.*

All my love,
Somin Starling

She held the letter for a full minute after she'd read his words. A wave of immeasurable sorrow shifted and changed into terrible urgency. *Balance.* They needed to restore the balance.

Rae reached into the box and wrapped her fingers around an elegant bracelet much like the one her father had worn. It was more delicate, made of twisting, silver vines that wrapped around a beautiful starling with its wings spread in flight. She turned it over, finding a name inscribed on the underside. *Gale Starling.* It was her mother's, likely a gift when she'd been lifebonded to Rae's father and had received the Starling name—an honor that wasn't always bestowed to bondmates. She slipped it on her wrist. She'd wear it with honor. And for now, she needed to set aside her melancholy. There was still work to do.

Gastel had begged to accompany Raemian to her father's residence. Instead, she made him promise to remain with Freya, saying she needed to do it alone.

"She's fine," Freya said, interrupting his pacing. "No one will hurt her. Even if someone tries, I hear she's a bit more than proficient with that sword of hers."

Gastel nodded, glancing over at Freya, who sat at a quaint dining table. She could have been Raemian's mother by appearances. She leafed through another manuscript. The woman was never without a book.

"Have you thought any more about Raemian's proposition?" Gastel asked. He tried to pull all the sharpness from his voice, but after spending nearly a week with him, Freya seemed able to see past every mask Gastel could wear.

"I have." She folded her hands on the table and gave him her undivided attention. "I'm flattered that anyone finds me qualified for such a responsibility, but I don't share your confidence. I've been guiding the Aequus for years. That doesn't mean I can lead the Shaylands."

"You'll be regent, not so heavy a title as queen. And you'll have every resource you could ever need at your disposal, including Legion Bowrhem's protection and my father's unyielding support," Gastel said. "You're the most suited to usher in a new era of peace between our people."

She shook her head, a wry smile crossing her lips. "You make it sound so easy."

"It is, and it isn't."

Her eyebrows drew together in a silent question.

"I can assure you my father is beyond ready to establish unbreakable terms of peace. That part is easy. Changing the rhetoric of hate ingrained in our daily life is the hard part." He smiled. "But I have every confidence in your abilities, and so does Raemian."

Freya's eyes twinkled with a curiosity that seemed promising. Her indomitable drive for equality was exactly what Rhend needed.

The door opened, drawing Gastel's immediate attention to Raemian. Her shoulders were hunched with sorrow; she clutched a wooden box against her chest. Gastel crossed the room in four long strides. He took the box from her fingers and swept her into his arms. She curled into him, burying her face against his chest.

"I wish I could talk with him one more time." Raemian took a long, soothing breath before pulling herself from Gastel. "There's so much more we have to do."

Before she could move farther from him, he captured her hand, entwining their fingers.

"Rae, you need to think about getting some rest," Freya said from her place at the table.

"I don't think ending a war is enough to stop the Sundering," Raemian said, the distinct look of concentration crossing her face. She pulled Gastel with her as she crossed to Freya.

"You just put yourself through so much; the least you can do is—"

"We need to open the rifts, don't we?" Raemian looked from Freya to Gastel and back.

Gastel hadn't realized how much Raemian knew of the situation. It was clear she'd managed to figure it out at some point, whether when she'd been in the Aequus compound or somewhere else, he couldn't know.

Freya shook her head. "What we need to do is figure out exactly how to go about opening them and not rush into anything. I'm hopeful Tor has found something." Freya's tone was heavy with intention. "The guild would have had information on how this could be done safely, but there are no members left to ask."

Gastel swallowed, clenching his teeth. "I know how to open a rift."

Raemian and Freya turned in tandem toward him.

"It takes an immense strength of Anam, one that the Elder Gods and perhaps the Great Wielder alone possessed," Gastel said as he set Raemian's box on the table, trying to ignore Freya's and Raemian's glares. "I've read my uncle's journal. He was a member of the Anam Guild and died closing a rift as all the guild members did."

Raemian's expression shifted from surprise to fear, and he had an inkling of why. If opening them was as dangerous as closing them, Gastel would risk his life. Not just once, but with every rift he opened. If true balance were to be restored, one for each Anam, Eishtala, and Svet would be needed. He'd already thought of this while pacing below the ground, helpless. He saw Raemian's understanding, like a razor-sharp kukri held to a throat.

"There must be other wielders possessing such power?" Raemian asked, her voice rising in pitch.

Gastel shook his head, noticing Freya look down at her hands. She knew the answer as well. There was only one Anam Wielder who had any chance of having the strength of power enough to open a rift. He couldn't hold Raemian's heavy stare and tried to find something else to look at.

"There has to be!"

"Now, Rae, it's going to be okay," Freya said. "We'll figure this out. We'll figure out how to do this safely."

"We'll? This is on Gastel's shoulders," Raemian said, the muscles in her neck tightening, her voice thick with fear.

"Rae." Freya tried to be calming but had the opposite effect.

"No, Freya. I won't allow Gastel to—"

"Raemian." Gastel was firm, raising his voice enough to cut her off without being disrespectful. He took a deep breath, focusing on how to make his point before he lost the nerve. "It's not about anyone allowing—or finding a safer way. It must be done, and I'm the only one who can do it."

Raemian gave him a look of absolute anguish.

"If you can stop a war, I can open a rift."

"Three rifts, Gastel," she said, panic lacing her words. "And how are we to know which ones to open and where they are, much less if there's anything that can be done to keep you safe? And what if this doesn't stop the Sundering at all?"

He shook his head as a smile turned up his lips. Her concern was endearing. "We'll figure it out. I promise."

FIFTY-SEVEN

Promise

Gastel plopped down beside Dulanii on the forest floor, breathing hard after going through several fighting forms. Shards of golden sun warmed the clearing where they camped, dancing in time with the breeze. It'd be a bit longer before Raemian would wake. She'd taken first watch and needed the extra sleep.

The gentle rise and fall of Raemian's chest captivated Gastel. There was something immeasurably calming about her uninhibited face when so often she tried to hide her emotions behind a mask. His eyes lingered on her parted lips, her waves of hair loose and chaotic around her head.

As though she felt him watching, she opened her eyes, tracing the forest floor until she found him. Gastel mouthed the words 'good morning' and grinned.

"The two of you are adorable," Dulanii said.

With shocking speed, Raemian retrieved a stick and threw it in Dulanii's general direction, but it fell short. He chuckled as he picked himself up.

"I'll find us some breakfast." He winked at Gastel and wandered off into the forest.

Raemian propped herself up on an elbow, a smile softening her sleep-touched face.

"He likes you," she said, voice rough from a night of disuse.

Gastel's cheeks grew warm. He hadn't realized how much he appreciated Dulanii's approval. He shook it away for more important topics.

"And what about you? Do *you* like me?" He bit his lower lip, then smiled, showing his teeth. He smiled so much when he was around her.

She rolled to her back, throwing her arms behind her head. "Maybe a little." He could just make out the gentle curve of her own smile as she gazed up into the trees, but then it faded. "We'll find the rift today."

He wasn't looking forward to it much either. Even though they wouldn't be walking into the same situation they had before, the rift was still terrifying. He had a general idea of what he needed to do, but he was going from memory of his uncle's journal and what little information Tor had provided.

He inspected his hands, weapons of fire that would wield the Anam needed to open a gate to another plane of existence. From his peripheral vision, he noticed Raemian roll to face him again.

"You don't have to do this, Gastel."

He cocked his head to the side. "I may be the only wielder who can."

"We don't know if that's true. Or if this will even help." Concern flashed in her eyes.

"Can we take the risk of not trying?"

"I...Gastel, I..."

Her hesitation was adorable. She blushed, sending butterflies loose in his stomach. Those magenta cheeks of hers reminded him of the burning sky at sunset.

"I'm not doing this for me." He closed his eyes and took a deep breath. "I'm doing this for Rhend."

She was on her feet in an instant. Gastel wasn't sure he could have moved so quickly after just waking. She planted herself in front of him, looking down with tight lips, hands on hips, expression drawn with frustration. Her hair was a splash of fire around her shoulders.

"There are a lot of things Rhend needs. Peace is still a long way off," she said. Her eyes were two sapphires burning with urgent intensity. "You made me promise not to do anything rash, but this feels beyond reckless."

She was beautiful when she was serious. Who was he kidding—she was always beautiful. Gastel leaned back so he could see all of her.

"If I didn't know better, I'd think you were terrified of losing me, Raemian."

"I am!" Her hands fell to her sides, her shoulders slumping with defeat. If she'd been blushing before, now her cheeks were on fire. "I...it's just..."

Dulanii stepped into the clearing with a handful of root vegetables and a small rabbit yet to be dressed. It was clear he was making as much noise as possible. What exactly did Dulanii think he'd be interrupting?

"Breakfast, anyone?"

They ate, then packed their bedrolls before starting out. Gastel felt heavily dependent on Dulanii's and Raemian's tracking skills. The two of them had spent countless hours scouting in these woods and knew where they were going. If it had been left to Gastel, they'd have gone in endless circles.

As they moved through a darker area of the forest, Gastel knew they were getting close. Raemian slowed her pace and looked back at him and Dulanii more often. But it was the silence that confirmed it. The first time, he'd assumed the rain was the reason, but now he realized that nothing lived in this part of the Middlelend Forest. It was too dark and foreboding.

"There!" Raemian pointed ahead and sprung forward. She deftly avoided the leafless lower branches that grabbed at pant legs.

Dulanii increased his pace, overtaking Gastel as the charred trunks of the trees surrounding the rift came into view. This place held nothing but a sense that something dangerous had existed. Perhaps it was the remnants of old magic that bled into their world when the rift had been opened before.

When Gastel finally caught up to Raemian, he looked down into the empty fissure, so deep that the bottom was black. Goosebumps crawled up the lengths of his arms.

"Gods. It feels strange here," Dulanii said, glancing around as he hugged himself. "Why exactly do we need to do this again?"

Raemian couldn't seem to pull her eyes from the emptiness of the rift, and Gastel struggled to pull his eyes from her.

"I should do what we came for so we can leave this place," he said.

A pang of nervousness rippled up Gastel's spine. Raemian had yet to see what he was capable of. He hadn't considered how she'd feel at the sight of him engulfed in uncontrollable soulfire.

Gastel did his best to keep his eyes on the rift. He was afraid he'd lose his nerve if he looked back. He knew what he'd see written across Raemian's face.

"Gastel. You don't have to do this." Her voice was strained with desperation.

He glanced over his shoulder enough to see she had stepped forward. He turned, taking in the urgency in her stance, the way her neck and shoulders were held tightly. She was a bowstring ready to fire.

He closed the distance between them and took her hands in his. Leaning forward, he pressed his lips to her forehead before looking deep into her eyes—their depths more beautiful than the Rahven Sea.

"I do. And I need you to promise me that you'll let me do this. That you won't interfere, even if you think something is wrong." He willed himself to remain calm and confident—for her, for himself. "And if something does go wrong, which it won't, you'll go to the Vail for Master Lorilay and take her to Freya before you do anything else. She may know more about the rifts."

Raemian closed her eyes. He could tell she was desperately trying to focus her thoughts. All her fear and trepidation simmered in her eyes when she opened them again. "I will."

"Promise me."

"I promise."

A tear slipped down her cheek, and it almost broke him. He wiped it away with his thumb, letting the backs of his fingers graze over her shaymarks. When this was done, he'd hold her in his arms, but for now...

Gastel glanced past Raemian to Dulanii, who wore a mask of seriousness, and nodded.

He was ready. Calm washed over him. He knew what he had to do.

He let Raemian's hands slip from his and turned to the rift.

⊢——— ———⊣

A tight ribbon of nervousness wrapped itself around Rae's throat as she held Freck's hand. Freck squeezed her in return, letting her know he understood she needed the comfort. The panic building in her stomach was hot. What if Gastel didn't walk away from this? Her chest felt tight, her eyes watering as a flash of memories washed over her. His long hair down his chest in the stream. Gemma as she'd held her notorious kukri to his throat. His silhouette as he had gazed up at the stained glass in the tower room.

If she lost him now?

She didn't know exactly what to expect. It was clear that he, Freya, and Tor all felt he was powerful enough to open a rift, but what did that mean? How could he think he could open the same rift that had rendered him unconscious before?

He pulled his mother's soul stone over his head before tucking it into a pocket.

Then every inch of him ignited.

He stood perfectly still as he was engulfed in white flames, arms outstretched, palms up, shoulders stiff. He threw his head back and looked to the trees above, the flames growing taller, reaching several feet above him, twisting and turning in a slow dance of raw Anam magic.

The reality of what he had to do to open the rift settled around her. Not so long ago, when she wallowed in bed recovering from an arrow wound, he'd sat next to her, telling her about Anam—how dangerous it was. That an Anam Wielder used their soul to create their magic, making it possible for a wielder to die from the effort if they weren't careful.

"Gods, this will kill him." She hadn't meant to say it aloud.

Freck held her firmly as she tried to pull away. "You promised, Rae. You need to trust him."

Gastel placed his feet at the edge of the crevice, turning his palms down. His shoulders rose and fell with a deep breath before he thrust his soulfire into the chasm with terrifying force.

She bit her lip as the pale flames faded from his legs and head, leaving only his torso and arms engulfed. He'd shared with her that his mother had died closing a rift—likely this exact rift. It stood to reason that he could die opening it. How much longer could she watch him throw his life away for a theory based on a prophecy open to interpretation?

The rift roared to life, looking as it had the day she and Gastel had stumbled upon it, the fire building to an incredible crescendo, casting eerie white light through the treetops that only encouraged her heart to race faster. His shoulders sagged with the effort; the muscles in his neck flexed as the flames died away from around his body, leaving only his hands surrounded.

She was watching him die.

It didn't matter if he thought he was restoring balance. She couldn't let him. She'd break her promise and apologize later.

He let out a bloodcurdling scream of agony and Rae snapped. She yanked her hand from Freck's, lunging forward, hands outstretched, regretting she hadn't made the decision sooner.

Her only thought as she barreled forward was to break his connection to the rift that seemed to take and take and take.

FIFTY-EIGHT

The Price

His life was quite literally being drained away, but Gastel was powerless to stop it. He was held firmly in place as the rift ripped whole pieces of his soul away. A terrible scream ripped past his lips as the pain overwhelmed him. The agony that coursed through every fiber of his being was more than he thought he could endure and remain conscious. Now he understood the price. Death was one thing, but this pain was so much worse.

He thought he heard Dulanii yell something, but all he could do was hope and pray to the Elder Gods that Raemian would do as she'd promised. If she interfered now, he didn't know what this magic would do.

He was knocked hard to the side. As he hit the ground, the connection to the rift was severed, his breath knocked from his lungs. The pain vanished instantly as he lay sprawled out a few inches from the rift's edge. He turned to see what had hit him, and his stomach dropped in horror as Raemian lost her footing, stumbling toward the chasm.

He scrambled around, reaching, his fingers just slipping past. In slow motion, she plunged into the ravenous soulfire. The last thing he saw of her was the surprise in her eyes as the angry, colorless flames of the rift swallowed her whole. He thrust his arms in after her, but there was nothing. Nothing but searing fire that reached with bitter thirst up his arms and toward his face.

"RAE!"

He stretched deeper, ignoring a new type of pain as his skin blistered. He tried to pretend he couldn't smell the acrid scent as the blood in his arms boiled in his veins.

She had to be there.

But there was nothing. *Nothing.*

"RAE!"

Dulanii's strong hands ripped him back and slammed him to the ground.

"NO!" He struggled against the Shay, trying to reach for her again and again, but his hands were useless. She had to be there. She had to be.

"NO!!" He thrashed, swinging wildly at Dulanii, but the man wouldn't release him.

Dulanii dragged him farther from the edge of the rift, hugging around his arms to keep him from striking. Gastel tried to free himself, clawing at the arms that held him, but the flesh on his fingers cracked and sloughed away, revealing bloody meat below.

"She's gone." Dulanii's voice cracked with despair. The man's body shook as he tried to restrain Gastel. "She's gone."

Dulanii finally released him, and Gastel collapsed, unable to move or think or breathe. His head fell back against the earth as his back arched, tears carving paths from his eyes as he squeezed them shut against the fire that still burned in his core.

She was gone.

He rested his charred hands on his chest, residual heat from the rift still sizzling up his arms. He refused to look at them. He knew they were decimated. *Good.* They were of no use to him if they couldn't even save the ones he loved.

Because he loved her.

And she was gone.

He tried to block out the sobbing Shay beside him—heavy, anguished sobs, thick with years of friendship.

What should he do? What *could* he do? The rift was open, but at what cost? His own life was a price he'd been willing to pay, but Raemian's? He rocked his head from side to side, trying to rid his mind of the vision of her sinking into the fires of the Great Sheol itself. She was gone.

He'd just found her, had just promised himself he'd never leave her side. *Never.* She was his light, his balance.

Damn the Elder Gods.

Damn the prophecy and the Sundering and the rifts and Rhend itself.

She was gone.

FIFTY-NINE

Treachery

For the first time ever, it fell to Belkin to maintain the order of the Bleck Larin kingdom. His youngest brother had returned with unusable hands, his mind broken by grief and his soul drained from opening a rift. Since then, their father had been at Gastel's side.

Belkin tried to take it in stride. This would, after all, be his life someday when he became king. He considered it a trial run. He corresponded with Legion Bowrhem of the Shay army regarding terms of peace. He graciously accepted the appointment of a Shay woman named Freya to the position of regent of the Shaylands. She'd been selected by Raemian. If Raemian had been anything, she'd been steadfast in her strategy for peace.

Now that things had settled somewhat, he needed to check in with Roulin and ensure the Bleck Larin soldiers had been properly directed. They'd been given strict instructions on how to handle any compromising situations that were sure to arise. Peace had a price. It didn't happen overnight. And this war had left a hatred hotter than molten metal between the races.

Belkin needed to brief his father, whom, in all honesty, he'd been avoiding. The loss of Raemian Starling had hit Mesmal almost as hard as Gastel. Even Belkin had to admit that in the end, she'd been a single elf swimming in a sea of adversity. Finding a way to dethrone a queen and bring a tentative resolution to thirty years of fighting was no small feat.

He rubbed his forehead as he sat in his father's chair in the strategy room. To see his father meant to see Gastel—an angry, lost soul. As much as his youngest brother frustrated him with all the trouble he caused, he didn't deserve this fate.

Belkin resigned himself to stop avoiding the situation. He was the commanding general of the Bleck Larin army, for Gods' sake.

"We need to talk."

Roulin had managed to slip into the strategy room without notice. His eyes glanced at something over Belkin's head. Probably the shortsword that hung with honor on the wall—a testament to the sacrifice of the House of Starling.

Roulin's brows were drawn, his lips a thin line of simmering anger— an expression Belkin was well acquainted with.

"Your expression speaks for itself, Brother," Belkin said, reclining in his chair so he could look up at Roulin, who stopped only a few feet from him.

"We have laid down our weapons, but these Shay monsters refuse to afford us the same courtesy." Roulin folded his arms. "I've lost more soldiers in the last week than—"

Belkin brought his brother to silence with a single raised hand. He pushed himself out of the chair to meet Roulin at eye level.

"Peace is never easy, and our role is even more difficult, knowing that there are many who didn't wish for it." Belkin held his brother's furious glare with what he hoped was a resigned, calm expression. "Your only responsibility is to protect civilians from the nefarious. You should not be pursuing Shay."

Roulin bared his teeth in anger.

"You disagree?" Belkin asked.

Roulin took a few steps back, a hand dropping instinctually to the pommel of his sword. "Peace is not the answer. It was never the answer," he spat. "You've all been brainwashed by a stupid girl. It's sickening."

Belkin couldn't help the left side of his lips from turning up. A few weeks ago, he had felt much the same way. Until he'd looked into the blue eyes of a Shay woman who had taken an arrow in the back to save his life. Perhaps he was brainwashed. He'd never thought he could be so soft toward any woman, Shay or Bleck Larin alike.

"Gastel's broken. Father has no ability to rule without his precious, spoiled elfling. You've grown completely complacent." Roulin threw his hands up with exasperation. "I'm the only one left holding the last of our Bleck Larin pride in my bloody hands."

"Wash them clean, Roulin," Belkin said, already tired of his brother's temper. "This is the path our father, our king, has chosen for us, and we—"

Roulin interrupted with an exaggerated, fake laugh. "You...you shall accept it. I'll be waiting on the battlefield." Roulin looked up at the sword again. "Find me when you grow a pair of fucking balls."

It wasn't the first time Roulin had used disrespectful language, but it was the first time Belkin noticed such a strong undercurrent of treasonous intention. He'd have to keep an eye on Roulin. Just another thing he'd have to do while he held the Bleck Larin kingdom in balance for his father.

He stood in the perfect stillness of the strategy room, eyes flowing over the tabletop map, a stack of correspondence yet to be read on the edge. This was a kingdom that needed its king. A kingdom that needed Mesmal's gentle touch as it navigated a new type of normal. Belkin wasn't gentle. He was a warrior, a battle strategist, not a sweet-tempered Bleck Larin in his millennial years. He was beginning to doubt his ability to fill his father's magnanimous shoes.

It wasn't the first time Roulin had met with Tace the tracker over the last several weeks. Tace was highly skilled at his craft and the only person Roulin could trust with the task. After his last encounter with Belkin, Roulin's conviction was even more justified. It didn't matter if what he wanted went against his elder brother's orders. It was the right thing.

The best for the Bleck Larin people.

Tace was seated at the back of the usual place—a seedy pub on the outskirts of Parth—lounging with a full tankard and several empty ones. He wore his typical snarky expression and black leathers. As an independent contractor, Tace wasn't at the mercy of Belkin's orders, and this was ultimately what Roulin needed—someone above his father's edicts.

"I had a feeling I'd be seeing you soon." Tace's eyes followed Roulin as he slipped onto the chair across from him. "I've been wondering how you'd be taking all this talk of peace."

"My younger brother is broken, my older brother has been brainwashed, and my father is fully entrenched in his own demons. How the fuck do you think I'm taking things?"

Tace leaned back, snickering through his nose. "And what exactly can I help you with, Highness?"

Roulin placed his hands flat on the surface of the table and drummed his fingers. If Belkin got wind of his plan. He cringed. Belkin had best not find out, and Tace was the best for that. None of the jobs Roulin had hired him for had ever come back to him. Not even the botched situation with the wretched Starling girl. He'd given his father and Belkin the perfect catalyst, a means by which to incite the final battle and annihilate the Shay. But they'd squandered it like everything else.

"I need you and your men to...shall we say...stir the pot." He narrowed his eyes. "I want these Shay shitheads to keep coming back with more each time. I need to prove that peace is pointless. Belkin needs some encouragement."

Tace's grin deepened. "With pleasure, Highness." He took a long drag from his tankard, emptying it, then wiped his mouth with the back of his hand. "One question. Have we grown soft on the subject of prisoners?"

The hair rose on the back of Roulin's neck at the hatred burning within him for the Shay abominations. Without their queen, especially, they no longer had the right to exist. He leaned back in his chair.

"Never."

Balance

Without knocking, Belkin slipped into Gastel's personal quarters, hoping to find his father. Instead, he found Gastel alone and sitting on the edge of his bed, hands unwrapped for the first time in days. The burns were healing, but the scars would be with him forever. On the side table sat Gastel's cuff, which had once held his hair, and his mother's soul stone.

When Gastel looked up, all Belkin could see was a broken man. Somehow, Gastel had opened a rift. No mere mortal had ever attempted it—with good reason. The rifts had originally been opened by the Elder Gods long ago when Rhend was new. It had taken its price, and Gastel had paid it with his soul. His powers had been tempered. He no longer needed the soul stone to calm the flames that had once engulfed him.

"I wouldn't have chosen this for you," Belkin said.

The sadness in Gastel's expression turned to rage that simmered under the surface of his flesh.

"I know you think I hated her, but at some point…" Belkin sighed, trying to craft the best words. "She cared too much for you, for father. For peace."

"She saved my life." Gastel squeezed his hands into fists. The scarred flesh around his knuckles turned white from being stretched taut. "She saved all our lives."

Belkin nodded. Perhaps she had. He wasn't one to dwell on the convoluted interpretations of the prophecy.

Gastel stood from the edge of his bed, a conviction in his eyes that Belkin wasn't sure he'd ever seen in his youngest brother.

"I'll be leaving soon," Gastel said. "There's someone I need to visit, and then I have rifts to open."

Belkin smiled, knowing how it felt to throw oneself into the next task to distract from something bigger.

Gastel held up a single ruined hand, palm to the ceiling. His fingers couldn't fully extend; the flesh was far too damaged. He concentrated, eyes closed, breathing smooth and deep. Even with ruined hands, Gastel was able to ignite his soultorch, shifting the amber flames to bright, hot white.

He met Belkin's gaze, and the fire in those amber eyes was undeniable. Belkin saw strength and confidence—everything his youngest brother had always been. There was anger and confusion and determination there, too. Mettle honed by grief.

And there was love.

"I have balance to restore."

Acknowledgments

When I was in college working on a degree in graphic design, my dad gave me Stephen King's *On Writing*. That was over twenty years ago. I like to think he knew something about me I hadn't yet learned about myself.

Keith Prescott, aka "KP," aka Dad, aka Grumpy Grandpa, your unwavering encouragement has been the driving force in my journey to finish this book. Maybe I've managed to inherit at least a little bit of your expert ability to tell a story about anything anywhere to anyone. Thank you for being the Hershal to my Ogg. I have a feeling this is only my first invention.

During the three-year process of working on this book, there were meals that went uncooked, clothes that went unwashed, chores that went undone while in the throes of inspiration. Thank you, Timmy and Myra for always picking up my slack around the house all while continuing to encourage me to "finish your book already!!!" Without your love and support this book would not exist FULL STOP

To my earliest readers, who had no idea what they were getting into, because I had no idea what I was getting into; Mike Binder,

Mike Ubaldi, Erica Row, Tiara Kitzler, and Jeff Brown, thank you for spending time with my words. Here's hoping this finished book is so much better than the first one you read.

Katrina Robinson, my editor extraordinaire! You've been priceless in cleaning up my drivel and helping me with clarity, smoothing my prose into what I hope is a truly magical reading experience. Prepare thyself! Book two is coming in hot.

Keko V., you will remain the biggest influence on my writing journey. I can't read the word "just" without thinking of you and how you tore my manuscript into manageable pieces, dusted off all my dirty prose, and helped me put it all back together into a beautiful story. I learned more from your feedback than any class I've ever taken or could ever take. Thank you, mate. Truly, thank you! I will cherish your friendship for the rest of my life!

Edith Pawlicki, your generosity of time and wisdom gave me invaluable insight into story structure, something I was very new to. Your encouragement pushed me through some serious imposter syndrome, and your wonderful feedback gave me the courage to keep going! I am forever grateful for you.

I had a crew of the most wonderful beta readers! Rose Thomson (also a sensitivity reader), Selena Martinez, Mariella, Luke Courtney (also provided me with a ton of grammatical feedback), Bron, Jayne Murray, and Ashley Thedford; your feedback and encouragement has made this book what it is. Thank you, thank you a million times, thank you! I'll be begging you to beta read book two so stay tuned!

My "IG Bestie" Zaid Hasan; never change. Never ever ever change. You probably thought I forgot you in the list of beta readers above, didn't you? Hell, no! Your play-by-play beta feedback kept me walking this road when I struggled most with doubt. Your constant encouragement and friendship has gotten me through some dark days. I can't wait until we're working on putting the finishing touches on *your* debut novel! 2024 is our year, my friend! We've got this!

And lastly, to the Instagram writing community! Thank you, always. You are my social media home, and I could never ask for a more caring and welcoming place on the internet. Three years ago, I started inserting myself and found nothing but kindness and encouragement.

Becoming an indie author has been the single most challenging learning experience of my life, and I've loved every minute of it. I wouldn't be writing my first acknowledgments if it weren't for the countless people who I've connected with along the way. I can't capture all your names here, but I do hope you know that I'm eternally grateful.

Thank you. *Truly.*

Glossary

Aequus | {*AY-kwiss*} An elf of any race holding no allegiance to any one sovereign.

Amfithere | {*AM-fih-theer*} One of the prominent Great Houses of the Bleck Larin.

Anam | {*A-nahm*} A form of magic used by Bleck Larin elves. Anam is created at the cost of an individual's soul, making it incredibly powerful depending on the Wielder's capabilities, but also very dangerous and impractical in battle as the cost to wield is quite literally one's life force. Proficiency is only possible for a small percentage of Bleck Larin. However, all Bleck Larin possess a minor form that allows them to ignite a heatless flame (see Soultorch).

Bleck Larin | One of the three elven races of Rhend. Usually tall, almost always over 6 feet in height, and very slender, making them deceptively strong. They are pale blue, green or cool gray fleshed elves with black, dark blue, or violet hair occasionally streaked with white or silver. Eye color ranges from yellow, to amber to warm orangish brown. They have much longer lifespans than Shay by several hundred years.

Bonded | A formal coupling of two elves akin to marriage.

Bondmate | A title bestowed to one another once bonded.

Dormshire | {*DORM-sheyer*} A Shay held city previously shared between the Bleck Larin and Shay before the current war conditions.

Effrin | {*EHFF-rin*} Training overseer of Anam magic.

Eishtala | {*EESH-tah-lah*} A form of magic used by Shay elves. Eishtala is the influence of outside life forces such as plant based or non-sentient living things in order to manipulate organic materials into desired structures or shapes. It can also be used to heal wounds of any severity, but at the cost of the outside life force. Generally thought to be possible for nearly a quarter of the Shay population to a minor degree, only a select few have enough skill to train to become masters of healing.

Great Sheol | {*ShOLE*} A place akin to the afterlife.

Rhend | The land of the elves, separated from the human domain by a magical and physical barrier known as the Wastelands, put in place by the Elder Gods after the 100 years war.

Shay | One of the three elven races of Rhend. Usually creamy pink or pale pink fleshed elves with platinum blonde, white, or red hair. Most of them have some form of red birthmarks (see shaymarks). They have pale blue almost silver irises, sometimes greenish blue or deep blue. Closer to average human height, they are naturally muscular and extremely strong. Even female Shay have defined muscles and are nearly as tall as the males. Average lifespan of around 1000 years.

Shaymarks | Bright red birthmarks possessed by Shay elves, usually lacy patterns or large freckles that run along the sizes of the face, neck and torso, sometimes down arms and rarely on to legs.

Soulfire | A general use term for the white fire Anam magic creates.

Soulflame | An advanced level of heated soultorch created by Anam magic.

Soultorch | A light source created by a simple form of Anam magic that can be created by most Bleck Larin.

Svet | {*Sveht*} A form of magic used by Trove elves. Svet can banish or return a life force to a corporeal body. While mostly associated with the resurrection of deceased sentient beings, it is also associated with having the ability to sense or "see" the life force of sentient beings. Those gifted with Svet are incredibly rare. Because Trove elves tend to isolate themselves from the other elves, there are very few Svet Priests known. Svet paired with Eishtala healing can fully restore one from death. Svet paired with Anam can destroy a life force and permanently kill.

Tremire | {*Treh-MEER*} A Shay held city. One of the prominent Great Houses of the Shay.

Trove | One of the three elven races of Rhend. Pale violet or white fleshed elves with only silvery white hair and pale almost white eyes. Much smaller than both Shay and Bleck Larin in stature, they are thin and petite in all aspects. They rarely grow to be taller than 4 feet. They live underground and have exceptional low light vision. They rarely come above ground unless needed and choose to isolate themselves from the other elven races. Lifespan is unknown.

Character Guide

Raemian Starling, Rae | {*Ray-MEE-ehn*} (Shay, age 35) Observant, Moral, Timid. Neutral Good

Dulanii, Freck | {*Doo-LAH-nee*} (Shay, age 34) Friendly, Loyal, Kind-hearted. Chaotic Good

Bowrhem | {*Boe-ray-him*} (Shay) No-nonsense, Strategic, Moral. Lawful Neutral

Gemma | {*Jem-Uh*} (Shay, age approximately 450) Self Centered, Ruthless, Manipulative. Neutral Evil

Mesmal | {*MEHS-Mehl*} (Bleck Larin) Calm, Patient, Impulsive. Neutral Good

Belkin | {*BEHL-kin*} (Bleck Larin, age 284) Battle hardened, Unwavering, Complicated. Lawful Neutral

Roulin | {*ROW-lin*} (Bleck Larin, age 267) Prideful, Bitter, Instigator. Lawful Evil

Gastel | {*Gas-TEHL*} (Bleck Larin, age 32) Confident, Curious, Naive. Chaotic Good

Tace | (Bleck Larin) Arrogant. Chaotic Neutral

Tildimin | {*Til-dih-min*} (Bleck Larin) Loyal, Intimidating, Steadfast. Lawful Neutral

Somin Starling | {*SAH-min*} (Shay) Kind, Conflicted, Easily Swayed. True Neutral

Inara | {*Ih-nar-ah*} (Bleck Larin) Timid, gentle, Respectful. Neutral Good

Jad | (Bleck Larin) Anam apprentice. Lawful Good

Rayken | {*Ray-Kin*} (Bleck Larin) Shrewd, Strict, Prideful. Lawful Evil

Kresha | {*Kresh-Uh*} (Bleck Larin) Seductive, Vicious, self serving. Neutral Evil

Kalbasen, Kal | {*Kal-bai-sin*} (Bleck Larin) Calm, Intelligent, Respectful. Neutral Good

Lorilay | {*Lor-ih-Lai*} (Shay) Gentle, Motherly, Intelligent. Chaotic Good

Geri | {*JAIR-ee*} (Bleck Larin) Aequus, Naive, Inquisitive, Trusting. Neutral Good

Freya | {*Fray-Uh*} (Shay) Aequus, Matronly, Understanding, Perceptive. Chaotic Good

Lokryn | {*Lok-rin*} (Bleck Larin) Aequus. True Neutral

Druevgar, Druev | {*Droov-gar*} (Shay) Aequus. Lawful Good

Tor | (Bleck Larin) Aequus, Geri's father. Lawful Neutral

Solena | {*Soe-lehn-uh*} (Shay) Sympathetic, Moral, Stern. Lawful Neutral

Neffriss | {*NEF-ris*} (Shay) Lawful Neutral

www.ingramcontent.com/pod-product-compliance
Lightning Source LLC
Chambersburg PA
CBHW031826310726
48972CB00005B/1172